See ~ Saw

A Novel

to Judy with Love! ♡

See ~ Saw
A Novel

by Lili Vincent

Scriptures marked NAS are taken from the NEW AMERICAN STANDARD (NAS): Scripture taken from the NEW AMERICAN STANDARD BIBLE®, copyright© 1960, 1962, 1963, 1968, 1971, 1972, 1973, 1975, 1977, 1995 by The Lockman Foundation. Used by permission.

Knoxville, Tennessee, USA
crippledbeaglepublishing.com

Cover design by Lauren Balmer
Author photo by D Stults Photography

Hardcover ISBN 978-1-958533-78-9, 978-1-958533-80-2
Paperback ISBN 978-1-958533-77-2, 978-1-958533-79-6

Library of Congress Control Number: 2024905075
Printed in the United States of America

For Jeremy—my husband, my partner, my best friend.
Thank you for walking every step of this journey with me.

For my girls.
Eleanor, because you asked, "Why?"
MJ, because you asked, "What?"
and Abigail, because you asked, "How?"

For my parents. Mama, I only wish you were here to read it.

1

Marie

April 2001

I can't tell you about all the times I've fallen in love, but I can tell you about the first.

Walt Mavin moved into my parents' subdivided apartment house the year I turned twenty-three. The late spring afternoon gifted us with the sweet smell of blooming lilacs, the sound of lawnmowers, and the squeals of children running wild. The warmth of the sun promised that the bitter cold days of winter were behind us.

Mama had already moved the stand fans up from storage, and their gentle hum was comforting, like crickets on a summer night. The unique rumble of a diesel engine and the crunch of truck tires on the winding drive interrupted Wednesday afternoon knit club, a tradition that went back long before I could hold a set of knitting needles. A heavy door opened and closed, and ladies' voices whispered around me.

"Well, as I live and breathe."

"Who on earth?"

"Is he here to fix something?"

"I don't think there's anything broken."

"Give me a hammer. I'll break something."

"Fifi!"

"Who are they talking about? These are just readers."

"Sssssshhhhh!"

I heard his work boots on the steps moments before he knocked on the screened door.

"Well, hello, hun," Mama said in a voice loud enough to cover the chatter of the dozen women on her porch. She set her project down on the cushion beside her and got up to meet him.

"Walter Lee…I mean, Walter Mavin," he said with a gentle drawl that was from nowhere near Roland Park or Baltimore City, for that matter.

"Greta Ricks," she said. The door latch made a tinkling sound as she flipped it, and the spring on the screen door groaned as she pushed the door open to let him onto the porch.

I cringed at the cliché that was my mother's Baltimore accent; the word *hun* sounded like "hon."

"Yes, ma'am. I think I spoke to your husband, William, on the phone."

"Oh, you call him Billy," she said, waving away his formalities. "And he's gone danny-ocean with Evelyn's husband, Mr. Colgate. He'll be back late this evening."

I shut my eyes to mentally translate. There was no way this man would understand the phrase meant *down to the ocean*. I imagined the bewilderment on his face and felt embarrassed for Mama. I prayed she'd just stop talking. I can honestly say I loved everything about my mother except how well she fit into the fabric of her hometown. I hadn't realized I'd stopped knitting to listen until she touched my arm with cold fingers.

"Wuder or lemonade?" she asked me.

I turned to face her. "Lemonade is good. Thanks, Mama."

"Yes," she said. The ice rattled in her pitcher as she moved among the group of women scattered across the porch to pour lemonade for others. Back toward the man's direction, she spoke, "My husband said you'd be here this afternoon picking up keys and whatnot."

"Yes, ma'am," he said from his spot just inside the door. "I'm sorry. I didn't mean to interrupt."

"We welcome interruptions!" The voice came from the far side of the porch and belonged to my mother's oldest and dearest friend, Delphine Probst. "Especially those of the young male variety."

The space erupted into laughter.

I heard the wicker couch creak when Mama sat down, and then Delphine continued.

"Now, dear, please come in. There's a space right here," she said as she patted the cushion beside her.

"Fifi!" came the scolding voice of Mable Turner. She'd been the last to arrive and had taken the seat beside me on the opposite end of the long blue couch. "It's my turn!" Again, the room filled with laughter, only now a man's low tenor was in the mix. I couldn't help but smile. These women were my world.

Mable and Delphine, or "Fifi" for short, had lived together in Unit 4 of Edgevale House since their husbands passed away over twenty years ago, just a few years before Mama and Daddy bought the manor house when I was nine years old. Fifi was about fifteen years older than Mama and had always been a surrogate mother to her. Fifi had suggested the purchase of Edgevale House to my parents as a property with a stable income. She was right about it being a great investment, and having her best friend close by was icing on the cake.

Becoming landlords had been a bit of a stretch for my parents and required some logistical gymnastics—Daddy had to leave his job in operations at Baltimore Metro, and Mama had to leave her job as a nurse at Hopkins. The re-signing of all seven renters for two years meant minimized risk. A completely full rental property with good tenants and over two acres in the middle of Baltimore was too good to pass up.

My mother was born and raised in Dundalk, Maryland, a congested northeast suburb of Baltimore. My dad grew up on a farm in Shelbyville, Tennessee, where they raised championship Walking Horses. Edgevale House brought together the best parts of their worlds—a bit of the country in the heart of the city.

Six months later, when I was diagnosed with retinitis pigmentosa, a disease inherited from my father, it was clear that their position at Edgevale House wasn't by accident. The flexibility enabled them to make their own schedules and take me to countless medical appointments and therapies. Without realizing it, they'd built a community around our family, and that community supported and sustained us through four surgeries. When total blindness was my quickly approaching reality, our community surrounded and protected us, especially me.

My doctors told my parents that I would likely lose my sight completely and they should start planning for that reality. Mama was at a loss and overwhelmed at the thought of navigating that transition with the special education department of the Baltimore City School System. They kept telling her that when I "achieved total blindness"—like the condition equaled perfect attendance or straight As—I would be required to go to an institution for blind children.

The knit club ladies were outraged.

Mom's good friend from Unit 6, Linda Morris, had a blind nephew who had been a residential student at MSB, the Maryland School for the Blind, several years before, so she offered to come with us to tour the school facilities and campus. I was terrified. Even though MSB was only thirty minutes from Edgevale House, I cried for days because I thought my family was sending me away. All I wanted was to stay home where I knew I was safe.

Linda checked out books from the library and talked to teachers at MSB. She got a braille slate and braille flashcards and even purchased herself a braille typewriter. She taught herself braille, and then she taught me.

She learned everything she could about teaching, especially teaching blind children, and then enlisted the help of Linda Brooks, a former teacher and principal.

Fewer than eighteen months later, at age eleven, I was completely blind. Together, "The Lindas" took over my education for the next seven years. They both lived at Edgevale House and aside from an occasional unit study with my parents, they were my only teachers. I loved them both deeply for this selfless and important gift. Linda Brooks wasn't much of a knitter but attended our club once a month to catch up with The Ladies. When she did come, she joked that she was there only for the dessert, which no one minded.

On the other hand, Linda Morris was steadfast in her attendance. The only time she missed our weekly get-together was when she had to reschedule her weekly visit to her mother's home in Mechanicsburg, Pennsylvania, an hour away. If Linda Morris was there, no matter where I sat in our knit circle, she always sat directly across from me. Her needles clicked as she updated us with news of her children, "No grandchildren yet, but maybe soon if the good Lord's willing and the creek don't rise."

Including Mama and me, our weekly knit club had fifteen members, but each week it brought together a different mix of ladies on my mother's screened porch. Most of them had been meeting together long before we called the manor house home. They affectionately called themselves The Ladies of Edgevale.

Lost in my reflective daydream, I did not hear Walt cross the porch. I jumped out of my skin when he sat down smack dab between Mable and me.

"I'll sit here for today just because it's closer, but next week, I'll have to start takin' turns." He lowered his voice. "I'm sorry," he said and touched my arm, "I'm Walt, and I didn't mean to startle you. I didn't realize you weren't able to see me comin'."

"It's okay," I said, trying to sound less embarrassed than I felt. "I normally do a better job listening." I felt my voice settle. "When I was little, Mama used to put bells on my shoes so Daddy could tell where I was." I reached out. "I'm Marie."

Walt took my hand and shook it. "Marie," he said, and there was a curious lift in his tone. "This is gonna sound weird, but your voice sounds familiar."

I raised my eyebrows and smiled. "I get that a lot," I said, sure he was messing with me.

"So, your dad, he's blind too?" he said. The question might have sounded rude, but it was simply a question from Walter Mavin.

"Yes. Well, visually impaired. He doesn't drive or operate heavy machinery, and we don't let him use a blow torch, but he gets around well when he's familiar with a place."

"I can't wait to meet him," he said, and I heard his smile.

For the next hour, he sat between Mable and me and allowed the knit club ladies to flirt with him and play an informal game of round table twenty questions. He answered every one of their probing questions with ease and without a hint of hesitation.

"Where are you moving from?"

"Knoxville, Tennessee."

"Where will you be working?"

"Bethlehem Steel as a structural engineer."

Sitting next to him that afternoon, I learned that he loved Italian food, that when he was fifteen, his pastor caught him ripping out pages in the hymnal and made him sing in his church's choir as punishment, and to everyone's surprise, he could actually sing. He played the piano and made his bed every morning without fail. He'd broken two bones in his leg when he was a kid because his brother, Chuck, convinced him to jump off the roof of their garage, and he shared that he loved sushi, sun tea, baseball, and East Tennessee in the fall.

The only question that caused him to pause came from Evelyn Colgate. She and her husband Pluto were the longest residents of Edgevale House and had lived in four of the seven units in the house. They appeared to have settled on Unit 2 across the hall from me, but I was sure they had their eyes on Unit 1, a sunny, southern-facing, two-bedroom that had been mine since I graduated from college two years before and moved out of the carriage house where my parents lived.

"Do you have a sweetheart?" Evelyn asked.

Even though I couldn't see them, I felt every single eye looking in our direction. He cleared his throat, and I felt him shift where he sat. "No." He waited and must have been gathering his thoughts before he went on. "For a short time, I was married, but that didn't end well." The bright spots in his voice had gone dull.

Before I realized I was doing it, I heard my own voice ask, "What happened?" I clapped my hand over my mouth. "I'm sorry! That's none of my business." My words came out muffled as I spoke through my hand.

"It's okay. I don't mind. You caught me off guard, that's all," he said. A low rumble filled the air around us, and I felt the vibration of the old porch through my feet. "Saved by the bell," he said. "Looks like my moving truck is here."

"Young man, you will be back soon to finish your story, right?" Evelyn asked, though I heard an instruction more than a question.

"Yes, ma'am," he said.

"So, you're planning on being a regular attendee at knit club?" I asked, just above a whisper.

"Do you come every week?" he asked.

"I do," I said. I smiled and looked in his direction, nervous about how he might react.

"You must have a pretty flexible job to get to take off every Wednesday and do somethin' you love."

"I do," I said, feeling awkward that my responses all sounded like the answers to wedding vows. I was also starting to second guess my judgment of his opening line about recognizing my voice. "Commercials."

"Commercials?" he said, and it was definitely a question.

"That's where you've heard my voice before. I produce radio commercials."

"Really?" he said, and he sounded impressed.

"Yeah, I have a little studio here at Edgevale House."

"That's…" He started but then stopped.

"What?"

"I was gonna say cool, but it didn't sound big enough when I said it in my head. I just was tryin' to think of a better word."

"Thanks," I said, blushing at his compliment. "It isn't fancy, but it works."

"If it works, that's what matters," he said, and this time, I didn't have to imagine his expression. I could hear his smile.

He leaned over, took my needles in one hand to keep them in place, and gently took my other hand in his. He leaned in close and whispered, "You dropped a stitch." Then he guided my fingers to a place on the square I'd been working on and by feel alone, I knew he was right.

"How—" my voice fell away in surprise, completely at a loss for words.

He laughed, "My mama had two boys and insisted we both learn to sew a hem, fix a button, and knit a potholder. I understand the hem and button, but I'm convinced that the potholder was just to keep us busy and out of trouble at her ladies' meetings."

The knit club laughed.

He touched my arm, where a thin silver bracelet rested above my wrist. "This is pretty," he said.

"Thank you," I said, flustered. Not quite sure what else to say, I blurted out, "My mother has one, too."

"Oh," he said.

And somehow, for some reason, unable to stop talking, I said, "Yes, all of The Ladies of Edgevale have them. It's sort of a thing." I felt myself blushing and turned the bracelet on my wrist a few times. I forced myself to stop.

"Who are The Ladies of Edgevale?" he asked. There was no judgment in his tone. I heard genuine curiosity.

I waved my hand, palm up like Vanna White, revealing the puzzle. "These are The Ladies of Edgevale."

"I see," he said and turned my bracelet once. "I like it," he said. He let go and touched my arm, and for just a moment, everything else in the world fell away. He lowered his voice. "I'll see ya next week."

"Okay," I said with a smile. "I'll see you next week."

I didn't have to wait a week.

Because everything he owned was in boxes, my parents insisted Walt come to dinner that night. Then, that night at dinner, they invited him to join us and The Ladies of Edgevale for our annual outing to Pimlico for Sunrise at Old Hilltop, a Baltimore Preakness Week tradition. He said yes without hesitation and even offered to drive.

The day started inappropriately early, and I was surprised when, rather than Mama or Fifi, Walt handed me my tea in a to-go cup.

"Thank you," I said.

"You're welcome." His voice sounded far more awake than I felt. "Fifi told me how you take it."

At Pimlico, Walt walked beside me as we took the guided tour of the stables, ready paddock, and winner's circle. I held his elbow as he narrated what he saw and sprinkled in a well-timed joke here and there. The tour guide led us over to the farrier and a training jockey and asked if anyone wanted to pet one of the escort horses.

Walt leaned down and whispered, "I'm terrified of horses."

"Seriously?" I asked.

"Seriously," he said. "So, you're gonna have to hold my hand."

"You know you don't have to pet the horse," I said.

"Oh, there's no way I'm gonna pass up the chance to pet a Preakness horsey. I mean, this guy might be on TV escortin' the winner of the triple crown," he said. His accent was foreign and endearing.

In the short time I'd known him, I'd noticed that the drop of a genuine "howdy," "y'all," and "ma'am" worked as accidental currency. His southern drawl, slow and sweet, was like a master key. It opened doors he hadn't even realized were closed to him.

He touched my back and moved us through to the front of the group. "I can tell people I knew him before he got famous," he said, like an excited child.

The trainer brought us to the horse's right side. Walt took my hand, gently pressed his on top of mine, and guided my fingers to the horse's neck. Surprised by the size of the animal in front of us, I drew in a quick breath.

"Isn't he incredible?" Walt asked like he was reading my thoughts. He ran our hands together down the side of the horse's body. He turned to the trainer and asked if we could listen, and with his blessing, we leaned in until I felt the silk of his coat against my ear. With each of the horse's breaths, I felt his chest press into my cheek. Completely naturally, Walt's fingers laced into mine. For a moment, the world stood still around this amazing creature, Walt, and me.

After the tour, we sat together with The Ladies in the grandstands as the sun rose over the track. We ate a picnic breakfast as the thoroughbreds' morning training sessions thundered around us.

Later, on our way out, I held Walt's elbow as he guided us with the crowds up the sloping floors. Before we reached the doors to the parking lot, someone handed me a glossy-feeling Preakness flyer, and I felt giddy as I folded it and tucked it into my jeans pocket.

I knew this was a day I'd never forget.

I knew then that I'd love this man for the rest of my life.

If only I'd known how much he'd love me back.

If only I'd known that our love would span time and space. If only I'd known our love would grow in ways I never could have imagined. I wish I'd known then that the decision to love this man, Walter Lee Mavin, would bring me happiness beyond my imagination. If only I'd known then that choosing to love him would give the world the most amazing girl I'd ever get to meet and never get to hold.

Make no mistake, I wouldn't change a moment. I just wish I'd known then that those would be my best two years.

2

Charlie

December 2018

I tucked the journal-sized book into a brown padded envelope. I scribbled the familiar Nashville address of my best friend in the center and my own in the top left corner—Charlie Mavin. I paused to consider the two hearts I'd used to dot my i's. I couldn't erase them, so I settled for filling them in instead. In the space where the stamp would have been, I neatly printed "Free Matter For The Blind" and carried the book, tucked inside my coat, out to the mailbox.

Back inside, my fingers were sweaty and shaking as I made the final loops in the hangman's knot. A few summers back, we were fixing up the old tire swing, and Dad taught all the kids all kinds of knots. Of course, back then he referred to the knot as a "tire swing knot."

Not until I started researching how to kill myself on the internet did I realize that my father taught me how to create a noose.

Tying knots had been something I'd excelled at naturally because the task relied more on feeling than seeing. I was the first girl in my troop to get that stupid knot-tying badge.

"Freakin' Girl Scouts," I said, yanking the knot as tightly as I could one last time. For a year, I endured being hated, just as much as the girl whose feet smelled like dog vomit, because I was different. Because I couldn't see well. Because I had to hold things really close. Because I wasn't a blonde-haired, blue-eyed clone. No one wanted to sit beside me. My heart sped up with the memory of the popular girls unzipping my hand-me-down uniform in front of the whole troop.

I pushed myself up off my bedroom floor and crossed to the door. I pressed my face gently against the door frame. The summer of the tire swing was the summer I'd also learned to take pictures with an old Canon SLR camera. Reading the dials on the lens was hard. I ended up just memorizing where things needed to be set for each sort of lighting situation. My pictures weren't terrible. The teacher said I had an eye for framing a shot, which was high praise, but then he followed it up by saying I ruined the picture by forgetting to turn on the autofocus. He said that we all have challenges, and mine was that I couldn't see well enough to know if the picture was in focus, so don't even try. He probably didn't think his comment was mean, but it was, and it stuck with me.

This part of the memory pushed me back to reality, reminding me not of the happy times of my almost sixteen years of existence but of the reason I was right here at this moment. The reason I was choosing to end my life.

Last year over Christmas break, a senior boy tried to kill himself. Rumors got out about his reasons. He didn't get early acceptance to Vanderbilt University. He got caught with pot in his car. He lost his starting spot on the basketball team. And surprise, surprise, his girlfriend broke up with him. Those were stupid reasons if you ask me.

Because of that, there was a parent meeting at school last week. Coach Gibbins was head of health and physical education. And he gave all the parents a flyer I found on the kitchen counter the next morning. It had a bunch of warning signs about teen suicide.

The flyer had all the normal stuff, like talking or writing about suicide and withdrawing from social situations. There was something about mood swings and alcohol or drug use. It also talked about changes in everyday routine and giving away possessions. I used it as a sort of checklist of what *not* to do. For the most part, the process was easy.

I haven't ever used drugs or alcohol. I don't really have any friends except Leia, who lives two and a half hours away. I did write about how I was feeling and thought the pages were in a place no one would find. The hardest challenge was not to give at least something to Wade and the twins. I wanted to reassure them that my suicide wasn't their fault.

The paper also listed random facts about suicide, and most of them were standard, but one stuck with me. Teens can think about killing themselves for months and even years, but the statistics show that once a teenager decides to kill herself, she typically does it within the hour.

Give or take thirty minutes, I'd have to agree.

I stuck my head into the hallway and looked in both directions and down the steps. To the right, at the end of the hall, were my older sisters' rooms. Nora and Margot, identical twins, got every ounce of our parents' beauty, talent, and all in all, good genetics.

Their rooms, on opposite sides of the hall, were as different in décor as the two girls were alike. Nora was prim, with the same white linen canopy bed that she'd gotten when she was twelve. She collected China dolls that lined the top of her walls on a shallow wooden shelf that our dad had built just for her. She also collected a silver spoon from every city she visited. She'd gotten the idea from our grandmother's collection of shot glasses, but according to our parents, this was a more tasteful alternative and was one she could show her friends.

In every way that Nora was light, Margot was dark. Against Dad's protests (namely that repainting her walls would take three coats of primer), she'd painted her walls navy blue and hung posters of the great rock bands of the late sixties and early seventies. And even though I knew for a fact that she was too much of a chickenshit to ever smoke dope, at seventeen and a half, she was the absolute coolest person I knew. I got back from summer camp the previous year to find a new-to-her Toyota 4Runner parked at our curb and a note on my bedroom door in her curvy artist scroll:

Charlie! I found the 4Runner on Facebook Marketplace and can't wait to take you for a ride! I might even let you drive! – M

I tightly closed my eyes and could remember how I'd traced the dark, oversized letters, the beautiful, loopy version of handwriting my sister created just for me. The thought made me both glow and fade at once.

To the left was our brother's room. The door was no longer on the hinges because he'd figured out how to work the old-fashioned bolt door locks (from the inside). My dad and our neighbor spent four hours and finally used a chainsaw to free him. Now, my brother sat in the middle of the floor. He rolled the *Little People* cars he'd gotten for his birthday through a matrix of roadways he'd built. He turned five years old a few weeks ago. His blond curls bounced as he contorted himself to reach the outer limits of the carpet city. I remembered the day he was born.

Wade had been a late-in-life answer to my dad's unspoken prayer for a son. He was the perfect snuggle bug and had been my pet since the moment he'd arrived. We were alike in many ways. We were double-jointed and had connected earlobes. I shook away the thought of all the things that made us alike and brought our eyes to the front of my mind, which were as different in function for each of us as they were in color. His were perfect, gigantic, curious, emerald saucers. Mine were deep almond brown, a color that I lovingly referred to as "broken brown" because they gave me the unwanted gift of seeing things differently, or *not seeing things* like my other siblings, and at that moment, the differences were just too big.

The differences were all I could see.

I gently pressed the door and felt it latch. I twisted the bolt closed. I let my hand rest on the old lock, feeling the ridges under my finger, letting my fingernail slide in and out of each groove. *No more broken doors*, I thought to myself. With only a moment's hesitation, I rolled the lock open again. This will be hard enough for my family when they find my body. Why make them break down the door?

I crossed my room for what I was sure would be the last time and gently touched everything I passed. The green and orange knit quilt at the foot of my bed was rough against my hand. I'd had it for as long as I could remember. The quilt was a baby gift from an old friend of my parents whom I'd never met. I felt the cold metal of my camera and the keys of my electric piano that had a magnetic pull on me. I touched the corduroy back of my desk chair, soft and welcoming as my fingertips brushed against its ridges. And finally, I grasped the warmth of the old glass doorknob on my closet door as I pulled it shut behind me. At that moment, the world beyond the door was gone. I was alone with my problem and the only solution I could see.

I set to work with the afternoon light pouring in from my closet window, one of the quirky features my parents chose to keep when renovating our 1920s colonial home. I remember being disgusted that women back then didn't wash their dresses. They just put windows in their closet spaces to "air them out." Why did I remember something so random when I was on the edge of something so intentional? Maybe my mind was trying to remember the good and trying to choose life.

From the corner of my closet, I slid a stack of twenty-five brown, spiral-bound, enlarged textbooks into place on the floor and directly under the square scuttle hole in the ceiling. I took the broom I'd taken from the pantry earlier in the day and used the handle to push the wooden attic access cover open. I flipped the broom to face brush end up, and as quietly as I could, I slid the cover away from the hole. I felt a cold rush of December air hit my face.

I hurriedly looped the rope over the broom handle, tossed it like a javelin through the hole, and held my breath as it clattered against the attic floor above. I listened to be sure no one had heard the noise.

When no one came to investigate, I gently eased the broom handle back across the opening. I pulled against it, lifting my feet from the stack of books, testing the whole of my weight against the handle and the rope. It held.

Until that moment, I hadn't noticed my heartbeat, but now I felt it slamming against the inside of my chest. This was really happening. I was choosing to die. I was choosing not to be a burden.

Through scary, dizzying, deep breaths, and before there was time to think or reconsider, I slipped the loop over my head, cinched it around my neck, and stepped off, feeling the stack of books topple away from my bare feet.

3

Nina

December 2018

I gripped my steering wheel to steady myself as I watched goosebumps appear, and the fine, blonde hair on my arms stand on end. I stopped at the traffic light and waited to turn left into our neighborhood. I shut my eyes as a chill passed through my body. For just a few moments, the world around me was still. Even the stereo sat silent, waiting for my phone to load the next song. This wasn't the gentle, welcome silence that I craved as the mother of three teenagers and a five-year-old. This was the eerie silence that preceded chaos.

When the twins were five and Charlie was three, we were deep into the construction of a 2500-square-foot, two-story addition to the back of our 1920s, corner lot colonial. I'd come home from work to find Bridget, our summer nanny, kicked back on our couch, talking on the phone, and watching *The Real World: Austin*. The living room was a disaster, covered in every Barbie and Barbie accessory we owned. She jumped like a startled cat when I dropped my bag on the floor and asked, "Where are the girls? Where's Charlie?"

We searched inside and out for fifteen minutes. Other than our voices calling their names, the house was that same eerie silence.

Bridget was sitting in the kitchen with her head in her hands, crying, and I was on the verge of calling the police when we heard Charlie squeal with delight from the closed and usually locked, basement door. We'd found the three of them in the mechanical room closet painting each other's hair University of Tennessee, Volunteer orange with old latex paint left by the previous owner.

Since that day, whenever I get that silence-before-chaos feeling, I see orange, and my nose burns from the odor of paint.

The phone rang, breaking the silence and bringing me back to the present. I pressed a button on my steering wheel. "You know that expression, 'A goose walked over your grave?'" I said to my best friend.

"Umm…Weirdo! No? Is that how you answer all your calls?" Suzie Vandenburg's voice made me smile and brought a settling peace in the way that only a best friend can.

"No. Just yours?" The light turned green, and I turned onto Cherokee Boulevard and past the stone sidewalk arches, welcoming me home to Sequoyah Hills.

"So, Nina, what's up with the funeral geese?" she asked.

I laughed and went on. "It's an old expression from the 1800s, I think. It's what people say when they get a whole-body chill."

"They say that a goose walked over their grave?" she asked.

"Yes," I said.

"Why?" she asked.

"I don't know. It's just what people say," I said.

"And it's like a shiver?" she asked.

"No, like cold from head to toe, the whole world gets quiet for a minute, sort of chill." I said.

"Good quiet or bad quiet?" she asked.

"Like the smell of paint, quiet." I said, knowing she'd understand.

"Oh…so a bad quiet."

"I don't know," trying to put what I felt into words. "Maybe not bad, just weird."

"Oh, so it happened to you?"

"Yeah," I said. "Just now. I was just sitting at the light getting ready to turn onto the boulevard." I shook my head, still not able to shake the feeling. "Anyway," I said, changing the subject. "Why'd you call? What's up?"

"No reason," she said, her tone bright. "You just popped into my mind while I was sitting here with the little girls waiting for Leia to finish up her piano lesson, so I thought I'd give you a call. So, how was your day?" she asked in a single breath.

"Not bad. I didn't have court or trial, so I got to wear comfy clothes," I said.

"Ooh, comfy clothes are good," she said.

"Oh, did I tell you that Spanx makes pants?" I asked her.

"Yeah, like leggings?"

"No, like actual pants."

"Like you can wear them to the office?" she asked. "Like on the outside?" she clarified.

"I've been wearing them all day," I said.

"And you're at work?" she asked.

"Yep!" I said. "I mean, I'm in the car now, but I was at work. I got in at about 7:45, was up and down doing trial prep for tomorrow, and had four consults this afternoon, so I was moving and shaking. They're the most comfortable pants ever!"

She was quiet for a moment, and I heard her tapping on her phone. "What size did you get?"

"Small petite, so you'd probably need a medium because you're tall."

"Adding them to my birthday list. Can you believe I'll be forty-five in two weeks?" she asked, more as a statement than a question.

"Nope, because that means Charlie will be sixteen next week, and I'll be forty-five in a month."

"Sweet sixteen!" she said in a dreamy sing-song voice. "What does she want to do for her big day?

"Oooh!" she said, hardly stopping to breathe. "Leia and I could come over, and we could do a spa day!"

"I asked her," I said. "She said she didn't want a big scene." I slowed down as I watched a couple cross the street diagonally ahead of me.

"Nina, a spa day isn't a big scene!" she said. I could imagine her making air quotes with her fingers around the word "scene" as she spoke.

"Agreed," I said, feeling my body relax at the mere mention of a spa day.

"John is on call Friday, and the girls have a half day of school before Christmas break, so I already have Anna scheduled. She texted me last week saying she'd be home from college and was hoping to babysit as much as possible, so I was like, well, this works out well for us both because I am so not ready for Christmas."

I laughed, knowing that my best friend's definition of "not ready for Christmas" was drastically different from my own. That wasn't to say we didn't do Christmas big. Our Christmas was just more "eclectic big." Suzie's version of Christmas was classic and could be in a magazine.

"Anyway, they get out at eleven-thirty, so all I'd have to do is drop Adah and Sylvie at home with Anna. Then Leia and I could be in Knoxville by three, and even with the time change, that still gives us time to squeeze in pedicures before the official birthday dinner, leaving us the whole day Saturday to play. Oh, what about Blackberry Farm?"

"She's turning sixteen, Suz, not getting married. Blackberry Farm would probably be overdoing it," I said, imagining the stunning, $1,000-dollar-a-night, luxury Smoky Mountain resort where Suzie and John got married and where she convinced Charles to take me for our twentieth anniversary. "But a spa day does sound nice. I'll ask her."

The couple who had crossed in front of me stepped over the grass and onto the gravel median. The path ran the entire two-point-seven miles of the boulevard and was one I knew so well I could probably run it with my eyes closed.

I met Suzie during my freshman year at the University of Tennessee. She was Suzie Sanderson back then. We were in the same English class and became fast friends when we realized that my roommate—Nancy Lynn Archer—had been Suzie's roommate at a prep boarding school outside of Atlanta.

We started hanging out regularly, having dinner together a couple of nights a week at the student center, and then Suzie got a wild hair and signed us both up for a half marathon in Nashville. I was so enamored by her and our new friendship that instead of telling her there was no way I could run thirteen miles, I went out and bought a pair of sneakers from a consignment shop near campus and started running.

We logged every training run together, and most of our miles were run on the gravel path that stretched the length of Cherokee Boulevard in my neighborhood, Sequoyah Hills. After three months of training in April, we headed to Nashville in her Jeep and ran every step of the race together. The photo of us holding hands as we crossed the finish line was framed and sat on my desk at work. A second copy rested on the middle shelf of the built-ins in Suzie's living room. That race was supposed to be it, but we enjoyed each other's company so much that we just never stopped. She found the races. I planned the training routes.

We spent hours and miles talking through roommate drama and boy drama, classes and grades, the GRE for her and MCAT for her boyfriend, John, the LSAT for me, and interviews for my boyfriend, Charles. We ran through our engagements and the planning of both of our weddings, which were scheduled just a few months apart during the summer between graduation and everything that came next.

We ran through their decision to live separately for the first two years of John's medical school in Memphis while she finished her master's degree in Knoxville and lived next door to Charles and me in Sequoyah Square. We ran through the surprisingly fast relationship of our mutual friend and former roommate Nancy Lynn to Charles's brother Walter and the announcement of their engagement and wedding three months later. We ran through the speculation that they were pregnant and then the guilt when we suspected but never confirmed that Nancy Lynn had miscarried. We ran through Suzie's struggle to conceive, and we continued to run until I was just over eight months pregnant with twins. Then, the running came to an abrupt stop.

It turned out that my obstetrician, Dr. Heart, a petite, spunky brunette and former University of Tennessee cheerleader, lived in one of the houses that overlooked the boulevard. She passed us one morning on her way to the hospital and did a U-turn to pull in front of us at Sunhouse Fountain. She blocked our path, got out of her SUV, and waited for us where the path met the road. She stood with her hands on her hips and wore the uniform green hospital scrubs and sneakers. I was at least six inches taller than her, but as we walked toward her, I was terrified—like we were walking to the principal's office.

With a perfect game day smile, she ushered both of us into her back seat and physically escorted us home. She sternly warned me that if she saw me running on the boulevard before I was pushing my baby girls in a stroller, she would personally admit me for observation until they arrived. Then she turned to Suzie and said, "You're John Vandenberg's wife, aren't you?"

With her voice shaking, Suzie had said, "Yes, ma'am."

"Has he decided where he's applying to residency?"

Nervous and unable to speak, Suzie just shook her head.

Dr. Heart reached into a side pocket of a leather bag that lay on her front seat.

She looked at Suzie in the rear-view mirror and said, "My husband and I lived apart for the first three years of med school. He was in law school." She turned to face Suzie and handed her a business card. Suzie took the card, but Dr. Heart didn't let go. "That was one of the hardest times in our marriage. It will get better," she said and then let go.

Suzie thanked her and took the card, holding it like it was something precious before tucking it into her run belt. Dr. Heart dropped us off at Suzie's front door and reminded me one more time to rest, then Suzie walked me home.

I crested the hill, and the Tennessee River appeared, stretching out in front of me beyond Sequoyah Park. This urban oasis joined me in patiently waiting for the arrival of spring and the promise of freshly lined baseball diamonds, flying kites, and picnics in the grass. When I reached the fountain where Dr. Heart had stopped us that day, I made a right onto Talahi Drive.

"Nina?" I heard Suzie say. "You there?"

"Yeah, sorry," I said. Lost in the memories, I'd completely forgotten I was talking to her. I slowed down again to ease through the roundabout as I tried to regroup. "I was just thinking," I said, following the road to where it dead-ended and made a right turn.

"About what?" Suzie asked, with a note of concern in her tone.

I knew that I didn't have to explain anything to Suzie. She understood me better than I understood myself at times. She'd have been okay if I'd said, "I don't really know," or, "Nothing really, just tired." She would also know if I were lying. I wanted to try to find a way to explain, at least.

"I was thinking about the day Emma Heart stopped us on the boulevard," I said and knew without a doubt that she'd remember that day.

"Oh," she said with a noticeable shift in her voice.

That was also the day Walter showed up at our door, suitcase in hand. He'd graduated with his degree in engineering that December and had struggled to find a job in the area. He'd been offered several positions in West Tennessee and one with the Army Corp of Engineers in Mississippi, but over and over, Nancy Lynn had refused to move, so he'd turned them down. She didn't want to leave Knoxville. Finally, he took a job in Baltimore, and she would not be going with him. After two years of marriage, they split up.

Over the next few days, Walt found a place to rent in Baltimore. Charles helped him pack his things from his and Nancy Lynn's Fourth and Gill bungalow. Neither of them was talking about what had happened, so while the guys did the heavy lifting, Suzie and I speculated and analyzed everything. Each time, it came back to that day. That was the day everything began to change.

Because the babies were due any day, Walt hired a guy to drive the moving truck to Baltimore and help him unload once he got there.

I hugged him goodbye, and he felt thin. When his taillights winked and disappeared around the corner for the last time, I leaned into Charles and confessed I was worried. He'd agreed but we didn't have time to dwell on that worry. I'd gone into labor around lunchtime, and the twins were born just before midnight.

I turned into our driveway and raised the garage door to see Charles had just arrived home. He was carrying two oversized Target bags, and when he saw me, he grinned. Busted! I eased into my space, turned off the engine, and held up a finger to let him know I'd be a minute. He must have seen something in my expression because he set his bags down. Still smiling, he leaned against his car to wait for me.

"I gotta go," I said. "I just got home, and it looks like Charles went Christmas shopping and bought all of Target."

"You okay, Nina?" Suzie asked, still concerned. "Should I be worried about you?"

"I'll be okay," I said, reassuring her. "It just always comes back to that day."

"I know," she said, knowing nothing else needed to be said and knowing this time of year was always hard. "I love you. I'm here," she said, "and, I'll be there in less than a week."

"I know," I said in a whisper because it was all I could manage. I ended the call without saying goodbye and gently pressed the heels of my hands against my eyes, still remembering. That was the day that changed all our lives forever. The day that set everything in motion and ultimately led us to Marie.

4

Marie

May 2001

I felt the braille dots under my fingertips as I slid them along the line of text for the third time in a few minutes. I was normally a quick reader, but I couldn't keep my mind from wandering.

Walt Mavin had been living at Edgevale house for a month, and true to his word, he came to Wednesday afternoon knit club every week. Some weeks he stayed for the whole time, and a couple of weeks, because of his work schedule, he was there only for the last hour. He did not keep his promise to Mable and Fifi to "take turns" sitting next to them. Each week, he either got there first to claim a spot on the blue velvet couch or, when he arrived late, the seat next to me was conveniently empty, even if it had been occupied the moment before.

It was sweet how well he fit in with everyone. Pluto, Evelyn's husband, was generally a quiet observer. He was always at knit club. Content to read his magazines and history books, he spoke up only occasionally to add tidbits to stories here and there. But once Walt moved in, Pluto appeared to come alive. He really enjoyed having Walt around.

The Ladies of Edgevale were still interested to know more about Walt's life and family. His brother's wife, Nina, had just had twins. The Ladies swooned over the pictures he passed around one week.

Linda Morris sat beside me and held a photograph. She described two babies with practically translucent blonde hair, tiny pink lips, and long, elegant fingers. "Marie, they're just the sweetest things," she said. "When they're together, they sort of curl into each other, and when they're apart, it's like they're looking for each other."

The last four weeks had been innocent fun. Walt and I flirted whenever we were together, and it was obvious to anyone paying attention that there was something between us that no one could quite put a finger on. I didn't have any experience in the arena of love and relationships, but the word I kept coming back to was *chemistry*.

Whether out of concern for me or driven by a level of curiosity that's just tolerated from women of a certain age, The Ladies of Edgevale made it clear that they wanted to understand more about his ex-wife, a woman named Nancy Lynn, whom he'd met in college. Yesterday at knit club, Walter gave them what sounded like the short version, but I was sure there was more to the story. I'd overheard Mable and Fifi talking to Mama and saying the same thing.

Mama didn't say much, but Fifi was worried I was going to get hurt. Mable snapped at them both, "You two need to settle down. Marie's got a good head on her shoulders, and we raised her better than that. I bet my girdle she sees right through his story." I had to bite my fist to keep from laughing out loud. I could imagine her fingers making air quotes around the word "story," just like they often did when I was younger.

I did see through his half-truth. I decided that no matter how good it felt to be near him and be admired by him, if he didn't tell me the whole story on his own, I was no longer interested in sharing a couch with him on Wednesday afternoons or any other afternoon, for that matter.

As though thinking of him conjured his presence, I heard the familiar sound of his boots on the porch. Without saying anything, he sat beside me on the swing. The chains above us jingled as we settled into a gentle rhythm. We sat for a long time in a silence that felt full. I wanted to ask him what he was thinking or if he was okay, but a small part of me, one that sounded like Linda Morris, told me to hold back. So, even though it wasn't easy, I waited.

"Nancy Lynn was pregnant." His voice was calm and deliberate, like he was telling me a story that happened to someone else in another life. "It was a really small service—only our family and a couple of close friends."

His words felt far away, and before I could stop myself, I said, "Walt, you don't owe me an explanation…"

"I wanna tell you. I need you to know that that's why we got married," he said.

"Oh," I said, in a voice so quiet that I wasn't sure he heard me.

"We'd been datin' for a few months," he said. "She said she was on the pill. I don't know if she really was. Either way, she got pregnant, and we got married."

I sat motionless, knowing there was more.

"About a month later, she miscarried, and from that point on, she turned all her focus on getting pregnant again." He stopped for a moment like he was trying to decide how to tell the next part.

"Even though I told her a hundred times I wasn't goin' anywhere," he said, "I think there was a part of her that thought that I'd leave if there wasn't a baby to keep us together."

I wanted to ask why she'd thought that, but all that came out was, "Oh." I couldn't help but wonder. He had just moved all the way from Tennessee and put five hundred fifty miles between them. Had there been some truth to her fear?

"I don't know why she felt that way," he said, answering the question I hadn't been able to ask. For a while, we sat listening to the swing creak as we moved forward and back.

I felt the swing shift as he leaned back, shaking his head. "My mom thinks it's 'cause, growing up, Nancy Lynn didn't really have anybody."

"She didn't have parents?" I asked, confused but wanting to understand.

"No, she has parents or had them at least. But no brothers or sisters," he said. It felt like he was still trying to find the right words to explain something he didn't really understand himself.

"Her mom didn't work, and she was—odd?" He paused to consider his words. "Maybe *eccentric* is a better way to say it. When she came to visit, she was over the top. Her dad was a lawyer at a big financial outfit. They lived in New York City until he died when she was nine."

"Oh my goodness!" I said, covering my mouth. I didn't even notice my braille copy of *Mr. and Mrs. Bo Jo Jones* slide off my lap. I jumped at the sound when it hit the floor and heard Walt pick it up. I felt him set it on the swing between us.

"I know," he said. "Her mom was nutty. She was gone a lot. She didn't work or anything like that," he repeated, and then his voice fell away, like it was searching.

"Nannies mostly raised Nancy Lynn. It's weird, but that sort of thing is normal up there. Anyway, her dad died when she was in third grade, and after that, her mom went completely nuts. She sent Nancy Lynn to a boarding school north of Atlanta. In the summers, Nancy Lynn went to a crazy expensive sleep-away camp in Maine. She never wanted for anything until she met me," he said. I heard sadness in his voice, and I knew what was coming.

"She wanted a family," I said, understanding. I felt sorry for this woman I'd never met.

"She did," he said. I felt the swing move as he nodded his head and went on. "We were married for just over a year when we were referred to a fertility place. We did two rounds of IVF and froze twenty-four embryos. That was enough for four transfers of six eggs."

I heard and felt the defeat in his voice.

"She got pregnant three more times. The first time was with twins. She carried them for sixteen weeks. The second and third were back-to-back, and both were just one baby." He paused and took a couple of slow, deep breaths. "We lost 'em all," he said in a whisper.

Tears slid down my cheeks, but I didn't move to wipe them away.

"I did everything I knew to walk through grief with her, but she wouldn't even talk about them." His voice broke. "I wanted to go to a counselor, but she didn't. I wanted to name the babies we'd lost, and she just wouldn't."

We sat together for a long time. Neither of us spoke as he let me process everything.

"I know it's a lot to take in, and I can understand if... I mean... Now that you know everything, I understand if you don't wanna have anything to do with me." He took a breath. "It's a lot," he repeated,

I reached out and found his leg exactly where I thought it would be. "It doesn't make me not want to have anything to do with you," I said. "It makes me..." I paused to find the right words. "It makes you more real to me."

He laughed. "You thought I wasn't real?"

"No," I said and pulled my hand back, embarrassed. "I just meant..."

He caught my hand in midair and squeezed it. "I'm sorry. I was just jokin'."

I thought he would let go, but instead, he held on. "The truth is, you're the one who doesn't seem real."

I wasn't sure how to respond. It felt like he had more to say, so again, I waited.

"The last year has been hard. I never expected to come up here and feel better. I just thought I'd feel alone," he said.

"Do you feel alone?" I asked.

"No," he said, still holding my hand. "No, I don't."

"Well, good. I'm glad you're here," I said, realizing what I'd said a moment too late. "I mean, we're all glad you're here, especially The Ladies," I said, trying to backtrack. "And Pluto. I don't think he's ever been happier to have someone new move in," I said, rattling with nerves. I willed myself to stop talking to keep from being even more embarrassed.

"Oh," he said, in a tone of mock surprise. "I was gonna ask you if you wanted to go to dinner sometime, but I guess… Should I ask Pluto?"

I laughed and didn't have to see his face to know he was smiling. "He'd probably say yes," I said.

He laughed. "Marie, can I take you out sometime?"

I shut my eyes and took a deep breath. I could hardly believe what he was saying. "Okay," I said, completely unable to hide my smile.

He squeezed my hand and bumped it against his knee a couple of times. "Okay," he said, and I was sure his smile was just as wide as mine.

The next morning, I was stirring cream into my tea when I heard a knock on my door. I set the spoon on a spoon rest beside the electric kettle and went to the door, "Who is it?" I called, expecting to hear Mama or Linda Morris answer back.

"It's Walt."

I stood frozen. Without thinking, I flipped the glass cover of my watch open and touched the hands. Seven fifteen. I took a quick mental inventory. I'd already showered, brushed my teeth, and pulled my hair into a ponytail. That'd have to be good enough. I unlocked the door and pulled it open, and I couldn't help but be thankful I'd opted for a T-shirt and linen drawstring pants instead of sweatpants.

"Mornin'," Walt said. His voice was low and sleepy. "Sorry, it's early. I was just on my way out and wanted to catch you before I left."

"Oh, Poky and I have been up for a while," I said, somehow sounding way cooler than I felt.

"Poky?" he asked.

I pushed the door back, positive my not quite two-year-old, fat, orange tabby cat was exactly where he was every morning at this time—in the corner of the couch and sleeping on his back with his belly splayed just in case anyone decided to pet him.

He laughed, "Now that's the life."

"I know, right?" I said.

"How have I known you for over a month and not known you have a cat?" he asked.

"You never asked," I said, with a playful confidence that I didn't recognize.

"So Poky, like Gumby's sidekick?" He asked.

"Like the Little Puppy from the children's book," I said.

He hummed his approval.

"Do you wanna come in?" I asked.

"I can't," he said. "I want to, but I can't," he said, correcting himself. It was like he'd realized it had come out too quickly. "Next time, I'll plan it better so I can, but I just wanted to see..." His voice shook as he cleared his throat and went on. "Are you free Sunday?" he asked.

"I think so," I said. "Why?"

"I wanna take you somewhere," he said.

"Okay," I said.

"Okay," he said. I heard his voice brighten with a smile. "I'll get ya at four. Oh, and wear comfortable shoes."

"Comfortable shoes? Where are we going?" I was unable to hide my curiosity.

"You'll have to wait and see," he said. Then, like it was the most natural thing in the world, he leaned down and kissed my cheek and said, "Have a good day."

Absently turning my bracelet, I stood for a long time in my doorway, half in and half out of the center hall of the old house. I tried to wrap my head around his invitation, the way my heart sped up, and how my skin sparked at his touch. Finally, I stepped back into my apartment, pushed the door closed, and let my head rest against its smooth surface. "Did that really just happen?" I asked out loud.

Poky gave a long yawning meow in response.

"Yep. He just asked me out."

5

Charlie

December 2018

The moment the rope went tight, I changed my mind. As soon as the heat of the rope began to tear into my skin, I wanted to take it all back. I stretched my toes out for the floor, but as the slick covers of the books slid further away, all I felt were the wisps of the top of the carpet on my outstretched toes. It was too late!

I reached for my neck and tried to slide my fingers between or underneath the rope, but there was no room. I reached above my head, found the line, and tried to pull myself up and take away the pressure. Out of the silence, I heard the robotic voice of my talking watch on my left wrist. It was bumping again and again against the rope as I pulled against it. Over and over, as I kicked and swung, side to side, round and round "4:47. 4:47. 4:47. 4:47. 4:48 …" My body went still. I used every ounce of strength to take away the pressure. The bright closet began to fade around me. Then, from another world, I heard a voice.

"Damn it, Charlie! Your watch battery is going dead again," Nora called. I heard her pushing through the door and moving things on my desk. "Charlie!" she called, moving closer.

I tried to scream, but nothing came out. I tried kicking for the walls and doors but couldn't reach them. Again and again, the watch screamed, "4:48. 4:48. 4:48. 4:48!" like a completely fucked up game of Marco Polo—her calling and the timepiece calling back, demanding that she keep looking, demanding that she find me.

"Charlie!" she shouted, shifting papers, moving things, looking, and then, under her breath, she said, "Ugh! Where is it!?" Then, as though she were touching my own skin, I heard and felt her hand touch the closet door.

The door swung open in front of me, and, at such a close distance, I saw the horror on her face clearly. Nora opened her mouth to scream, but before any sound could escape her lips, her twin clamped her hand over Nora's mouth from behind.

"Wade will hear," Margot said in a panicked whisper as she pulled her into the closet and, with her free hand, pulled the door shut behind them.

"Wade will hear what?" he shouted from his room, and when no answer came, his feet hit the carpet at a trot.

The door latched shut just as he appeared in my doorway. Nora grabbed my legs and lifted me. Both girls were crying and hissing instructions at each other, but all went silent when we heard his palms hit the door with full, five-year-old force.

"Wade, no!" they both shouted in unison.

"Why? What are y'all doin'?" he whined. "I wanna do it, too. I can help! I had by birthday *lasterday*, and I'm not too little. I'm a good helper," he insisted, pressing his face and mouth to the door, muffling the sound of his last few words.

Nora and Margot exchanged panicked looks and, without words, put together a plan.

"Wade, you can help. You're a great helper. Can you get me the scissors?" Margot asked.

We heard his hands squeak against the door as they slid down. "But I'm not 'pose to touch the scissors since when I cut my shirt, remember?" he said.

"Oh, I know," Margot said, thinking on her feet, still pulling back hard on the doorknob. "This is sort of a special time where I can give permission, so can you please, this one time, go get them and push them under the door?" she said, doing her best to take the tears and fear out of her voice.

"Okay!" he said with instant glee. We heard him tear from the room on a mission, chanting, "Scissors, scissors, gonna get the scissors. A secret mission, gonna get the scissors."

Margot let go of the door handle and joined Nora in lifting me. "Can you loosen the knot?" she cried in a whisper.

I shook my head wildly and clawed at the rope, feeling sweat or maybe blood smear over the line as it dug deeper into my skin.

Margot dropped to her knees, and together with Nora, they held me up. I felt their tears soaking into my jeans.

In no time at all, Wade was back, pushing the blue-handled scissors under the door. "Here ya go," he sang.

Margot let go of me and grabbed the door handle with both hands. Nora let go to scoop up the scissors. I heard myself squeak when, for a brief moment, my full weight was again pulling against the rope.

"Get her down!" Margot hissed through tears.

"I'm trying!" Nora cried as she worked on her tiptoes with the scissors, gnawing and chewing at the rope until finally, against the force of the scissors blade, the rope broke. We fell to the floor in a pile. Nora and I both pulled, and the knot slid loose. She pulled the rope from my neck and threw it across the closet as though it were a snake. The air hit my throat and lungs and burned like fire going down. *Sweet, life-giving fire*, I thought as they pulled me between them and held me close.

"What are y'all doin' in there?" Wade gasped, and we all looked at the door. "Are y'all cutting hair?" he asked in surprise. "Mom said no cutting hair," he said, shifting his voice to a falsetto impression of our mother. "You're gonna be in so much big trouble if you're cutting hair."

We heard his weight slide down against the door again. The shadow of his body blocked the light, and then his fingers appeared in the gap under the door. "Margot, can I play too?" he begged.

Margot reached out and touched the tips of his fingers. "No, buddy," she said in a tone that was entirely out of character—gentle, sweet, and full of tears she could no longer remove from her voice. "Not this time." She drew me closer as Nora stroked my hair.

6

Nina

December 2018

Tears pricked my eyelids, and I held the steering wheel like a life preserver. I heard the voice of my therapist—Mitchell Kent—in my mind. *Slow, deep, intentional breaths...* I just needed time to collect myself and calm my anxious heart.

I looked up to find Charles had tucked his Target haul into the space between his workbench and the cabinet where he stored all his clothes that I'd banished from our shared master closet, like Carhartt jackets and heavy flannel that would forever smell like the outdoors. Work boots, baseball caps, and coveralls that reeked of gasoline, lawnmower oil, and a myriad of other totally offensive smells that didn't belong anywhere near the suits I wore to court. Thinking of other things slowed my heart and settled my feelings. *Sadness is a feeling.* I heard Mitch's voice as I whispered to myself, just barely moving my lips, "Sadness is a feeling I can control."

Charles waited by the door to the house with his hands in his pockets, undoubtedly fiddling with his keys, coins, or the three hair ties that I knew he kept clipped to his keys.

I thought the hairbands were a "my dad" thing, but it turned out they're a "girl dad" thing.

Charles had picked up the habit of always having a hair band on hand from my dad. Even though my dad and I hadn't lived in the same town in years, he still carried an extra hair tie or two in his pocket and always had at least one looped around the gear shifter in his car. At our rehearsal dinner, he'd gotten up and presented Charles with a huge pack of them. Dad told him that I'd need one at least once a day. Dad also told Charles that he had no idea how I lost them or where they disappeared to. Then he clapped Charles on the shoulder and told him those would probably only last a year. He told him that he would cover the first year, but after that—as far as hairbands were concerned—Charles was on his own.

When he realized it was going to be more than a moment, he hoisted himself onto the workbench with his feet dangling like a kid and watched me. His eyes said, "Take your time," but I knew his heart well enough to know he was asking, "Are you okay?" He knew better than anyone that this time of year, the weeks before Christmas, were always, and would always be, hard. His patience astounded me, especially over the last eighteen months when my sadness had been worse than it had ever been. A lesser man would have given up, knowing that the deep, exhaustive waves of depression that crashed over me without warning were something he couldn't fix. Charles Mavin wasn't a lesser man, and I was grateful he'd chosen me over two decades ago and grateful that I'd let him choose me.

I reached up and pushed the button to close the garage door, gathered my coat and bag, got out, and crossed the space between us.

Charles hopped down from the workbench, hugged me, and let me lean into him.

"Long day?" he asked.

"Not terrible," I said, breathing in the smell of him— Tide and the faint hint of Dolce & Gabbana Light Blue he'd put on that morning.

"You smell good," I said.

"It's Ho Juice," he said.

I couldn't help but laugh out loud at what he and his brother had called cologne in college. Despite how I felt inside, he could always make me laugh.

"Client meeting," he said.

I nodded, knowing that cologne was generally not something he wore every day but only for weddings, date nights, school stuff for the children, and client meetings.

"Anyone I know?"

"Actually…yeah…probably so," he said. I heard something in his tone, like there was something he'd been hanging onto all day that was meant just for me.

I stayed where I was, ear pressed to his chest. He spoke, and I felt his East Tennessee drawl, easy and smooth, as I listened. He wasn't hard to understand at all.

His southern accent was one of my mother's favorite things about him when I introduced them a few months after we started dating. A few days later, I overheard her on the phone describing him to someone as "easy on the eyes, with a voice slow and sweet like honey."

She was right. Charles never rushed. She'd told whoever she was talking to that she hadn't even realized it, but she caught herself leaning into him like he was a storyteller as he talked about his parents and how he grew up. That memory still made me smile because it was true.

"Who was it?" I asked.

"A home renovation over in Nashville for Allie Quick."

I pulled back from him at the mention of the young country music singer-turned-pop mogul and watched his blue eyes spark and a grin spread across his face.

He knew that I and our three teenage daughters owned every single one of her albums. I still had my stadium tour concert tickets from the previous August tucked into the edge of my vanity mirror. She was one of my all-time favorites.

"Allie Quick, like *the* Allie Quick?"

"Yep," he said, playing it cool.

"You're serious," I said, more as a statement than a question.

"Yep," he said in an unnervingly casual way. He took my bag from me and moved us toward the door to the house.

"She was just there," I said as he bumped me from behind to get me moving. "Like, in your office?"

"Well, not in my office," he said as I opened the door, and he followed me inside. "But definitely in the conference room."

"Charles, that's..." I stopped, looking for a word that was good enough but coming up short.

"I know," he said, not needing me to finish.

Our conversation was interrupted by what sounded like a bowling ball rolling down the stairs. We turned to see our five-year-old son appear in the door.

"Wade," Charles said, running his hand through Wade's wavy blond hair as he ran past.

"Hi, Daddy—secret mission!" he offered the two words as an explanation and kept going.

Maybe it was that he was our only boy after having three girls, but he was such a mystery to me. He didn't just walk places. He stomped. When we'd take long walks in Sequoyah Park down by the river, he could never just walk beside me. He had to carry a stick of some sort and launch rocks into the water. He couldn't resist hopping onto every tree stump and doing a crazy spin-jump off it. And when he spoke, like today, his voice was always a growl.

Charles opened his arms, expecting Wade to barrel into him for a hug, but was surprised when he passed him without a glance. Wade crossed the kitchen, opened the utensil drawer, retrieved the blue-handled scissors, closed the drawer, and turned around. He stopped and finally looked up at us, holding tight to his prize.

"Whatcha doin' bud?" Charles asked.

"I am not cutting anyone's hair!" He waved his right hand wildly with the word *anyone's* and then returned his grip to the scissors.

Charles crossed the kitchen and gently removed the scissors from his hand.

Wade's face fell in defeat. He watched Charles turn the scissors from blade end up to blade end down. Then Charles tucked them back into Wade's palm. His giant green eyes met Charles's, and he smiled.

"Always like this buddy, okay?"

"Okay," Wade whispered.

Charles held him there with only his eyes. He lifted his eyebrows and tilted his head sideways, waiting.

"Yes…Sir," Wade said, taking a deep breath between his words. I could tell he was proud he'd remembered.

Charles ruffled his hair and stepped aside to let him pass. When Wade reached the steps, Charles asked, "Whatcha cutting, bud?"

"Not me cutting, Nora and Margot and Charlie, and they're in Charlie's…" The rest of his words faded away. He never even slowed down as he climbed the steps, rounded the corner, and disappeared.

We stood in silence for a moment as we listened to his footfalls on the carpeted floor above. "It's crazy how much he looks like Walt," Charles said in a whisper.

I flinched at his words, knowing he didn't mean anything by it. It was probably one of those moments where you just say what you're thinking out loud, but I was glad he wasn't looking at me. When the house was silent again, he turned to face me. "Well, that was weird," he said, confirming that he hadn't realized he'd said it out loud.

"Who knows," I said, still staring after our wild boy. I shook my head to clear the cobwebs and turned my focus back to Charles. I did my best to let the echo of his words go. "So, Allie Quick? For real?"

"Yeah," he said. He opened the refrigerator and took out a Coke. "It was sort of wild, because none of us knew she was going to be there." He poured the Coke into a glass he'd filled with ice and waited for the fizz to settle before he emptied the can, tapping it on the rim of the glass. "We didn't even know it was her house. It was purchased in her manager's or somebody else's name. So, when we pulled everything from the city to start planning the project and getting permits, she wasn't anywhere on anything. And then she walks into the lobby with her big ol' sunglasses. It was nuts." He took a sip of his drink, set his glass back on the counter, and crunched a piece of ice between his teeth. "She's a lot taller than I thought."

"Yeah, she's like five-ten or something," I said, hoping it sounded like a guess, even though I knew it to be fact.

"Uh-huh," he said, grinning and crunching more ice. "You should've seen Tullie," he said, referring to Natalie Smith—his office manager—a no-nonsense woman with organizational skills that would rival those of a submarine designer. She was a huge part of the success of his mid-sized architecture and design firm.

"Oh yeah?" I said, imagining her stern, middle school principal demeanor.

"Yeah!" he said, laughing. "She walked Allie back to the conference room and announced to everyone, "People, this is Allie Quick, and she puts her pants on one leg at a time, so don't treat her otherwise."

"Then, totally stone-faced, Allie said that she didn't actually put her pants on one leg at a time. She told the whole room that she lays on her bed, puts both legs in together, and then jumps off the side of the bed to pull them up."

I smiled as he took another drink.

"I didn't think Tullie could blush, but I was wrong. She sure did today!" He leaned back against the refrigerator, crunched another piece of ice, and grinned at me, proud of himself for making me smile.

From above, we heard a thud that caused us both to look up and the glasses in the cabinet to rattle. I started for the steps but didn't get far.

"Babe, let it go," he said, taking my hand and pulling me back to him. "Listen," he said, "Nobody's cryin'.""

We both stopped and looked up again to make sure he was still right. After a few moments of silence, I stepped back and rested my back against the island.

"What's goin' on?" he asked.

"I don't know," I lied.

He ignored me and went on, "I know Charlie's birthday is next week, and that's always hard."

He paused, and I braced myself for what I felt coming next.

"Maybe—"

I started shaking my head, knowing I didn't trust myself to speak.

"Just hear me out," he said and held his hand up, hoping I'd let him finish, but I couldn't.

"I can't," I said, swallowing back tears. "I'm sorry."

We stood there for a moment.

"Are you still seeing Mitch?"

I felt my heart speed up in defense, and I turned my back to him and started pulling potatoes from the bin, scrubbing them, and setting them on a cutting board a little harder than necessary.

"Nina?"

"Yes!" I said and slammed the last potato on the counter so hard it split.

"Monday…I'm seeing him on Monday." I clenched my teeth and counted backward slowly.

"Okay." He stepped closer. I felt him behind me even though he wasn't touching me. He kissed the top of my head, and I heard him turn to leave the room.

"I'm just sad," I said, knife hovering above the potato, feeling tears on my cheeks. "I'm just really fucking sad." I took a slow breath, knowing he would wait for me to get the words out. "It just feels so wrong that she doesn't get to be here for any of this," I said, only able to manage a whisper. "I just miss her. I miss her so…fucking…much."

7

Marie

June 2001

The light from the glass in the front doors warmed my legs. Walt and I sat on the stairs in the center hall just outside my apartment. Opal and Gene Odell from Unit 5 had their granddaughters over for the afternoon. We listened as they sang a hand-clapping game.

"Double double this this,
Double double that that,
Double double this,
Double double that,
Double double this that."

I remembered the game from childhood when I bumped the ends of my fists together with my partner's fists. Then we flip-flopped our hands. The trick was to remember which way your hands were supposed to turn when you said the word "this" and then turn them the opposite way for the word "that."

Without thinking, I moved my hands on my knees along with the song. A moment later, I laughed with the girls, who apparently fumbled the motions because they burst into hysterical giggles. They settled quickly and started the rhyme over, but this time, they only made it through the first line before they started giggling again.

"Do you think they're lost?" I asked, still smiling at the silliness going on two floors above.

"I'd guess so," Walt said, tucking his arm around me and pulling me close. "Chuck doesn't ask for directions."

He kissed my hair, and I heard him breathe in—slow and deep.

I let my cheek rest against the worn flannel of his shirt. I knew without asking that it was the shirt he'd worn on our first official date. I closed my eyes and let the aroma of cologne and dryer sheets take me back.

Walt had asked me out early on Friday morning, and the rest of that day and Saturday crept by. I felt like a kid in the days leading up to Christmas. Poky tried to convince me to take a Sunday afternoon nap, but I couldn't. My excitement filled every corner of my apartment. I finished up two small recording projects for work. I cleaned out my purse and reorganized my kitchen drawers. I washed the sheets on both my bed and the guest bed, mopped the hardwood floors, and vacuumed the couch cushions.

Poky followed me through the apartment, meowing in protest until I turned my nervous energy in his direction. He let me trim his nails and then sulked under the living room chair while I changed his litter box and vacuumed his cat tree. He reappeared only when I filled his bowl with a can of soft food. I knelt by his bowl to listen to him purr as he circled me and rubbed against my legs. He still chattered his annoyance but was willing to be friends again because there was food involved.

Mama and Fifi stopped by around three, and I had them double-check my outfit. Forty-five minutes later, I pushed them out the door, brushed my teeth, sprayed my wrists with perfume, and rubbed Poky's belly for luck. Then it was four, and Walt was knocking on the door.

Before I had a chance to ask who it was, he said, "It's Walt."

I opened the door. "Hey, come on in. I'll just get my jacket," I said, stepping to the side to let him into the living room.

He stopped just inside and touched my shoulder. "I brought you somethin'," he said.

"You did?" I said, surprised and excited.

He took my hand and turned it palm up, "Hold still."

"What is it?" I heard a gentle rattle. "Oh goodness," I said, feeling my heart speed up. "Is it alive?"

"No," he laughed and placed what felt like a crumpled piece of paper in my hand.

"What is it?" I asked again, only this time excitement formed the edges of my words.

He took my free hand in his and said, "See for yourself." He brought the tips of my fingers to the edges of what I discovered were the delicately rolled edges of a folded rose.

"It's made from a page of the flyer from Pimlico," he said, knowing I'd understand the significance.

"How…" I said, astonished at the sentiment and even more at its intricacies.

"When Chuck and I were younger, we'd make contests out of everything. We'd call them "Betcha Can'ts." With a sort of faraway tone in his voice, he went on. "It was mostly stupid stuff like 'Betcha can't eat this whole sandbox,' or, 'Betcha can't jump off the roof and land on your feet.' In case you were wondering, neither of those turned out well."

"Oh no," I said and covered my mouth to stifle a laugh.

"So," he said, trying to sound serious but not really succeeding. "In high school, one of Charles's girlfriends was doin' the debutante thing. She asked him to take this paper art class with him. Of course, he didn't want to be the only guy in the class, so he walked into my room on a random Sunday afternoon and said, 'Betcha can't make a paper swan.' And I was like, "The hell I can't!"

My shoulders shook with laughter.

As seriously as he could manage, Walt took my hand and went on. "I learned to do the crane, a pig, a sailboat, one of those spinning wind things..."

"A windmill?" I offered.

"Yeah, a windmill," he said, snapping his fingers. "I also learned to make paper roses. I wanted to give you somethin' that you could touch and that wouldn't die, and that would mean more than just flowers."

"You did good," I said, and with a boldness, I'd not felt before, I stood on tiptoes to kiss his cheek.

We drove down to the water and parked in Camden. We walked and talked our way down to Fells Point.

He told me that except for him and Chuck's wife's best friend, Suzie, no one called his brother Chuck.

Since I'd never had a brother or sister, or really any other kids my own age around to play with, I asked him about the rules of siblings.

"What do you mean?" he asked.

"It just feels like there are so many rules with siblings. Like how someone can say crazy stuff about their own sisters and brothers, but nobody else can," I said.

"Oh, that's totally true," he said.

I nodded and went on. "Or how you seem like a person who isn't really competitive at all, but when it comes to your brother, you totally are."

"True again," he said with a laugh. We walked for a bit in comfortable silence, and then he stopped walking and turned to face me. "So, you remember when I told your mom and Fifi about the potholders?"

"That your mom taught you to knit them to keep you and Chuck busy?" I asked.

"Yeah," he said. "That was a Betcha Can't from mom. She bet us both that we couldn't knit 100 potholders in twenty-four hours."

"Did you make it?" I asked with a laugh.

He laughed, and we started walking again. "Neither of us won, but she still tells the story, and Chuck swears it's how he got the scar above his left eyebrow when he fell asleep and landed on his knitting needles."

When we'd both stopped laughing enough to talk again, he said, "Now that we're older, most of that competitive stuff is gone. He's my best friend. One of the best people I know."

"He sounds great," I said, and my voice sounded far away as I imagined them.

"They're comin' up in a couple weeks, and I really want you to meet 'em," he said.

"Oh," I said, surprised but excited that he was thinking farther ahead than the next day or week. "You'd better hope this date goes well."

He laughed and squeezed my hand. "I know, right?"

Somehow, without realizing it, half an hour had passed. He slowed us down and led me through the narrow doors of what I'd later learn was Dudas', a restaurant in an old, converted row home. It smelled like crab cakes and hush puppies with the unmistakable spice of Old Bay. The space was filled with the hum of a crowd, not rowdy but friendly and familiar.

"Walt!" A booming voice called through the crowd. "You made it!'

Walt leaned close, "My boss's son tends bar here," he said, leaning in so I could hear him. "I don't ever eat out, so when I asked about good places to eat, he said I had to bring you here."

And then the man with the booming voice was between us. He rested a gentle hand on my shoulder and clapped the other on Walt's with a loud slap. "Pop told me y'all might be in and said to take care of ya tonight," he said, steering us through the main room to a table at what sounded like the back.

"Margie!" he yelled over the noise. "Get 'em a bucket, a Natty Boh, and a dozen oysters on a half shell!" The word oyster came out like *eer-ster*, and he was so close that I could smell his cologne, cowboy boots, spearmint gum, and the hint of stale beer. The smell wasn't unpleasant, just distinct and memorable.

"And crab cakes—ya like crab cakes, right? What am I sayin'? Of course ya like crab cakes," he answered for us. "Margie, get 'em some crab cakes!" His laugh bounced between us and came from somewhere deep in his belly. He was a character in a movie, too big for the room. "Margie, get 'em both the crab cake dinner," he repeated.

We settled into our table, and Walt leaned in and said, "They say these are the best crab cakes in Charm City."

"Who's they?" I asked with a playful smile.

"That's a great question. I saw it on the sign outside."

The crab cakes didn't disappoint. In fact, the meal was one of the best I'd had in a long time, partly because of the food, partly because of the company, but mostly because of the whole experience.

After dinner, we talked and walked back the way we'd come. Walt stopped to get a blanket from his truck, and we found a spot on the grass in Patterson Park just as a young singer was taking the stage in front of the pagoda.

The whole night, I sat tucked into him. I can't tell you a single song she sang or even what her name was, but I can tell you everything about the way he made me feel—safe, wanted, and for the first time ever, like I was enough exactly as I was. I felt Walt squeeze my shoulder, which brought me out of my memories and back to the present.

"They're here!" he said and took my hand to pull me gently to my feet.

We stepped out onto the porch when I heard a door shut and, seconds later, feet on gravel, then cold hands taking hold of mine.

"Marie!" It was a man's voice, and without even being introduced, I knew he was Chuck.

I reached out my hand to him, and he took mine. He didn't shake my hand but held it tightly. "We are so excited to meet you."

"You, too," I said, and I meant it. All the anxiety I'd had leading up to that moment was gone.

"This is my wife, Nina," he said, taking one of my hands and joining it with hers.

"Marie," her hands were cold, too, but her voice was so warm that I caught myself leaning in. I started to shake her hand, but she surprised me by pulling me into a hug. She pulled away and then held me at arm's length. "We're just so happy to be here and so happy to meet you!" She hugged me again. Everything about her felt good.

Chuck laughed and said, "That might have something to do with the fact that we've been circling the neighborhood for the better part of a half hour, and she made me stop to ask a jogger for directions." His voice was friendly, like Walt's, but his accent was less southern.

"Nina, this is one of the many reasons I'm glad he married you," Walt said and gave a quick hug.

"Marie, you're going to learn very quickly that with the Mavin boys, it's the little things," Nina said, still holding my hand.

I laughed, feeling a million things all at once—relief, excitement, happiness, but most of all, at home. Yes, physically, because we were in my home, but also home and comfortable with Chuck and Nina.

8

Charlie

December 2018

That night, Nora and Margot agreed to tell Mom and Dad I'd had a migraine and had gone to bed. In return, I swore I was okay and promised I'd explain everything in the morning. They left my room but cracked the door. A few hours later, when I suddenly woke from a nightmare, I found them both in sleeping bags on both sides of my bed.

I slid gently from my covers and off the end of the bed. As I reached the door, Nora sat up like she'd been wide awake.

"You okay?" she whispered.

"Uh-huh," I said, embarrassed. "Just…" I gestured to the door. "Bathroom."

"Okay," she nodded. "Need anything?"

I shook my head, "I'm okay." I said, looking up from the floor and seeing the outline of her head and shoulders in the dark. "Nora…?"

"Yeah," she said. "I'm…" I started. "I'm sorry."

"I know," she said, and even though I couldn't see her face, I heard relief in her voice.

As I stood in the dark bathroom, I couldn't avoid my reflection in the moonlight that poured through the window. I splashed water on my face. I touched the marks around my neck, and the full weight of what I'd done settled around me. I couldn't help but be thankful it was winter, and I had a closet full of turtleneck sweaters. Hiding the bruises from my parents would be easy, but keeping what I'd done a secret would be more difficult.

That truth rested with Nora and…

"Margot!" I said, finishing my thought out loud, startled by her appearance in the mirror. I knew what was coming and shut my eyes. I gripped the sides of the sink to brace myself for what I was certain would be a fight. There was never a middle road with Margot. With her, it was love or hate, enthusiasm or indifference. With her, the water was raging, or the pool was empty. If the river was raging, the ride would either be exciting or terrifying. Either way, the conversation was guaranteed to be memorable.

"Why'd you do it?" Margot asked from the door. Her tone was not unkind, but a definite edge scared me.

I was sure that if I didn't tell her the entire truth, she'd still know, and then I'd have no choice but to explain everything to our parents.

Fear settled into knots in my stomach. Giving it a name, saying it out loud, that made it real. *Suicide attempt.* The secrets would no longer be just mine.

She stood motionless in the door as her question hung in the air between us. Her need for an explanation and the weight of my secret was so heavy that carrying it alone was exhausting.

"My vision is changing," I said. I didn't turn to face her. I was afraid of her response. "I'm starting to lose my sight."

Margot didn't move and didn't speak. I think she stopped breathing. Time stretched for so long that I couldn't help but say something to fill the silence. "Before, I just couldn't see well," I said, shutting my eyes again so I didn't have to see her looking back at me in the mirror as I tried to explain. "Now, I know it's the RP advancing," I said, dropping my chin to my chest. "I'm going to go… I'm going…" My voice fell away as tears came. I was angry at my weakness. I balled my hands into fists and pushed through the knot in my throat.

In my mind's eye, I backed out, hoping to try a different approach.

"There was a girl…at school…"

"What girl?" Margot asked, confused and disoriented by my change in direction.

"Porsche Holt," I said, knowing the name would strike a nerve because Porsche's older sister Penelope was in their grade.

In the mirror, I saw her cross her arms over her chest like she was physically holding herself back. She didn't speak. She just waited for me to explain.

"Something fell out of my bag," I said.

When I didn't elaborate, she said, "What? Like a tampon or something?" I heard and felt her irritation.

"God no!" I said, shaking my head once, frustrated that she wasn't connecting the dots. "Do you seriously think something that stupid would have gotten me where I am… where I was?" I corrected.

She stood there waiting, not accepting silence as an answer.

"It was way more personal than that," I said, hating myself for what came next.

"Well?" she said, her anger barely restrained.

"The Book. Somehow, she got her hands on The Book," I said, imagining it in the brown envelope inside the mailbox where I'd placed it this afternoon. The words had taken the wind out of me.

"The Book you and Leia share?" she whispered, understanding the gravity.

The Book was a small journal passed back and forth weekly between my best friend Leia Vandenburgh and me. Leia lived in Nashville, and we'd been writing to each other since she was nine and I was ten. The current Book was a simple red bound book with lined pages and an elastic band that wrapped from top to bottom to keep it closed, but there were twenty-three other unique volumes that were tucked away in a trunk in the attic less than ten feet from the scuttle hole in my closet.

Leia was my person, and I was hers, and every important thing that had ever happened to either of us was written in those books. We shared crushes, movie tickets from her first date—even though her mom completely set it up—the dates we got our periods, when Wade took his first steps, and when she thought her sister Sylvie was going to die when she'd been rushed to the hospital with a ruptured appendix. Everything was in those books. We left nothing out. We sugarcoated nothing. The pages were filled with every worry and wonder, every accomplishment and disappointment. The Book's pages held pure joy, devastating sadness, and everything in between.

"I wrote about how I was feeling—everything," I said, my voice breaking. I swallowed hard, pressing down my tears and rage, then kept going. "Somehow, Porsche found it. I don't know if she took it from my bag or if it fell out, and I didn't notice. It doesn't matter."

I wiped my eyes, frustrated that I couldn't get through this without falling apart. I took a deep breath in and blew it out to settle my thoughts.

"Today, after school when I was leaving, I saw her holding court on the lawn outside. Of course, there weren't any teachers, but she was reading from a book like she was auditioning for a play or something. When she saw me, she called me over and told me I had to hear what I'd written. She said it was like sad poetry. At first, I didn't understand, but when I saw up close what she was holding, I knew. She read every private thought I had about everything!"

"About a boy?" she said, still confused.

"No!" I said in a whisper that sounded like a hiss. "God! Do you seriously think I'd kill myself over a boy?"

"No! I don't know!" she said, equally frustrated. "Honestly, Charlie I never thought you'd try to kill yourself in the first place, so cut me some fuckin' slack!"

"She read about how much I hate myself!" I said, spitting the words out. "About how I wish I hadn't been born! And how much I hate being such a burden. How my family would be better without me. About how every teacher hates that they have to deal with me and how I've overheard them saying teaching blind kids in public school is a waste. How I will always be broken, and I'll never be enough! That I'm a waste, and it'll never be okay to be me, exactly how I am!" I shut my eyes, knowing I hadn't even gotten to the worst. "All I could do was stand there," I said.

"You could have walked away," Margot said through clenched teeth.

"I'm not strong like you," I said, shaking my head, "and I couldn't lose The Book. I had to wait for her to get bored of humiliating me. When she was finally over it, she tossed the book in the dirt."

I dropped my chin to my chest as tears flowed into the sink. I spoke her words from memory:

"'You know Charlie, I was just thinking…' She tossed her blonde hair over her shoulder and kicked the book toward me with the toe of her Uggs. 'Have you ever thought about un-aliving yourself?'

'What?' I tried to say, but it came out like a squeak, just louder than a breath.

'Yeah, I mean, you're a lot like all those famous poets and artists.' She reached down, picked up the book, and held it out to me. I reached out to take it from her but when I grabbed hold, she didn't let go and let me pull her close. She let go and leaned in so only I could hear her. 'Basically, you're nobody until you're dead.'"

I opened my eyes and watched Margot in the mirror. Every word I'd spoken connected with her like a physical blow, knocking the air out of her and leaving her speechless.

"Blind—" I whispered through clenched teeth, finally able to get there. "I'm going blind, and I'll always be a burden on someone."

Margot took a small, quick breath, unable to hide her surprise. "First of all, Porsche Holt is a bitch, and second— none of that shit is true," she said, shaking her head.

"It is true!" I said, needing her to understand. "Margot, it was like a deleted scene from the movie *Mean Girls*, except in this nightmare Regina George wins. And every thought or feeling I've ever had about going blind was read out loud on the high school lawn like a fucking flash mob from that Broadway show *Hamilton*."

"No, I meant the other stuff. You're not a burden—you are enough—you're okay exactly as you are."

I shook my head, not able to believe her.

Margot wrapped her arms around herself. "How long have you known?"

I ran my fingers through my hair and knotted them into fists at the nape of my neck. "A few weeks," I said, knowing exactly what she would say next.

"You should have said something." Margot took a slow, deliberate breath and stepped forward. She was close enough to touch me but she stayed still, rooted, where she stood. "You shouldn't have waited. You should have let us walk through this with you!"

In a move that surprised us both, she put her hand on my shoulder and turned me to face her. "I'm serious," she said. She took her hand away from my shoulder, then reached down and took my hand in hers. The gesture wasn't lost on me. Margot wasn't the type to unnecessarily touch anyone. Holding hands was reserved for potluck dinner prayers and deathbed goodbyes.

"Don't think for a minute that you're alone in this," she said.

We were so close now that I felt the heat from my sister's body as we whispered in the dark.

"Charlie, you were diagnosed when you were nine years old. We've been waiting for this. We've been preparing for this." She wiped a tear from her cheek. "Charlie Bee..." She spoke my childhood nickname with emotion deeper than any I'd ever heard from her before—a sweet melody, a lullaby that slowed my pounding heart and eased the thumping inside my ears.

At that moment, it occurred to me that as much as Wade was mine, as much as I doted on him and tried to look out for him because he was forever my unspoken favorite—in the same way, I belonged to Margot.

With these realizations tucked into my pocket, I reached for her. I thought about what it would feel like to lose Wade. I thought about the reality of what I'd done. I thought about what I'd put my sisters through. What I'd put Margot through. The weight pressed into me. And, even though I knew she would draw away, I still pulled her close and held her tighter than I'd ever held her before.

I felt her shake inside my embrace. It was right then that I made a silent promise to fight. And when my fight wasn't enough, I would ask for help. When my body failed, like I knew it would, I would ask for help. When I felt like running away, I would ask for help. I would let them walk through this with me.

The following night was Saturday, and Nora and Margot came to me insisting that we had to tell Mom and Dad what had happened. I asked them for more time. They reluctantly agreed to wait one more day.

The next night, after Wade had been put to bed, I made my way down the old L-shaped closet back staircase. These features were another original detail of the house that my dad refused to part with in the remodel.

I sat out of sight on the last step before the landing and listened to my parents in the kitchen. I knew without seeing them that Mom was wiping down the already clean counters in slow cathartic circles as Dad read to her. I leaned forward and rested my head in my hands and put my elbows on my knees. I let the quiet of the house settle around me and shut my eyes while his words came into focus.

It was their time together and had been for the last year. They'd never talked to us about it, but we all knew that they'd gone through something that started sometime last year between Thanksgiving and Christmas. Mom had gone weeks without speaking to anyone unless it was absolutely necessary. She left early in the morning and stayed away late. She told us that it was for work. Her fuse was short with everyone. Then, on a Saturday morning in early February, when we should have been sleeping in like normal teenagers, Nora, Margot, and I listened from the top of the steps. Mom cried, and Dad told her to stop, his voice somewhere between frustration and sympathy. He said he was glad she was going and that she needed help.

She was gone for fourteen days. She didn't call. She didn't write. Dad said she and Aunt Suzie had gone on a girls' trip, but Wade was the only one who believed that lie. I knew it wasn't true because I saw Aunt Suzie in the background when I was FaceTiming with Leia. It was the first time I could remember them lying to us, other than the normal stuff that parents lie to kids about. Then, two weeks later, it didn't matter where she'd gone, because she was back, and she was better. And now, every night after dinner, without fail, he reads to her while she cleans the kitchen and listens.

I felt Nora sit down behind me and rest her chin on top of my head. "Are they still on Jodi Picoult?"

"No," I said, shaking my head. "They finished *House Rules* over the weekend and started *11/22/63* last night."

"Is that Grisham?" she asked.

I rolled my eyes. "No, Stephen King!"

"Oh, excuse me!" she said, and I felt her jaw tighten into a smile.

"With all that *America's Next Top Model* in your brain, there's no room for the good stuff, like telling the difference between John Grisham and the one and only Stephen King," I said.

"You know you like it, too!" she said.

A silent laugh escaped my lips as she pulled me into a gentle hug, neither of us taking our eyes away from our parents. Watching them felt like catching them kissing. With four children at home, those moments were stolen and precious. We knew we should probably turn away to give them privacy as they shared what felt like an intimate moment together. At the same time, we couldn't leave because this was a glimpse into the heart of what we each dreamed of in our future husbands.

Margot slipped in beside us just outside the kitchen. "Grisham?" she asked.

"King," Nora said.

"Really?"

"So says Charlie, but it sounds way too normal for Steve," Nora said in a playful whisper.

I rolled my eyes and said with a smile, "Y'all need to read more!"

"Is it too soon to ask if we'll still get those priceless looks even when you're blind?" Nora asked and kissed my cheek.

I wasn't surprised that Margot had, as the spokesperson for the twins, insisted we tell Mom and Dad everything. Nora had talked her down to reveal only the essentials of the situation, insisting that the details of what had happened in my closet would hurt more than help. She said that telling them everything would cloud and redirect their focus away from my physical health toward my mental health.

I'd sworn to them that it would never happen again, and Nora had taken me at my word. But every time she looked at me, Margot's eyes revealed the fear and anger that remained.

"May we help you?" Dad asked.

The three of us looked around the corner and down into the kitchen. He hadn't even looked up from the hardcover that rested open on the table, but somehow, at the same time, he had been able to peer over the top of his slim, silver-framed glasses to spot my socked feet on the landing or maybe he'd heard us. His blue eyes sparkled with a hidden smile even though we'd interrupted.

"We wanted…" Nora started.

"…needed to talk to you about something," Margot corrected. Then they both looked at me, expecting me to pick up where they'd left off.

With all eyes on me, my knees began to shake, and I felt my whole body blush.

Dad tucked an index card between the pages and closed his book. He pulled out the chair next to him for me and then gestured with a gentle nod for Nora and Margot to sit on the bench on the other side of the table.

I looked at Mom and saw that her eyes, which had been warm and engaging moments before, were now ice blue and full of fear. I pressed my lips together annoyed. Why did she always react like this whenever we asked to talk to her? It was so frustrating. She made us feel like we couldn't talk to her about anything.

She folded her towel into thirds, hung it on the edge of the sink, and put her hands on the counter. With tentative apprehension in each step, she moved around the kitchen island and sat at the end of the table. I say 'sat' loosely. *Perched* is better. If I said something wrong, she'd take flight.

We sat for a few moments without speaking, locking eyes with each other and waiting for someone to ask—for someone to tell—for someone to break. I couldn't bear it any longer and dropped my gaze to the table and then my lap to where my hands were clenched so tightly together that my knuckles had turned white.

Dad cleared his throat and looked at each of us with a mix of questions and concern. "Sometimes," he said, bringing his eyes to rest on me, "when there's something that's hard to talk about, it's easier," he paused, turned to me, and leaned close to finish his sentence as a whisper in my ear, "if we close our eyes." He pulled away and looked at me, letting me know that whatever I had to say, they could handle it. He wanted me to let them take the weight of what I was carrying.

I shut my eyes and felt tears slip down my cheeks. I shook my head in frustration and wiped away my tears with the back of my hand. I was so angry that I was crying again. I opened my eyes and tried to start again, but when I opened my mouth, I still couldn't speak. I dropped my clenched fist to the table with a thud, cleared my throat, and started again.

"I think…I mean…I believe that," I began, the words shaky, but at least they were there.

I continued, "For the last few weeks, I've noticed that my...my vision...I mean...I don't know for sure, but I think the RP is advancing." I looked up from the table and saw sadness in Dad's face.

"What makes you think that?" he asked.

"At first, I wasn't sure. Back in October, when we went to Boo at the Zoo, things were so cloudy. I mean I can't ever remember being able to see well at night, but it was worse."

Dad laced his fingers together and pressed them to his mouth. He nodded but didn't say anything, so I went on.

"Then, when we went to Dollywood for the pumpkin thing a couple of weeks later, as soon as the sun went down, I couldn't see anything except blurry light." I looked at Nora and said, "I don't know if you remember, but I came out of the bathroom and was completely freaked out. This lady touched my arm, and I screamed."

Nora nodded.

"The lady said she was sorry for scaring me and asked if I was okay. I apologized for screaming and told her I was fine and I'd been waiting for my sister; she'd startled me."

Nora nodded again, "That must have been right before I walked up because I remember you talking to a woman."

As Nora spoke, I looked over at our mother and saw her shoulders relax with relief. Why was she relieved?

We'd talked about this possibility in the past, and there was a loose plan based on the typical progression of RP. Those plans included things like surgery, a guide dog, occupational therapy, and even the possibility of a boarding school for the blind where I could learn the normal school stuff but also braille and basic life skills. Everything we'd talked about and planned for would alter life as we knew it, and she had the nerve to look relieved. From where I sat, it looked like she was barely able to contain a smile.

"Charlie, this is okay," she said. Her eyes were shining, and her voice—there was a lift in her tone—an audible joy at the edges of each word. Every word she spoke made me feel like she was happy to be done with me.

The next week was business as usual. I went to school while Mom worked her magic. Somehow, she'd managed to make an impossible appointment in Nashville with a retina specialist at Vanderbilt University Medical Center, whose waiting list for new patients was over four months long. Her parents, Nana and Papa Doc, had materialized Wednesday morning after a last minute, overnight flight from Oahu, Hawaii, where they'd settled when Papa Doc retired from the Army. Mom scheduled time off work, and she, Dad, and I were leaving for Nashville in the morning. While we were gone, my grandparents would take care of things at home and get things ready for Christmas.

That night, I had trouble falling asleep, and once I finally did, my dreams were filled with ropes that turned into snakes. I saw dark rooms and sliding floors. Hot sand and the touch of cold hands against my skin caused my eyes to snap open. I woke up breathless and sweating. Even with my eyes open, I still lay in darkness. It occurred to me that one day soon, darkness would be my daily reality. My life, at best, based on my research, would be a life spent looking for lines between light and shadow.

I shut my eyes and felt the edges of my world blur. My thoughts pressed so deeply into my chest that I couldn't help but cry, and the sound was one I didn't recognize. The reality, both of what was happening to me and what I'd almost done to myself and my family, filled me with pain that burned from the inside out. It came from far inside, a place where the deepest, darkest parts of my fear lived. A place where I felt so alone. A place I couldn't help but be washed into but also a place where I couldn't allow myself to stay. I promised myself not to go there anymore.

That promise nudged at me and pushed me to get up, to push away the darkness and rise.

I rolled to my side. I reached for my phone on the dresser and the screen lit up, showing the time, 4:06 a.m. Knowing that there wasn't a chance of sleep, I decided on a shower, praying that the water would rinse away this blameless hurt.

Heated bathroom tiles warmed under my feet as I rolled the shower faucet handle all the way to hot and then pulled it gently back to warm. Steam began to rise and fog the mirror. I pulled a towel from the cabinet and tossed it gently across the top of the shower's glass door. I pulled off my pajama top and bottoms and dropped them into the laundry basket. Even with the heat under my feet, the chill of the air made goosebumps appear on my skin.

The shower was everything I needed it to be. The coconut-scented shampoo filled the air, and my thoughts drifted back to a day six years before. I saw the image of Nora and Margot splashing in the Pacific as I woke up under a beach umbrella next to Nana.

I touched my face the same way I'd done that day and remembered the indentions the beach towel had left on my cheek. I remembered looking around and waiting for the world to come into focus. The smell of sunscreen and the texture of sand were so vivid as the hot water rolled through my hair and down my back.

I remembered trying to blink the gray away. It was like I had water in my eyes, but no matter how much I tried, the gray just wouldn't clear.

"Hey, sleepyhead. Did you get sunscreen in your eyes?" Nana had asked as she watched me rub my eyes.

I pushed the heels of my hands deep against my eyes, just as I'd done that day. For a moment, the world went black, and bright stars of light appeared as I pulled them away, but just like that day on Ewa Beach, the world never came back into focus.

I shut off the water, pulled my towel to me, and pressed my face to the warm terry cloth. I stepped out and felt the autopilot of my "getting ready" routine take over. Without thinking, I applied lotion to my face, arms, and legs, put on foundation, added a touch of eyeliner, and swiped mascara over my lashes. As I capped the lip gloss, I wondered how much of this I'd be able to do from memory. I pulled my wet hair from its towel and looked at myself in the mirror as I let my hair fall over my shoulders, framing rather than canceling the red marks around my neck. I tried not to look at them and instead tried to think about what parts of my incredibly simple routine I would have to give up.

I pulled a robe from the back of the bathroom door and hung my towel on the hook in its place. Without a sound, I left the bathroom and crossed the hall. When I stepped into my room, I was stopped cold. I found my mother sitting on the end of my unmade bed.

9

Nina

December 2018

I watched Charlie appear through her bedroom door. Her wet hair fell over her shoulders. The skin on her face and neck was red from the shower. Startled, she pulled her robe tighter around her body and further up around her neck. I saw the surprise on her face a split second before she was able to hide behind the mask of wanting to be so much more grown-up than she was. There were so many secrets between us.

For sixteen years I'd been able to ignore them and pretend that she was mine. But as I sat on the end of her bed in the quiet hours of the morning, I felt the tangible truth racing toward us. Every lie Charles and I told—every wrong choice we'd made—they all crowded the space between us.

I had no doubt that she'd seen something in my face the night she'd shared the news of her declining vision. She'd seen the relief that had washed over me. It was so stupid. I'd been so transparent. I thought, just like I had with every confession or revelation before this one, that she'd figured out the truth. Somehow, despite how careful we were in concealing it, I thought she'd found out about Marie.

"I heard you shower and figured since we were both up, you might want some company," I said.

Charlie nodded, and by her expression I could see her mind turning. I could pinpoint the moment she decided not to be angry with me. At that moment, I allowed myself to relax.

She crossed the room and stepped into her closet, out of sight.

"Do you want me to fix your hair?" I asked. "Maybe a Dutch braid that comes across the back and onto the side?"

She reappeared in loose fitting jeans, a turtleneck, and a zip-up hoodie with her high school's logo on the front.

"Sure," she said.

"I hope I remember how. I haven't done one in a while," I said with a wink.

"You could probably braid in your sleep," she said with a playful eye roll.

"Grab your brush and no complaining."

Charlie nodded in agreement. "Do you remember what you used to tell me when I was little, and I would scream that you were hurting my head?" She picked up a brush from her dresser and began to work through her long strawberry-blonde hair.

"Of course! I told all you girls that if you didn't stop screaming, I'd stop and leave your hair exactly as it was. And..." I held up a finger, "if you remember, I only had to do it once to Margot when she and Nora were seven or eight years old."

Charlie nodded with a laugh. "Yeah, Nora and I were so scared after that!" She handed the brush to me and sat down with her back to me. "You even left the brush in her hair!"

I laughed, "I completely forgot about that!"

"Really?" Charlie said with surprise. "How could you forget leaving the brush? That was the worst part! It took Nora fifteen minutes and some mad scissoring skills to get it out without removing a big chunk of Margot's hair!"

"I must have blocked that part out," I said in a tone that conveyed exactly the opposite. I did remember. It was like most of the harder parenting moments I'd had to walk through. I could recall every detail, and I sufficiently beat myself up over it on a regular basis.

Charlie held her brush out to me, and I gently pulled through her hair and separated it into three sections on the right side of her head. Before I had a chance to ask, Charlie held an alligator clip over her shoulder, knowing exactly what I would need before I even asked for it. I took the clip and secured her loose hair in two sections on the left.

I made quick work of the braid as Charlie recounted Nora's removal of the brush from Margot's hair. She described in detail with accuracy how her hair had looked that day and how all three girls had cried on the way to church. She described everything so perfectly. As she spoke and I braided, I was reminded how Charlie was able to bring a memory to life and draw such a complete picture with her words. I wished again that this part of her had come from me.

As I drew her hair together at the base of her head, Charlie turned to face me. My fingers worked quickly as I wove them underhanded over Charlie's shoulder, wrapped the end tightly in a hair elastic, and let it rest against her chest. She looked up at me, holding my gaze.

"So, Leia said something earlier in the week about them coming here on Friday for my birthday."

A voice inside my head was screaming, *"Tell her! Tell her now! This is truly your last chance!"* In my mind, I heard my own voice crying out, *"I lied! We lied! I am so sorry! You aren't our real daughter, but God, how I wish you were! God, how I wish you were truly mine!"* But my lips stayed tightly closed, and the promises we'd made over sixteen years before held; the secret was safe. The truth stayed hidden, and the moment passed. My chance was gone.

She watched me, waiting for me to respond.

"Yes," I said, shaking my head. "Sorry, just lost in thought, I guess."

"About what?" she asked.

"Nothing really," I lied.

"So, my birthday?" she repeated. "Will we just do it another time?"

"No, I think since we're staying with Suzie, we'll just relocate the celebration," I said, "If that's okay, of course."

"Sure," she said, in a tone that was hard to read.

"If it's not, we can do something else, or—"

"Mom, it's fine," she said. This time, her tone wasn't hard to understand. "I'm gonna go make tea." She reached for her braid and twisted the end around her finger, appearing distracted by her thoughts. "Thanks for the hair," she said and bit her bottom lip. "Actually, I think I need to...I mean, I want to have it down." She slipped the elastic off and undid the braid I'd just put in. Then she pulled her damp hair over her shoulders.

I stood up. "Oh, you'll need to—" I started to say but stopped short in shock when she stepped away from me and back toward the door.

"Mom, it's fine!" she said, taking another step back. "I'll just blow dry it and run the flat iron through it. It'll be better for the drive." Then she turned on her heel and was gone.

10

Marie

July 2001

We moved to Edgevale house in the summer of 1986. I was nine years old and had just finished third grade. We made our way up the long, wide, sweeping driveway. I sat in the back of Mom's new Chrysler minivan with my face pressed against the glass. I can still remember the way the gravel sounded as it crunched under the tires and how the house looked with the red brick and white trim as it peeked through the trees. I'd heard them describe the house as *the lady on the hill*. The lawn opened in front of us, and she came into view, and I knew that was the perfect way to describe her.

Those early days at Edgevale were such an adventure. I met every person there and explored every nook and cranny of the house and grounds. The house sat at the top of the hill like a proud lady and the grounds sloped away from the *lady* like the skirt of an old-timey ball gown. My favorite spot was a flat grassy area at the base of the lady's skirt that Daddy called the *hem*.

On a hot Sunday afternoon in early July, I'd taken Walt down to the *hem* and spread a blanket in the grass. He was holding my hand as we rested in the hazy space between asleep and awake.

"I was thinking," he said. His voice was slow and sounded far away to me as I dozed.

"What?" I said, trying to focus.

He squeezed my hand and rolled onto his side. He pushed my hair off my cheek and went on. "It's my parents' thirtieth wedding anniversary next month."

He kissed my fingertips, and I felt my skin tingle and electricity touch me just behind my belly button.

"I thought you might wanna come down to Knoxville with me," he said.

"What?" I asked. I pulled my hand away and covered my face smiling, embarrassed that I still hadn't heard him and had no idea what he was talking about.

He laughed again.

I sighed and ran my hands through my hair. "I can't think when you do that?"

"Do what?" he said, with a playful tone at the edges of his words. He scooted closer and kissed my neck.

Like a reflex, I felt myself stretch into him and heard myself practically purr.

"That," I said and turned to him. I brought his lips to mine, and just like every time we kissed, I felt a piece of me slip into that space that was quickly becoming "us."

I pulled away to breathe. "So, you're going somewhere. I'm listening now."

"Yeah, so my parents are having this thirtieth anniversary party next month. I thought maybe we could go down there and stay with Nina and Chuck. And then maybe you could meet my mom and dad."

"And they invited me?" I asked.

"They invited you and said I could come if I wanted to. You're all Nina and Chuck can talk about," he said.

"And they know about me," I said, knowing he'd understand.

"They do," he said, answering the question I hadn't asked.

"Okay," I said, feeling the beginning of apprehension creep in. "So, we'd be staying with Chuck and Nina?"

"Yeah, I mean, we could stay at Mom and Dad's, but I thought since you and Nina got along so well and y'all have kept in touch, you'd wanna stay with them."

"No—yeah—I do," I said, trying to keep my nerves at bay.

He pulled back, and I felt him looking at me. "So, is that a yes or a no?"

"Sorry—yes," I said, trying to shake away...myself.

He slid his hands around my waist and pulled me back to him. "You okay?"

His hand slid up my back just under my shirt, and without thinking, I hooked my fingers into his belt loops and pulled him even closer, trying to push away my inexperience. I didn't think about how it would affect either of us. I just brought our hips together. He groaned in the same way I had a moment before, and I felt him against me in a way I'd never felt anything or anyone before.

He slid his hand to my hip, squeezed it gently, and then pulled himself away. He leaned in and touched his forehead to mine. "I can't think when you do that," he said, repeating my words back to me.

I felt myself blush, embarrassed.

"What?" he said, not letting me hide my face. "I was just teasing."

"I can't—" I said, shutting my eyes, pulling one hand free and covering my face.

"Can't what?" he said, sounding confused. "Marie, don't." He pulled my hand away from my face and kissed it. "Talk to me. What?"

"Ugh! Walt—this is so embarrassing!" I said and sat up.

"Why?" he said and sat up, too. "What?" He crossed his legs between us and pulled my legs over his. We weren't as close as we had been before, but we were still close.

I dropped my head, and my hair fell over my shoulder between us. "You can't look at me when I tell you this," I said.

"Okay," he said. "I'll shut my eyes."

He took my hand and drew an *X* on his chest. "Cross my heart. I'm not even gonna peek."

"It's two things," I said, letting him put his arms around me and pull me closer. Everywhere he touched left the heat of his fingerprints behind. I had to shake away the dizzy, drunk feeling and refocus physically. I'd never felt any of this before, and somehow, I had to tell him this, knowing he'd felt it all before, but with someone else. "Walt, it's possible I have been the most sheltered person on the planet."

He laughed. "That's part of what I love about you," he said, taking the end of my hair and twirling it around his finger, and giving it a gentle tug.

"Seriously, Walt. I was homeschooled and raised by a house full of old ladies, and don't you dare tell them I said they were old!"

"Your secret's safe with me," he said, matching my shift in tone. "Now keep goin'."

"Walt, I produce radio commercials from my guest bedroom. Not counting driving through the corner of Delaware to get to the Eastern Shore, I've only left the state of Maryland a few times. I have no experience with…this stuff," I said, gesturing at the tiny space between us. I put one hand on his chest and the other on mine. I felt our hearts beating, mine fast, his strong and steady. "In my head, I don't know how to do any of this. But my body…" I shook my head. "That's a different story. My body feels like it's trying to make up for lost time. It scares me."

We sat for a bit, with my hand on his chest, his heart thumping. Neither of us said anything while he absently traced my back along the inside of the waistband of my jeans.

"What was the other?" he said.

"What do you mean?" I asked, confused.

"You said it was two things."

"Oh, right. Like I said, I can't think when you do that."

I took a handful of his T-shirt and made a fist, hoping I could find the right words.

I didn't want this to come out wrong and sound mean. "The second is that I have no experience, and you do." The last part came out like a whisper.

"I do what?" he said, playing dumb.

"You're not making this easy for me," I said.

"Nope," he said. "Marie, if I've learned anything, it's that you gotta say what you're thinkin'. I can't be in your head. I can't read your mind. If this is gonna work, you gotta talk."

He was right, but that didn't make it any easier to say out loud.

"You've already done all this before. I feel like maybe it's all not a big deal to you or like you'll just expect me to do things because...maybe...you're..." I stumbled over my words and tried to regroup. "Like maybe because you and Nancy Lynn have—I mean had—" I felt my face getting hot and tried to finish. "I mean you were married—so sex. Because you did sex—I mean had sex. You've had sex." I covered my face again, blowing out in frustration. "I sound so stupid!"

"You don't," he said, and he sounded like he meant it. "Just keep goin'. You'll get there."

"It wouldn't be a big deal for you...I mean I know it would be something you'd want to do... I don't know if you'd sort of expect me to do it, and I..."

He took the hand that was holding his shirt, and I stopped talking.

"Marie, you don't have to—"

"Wait, no, I need to finish this," I said, interrupting him.

"Okay," he said, not letting go of my hand.

"What I'm trying to say is...you make me feel stuff...and I mean in a good way, but in a way where I don't trust myself. I don't know how to do any of this, and I'm so worried I'll do it all wrong. It's scary to me that in my head, I don't know how to do any of this stuff, and then my body...does. I don't want my body to tell you I want to do stuff when my head and heart aren't ready."

"So, you don't want to…" he said, and now he sounded confused.

"No, I do…it's just I don't—ugh…" I said, burying my head in my hands again. "This isn't coming out right." I tried to start again, only this time I tried to slow down. "Walt, I want to do everything with you. This is all so new. I don't want to rush through any of it. I know I'm not your first *anything,* and that's okay, or at least it's something I think I can get through, but you're my first *everything.* Every time you touch me, it's like that moment on a rollercoaster when the bottom falls out, except, try riding the rollercoaster with your eyes closed. It's scary as hell."

"I didn't think about that," he said. His voice was soft and thoughtful.

"It's like this," I said, getting an idea. "Take off your shirt."

'What?" he said and laughed.

"Seriously, I wanna show you," I said.

"And you need my shirt?" he said, and now I could tell he was grinning.

"No," I said. "I need you without your shirt." I held my hand out to him.

He pulled off his T-shirt and put it in my hands.

I took it, folded it neatly, and set it on the blanket. "Okay, now lie down," I said and touched his bare chest and pushed him gently back.

I reached for the small bag we'd brought with us that had a Nalgene bottle of ice water. I unscrewed the cap and dipped my fingers in to retrieve an ice cube.

"Close your eyes," I said.

"Okay," he said, and I heard something different in his voice. Maybe reverence. Like he was taking me seriously, he took my free hand in his and set it on his stomach. "I'm all yours."

I already knew his body so well and from memory I moved over him. I took the ice cube and touched it to his forehead.

"Oh man," he said and let out a laugh.

I laughed, too, and pulled the ice cube away. I touched it to the space just behind his ear. Underneath me, I felt him jump and shiver.

He reached up and rested his hands on my hips where I sat just below his waist, but I took them and put them back by his sides.

I drew a line from one side of his chest to the other, and he drew in a sharp breath as he held on tight to the blanket. I lifted the ice and felt it drip twice as I brought it down to the smooth channel that ran just above his hip and sloped down. With each drop of water, I felt him squirm under me. Finally, he took the ice from my hand and pulled me down and over him. We were so close that I could have tilted my head and kissed him, but I needed to wait for him.

"Marie," he said, and touched my face, then my shoulders, then my arms, and then my hands, lacing our fingers together. "Every first we have together means something to me. You're pretty much my favorite person in the world, and I'm not gonna do anything you aren't comfortable with."

"Even sex?" I asked. "What if I want to wait?"

"Marie, I don't ever wanna have sex with you," he said.

I pulled back, surprised. "You don't?"

"Nope," he said and tucked my hair behind my ear. "When we get there. If we get there, it's gonna be so much more than that."

"Not if, when," I said, trying to reassure both of us.

"Marie," he said, and his voice was low and serious.

"I love you."

"You do?" I said, a smile spreading across my face.

"Uh-huh."

"You love me," I said.

"I do," he said, and finally, he kissed me.

11

Charlie

December 2018

The mile markers slid by in a blur as we rolled down Interstate 40, somewhere between Knoxville and Nashville. I was nestled into the back passenger corner of my dad's beloved and ancient 4Runner, comfortable with my pillow and a fuzzy blanket. My earbuds were piping in Allie Quick's newest—a pop mastermind album that was rumored to be a response to celebrity haters. It was epic; somehow, every song felt like it was written inside my head. The volume was low enough that I could eavesdrop on my parents' conversation.

They'd been married for twenty-one years. They weren't perfect. They argued about dumb things like the toothpaste tube to the point that they now used separate tubes. They had epic standoffs about big things like what the twins would do after high school—college versus a service year. Through all of that, though, there was a constant and palpable love between them. Even now, as the miles slipped away and we drew nearer to Vanderbilt and what was sure to be an emotionally and physically draining weekend, they held hands. Despite what was coming, they continued to choose each other.

This was sure to be an emotionally and physically draining experience. They sat, holding hands, talking about the details of the model home show that Dad's company was putting on in the spring and a new celebrity client he had. They kept calling the person Q like he was James Bond or something. It was so annoying, I had to force myself not to roll my eyes every time they said it.

I leaned my head against the glass, hypnotized by the broken white line that divided the lanes as it sped by, and wondered, not for the first time, why they weren't as consumed by my blindness as I was. Then again, there was another part of me that wasn't surprised at all.

My mind drifted back to six years before when we'd made a similar road trip west. On that trip, my mom was pregnant with Wade. Instead of listening to Allie Quick through earbuds, Mom had surprised me with Quick's album, *Stand UP*. We made Dad listen to the entire thing.

We had a heated debate about the importance of all four food groups at every meal, and I remember my dad's reaction when I told him the four food groups were practically prehistoric. All the teachers at school had been talking about how First Lady Michelle Obama had thrown out the food pyramid and replaced it with a Food Plate.

We sang the entire Broadway cast recordings of *Wicked* and *Legally Blonde* and were about to move on to *Phantom of the Opera* when Dad refused to play another musical. He'd taken control of the stereo and played Journey's Greatest Hits album for the rest of the drive. Things were so much simpler back then.

As I reflected on that trip and compared it to this one, it occurred to me that both of my parents were experts in distraction and redirection. It also occurred to me that they employed their talent just as much for their own benefit as they did for mine. It seemed like they were also trying to avoid the truth.

As I waited with my stomach in knots, I made the decision that I wasn't going to play their game.

Even if it hurt them, I needed to talk. I needed to work through what was about to happen. I needed to acknowledge the inevitable and walk through the logistics. I needed to start talking about how I was supposed to do life.

I tapped the screen of my phone to pause the music and said, "So, will I see the same doctor as before?"

They'd probably thought I was sleeping because the sound of my voice appeared to catch them off guard.

"No," Dad said. He looked over at Mom with a smile, and she laughed.

"What's funny?" I asked, annoyed at what I felt was an inside joke at my expense. I didn't see anything funny about any of this.

She turned sideways in her seat and looked back at me. "So, you know Dr. Graham, the older doctor you saw the first time we were at Vanderbilt?"

I nodded, knowing it would bug her but not caring.

Even though nodding instead of speaking was one of her biggest pet peeves, she went on like I hadn't even done it.

"He retired about three years ago," she said. "They let me know when I called the other day to make your appointment. I was frustrated that they hadn't let us know since you're still connected with them through your ophthalmologist back at home, but anyway, that's another thing entirely." She looked back at Dad.

I smiled, imagining her slipping into 'lawyer mode' and giving a bunch of nurses hell, but when I saw her watching me, I let my face fall again.

She shifted so she was turned backward in her seat. "They let me know that a new Head of Low Vision had been brought in shortly before Dr. Graham retired, and she was amazing." She took a breath, building suspense.

"She assured me that we'd be pleased with Dr. Peepers." She paused for effect, but I kept my face expressionless.

She went on. "Dr. Peepers did her residency at Wilmer Eye Institute at Johns Hopkins in Baltimore and then did a pediatric ophthalmology fellowship at Kellogg Eye Center at the University of Michigan."

She grinned and raised her eyebrows, "So you, my dear, will be seeing Dr. Audrey Peepers, the ophthalmologist," she said with air quotes around the doctor's last name.

"So," I said, matching my mother's expression of raised eyebrows but not her enthusiasm, "is that her maiden name, or did she marry into that irony?" I smiled, unable to hold it in anymore. The two of them exploded into laughter, and the moment instantly thawed my icy mood.

We spent the final hour of the trip making up more ironic doctor names and creating entire stories about their families. We even named their pets. A lady anesthesiologist named Dr. Goodnight was married to an orthopedic surgeon named Dr. Bones. They lived in Scarsdale, New York. They were both so busy that they didn't have time for kids, but they did have a bulldog named Butcher and a cat named Stitches.

There was a cardiologist named Dr. Love, a dermatologist named Dr. Whitehead, an ear, nose, and throat doctor named Dr. Achoo, and a geriatric doctor named Dr. Wrinkle.

Each silly name sent us deeper into fits of laughter until we pulled up in front of a beautiful, cottage-style Sylvan Park home that I knew as well as my own. While we were in Nashville, we'd be staying at my mom's best friend's house, a woman I affectionately called Aunt Suzie even though we weren't at all related.

Just as she always did when we arrived, Suzie Vandenburg stepped onto the front porch and waved big. She was dressed in heels, skinny jeans, a fashionably loose sweater, and a pink apron that read "Kiss the Cook" in gigantic white letters. This apron was only one in a collection of more than thirty that were ironed, folded, and tucked away in the back of her enormous walk-in pantry.

Dad stopped the truck at the curb, but before he had a chance to turn off the engine, Mom was out of her seat and hurrying to meet Suzie halfway.

Suzie was one of those people who is always put together. She had a wicked sense of humor and absolutely no filter. She was loud and over the top, and I loved everything about her.

I'd hurried to catch up and was right behind Mom, being pulled into a warm and welcoming embrace. I breathed in Suzie's sweet perfume, a mix of honey, and whatever was currently baking in her oven. She let go of us, and I was surprised when Suzie brought her hands to my cheeks and kissed my forehead. She pulled back and held me at arm's length and locked her bold blue eyes with mine. I couldn't have looked away if I'd wanted to.

"Sweet girl," she said, forgoing formalities and simply cutting to the chase to dispense what I was sure would be unarguable wisdom. "I don't want you to forget what I'm about to say," she said, waiting for me to agree to the terms of what was coming next.

I nodded, but Suzie shook her head.

"No, Kitten," she said, using a nickname she'd given me when I was a baby. "You have to promise." Again, she waited, "You have to say it."

I found my voice. "I promise," I said, just above a whisper. I felt the intensity of what would come next pressing in and was surprised by how fast that feeling had come over me.

Suzie pulled me close, bringing her lips so near to my ear that only she and I would ever know what she had said. "Everything will be okay! This will not break you, beautiful girl!" She paused to gather her next words. "Whatever happens, this will *make* you." With her thumb, she wiped away a tear I hadn't realized was there and kissed me one more time. She let go and said, "Leia's waiting on you. She's upstairs in her room." She turned me gently by the shoulder. "Go on," she said and nudged me forward.

Suzie dropped back and wrapped her arm around Mom's waist. She called over her shoulder to my dad, "Chuck," a pet name that Dad allowed only Suzie to use, mainly because there was no stopping her, so why try, and partially because I think he liked it, "I made cinnamon rolls." She waved a hand over her shoulder for him to come on!

I didn't have to look back at Dad to know he was pulling our bags out of the back of his truck and grinning when he called back to Suzie, "Yes, ma'am!"

The moment I was through the door, I heard a familiar sound, like a baby elephant barreling down the steps. The girl behind the sound hit the kitchen floor at a run and rounded the corner. Without slowing down, she squealed my name and launched herself into my arms.

Leia Vandenburg was a carbon copy of her mother. Just like her two younger sisters, Adah and Sylvie, she had straight blonde hair that was long for the winter. She smelled of the tea-tree oil shampoo from Trader Joe's that I knew was stocked in every bathroom in their house because of Suzie's phobia of head lice.

She pulled back from me, and I saw pink cheeks and a radiant smile. I couldn't help but smile back at her. She was the only person on earth who completely understood me and was always happy to see me. Today, that felt particularly good. She was dressed in a white polo shirt with her school's logo, a red plaid uniform skirt, white knee socks, and saddle shoes that looked so clean they could have been brand new, even though I knew they weren't.

"Mom didn't tell me until this morning you were coming," she said, out of breath from how fast she'd come downstairs. Without a break in the conversation, she pushed her hair behind her ears, pulled a red knit headband from around her neck and into place atop her head, and pulled the hair back over her shoulders. Her excited chatter filled the space around us. "I was hoping you guys would get here before we had to leave for school, and you did!" She clapped her hands. "Ten minutes to spare." She took a quick breath. "Mom made cinnamon rolls, but I'm sure you can smell them all the way down the block. So freaking good!" she said, rolling her blue eyes back into her head.

She took my hand and pulled me deeper into the house. "Dad's already at the hospital, as always, but I think we might walk up there after school." Another quick breath. "Mom said y'all were going up there this morning for an appointment. She didn't tell me anything about it, and she told me not to be nosy, but seriously, it's like she doesn't know that we're friends." She held her hands up with her fingers spread wide. "Like best friends, and you'll tell me anyway!" She rolled her eyes with extra drama and then dropped one hand and threw the other hand into the air, making a big circling gesture over her head. "I told her I wouldn't be, but seriously." She stopped and turned to me with a jerk, her blonde hair swinging like a fan. "I mean…" For a brief moment, she was quiet, as though she was refueling. "…there's only one thing that would bring you back to Vanderbilt practically overnight. And on top of that, I got The Book yesterday, so I already know."

I opened my mouth to speak, not really sure what would come out. Leia stopped me with a quick hand up like a crossing guard, but close to her chest, and then a finger to her lips as our parents appeared in the front hall. "Eat," she said, producing a cinnamon roll on a plate. "We'll talk later," she said with a wink and a grin.

"Leia, Adah, Sylvie," Suzie called, clapping a few times. "Three minutes."

"Gotta go," Leia said, throwing her arms around me again. She stepped back. "I'm so glad you're here!" Then she smiled a smile that lit up the room. She turned, hurried to the mudroom, pulled on her navy winter coat and backpack, and with a wave over her head, she disappeared into the garage.

Behind me, I heard seven-year-old Adah as she scooped her homework off the kitchen table and, without even looking up, said, "Hey, Charlie."

"Hey, Adah," I said and reached out to tug at one of her French braids. "Your braids are gettin' good!"

She looked up at me and beamed like I'd said exactly what she needed to hear. She took the braid I'd just pulled between her fingers and inspected it. "You think?"

Leaning against the counter, I shook my head, put a bite of cinnamon roll in my mouth, and with my mouth half full, I said, "I know." I'd learned in the last couple of years that offhand comments meant more to Adah than something that was overdone. My two-word compliment meant more to her than an hour of praise from Leia or their mom.

She pulled her giant backpack onto her shoulders, held a strap in each hand and then nodded once.

Five-year-old Sylvie slid into the kitchen like she was wearing skates and swung around my legs like someone would swing around a lamppost. "Charlie Bee!" she squealed as she made a second circle around my legs. "Where's Wade?"

"Oh, he couldn't come this time," I said.

"Why?" she asked, making a third trip around my legs until Adah snagged her hand and helped her into her identical blue pea coat.

"Oh, he has school, but probably next time," I said.

"Okay," she said, as Adah lifted a glow-in-the-dark backpack, and Sylvie slipped her arms into the straps. They turned and walked through the mudroom into the garage.

I stood still as the house whirred around me. Suzie took my plate from my hand gently and eased me to a stool at the counter. She kissed my cheek. "Be back in a flash," she said, collecting her purse from the countertop and slipping through the open garage door that Sylvie had forgotten to close, only to reappear a moment later to pluck her keys from a hook on the wall marked "Keeper of Keys" and then pull the door shut behind her.

That entire scene couldn't have been scripted better as an illustration of the exact reason I loved this family and loved this house. Always busy. Always full of life, noise, and love. I cut away another bite of my cinnamon roll to reveal a section of the message printed on the plate that I knew would eventually read "Clean Plate Club." I smiled.

"It's better than the 'Eat Me' plates." My mom sat down beside me.

We both laughed, thinking about how so many things that Suzie owned made a statement, not just in style because it was definitely stylish, but also literally. Like the 'Kiss the Cook' apron she'd hooked on the wall before she left, Suzie had an apron for every occasion and mood; "I cook for shoes," "Leftovers," and, "You get what you get, and you don't pitch a fit!" She had pillows that said "Home" and "Dream" and "His" and "Hers" tossed on both of their favorite spots in the living room. Her children's names were shamelessly embroidered, stenciled, labeled, and ironed on everything they could potentially lose or fight over. Their heights were written on the wall just inside the mudroom.

A few years before, for Christmas, Suzie's husband, Uncle John, had found a door company and had them make a paneled swinging door that had the word *Pantry* etched into a frosted glass panel. There was even a light switch in the living room that, unfortunately, controlled every wall outlet in the room. Instead of trying to figure out how to change the switch, Suzie had physically stenciled an arrow pointing to the light switch and the words "Don't Flip My Switch," hoping that people would stop turning off the power to the room. Some might consider her love of labels an unhealthy obsession, but to us, this was just Suzie.

"What time's my appointment?" I asked, breaking the comfortable silence that had settled around us.

"Ten," Mom said, taking two plates from the stack and transferring a cinnamon roll to each from the pan.

"Tell me again how y'all met and became friends," I asked.

"Maybe another time," she said and patted my knee. "I'm really tired."

I rolled my eyes and picked up my plate. "Whatever," I mumbled under my breath and walked to the living room. I'd heard their story a hundred times before, so it shouldn't have been a big deal, but it was. I knew it was a story she loved to tell, but now it was a story she just didn't want to tell me. If I'd been more observant and less self-involved, I'd have seen that my words hurt her and that she did look tired, but under that, I would have seen that she also looked sad.

Two and a half hours later the exterior of Monroe Carell, Jr. Children's Hospital came into view as we turned the corner onto "Children's Way." The building was a mass of glass and bright color. I wondered why a designer somewhere thought that slapping bright colors on a Children's hospital made it fun. That might work on other kids, but I was positive that within those brightly colored walls, nothing fun would ever happen for me.

Dad eased his truck into the valet drive at the front of the building and stopped under a curved awning that looked like a giant glass wave. He unbuckled his seatbelt and looked back at me. "You ready?" he asked.

I nodded and attempted a smile. I wrapped the cord of my headphones around my iPhone and tucked it into the pocket of my hoodie. I checked the collar of my turtleneck. It was still high and tight, hiding the bruised skin of my neck.

Dad opened my door. I took his outstretched hand and slid out. The frigid December air hit my cheeks, and the wind that whipped through the buildings took my breath away. I pulled my beanie cap down over my ears and tucked my chin low. Dad took my backpack from me and handed it to Mom, who swung it over her shoulder. He put his arm around me and guided me inside and out of the cold.

As we stepped through the double sliding doors of the hospital's main entrance, the warmth of the lobby made my face tingle. Despite my fear and anxiety, it was as though we'd entered a magical place. There was a grand staircase with pillars that stood before us and stretched out and up into the hospital. The staircase offered handrails of both child and adult height, and of course, there were bold colors everywhere. Main Street, where all the hospital shops and food court were, was a flurry of activity and chatter off to our right. In an instant, we were in a different world. All the sullenness I'd felt on the short drive from Suzie's house began to thaw. Maybe there was something to the colors.

12

Nina

December 2018

Everything around me brought back memories of the last time we'd stood in this lobby and the events that led us to that point. As my husband and our youngest daughter walked ahead of me, I paused. For a moment, I let the memories consume me and hold me in place at the bottom of the grand staircase. Then, I was seven months pregnant with Wade, and Charlie was two weeks short of her tenth birthday.

A few months before, we'd gone to Hawaii for my dad's retirement ceremony from the Army. As a splurge, Charles and I island-hopped over to Maui for a couple of days and left the girls with my parents. The twins were about to turn eleven, and Charlie was nine. While we were gone, Charlie had started to complain about things being blurry and that she wasn't able to see clearly.

Having no idea of the secrets between us, my mom just thought that Charlie was tired or that maybe she'd gotten a bit of sand or salt water in her eyes. My mom never mentioned Charlie's complaints to me.

When we got back to my parents' house and were packing for our trip back to Tennessee, I noticed Charlie rubbing her eyes excessively and asked her what was wrong.

"Everything is still really blurry," Charlie said.

Her response caused Charles to look up from his book. He looked at me, and there was no way to hide the bolt of fear that passed through my body.

From the kitchen, Mom said, "Yeah, she's been talking about that for the last couple of days."

A silent message passed between Charles and me. He's always been able to read my mind. He sat beside Charlie on the floor and spoke to her in a completely normal voice, so he didn't alarm her or anyone else.

I looked at my phone, and even though it was after seven o'clock and our flight left the following afternoon, I knew, without hesitation, exactly what had to come next. I lifted myself off the floor where I'd been folding our clean laundry and packing. As I walked past my mom, I heard her say, "She probably got sand in her eyes or some sunscreen."

I slipped into my dad's office and shut the door behind me. My stomach was in my throat, and my heart was pounding. I knew our perfectly knit lie was about to unravel.

"Daddy?" I said.

He grunted without looking up from the medical journal stretched across his desk.

"I think Charlie needs to go to Tripler," I said. When he didn't respond right away, my tone grew more insistent, "Like now!"

He looked up with confusion. He looked around as though he'd expected to see his third granddaughter lying on the floor, unconscious or bleeding out, around the corner, just out of sight.

When I didn't give an explanation, his confusion grew. He cocked his head sideways and really looked at me, his only daughter, wringing my fingers at what would have been my waist had I not been so pregnant.

"Nina?" he said and leaned back in his leather chair, causing the springs to creak. "What's goin' on?" he asked, letting his southern drawl and rural Tennessee roots seep through. His only tell was a tiny crack in his iron façade that revealed his growing concern.

I walked back to the door, locked it, and crossed the room to sit on the couch that was against the wall beside his desk. He turned his chair to face me. It squeaked as he leaned forward with his forearms resting on his knees to listen.

I'd never forget the way the creases slowly appeared along his brow as the truth came tumbling out—the true story of Charlie, her birth, her birth mother and father, her genetic medical history, and how she came to be with us.

I knew better than to leave anything out, and more importantly, I knew not to cry as I told the story. Being raised the daughter of a full bird colonel, I'd learned to make my bed daily, always be on time (which meant be early), and never cry if it hindered the transfer of information.

When I finished and there were no more secrets between us, my hands rested motionless on top of my belly. All I could do now was watch and wait as he took several silent moments to put all the pieces into place.

Without a word to me, he turned away and punched numbers into the old phone that rested on the far corner of his desk. "Yeah, Crutchfield," he barked into the receiver. There was a quick pause, and then, "Tell 'em Hawkins."

He shortened his consonants and drew out his vowels. My heart sped up as it always did when I saw my father in action. He was a different man when he was at work. He was a different man when he worried.

The room was thick with silence for several minutes as he waited. Then he shook his head, "Nope, he can't get back to me." He paused to listen, then said with irritation in his voice, "Specialist Stephens, that information is as useless to me as a knitted condom. Tell him to un-fuck himself from wherever the hell he is, put on his Go Fasters, and get his ass to the fuckin' phone."

Another pause—longer than the first. Finally, Crutchfield was on the line.

"Hey... Yeah... Doesn't matter... Look, I'm gonna be arriving in fifteen... Yeah, Tripler... No, to the ER." His voice was solid, the tone steady and unchanging. "Yeah, at nineteen thirty with my granddaughter." There was silence for a moment as he listened, "She's…" he paused, turning to me.

"Almost ten," I mouthed, holding up one index finger and making a zero with the other hand.

"She's nine," he said and turned his back again and continued. "Charlotte Mavin."

There was another brief pause. He took his reading glasses off and laid them on the journal on his desk. He sighed deeply and rubbed the bridge of his nose. "I need you to call in Miller from opthi." He ran his hand through his short gray hair and took another deep breath. "Yeah, I know. She's not gonna mind." He let out a chuckle at something Crutchfield had said. "No, she's alright, just high speed." Another laugh. "She and Colleen are close. I'd call her myself, but I gotta get rolling in that direction." He nodded to himself. "Alright, see ya in fifteen," he said and cradled the receiver.

He stood up, letting his full height of six feet three inches tower over me. He shook his head and sat back down. He leaned toward me and rested his hands on my knees. He looked directly into my eyes and said, "I will not keep this from your mother!"

I nodded my head.

"You and Charles will tell her by the end of the night, or I will, and I can guarantee that if I have to tell her, it will not be good."

All I could do was continue to nod and do everything I could to not burst into tears.

He rolled his chair forward. He was so close that I could smell his aftershave. I feared what was coming next and was on the edge of apologizing again for our dishonesty, but before I had the chance, he surprised me when he took both of my hands in his. He was full of emotion and steadied himself before he spoke again.

"Nina, y'all did a good thing," he said with more restraint than I thought was possible. "I just can't help but feel like we, your mom and I, like if we'd been there for you, if my job wasn't what it was, and if we'd lived closer..." His voice broke and he closed his lips in a line.

"Oh, Daddy, no, please don't," I said, struggling to keep myself from coming undone. "This was us, Charles and me."

"But an entire pregnancy?" he said, shaking his head. "How did we not question that?"

"We didn't let you," I said. "You'd just gotten back to Germany after deployment to Afghanistan. You and Mom were getting ready to move home to the States. Charlie was a month early. We let you fill in the gaps and ride the wave of happy surprise that comes with a new baby. This was all us."

I watched him nod to himself as he processed and reconciled everything like a checkbook ledger.

"I don't care what blood says. That girl," he said, visibly biting back his own tears. He swallowed hard, "that girl is yours. There isn't any way to know how all this is gonna come out." He shook his head again, still wrestling with his new reality. "She's got a right to know and she's gonna need to know her story, where she came from." He shook my hand for emphasis. "But don't you think for one hot minute that her story, where she's from, changes who her Mama and Daddy are or who your Mom and I are to her."

He took one hand and wiped away his tears while I finally let mine fall.

"This lie y'all told," he said, shaking his head, "which I do not agree with at all," he paused and held up his hand, "is not good, but I understand why you had to," he said, interrupting himself. "This lie is gonna come apart, and when it does," he shook his head again, "she's gonna question you and Charles, but especially you. And you're going to question you." Still shaking his head, he continued, "It's gonna be a mess however it unfolds, but your mom and I are gonna be here. And we'll help you put life back together, okay?"

I nodded and managed a shaky, "Okay."

"Okay," he said, slapping his hands on his thighs and standing up. "Let's dry those eyes and get rolling." He pulled a lightweight jacket from the back of his office door and dropped his keys into his pocket. "You ready?" he asked, reaching for my hand.

I nodded and let him help me up and into a hug.

That first night in the emergency room of Tripler Army Medical Center was torture. Even though there were perks to having my dad with us, the night went on until Charles and I saw the first peeks of sunshine winking through Charlie's hospital room window. Those first forty-eight hours were hard to walk through. We got the diagnosis we knew was coming and we were able to get on a plane and fly home, knowing her vision was stable for now and we had some time.

Over the next several months, we made small adjustments to shift our world and meet Charlie's needs, but to say that life as we knew it changed dramatically or that this diagnosis had flipped our world upside down would be wrong. In fact, the way Charlie handled the change was nothing short of extraordinary.

With Dr. Graham's help, we found parent support groups through our local chapter of Alliance for the Blind and started going to monthly meetings. We learned that sight loss could be painful and confusing for anyone, but more so for children. Dr. Graham warned us that during the worst times, we could expect emotional outbursts and tantrums that could go far beyond what would be considered normal for a child. We'd expected and prepared for the worst, but the worst hadn't come. When Charlie got to the point where she could no longer self-correct a situation, she didn't throw tantrums. She simply asked if something could be made bigger or if she could move closer to see it better.

Last year in ninth grade, when most of her coursework became more computer-based and the glare from her school-issued computer screens became too much to handle for long periods, she took matters into her own hands.

Charlie came to us and presented pages of research about how buying a MacBook laptop would help. MacBooks had something called a *retina display* and a ton of integrated accessibility features. Even though the computer was expensive, she'd sorted out the education discount program and presented us with a bottom-line price for the machine she thought would work best for her needs.

Charles and I took her to the glossy computer store in the mall. For an hour, we watched her dazzle the clerk, showing him all the accessibility features that had been built into the three-pound machine that sat on the table between them. Charles and I stood back and watched as our quiet girl became a gentle teacher and an advocate for herself.

I felt a hand on my shoulder and turned to find Charles at my side. "She's all checked in," he said, and I knew he could see the distant look in my eyes.

While he'd been present for and taken care of our daughter, I'd let myself get lost in the past.

He put an arm around my waist, and I let him pull me closer. Together, we found our girl standing on the landing of the grand staircase, people-watching.

I tucked myself into Charles's side. There was so much churning between us. The reality of our secrets and the knowledge that everything was about to change rested in suspension. We'd lived this lie for so long that the lines of truth were a blur.

"Everything's about to change," he said.

I nodded. He had read my thoughts.

"We have to manage as best we can," he said.

"We could lose her," I worried through a whisper. Nothing he said could change our reality. There was no stopping the approaching wave.

13

Marie

September 2001

Labor Day came and went like it always did, and the summer all too quickly turned to fall. The cool snap ushered us into boots and sweaters. I even tucked a scarf into my bag when Walt and I took Nina and Chuck down to see the tall ships in the harbor the last time they were in town.

For the last few weeks, Walt traveled often for work. He was back and forth between New York, where they were wrapping up work on a Ritz Carlton Hotel project, and a new contract he was calling the St. James build that was about to start in Philadelphia.

Work had kept me busy as well. All the new fall lineup commercials and public service announcements had to be ready to air next month. Also, last week, Evelyn knocked on my door and asked if I'd start walking with her in the mornings.

I stepped into my sneakers, slipped my watch on, and opened my apartment door to leave when I heard something hit the floor in front of me. I knelt to find what had fallen as Evelyn stepped into the hall.

"Three o'clock, honey bun," she said as she locked her door. Her words directed me to where I'd find the fallen object.

"Thanks," I said, moving my hand to the right where the number three would be if I were in the center of an imaginary clock. I found an envelope and smiled.

"That boy?" Evelyn mused.

"That boy," I repeated as an answer. Walt had left me a similar envelope a few days ago, the last time he was home.

On Wednesday, Linda Morris sat next to me on the porch and had let slip that she'd been helping him with a "project." It turned out she was teaching him to write braille.

I sat down on the steps, slid the envelope open, and pulled a single sheet of thick paper from inside. I rested it on my lap and started to read.

> *Dear Marie,*
> *I hoped to see you in the morning, but my Friday afternoon meeting in Philly got moved to Friday morning. I should be home late Saturday. I'll need to head to New York on Monday to wrap that one up on Tuesday. Sunday, I'm all yours!*
> *I love you!*
> *Walt*
>
> *P.S. I think I'm getting better. This one only took me an hour and twelve sheets of paper to get just right.*

I sat for a moment to let his words settle around me. "That boy," I said again with a smile.

"Come on, love bug," Evelyn said. "Let's walk! Fifi's gonna make fun of me for buying this jogging suit off of that Amazon dot com if we just sit here in the hall with goo-goo eyes."

"Yes, ma'am," I said and reached out for her arm. "Hills first or the flats?" I asked.

"Let's get the worst over with," Evelyn said with a playful groan.

We turned onto the gravel path that went along the driveway. "It smells like rain."

"It looks like rain, too," Evelyn said.

"Do you wanna speed up?"

"I do not," she said with a laugh and patted my hand where it rested on her arm. "Dr. Gable said I needed to move *more*. She did not say I needed to move *most*."

I laughed and let her set our gentle pace.

"Pluto asked me if you would be here on Tuesday?" she said.

"I should be," I said, "Walt said he goes to New York to finish up on Monday. What's Tuesday?"

"That's the only day the piano tuner can come next week, and Pluto's got some things to do with your daddy over in Owings Mills."

"I can meet the tuner," I offered.

"And you're sure it won't be a problem?" she asked.

"No, not at all." I said, "I'll be here."

"So, tell me about Knoxville?" she asked, making a hairpin turn with the conversation.

I laughed, "It was good. His parents are so nice."

"Nice is good," she said.

"I got to hold the babies," I said.

Patting my hand, she said, "There's nothing sweeter than new babies."

"They are sweet, and they're getting big! Even from when they were here a few weeks ago."

"I hate that I missed meeting them," she said.

"That's right," I said. "I forgot you were at the shore."

She and Pluto had several rental properties in a canal community in Ocean Pines, and their adult son managed them. They went over to see him and check in every month. They were in Ocean Pines when Chuck and Nina brought the babies to Baltimore for the first time.

"So, how is Paul?"

"Oh, he's fine. Single, always tidy, nothing new," she said. "But never mind our Paul. Tell me more about Knoxville and the Mavins."

I rubbed her arm and laughed.

"What?" she said, laughing with a gentle elbow. "That boy of mine's never gonna get married. I'm living vicariously through you."

"Oh Evie, we're nowhere near marriage," I said.

"Really? The two of you looked cozy on the lawn a few weeks ago." The tilt in her tone turned her statement into a question.

I smiled and felt myself blush. "I didn't realize we had an audience."

"Never mind that. What makes you think you're nowhere near marriage?" she asked.

"He told me he loved me that day," I said, trying to decide if I should tell her the rest and how I really felt.

"But?" she asked.

"But I'm afraid," I said.

She didn't say anything. She just hummed and patted my hand.

"That I won't be enough. That I'll do it all wrong."

"Do what all wrong?" she asked, surprised.

"It!" I said in an embarrassed squeal.

She laughed her deep, familiar laugh that was full of wisdom and snark. "Sweet Marie, this may come as a surprise to you, but there is virtually nothing you can do to mess "it" up aside from not showing up."

I felt my cheeks burn. "But he's been married before."

"And he isn't anymore," she reminded me. "Sweetie, we weren't so sure about Walt when he first arrived, but now that we know him, we know he's a good man who was put in a tough spot."

"He is a good man," I said.

We walked together for a bit, neither of us speaking, just enjoying the quiet of the morning.

"I met Suzie," I said.

"Remind me who that is," she asked.

"She and her husband John are Chuck and Nina's best friends. I thought it would be weird because they'd been friends forever, and I'd feel like an outsider."

I continued, "But it wasn't like that at all. In fact, I think Suzie might be the most welcoming person I've ever met! I sort of feel like I've known them all forever. There wasn't any of that awkward stuff when you first meet people. It's like we all just fit."

"That's so good."

"And she gave me a nickname," I said, embarrassed that this was a highlight.

"Oh?"

"Yeah, 'Me,'" I said. "I know it probably sounds sort of silly, and maybe you had to be there for it to make sense, but the day we got there, she'd gotten a dental filling. Her mouth was numb. She kept trying to say 'Marie' but kept saying 'Me.' The nickname stuck."

Saying this out loud made the story sound like I was making a bigger deal out of it than maybe I should have, so I felt compelled to back track. "I think maybe she gives everyone nicknames to help her remember their real names." I shut my mouth. I was sure I was rattling. I was sure I was trying too hard. I just really wanted her to understand.

"Yes," Evelyn said. "I've heard that can really help with remembering names."

"I don't think I've ever had a nickname," I said, thinking out loud.

"It's lovely, Marie, and that's not just a polite, southern lady 'lovely,'" she said, patting my hand where I held her arm, letting me know without words that she could tell how much this meant to me. "And if you've ever had a nickname, I can't remember it." She went on. "Your mom was nervous for you to go, so I'm glad everything went well," she said. "When will that boy be home?"

"His note said tomorrow night, but he has to leave again on Monday.

"So just one more day," she said.

"Just one more day," I said, but it ended up being longer than just one more day.

After another delay, Walt didn't get home from Philadelphia until late Sunday night. After a restless night of sleep, I woke up early Monday morning hoping to catch him. Maybe there would be time for breakfast or lunch before he had to leave again.

I made my way down the steps to Walt's garden level apartment and knocked on his door. It had been over a week since he'd been home, and I could hardly contain my excitement.

I waited for a moment, but when he didn't answer, I knocked again and harder. I hadn't thought of it before, but maybe he was still asleep. I stepped back from the door, thinking I'd come back at a more normal time, or maybe I'd leave him a note, but before I turned to go, I heard a voice from inside his apartment, and an unfamiliar woman answered the door.

I froze, unsure what to do.

"May I help you?" the woman said.

"I'm sorry," I said, and I felt my entire body go hot and then a moment later when I heard his voice, I felt the blood rush from my face, leaving me dizzy.

"Are you okay?" the woman asked, and somehow her tone made me feel small.

"I'm sorry. I was looking for…" I took a step back. "Walt," I said, and his name came out just like I felt, small.

Her voice brightened, "I think he's just getting out of the shower, but maybe I can help you. I'm Nancy Lynn." She waited. I knew her eyes were on me, and even though I'd never met this woman before, I was sure her pause was intentional. "I'm Walter Lee's wife." The brightness in her voice turned dark. I imagined her baring her teeth.

From inside I heard Walt say, "Jesus, Nancy Lynn. I said I'd get it." His voice went from muffled to clear as he opened the door and stopped short.

"I'm sorry. I didn't mean to." I said, taking another step backward. My mouth was completely dry, and I couldn't have said another word. I didn't want to. My heart was pounding, and my stomach was churning. I wanted to go. I needed to go.

"Marie, wait," Walt said.

"Wait, you know her?" the woman asked.

Nancy Lynn. Wife. His wife. The words rattled and jangled in my mind. I had to shake my head to make them stop.

"Marie, I can explain," he said, and I heard him step out the door. An instant later, I felt him take my hand. His touch gave me strength, but not the strength he was expecting. I found my voice.

"Your wife?" I said, looking right at him, needing no vision to see right through him.

"My *ex*-wife," he said, holding my hand tighter like he could feel me slipping away.

"That's not what she said." I jerked my hand away. "She said wife!" Angry tears rose, and I shoved them down. "She said Walter Lee's wife!" My anger froze the space around us while Nancy Lynn put the pieces together.

"Wait..." she said, sounding amused. "Are y'all fucking—"

"Jesus, Nancy Lynn! Knock it off!" Walt said, cutting her off.

I took another step back. I had to get out. I turned for the stairs and misjudged where I was in the hall. I bumped the banister hard and knocked into a small table, causing something to fall. It hit the floor, shattering into a thousand pieces.

"Good God," Nancy Lynn said, and she laughed at me.

Holding tight to the rail, I made my way upstairs, past my apartment, and out the front doors. I pushed open the screen door and heard it bang closed behind me. I was down the steps and on the gravel path before I realized it was raining. I turned where I stood as I realized there was nowhere I could go to escape. This was my house.

I heard Walt, barefoot, running across the porch. He was beside me. "Marie, please let me explain."

"No!" I said, shaking my head. "I'm done!"

"Please!" he said, pleading. "I know this looks terrible, but please let me explain!"

"No!" I screamed, swinging my arm to make my point clear.

He caught my hand in the air and held it, "Please."

I yanked my hand back again. "Did you sleep with her?" I was completely unable to filter my thoughts.

"What?"

My words stung him. I pressed on. "Because I wouldn't sleep with you. Did. You. Sleep. With. HER?" With each word, I slapped the back of my hand into my palm.

"No!" His words were firm and steady, and he kept my hand tucked into his.

"Marie, honey, are you okay?" Pluto was on the porch; if I knew anything about my people, I knew he wasn't alone.

"I'm okay," I said with forced calm. "Walt was just introducing me to his wife. I'm sorry we woke you."

"Honey, you know, with Pluto's blood pressure pills we were up," Evelyn said.

Just knowing they were there helped me slow down.

"Marie, please," Walt said again. This time, I listened.

"What?" I said, lowering my voice. "Walt, it's not even seven in the morning, and your wife is in your apartment? What could you possibly say?"

"Nancy Lynn just showed up," he said. "Honest to God Marie, I had no idea. I came home last night. I was gonna drop my stuff off and come to you. I was comin' to you, and she was sittin' in the upstairs hall on that old church pew."

In my mind's eye, I could see the old pew in the main floor hall and realized she'd been just feet from my door.

"She came in. We talked. That's all. It was late. I made up the pull out. I called her a cab this mornin' before I got in the shower. That's all," he repeated.

"I thought..." my voice fell away. His words washed over me like the rain that was now pouring down on us.

"Marie, I love you! I only want you!" he said.

I shook my head. "I thought..." I said, letting myself cry with relief.

"Don't cry," he said. Now, he was close enough to touch.

"Please don't cry." He put his arms around me, and I let him pull me in. I let myself lean into him, and I let myself believe him when he whispered, "Marie, I want to spend the rest of my life with you."

Neither of us noticed the taxi arrive, and neither of us saw the look of hatred on Nancy Lynn's face as she threw in her overnight bag, slid inside, and slammed the door behind her.

14

Charlie

December 2018

The corridor was quiet as I made my way to the water fountain. As I walked, I let my fingertips brush the wall just like the occupational therapist I'd met with that morning had shown me how to do. She suggested I make the behavior a habit.

As I walked the hall, I thought, not for the first time, about how different it is to be in the hospital for your eyes. There aren't any gowns or visible ports or tubes jutting out from completely unnatural places.

When we checked into Monroe Carell two days before, I passed countless kids dragging tagalong IV poles and wearing masks and knit stocking caps. Even though they were in a form of isolation, the world around them had been made beautiful and fun.

Even though I could still see, I shut my eyes to see if I could manage in the dark. I counted my practiced steps from the corner and felt the metal of the water fountain against my fingers exactly when I was supposed to.

I smiled to myself, opened my eyes, and took a drink. I used the collar of my shirt to wipe my mouth and turned to face the waiting area to find a boy I hadn't noticed before. He was sitting in a row of chairs in the middle of the room.

He was close to my age—maybe a year older. I turned to see who he was with, but he appeared to be alone.

His eyes were focused on nothing. He had a gentle smile and an upward tilt to his chin. I'd seen this posture enough in the last two days to know that he was blind.

Without thinking, I left the wall and crossed to the center of the room without making a sound. I stood in front of him.

His hands rested palm down on his lap and, compared to my lived-in distressed Levis, his jeans were crisp and bright blue. There was an ironing crease that traveled straight over the bend of his knee and down to the smooth hem that rested at the top of his Chuck Taylors.

I held my breath as I leaned toward him to the point that our faces were only a few inches apart. My hair fell over my shoulder until it almost touched the top of his hand, but he continued staring, not *at* me but *through* me. He had an imperceptible front-to-back rock. The angle of his jaw was strong, and his eyes were cobalt blue.

I wanted to touch him but stood up and backed away, afraid I would actually do it. Not turning from him, I felt my way back down the hall until I heard the familiar voices of my parents and Dr. Peepers float through the exam room door. "Yes, but Charlie's case is different." Dr. Peepers said.

My hand rested on the door handle, but something pressed into me and said to wait.

"We don't need to do all the probing discovery tests. We're lucky because even though we don't know all the facts, we do have her genetic history."

What I thought was silence filled the air, but when I brought my ear closer to the door, I heard my mother's voice through tears and wondered what detail had made her cry. In general, it was me. I made her cry.

Dr. Peepers spoke again, her words clear and confident. "Nina—may I call you Nina? And may I speak frankly?"

There was a pause where, in my mind's eye, I could see my mother nodding for Dr. Peepers to continue.

"Nina, I knew the details of Charlotte's history when Suzie asked me to see you so quickly, but I was clear to her, and I'll be candid with you both as well. My obligation is now and will forever be to Charlotte. With her genetics and family history of retina disease, you'd be doing her a disservice by not telling her everything. She needs to understand what's happening to her and why."

Again, I thought the room had gone quiet, but when I leaned in, pressing my ear to the door, I heard the broken whispers of my mother's voice.

"...know everything will change...where to start...hurting her..."

And then, as clearly as if he was standing right next to me, my dad said, "When everything fell apart for Walter Lee, the agreement was made to protect Charlie. We've only ever wanted to protect her."

My head began to spin as his words bounced around. My parents' words lit up everything they touched, like the silver ball inside a pinball machine, but they were so scattered. Nothing made sense.

A chair scooted across the floor. "Are there grandparents?" Dr. Peepers asked in a voice that had shifted from strength to compassion.

"Yes," I heard my dad say. "Nina's parents know everything, and just like you, they think we should have set it all straight a long time ago."

"I'm sorry," Dr. Peepers interrupted. "I should have been more clear. I meant to ask if you, or even..." Pages turned. "...Walter. Has he kept in contact with Charlotte's maternal grandparents?"

Her words opened a hidden door inside me, like the ones behind bookcases that conceal a secret staircase, passageway, or, in this case, trap door. Her words shoved open a space that I hadn't known existed before now. A cavernous space cracked open, and the floor shifted under my feet. I pulled myself away from the door, away from their words like they were scalding my ears, and stepped back until I felt the cool wall behind me. It steadied me as a wave of dizziness washed over my body. I slid down until I was sitting, knees to my chest, heart slamming, blood thumping through my ears.

I heard him before I saw him. He slid down the wall to sit beside me and crossed his legs. I heard Wade's singsong voice in my head, "Criss cross applesauce...Criss cross applesauce."

I turned to face the teenage boy next to me. The eyes that met mine were those of the boy from the lobby. Only now, instead of looking through me without seeing me, they were looking right at me, straight into the deepest parts of me.

I opened my mouth to speak, but before I could say anything, he lifted his index finger to his lips. The universal symbol for quiet. He pulled a pen from his pocket and took my hand. Turning it palm side up, he wrote something and closed my fingers shut without letting me see what he'd written. Then, with the same gentle touch, he reached in and repositioned the collar of my turtleneck where it had slipped down to reveal the fading marks left by the rope. Then he took my hand again and gently pressed it flat on the tile floor. With his other hand, he made a walking motion with his fingers. I blinked and felt it, a rhythmic tapping on the floor against my palm.

Putting the two together, I realized it was footsteps. Our eyes met again, but before I had a chance to ask how he'd known to do that, the door to my exam room swung open, and Dr. Peepers appeared in the doorway.

She looked from me to the boy beside me, and with a grin, she said, "I see you've found a Walton."

15

Nina

December 2018

"What's a Walton?" I asked, lifting myself from the chair I'd been perched on to walk toward the exam room door where Dr. Peepers leaned against the door frame.

Of all the things I expected to see when I looked past her through the exam room door, Charlie sitting on the floor beside a handsome teenage boy wearing a Farragut High School sweatshirt was not on my radar. But there she was, folded into herself and pressed against the wall. They were so close that they could have been touching, but there was a distinct, intentional space between them.

And this boy. He was trim, dark-haired, and looked up at me from behind stylish, shaggy bangs. There was something in his deep blue eyes that I couldn't quite understand, but before I could figure it out, he dropped his gaze to his lap and then looked at Charlie.

I looked at her, too, and the expression on her face made me feel lightheaded, and my fingertips tingled. She'd let her guard down, and in that heart-pounding instant, I knew the walls were thin, and she'd been there long enough to have heard everything.

Dr. Peepers turned to face me as I leaned on the opposite side of the extra-wide doorway. "A Walton isn't a 'what.' A

Walton is a 'who.'" She smiled. "I always forget that Knoxville is the biggest small town. You two probably know each other from school."

I turned to him, our eyes locked, but neither of us spoke.

Dr. Peepers went on. "Nathan and Andrew have been terrorizing the halls of Monroe Carell for, hmmm, how long is it now?" she asked with a grin.

"Five years," the boy on the floor said with a smile.

"And she still can't tell us apart," said a matching voice from the end of the hall.

Charles had appeared in the doorway behind me. The five of us turned to see a boy gently tapping his way toward us with a white cane. He bore a strong likeness to the boy sitting beside Charlie.

"Not so!" Dr. Peepers said, taking mock offense. "Charlotte, Nina, Charles," she gestured toward the boy who'd stopped beside her and set her hand on his shoulder, "this is Nathan Walton." Then she turned toward the boy who sat beside Charlie on the floor, "and this is his younger brother, Andrew Walton."

The boy on the floor gave a polite half-wave. "Ma'am," he said.

"Nice to meet you," I said without taking my eyes off Charlie, who hadn't taken her eyes off of Andrew.

"All right," Dr. Peepers said with a clap. "Mavins, you've got decisions to make before we can move forward," she said, gently squeezing my shoulder. "And Waltons," she said, speaking directly to Andrew without looking at him. "That's enough eye-gazing. We've got work to do." She extended her left elbow, and Nathan slipped his right hand in to rest just above the bend. Dr. Peepers and Nathan started walking down the hall, and as though an invisible string connected the two boys, Andrew silently and seamlessly lifted himself off the floor and followed his brother.

Before he turned the corner, he looked back at Charlie. He grinned and gave us all an open palm wave. He tapped his finger twice on his hand and was gone.

We waited in silence, daring someone to speak first. The weighted space between us was tangible. A million conversation starters swirled in my head, but when I opened my mouth to speak, nothing came out. As much as there was to say, I couldn't find the right words. It shouldn't have surprised me in the least when Charlie's voice broke the silence.

"You could start with the truth," she said. She was still sitting on the floor, looking up at us, her brown eyes filled not with anger but anticipation and a desire to know.

"Do you wanna go back in?" I asked and nodded back to the exam room.

She looked down at the floor and shook her head. "Yeah...no—I think I'm fine here."

I was surprised by her response, but when Charles, without hesitation, moved from the exam room doorway to sit cross-legged beside her on the floor, I had no choice but to do the same.

"It's not as simple as just 'the truth,'" I said, trying to hide my frustration at the fact that we were about to have this conversation in a hospital hallway. This wasn't how it was supposed to happen. I sat down to face her. "There are so many pieces that—"

"Lies," Charlie interrupted with a sharpness in her tone that I had never heard before. "You mean *there were so many lies*, not *pieces*, right?" Her voice had softened, but her words still stung.

I tried to begin again, to explain, but when my tears began to fall, and I couldn't continue, Charles covered my hand with his. "I think we should start with this," he said, his voice steady and strong. "There hasn't been a day of your life that we haven't loved you. You're our daughter."

She turned to him, and her expression eased.

He shook his head. "You know, it's funny. I imagined having this conversation with you a million times, but..." he paused, looking around, "I never, ever thought it would be on the floor in the hallway of a hospital in Nashville."

He closed his eyes, bowed his head, and took a slow, intentional breath, "But ya know what, kid?" he said, reaching out to gently lift Charlie's chin so he could look her in the eyes. "It doesn't matter where we have it, it matters that it's happening."

Without warning, the words began to tumble out of me. "You were born on a Monday. We got to the hospital, and they told us that it would be hours and we might as well go home. At least at home..."

"I know," she interrupted. "You've told me that a million times."

I swallowed hard and nodded, "But what we've never told you is that, even though we were there, I wasn't pregnant with you."

I turned to Charles, and without pause he picked up where I'd left off. "Your mother was incredible," he said and closed his eyes for a moment to remember her.

"Did you..." Charlie looked at her dad. "Did you have an affair?" Her voice trailed off at the end as if she was embarrassed to say the word. She turned to me for the answer.

"Oh! No!" I said, shaking my head in his defense. "No, no, no! It wasn't that at all," I said, watching her face fill with even more confusion.

"No," Charles said, looking at me and then back at Charlie. "No, I didn't have an affair," he said with a gentle smile. "It's complicated, but your biological father is my brother. He was married to a woman before Aunt Nancy Lynn."

I reached out and put my hand on Charles's shoulder to stop him. I knew deep inside me, down to my core, that I had to be the one to tell her.

Charlie looked back and forth between us, waiting.

"Your mother's name was Marie."

16

Marie

September 2001

My wet footprints made their way from the front door down the hall to my bedroom. After standing in the pouring rain, we were both soaked to the skin. I told Walt I needed to get cleaned up. He said he did, too. I asked if he'd come back, and he said he would.

I was pulling on jeans and a T-shirt, hands still shaking with fear and excitement, when I heard his knock on my door.

"Come in," I said, hoping he could hear me. My wet clothes were still in a pile on the bathroom floor. I heard the door open and close. "I'm back here. I just need to get this wet mess out of the floor." I said, trying to take the nervous sound out of my voice. I hung my clothes in the shower to let them drip dry.

Walt met me at the door to my bedroom. He hooked his fingers into my belt loops and pulled me to him.

"Hi," he said in a whisper, stepping us back until my back touched the door.

I tilted my head up, knowing his mouth would find mine. I felt an electric current pulse through me as we kissed.

"I'm not gonna go," Walt said.

"Go where? New York?" I asked. "But it's for work."

"I don't really need to be there. It's just a handover meeting from construction to design," he said. "Julia's better with those Ritz Carlton people anyway. They're too up in the air for me."

"And you're sure that's okay?" I asked. Even though it meant he wasn't leaving, the cancellation unsettled me.

"Yes, I called the team this morning, and I'm just waiting for a callback, but it's fine." His words were firm and confident as he pulled me close. "This is where I want to be," he said and kissed me again.

As though on cue, his phone buzzed in his pocket. "That'll be Julia." He touched my arm. "I'm gonna take this," he said and left the room.

From where I stood, I caught only bits and pieces of his side of the conversation.

"Unexpected...Yeah...I figured...no...everything on the drive...auto cad..." and then a word that sounded like "fiancé." I was sure I'd heard wrong or that it must have been the other person's fiancé, but Julia was a mother of four, and her husband was a stay-at-home dad. My heart sped up.

Walt came back to the bedroom, and I heard him set his phone on the dresser. I then felt him sit beside me. He took my hand and flipped it palm up, just like he'd done before our first date. He set something in my hand. This time, it wasn't a paper rose.

I took it in my hands and recognized the shape immediately. I relaxed and smiled. "This is one of my dad's puzzle boxes."

"It is," he said, matching my tone. "Marie, I went to him and your mom last week."

I gripped the familiar cube to keep my hands from shaking.

He put his hands around mine as I held the box. He said, "This isn't how I'd originally planned it, but honestly, this is probably better," he said. I could tell he was smiling.

My mind was spinning as I found the slide hidden in the top of the cube and moved it a quarter inch forward. I twisted the top of the box and lifted its lid. Inside, I felt the top of a smaller velvet covered box. Startled, afraid, and excited all at the same time, I drew my hand back.

Walt took the box from my hands as I covered my mouth, willing myself to breathe, willing my heart to slow down, willing myself to mentally record everything. I heard the velvet box click open. He took my hand and led my shaking fingers to touch the diamond resting inside.

His voice was calm and grounded my spinning head and thumping heart. "Marie, I've spent most of my adult life thinking I wasn't enough. Since I left my parents' house after high school, I've never felt like I was home until now. You feel like home. I didn't come to Baltimore looking to find somebody, but then came you." He ran a gentle hand up my arm and over my shoulder, then cupped my cheek in his hand, never breaking contact, always letting me know he was there. "You're the first thing I think of in the mornin' and the last thing I think of before I go to bed. You are the most beautiful person I've ever known, inside and out. I love everything about you!"

He took my hand in his again. "Marie, I want to marry you, and Lord willing, I want to make babies with you. If that's not in the cards for us, that's all right. I've made peace with that. Either way, I want to make love to you and only you forever."

His voice broke with emotion, but he kept going. "I want to sit beside you with The Ladies at knit club every week and get old with you. I want to spend the rest of my life with you if you'll let me."

Before he could finish, I nodded, tears running down my cheeks.

He laughed a deep, sweet laugh. "You gotta let me actually ask you first."

"Okay," I said, laughing through my tears, wiping them away with my hand. "Start over. I promise I'll let you finish," I said, holding his hand tight.

"Okay," he said.

I raised my eyebrows and smiled. "Okay."

"Marie Collie-Ricks, will you marry me?"

My tears were gone, replaced with the confidence that
from this moment forward, I would be his, and he would be
mine. With certainty, I said, "Yes."

We didn't leave my apartment. Other than his call that
morning, we didn't speak to anyone. We spent the day
together. We talked and dreamed. We also decided to get
married on February thirteenth, the Wednesday just before
Valentine's Day. We were sure that The Ladies of Edgevale
would trade a Wednesday Knit Club meeting for a
Wednesday wedding.

Around eleven, Walt cooked us breakfast. At three,
someone knocked on my door while we lay dozing in the
afternoon sun with Poky tucked beside my feet. My back
was pressed against Walt's chest. His arms were wrapped
around me. I'd remember later that it was the piano tuner I'd
promised to meet, and even though he knocked twice,
neither of us moved. The world and everything else could
wait. He stayed with me that night, and I slept tucked into
him. I had never slept so peacefully.

The next morning, I woke up just after seven to the sound
of a sports announcer on the television in the living room. I
got up, brushed my teeth, put on my robe, and joined Walt
on the couch. I tucked myself in beside him.

He pulled me in close and kissed me. "Good morning,"
he said. "Did I wake you?"

"Yeah, but it's okay. Remember the knocking
yesterday?"

"Yeah?" he asked.

"It was the piano tuner. I feel bad because I told Evelyn
I'd take care of that for Pluto."

"Oh man, can you reschedule?" he asked.

"Yeah, I just need to call."

He kissed the top of my head and said, "You gonna hang
with me today?"

"I can't," I said, letting myself relax into him. "I have to
work today," I said, teasingly drawing out the word *I*.

"You're in good company," he said.

"Oh yeah?" I asked.

"Michael Jordan's goin' back to work today, too," he said.

"Man!" I laughed. "Great minds think alike!"

We watched the news for a while. There was a segment about stem cell research funding. Al Roker tracked the progress of Hurricane Erin off the New England coast. There was a lot of political talk about money and taxes while President Bush was in Florida reading to school children. And there was a teaser for Macy Gray being the performer for the Friday concert in Times Square. At seven-thirty, my alarm clock began chirping, and I moved to get up.

"Nooooo," Walt said, playfully pulling me down and onto his lap.

I laughed and kissed him. "I gotta get to work, but first, a shower," I said.

"Fine!" He said and kissed me again and let me go.

In the shower, I let my mind drift through the last few days. The life I thought would be had taken a sidestep. That shift brought so much excitement and possibility that I'd never allowed myself to imagine before, but it also brought with it a whole list of questions. Children? Work? Home? All those questions carried with them a whole bucket of uncertainty. I had worked so hard for my independence and was confident in my autonomy. I didn't want to lose that and become a burden to anyone. When I made the decision two years before to move out of my parents' home, it was huge and surprised everyone except Linda and Fifi.

Mom and Dad's three-bedroom bungalow sat at the back of the Edgevale property. We'd nicknamed it the cottage. There was more than enough room for the three of us, and I know they felt a certain level of peace knowing they were right there if I needed anything. They were familiar and easy to live with, and I truly loved being there.

The idea of getting my own place first crossed my mind shortly after turning twenty-one. I'd mentioned to someone that I still lived at home with my parents, and the person's response had been, "Well, of course you do."

Even though the comment wasn't meant to be insulting, I couldn't let it go. People didn't expect me to do much, and they didn't take me seriously. The need to prove myself and prove people wrong grew.

When I finished college, I applied for graduate school at the University of Baltimore and was accepted. It might have been a pity acceptance, but that only pushed me more. I finished that program with honors and accepted a job with the communications firm I interned with. I started producing commercials for radio, and in the last year, I added a few national brands to my portfolio.

On a Wednesday, a couple of months before I graduated, I found Linda and Fifi in their corner of the porch. I shared with them what I was feeling and asked what they thought about me moving out. They were encouraging, but I could tell that Fifi was thinking about what my mom would say. Linda sat quietly and listened while Fifi and I spoke. When there was a lull, I turned to her. For so much of my life, Linda's opinion had been the one that mattered most to me. For so long, she was the voice I heard in my mind when I made important decisions. She touched my knee, and in her sweet and confident tone, she asked, "Have you considered Edgevale House?"

"How do you mean?" I asked.

She scooted closer, lowering her voice. "It isn't public knowledge, but it is my understanding that an apartment on the first floor will be available in the next year. Mind you, I don't know exact details or dates, but, if you can be patient, this may be an option that would be agreeable to everyone."

For a moment, we sat in silence. Fifi and I were stunned by what Linda had revealed. I heard the wheels in our minds turning. It had never even crossed my mind to consider Edgevale House home.

Edgevale House was a three-story, 11,000-square-foot, center-hall colonial mansion. The home had remained a single-family home until the early 1980s, when it was artfully converted into a seven-unit apartment house. Units one through six were above ground, with sunrooms or balconies. Unit seven was at basement level with a walk-out terrace. Each floor was divided into two large apartments. When the house was divided, the center hall on each floor was left as a common space. The third floor held the library. The main floor was full of cozy couches. But the second floor was my favorite because it was home to a black baby grand Baldwin piano that Evelyn and Pluto brought with them when they moved to Edgevale House.

I fiddled with my bracelet, turning it round and round as I turned the idea in my mind. Sitting with two of my favorite people on earth, I felt the pull of Edgevale House calling.

Fewer than six months later, Unit 1 was home. Mom and Dad still had me close, but I was on my own in every other way. That gave me confidence I had never known before.

Edgevale House was a big part of my independent life that I couldn't imagine leaving. I belonged there, and now so did Walt.

I turned off the water in the shower and stood for a moment, absently turning my bracelet and letting myself remember yesterday. The sound of Nancy Lynn's voice and the syrupy, condescending way she'd spoken to me bounced around my mind. If Edgevale House didn't choose you, then you had no business being there.

A sharp knock on the bathroom door yanked me from my thoughts.

"Marie," Walt said, but something about his voice sounded off.

I wrapped myself in a towel and cracked the door. "What's up?" I said.

"A plane. Two planes," he said, and his voice sounded slow and scattered but also frantic at the same time. His words were disjointed and somehow lost, so different from when he'd been teasing me half an hour before.

I let him take my hand. He led me toward the living room.

"Walt, I'm in a towel," I said, but it was like he hadn't heard me. I pulled my hand from his, "Walt, wait."

"Airplanes. They hit the towers."

"What towers?" I said, confused. "Wait, I need to put on clothes. The curtains are open in the living room."

"The tallest two," he said. He stopped in the hall, and I reached out to touch the corner where it met the living room.

"Walt, you aren't making any sense. Planes hit the tallest two what?"

He held his hand over mine on the wall, and I felt tension as though he were holding himself up. He drew in a measured breath. "The World Trade Center Twin Towers in New York City."

"What?" I said, stopping short as my hand slipped from the wall, and I swayed where I stood.

He reached out and took my arm to steady me.

"Are the towers close to your building?" I covered my mouth and froze. "Oh, Walt—your building—where was your building?" I started to shake and struggled to breathe. "You were supposed to be there," I cried.

He pulled me to him, and I held onto him, like holding him would keep him there with me and not in the city where he should have been.

"No, no, no. It wasn't close. It was ten blocks below Vesey near Battery Park," he said, his fingers tangled in my wet hair, holding me just as tightly as I was holding him. "It wasn't close. I promise. It wasn't close."

His voice shook, and I couldn't tell which of us he was trying to convince as he repeated over and over, "It wasn't close."

17

Charlie

December 2018

Part of me didn't want to be there anymore. Part of me was going to be sick. Staying in the hallway had been such a stupid way to gain a tiny piece of control.

I wanted to run, but the smallest part of me was screaming, demanding that I stay, if for no other reason than to understand who I was and how I'd gotten here. So, I stayed rooted to the gray tiles that made my sneakers squeak as I shifted my feet and slid my knees closer to my chest. I held myself together as tightly as I could to keep from flying apart.

After letting me take a moment to digest what he'd said, my dad continued.

"I want you to understand that I'll always call myself your daddy, and this beautiful lady right beside me will always be your mama."

His eyes stayed locked on mine as he took Mom's hand. "This story doesn't change who you are to us, and it shouldn't change who we are to you."

My eyes were so full of tears that all I could do was nod. I felt my world crumble around me but knew that if I didn't agree, he probably wouldn't continue.

"A couple of years before you were born, your Aunt Nancy Lynn left your Uncle Walter." He paused, and his face told me he was looking for gentler words to explain the truth that was right in front of him. "I think, well, I think she sort of got, well, lost. She had a really," he paused again, "lonely childhood. I think you know she lived at a boarding school from the time she was five or six years old." He looked over at Mom for confirmation.

She nodded. He went on. "Mom actually knew Nancy Lynn in college before she ever knew Walter." He shook his head. "Anyway, when Nancy Lynn left Uncle Walter Lee, my brother, he was devastated. He had a hard time finding a job nearby. He ended up leaving Knoxville. He moved up to Baltimore, where he had a really good job as an engineer at a place that made steel. There was a lot of stuff that happened to lead up to the situation, but the short story is that Nancy Lynn told Walter Lee she wanted a divorce. He signed papers and gave them to her to file. When Walter left Knoxville, he was completely broken. We were really worried about him."

"Mom was pretty far along pregnant with the twins at the time. When they were three months old and big enough for her to leave them for a few days, Mom and I left Nora and Margot with Grandma and Grandpa and took a few days to go up and see Walter Lee. We wanted to make sure he was all right."

I looked over at Mom and could see his words brought back memories. She was sitting with us, but looked like she was in a completely different world.

18

Nina

December 2018

As Charles spoke, his words brought back the memory of that day.

Walter Lee had rented an apartment in an old mansion that had been divided into apartments I remembered the first time Charles and I navigated the tree-lined streets of the Roland Park neighborhood we would eventually come to know, as well as our own, back in Knoxville. This was before GPS in cars was a thing.

The historic neighborhood was full of narrow, one-way streets with shaded sidewalks. After circling for ten minutes without any progress, we had to ask a jogger where to find 201 Edgevale. The jogger laughed as he lifted his T-shirt to use the hem to wipe sweat from his face. He asked, "The Ricks place?"

We said, "Yes."

He pointed to the driveway directly behind us and said, "It's right up that drive, top of the hill. You'll come to the big house first if you're lookin' for one of the renters. But if you're lookin' for Mr. Bill or Mrs. Greta, they are in the second house you come to." In true Baltimore native fashion, the word *to* rhymed with *ewe*.

Pulling on the bill of his Tennessee baseball cap, Charles thanked him, backed up his truck, shifted into drive, and eased into a skinny driveway with a brick wall on one side.

I remember how the sound of the tires changed when the road switched from pavement to poured asphalt and then to gravel.

"Like Dad said earlier," I said, my mind between the past and the present. "Walter Lee was a mess when he left Knoxville, so you can imagine our surprise when we pulled your dad's truck down the long, winding driveway. We were worried about the state we'd find him in, and then he walked out of this huge old mansion onto the front porch with a gigantic smile on his face and a really pretty girl by his side."

Charlie looked up from her lap, "Marie?"

I nodded and felt a new wave of grief for the friend I'd lost. "Yes, Marie," I whispered and felt myself slipping away.

"She was pretty?" I heard Charlie ask from somewhere far away, but I was lost in another memory.

Suzie and I went to Baltimore in late September to help Marie and her mother pick out a wedding dress. That was just over two weeks after she and Walter had gotten engaged. That was also just over two weeks after the World Trade Center towers in New York City had been hit by airplanes and crumbled to the ground.

Suzie was the one to spot the dress and pull it from the rack. On the hanger, the gown looked too simple to be a wedding dress. But, when we helped Marie slip the white satin gown over her head and let it settle on her slender frame, there was no doubt that it was the one. The neckline went straight across and rested just below her collarbone. The fabric followed the curve of her hip and lay against her body like a second skin.

"I love how this one feels," Marie said, gently running her fingers across her stomach to her waist and down her hips. "But the back," she said, reaching around to try to get a feel for it. "Is it too much?" She turned her back to us.

"Oh, Marie!" I said.

I turned to see Suzie's hand over her mouth. For once in her life, she was speechless.

"Is it 'Oh,' good? Or 'Oh,' bad?" Marie asked with a nervous smile at the corners of her mouth.

"Definitely 'Oh good,'" Suzie said, finding her voice. She stepped forward, took Marie's hands from behind, and let them rest at her sides. "I'll show you," Suzie said. Suzie began to describe the dress in detail, how its simple lines and seamless construction fit her body in a way that looked like the dress had been designed specifically for her. Suzie touched the delicate straps that rested on Marie's shoulders and ran her fingers down, drawing a line along the edge of the fabric where it draped into a deep curve against the lowest part of her back.

I looked over at Marie's mother to see tears run down her cheeks. I shut my eyes and tried to put myself in Marie's position. I wanted to see the dress like Marie saw it—through Suzie's words and touch. The moment was intimate and special. None of us would ever forget the experience.

Charlie's voice brought me back to the present, as she repeated her question—this time more insistently. "Was she pretty?"

Charles laughed and reached into his back pocket and pulled out his wallet. He was probably one of the only people who still kept real photos in his wallet of all the important people in his life. I watched Charlie's face light up with interest, knowing and also fearing what was coming.

He flipped past a professional photo of our four children taken in the fall that had made its debut on our family Christmas card. He passed one of us together on the beach the summer before. Then, he passed four individual class photos of each of our children and stopped at Charlie's.

He slid his fingers behind our daughter's school portrait and gently pulled out an old, folded snapshot. He held it out to Charlie. "See for yourself."

19

Marie

February 2002

I heard the guest room door latch. Nina tiptoed back down the hall and closed my bedroom door.

"Did they say it?" I asked.

"No," she said and flopped down beside me on my bed. I felt Suzie shake with laughter on my other side.

"I told you they didn't. I told you not to go in there," Suzie said, still laughing.

"I just thought they might…"

"Those babies are gonna be five years old before they say *mama*," Suzie said, still laughing.

I couldn't help but laugh, too. Nina had been with her twins since they were born, and even though they'd been saying *dada* for over a month, they weren't even trying to say *mama*.

Nina covered her face with a pillow and growled with frustration. "I know," she said, taking the pillow away. "I bet Chuck promised to buy them Power Wheels if they hold out until they turn one."

"The funniest part is, they look at you, and you think they're gonna do it," Suzie said. "They press their pouty lips together and then—"

"Da da da da," Nina said, finishing Suzie's thought.

For a few minutes, we lay together, neither of us speaking until Suzie took my hand. "I can't believe you're getting married tomorrow! I feel like these last five months have just flown by," she said.

"I know," I said, unable to keep a smile from spreading across my face.

Nina took my other hand and laced her fingers with mine. "I can't believe we got everything done," she said, "and your dad and that gazebo! You seriously had no idea?!"

"No!" I said, still astonished that everyone had kept secret the elaborate structure that now sat on the *hem* in the exact spot Walt had told me he loved me for the first time. "Those two," I said, thinking of my dad and Walt and how close they'd become.

"I think Billy may like Walt better than he likes you," Suzie said with a giggle.

"You may be right," I said. "He's definitely more useful than I am."

"He's not as pretty," Nina said, and we burst into hushed laughter.

We settled into another comfortable silence. I let go of their hands and got off my bed.

"I was going to wait to give these to you tomorrow, but I think now is better," I said, crossing the room and pulling two gift bags from my closet. When I returned I heard Nina pat the bed where we'd been lying to let me know they'd sat up and scooted back to make space for me.

I handed them each a bag and sat down with them. The bags rattled, and the tissue paper rustled.

"Oh, Me," Suzie said in awe.

"Beautiful!" Nina said, with the same tone. "Are these handmade?"

"They are," I said. "My dad makes something similar for this guy in Harpers Ferry. His family has a stand down there and they sell all kinds of stuff, like homemade kettle corn and saltwater taffy and local crafts. Who knows where he found the puzzle boxes in the first place, but he loved them. Then he found out my dad was blind, and he went nuts. He bought every one they had on hand, and when they sold out, he ordered more."

"They're normally empty," I said, picking up the one Walt had given me. I showed them how to find and push the slide. Then, I twisted the lid and lifted it away.

"This is where Walt put my engagement ring," I said, tipping it so they could see the box inside.

I heard them both mimic the motions I'd shown them on their own puzzle boxes.

"I asked my dad if he could make a photo ladder for yours."

"Oh, Me," Suzie repeated, but this time there were tears in her voice. She leaned across the bed and pulled me into a hug. "I love it, and I love you!"

Nina joined our hug. "I'm just so happy!" she cried. I know you're marrying Walt, but I sort of feel like that's like a side thing."

We all laughed, and she went on.

"I'm serious though. I feel like I'm getting the sister I've always wanted!"

I reached out for her hand, and she held it tightly. I didn't have to say anything for her to know I felt exactly the same way.

20

Charlie

December 2018

I took the photo, praying that the sweat from my shaking hands wouldn't destroy what I thought would be a seventeen-year-old photograph of my biological parents or at least my biological mother.

I looked down at the picture and was surprised to see my parents on the top of the fold. They were standing beside each other just as they were today, with Mom on the right and Dad on the left. I gently lifted the fold to reveal a younger version of the man I knew as my uncle, Walter Lee. His face was bright and full of life, a far cry from the man I knew, who, at best, was present and cordial but mostly just wasn't around. He wore a baseball cap, but even with the cap, I could see that his hair was longer than I'd ever seen it before. To his left, tucked into his arm, was a young woman who looked so much like me that I couldn't breathe for a moment.

She stood so close to my mom that you couldn't help but know that they were good friends, maybe even best friends.

She was the shortest in the group by several inches. Her skin looked healthy but pale, just like mine. Her eyes were brown and bright, and she smiled with her whole face. Her strawberry blonde hair was pulled into a low ponytail and drawn over her shoulder on the right side, a mirror image of how my hair currently fell over my own shoulder as I looked down at the photograph.

"She looks just like me."

I wasn't the same person I had been even ten minutes before. I knew there were a million things I wanted to say and a thousand questions I wanted to ask, but they were all so jumbled that I couldn't make anything sensible come out. I had to force myself to look away from the photo and at my parents, but I couldn't keep from looking back down. The details around the four of them started to come together.

They were all wearing fleece jackets. Mom and Dad were even wearing stocking caps, and Marie wore a fuzzy headband covering her ears. They were huddled together, and their cheeks were pink from what could only be the cold. They were standing in an arena of some kind. I brought the picture closer and saw what looked to be white railings in the background and maybe a track of some sort just beyond the fencing. With all the questions floating in front of me, the only thing I could manage to blurt out was, "Where was this?" I looked back up at them. And said, "Y'all look cold."

They both laughed, "We were in the hood of Baltimore," Dad said. "And it was cold as a witch's—"

"Charles!" Mom said, cutting him off and smacking his knee. "Lord," she said and rolled her eyes. "Daddy thinks everywhere in Baltimore is the hood." She smiled and slid around beside me to look at the photo right side up. She closed her eyes and took a slow, deep breath like she was physically pulling this particular memory back to the surface of her mind. "We were at Pimlico, the horse track. They had these early morning tours a few days before the Preakness."

"Sunshine on the Hill or something like that, right?" Dad asked.

Mom laughed, "Close," she said. "Sunrise at Ol' Hilltop."

He laughed back at her, "That's what I said!"

He reached over me and touched Marie in the photo. "You can't tell because she was so tiny, but she was about three months pregnant with you when this picture was taken."

I looked back down at the picture, and he was right—I couldn't tell. "You all look really happy," I said.

"We were," Mom said in a voice that I didn't recognize. "That was truly one of the best springs and summers of my life." And even though she was sitting beside me, and I felt the warmth of her body and the shift of every breath she took, she sounded seventeen years away. "Marie was my best friend."

And just like that, all the noise in my mind fell away, and there was only one question left to ask. Only one question mattered. "Where is she?" I asked. I looked back and forth between my parents. "What happened?"

I will never, for as long as I live, forget the look on my mother's face when I spoke those words. Even if I'd tried to reach for her and pull her back, it would have been like trying to grasp running water. She slipped away into a dark space.

I looked at my dad for his reaction and for help. He'd seen the change in her face just as I had. He reached out and took her hand in an effort to reconnect, but she was already gone.

Her eyes went blank, and when she opened her mouth to speak, the voice that came out was deep and unfamiliar. "I... I can't do this." She looked at me and gave away a glimpse of what was inside: sadness, pain, loneliness, fear, love, hate, and hurt. I wasn't sure what was meant for me and what was meant for the world.

I watched her push herself off the floor and ball her hands into fists, holding onto what was left of her composure while simultaneously holding in everything that threatened to break her apart. She looked at Dad for a long moment as though she was begging him to take away what was consuming her.

"Nina," he whispered, "don't." His voice was gentle, like the time he caught Wade climbing the outside of the staircase to the catwalk at church. If he'd shouted, Wade may have been startled, let go of the railing, and fallen. That was exactly how he was talking to Mom—like she was in an unsafe place, and a harsh word could cause her to fall.

She looked at Dad and kept backing away. She shook her head once, "Charles, I can't." She reached out to touch the wall to steady herself. "I can't," she said again. She turned and disappeared around the corner.

He reached for me. "Charlie, you have to understand that this isn't about you." He took my hand in his. I felt small within his grasp. Like I might slip through his fingers. I could still hear her sneakers echoing in my ears as he and I sat together. We were both stunned that she was gone and not sure what to do or where to go next.

"Where did she go?" I asked. My voice shook as I spoke.

He dropped his chin to his chest.

"I don't know," he said, lifting his eyes to meet mine.

I looked at him, trying with everything that I had not to cry. "Is she going to come back?" My voice sounded so small like I was a little girl.

He scooted close. "I don't think so."

I felt his words echo around my heart. In that moment, with the honesty of his words, I let myself feel the weight of everything. I reached for him and let myself fall apart in the arms of the man who would always be my dad.

21

Nina

December 2018

My sneakers squealed in protest with every step I took down the hospital corridors. I knew I would have to apologize for every one of them later, but I couldn't stay.

My heart was pounding in a way it hadn't in sixteen years. I knew I was running away, but I was also acutely aware that my heart rate slowed with every step, and the thumping in my ears died away. Even though every step might be doing irrevocable damage, I'd made a promise to myself that I would never go back to the place that had broken me. I was trying, with every muscle in my body, to keep that promise.

I hardly noticed the chill of the late December afternoon as I slipped through the main lobby doors. Suzie and I had run this route to and from the hospital so many times that my body shifted into autopilot. I didn't notice as the road transitioned from Blakemore to 31st Street. I didn't notice as the stone buildings of Vandy slipped past. I crossed street after street without looking once for cars and never even slowed down as I made the typically tenuous left onto West End, a busy intersection at any hour of the day.

Runners were commonplace on these streets, but not a runner in jeans and a T-shirt. To keep people from staring, I picked up the pace. My T-shirt was no match for the chill quickly setting in with the sinking sun. I ran faster as I made the quick half-mile climb to Murphy Road. My lungs were on fire, and my cheeks were numb by the time I reached the row of old converted homes that housed various law offices and boutique clothing shops. There was no way I could outrun the hurt that was on the verge of swallowing me whole, the hurt that had nothing to do with physical pain and everything to do with the pain of loss that consumed me.

By the time I reached the I-440 bridge, I could no longer feel the tears running down my cheeks, and I no longer cared as I let gravity and anger carry me down the hill into Sylvan Park.

I pushed through the light near Greenhill Church and finally, as I slipped under the graffiti-covered railroad bridge, I felt the tiniest release in the knot of anxiety in my chest.

The shop owner of Ellie Gray's was pulling in clothing racks in preparation to close for the day, and she waved as I passed. The sweet and salty smell of Local Taco reminded me I hadn't eaten in hours.

When I reached the roundabout that joined Murphy, 46th, Westlawn, and the Richland Creek Greenway, the sound of a blaring car horn brought me to an abrupt stop. The car passed so close to me that the air between us pressed me backward, and then the vacuum from it sucked me toward the street. My arms pressed out reflexively, and the toes of my shoes hung on and off the curb at the same time. I didn't remember passing my turn, but there I was, blocks away, standing in the rush of early evening traffic. Then, through the cold, I heard my name,

"Nina!"

I turned to look for the source.

"Nina!" louder and more frantic.

I turned once more before my eyes came to rest on a woman with her hands full of carryout bags on the other side of the roundabout. She handed them to a Local Taco server standing just inside their patio area. She stopped traffic as she stepped into the street and hurried toward me.

When Suzie's gloved hand touched my arm to pull me away from the curb, I was finally able to focus but unable to speak more than a stammer of broken words.

She eased me farther onto the sidewalk and put herself between me and the street like a parent might with a child.

"Hun?" Her single word, one she'd perfected in Baltimore and effortlessly transitioned to the south, was filled with a hundred questions.

'I—they—know—we—" Every word was paired with a heaving breath as I waved my arms wildly. "Everything—" I wiped my face with the cuffs of my sleeve. "Except— Marie—I can't." I dropped my hands to my side.

"Wait." The comprehension of my scattered words hit her all at once. "You and Charles told her everything?"

And right there, in the middle of the street, like every absolutely crazy and wonderful best friend would, she pulled me by my shoulders into her arms. I hooked my arms up around her shoulders and collapsed into her and cried like I hadn't allowed myself to cry in sixteen years when our worlds were ripped apart and knit back together by the same girl and the same truth I'd literally run away from.

And then we were moving. Somehow, without words, Suzie got the waiter holding her bags to follow us as we walked in silence the three blocks to her house.

I waited in the entry as she ushered him in. He placed the carry-out bags on her farmhouse table, and Suzie pressed a folded bill in his hand in thanks. The young man thanked her by name, smiled kindly as he passed, and pulled the door closed behind him. From across the room, she pointed at me and, in as gentle a voice as I'd ever heard her use, said, "You go there." She swung her arm toward her bedroom.

Her words gave me permission to move, but I stood where she left me.

"Leia, Adah, Sylvie," she sang as she unpacked to-go containers. "Supper!"

She pulled plates from the open shelves and set them on the counter. She touched my arm and gave me a nudge. "I'll be in as soon as I get them started. There's something I need to show you."

I nodded and let her words carry me forward. I heard her daughters' footsteps on the stairs as I opened Suzie's bedroom door and pushed it closed behind me. As my eyes adjusted to the darkness, I was surprised to see the outline of her sleeping husband in their bed. Not daring to leave the room, I sank onto the bench in front of Suzie's vanity table and listened to the girls as they sang a familiar mealtime prayer.

A few moments passed as I heard Adah chatter about the diet of a panda. Without warning, the door eased open, and with practiced stealth, Suzie stepped through and shut the door without a sound. She waved for me to follow. I stood, crossed their bedroom, went through their bathroom, and stopped in their massive walk-in closet. When she reached the back, she slid clothes away to reveal a pocket door. If I'd been in her closet once, I'd been a hundred times, and I had never in my life seen this door before.

She slid the door open without a sound and then turned and reached for my hand. I took it and let her pull me in behind her. She touched a light switch on the wall just inside the door, and a small room materialized before me.

I stood in stunned silence as the space around me began to come together. There were eclectically framed photos, ribbon boards, and pinboards everywhere. A carved stump sat as an end table between two cozy, white, upholstered armchairs. The crushed pillows and seat indention made it clear that, even though they were identical, one chair had been used far more than the other. Picture frames, a lamp, a stack of coasters, and what looked like a Bible and a journal rested on the table. There was also a familiar, lightly stained wooden box that made my heart speed up and tears form. I looked to her for understanding or some kind of answer to a question I didn't even know how to ask.

I knew what would be inside the small wooden box, but I had to ask to be sure.

"Is that—?"

As it often was with Suzie, words weren't necessary. Suzie pressed her lips together and nodded.

I moved farther into the small space until I felt the familiar, silky, soft, wood top against my fingertips. I felt the delicate slide shift with the slightest amount of pressure and, with a final twist, like stepping back in time, a length of folded small square photo frames from our shared past. I lifted them from the box. And there she was with her flawless pale skin, radiating smile, strawberry blonde hair, and knowing brown eyes.

They were the eyes of a woman whose friendship I cherished so deeply, and at the same time, they were my daughter's eyes. Each image held some combination of Marie, Suzie, and me from a time so long ago that the memory was a dream.

"I put everything that reminded me of her away," I said, sinking into a chair. "I felt so guilty. I still feel guilty."

Suzie sat on the edge of her own chair, leaned in toward me, and rested her hands on my knee. "Nina, sweetie," her soft southern lilt felt warm around us. "Hun, you had to function. You say you put everything away or got rid of everything, but you didn't. You had Charlie." She covered her face with her hands, perhaps trying to control her emotions. "And every time I see her, Nina, I see a ghost," she whispered.

We sat in silence for a long time.

A million thoughts swirled around in my mind, but I kept coming back to this. "We should have told her."

"You can't dwell on what you should've or could've done," she said, pushing me with her words. "Nina, we'd lost our best friend. Walt was..." She waved her hand as though waving away a gnat. "And then there's Nancy Lynn, which, well, you know how I feel about every bit of that." She rested her chin in her hand, puffed her cheeks and blew out in exasperation at just the memory of Nancy Lynn and the person my sister-in-law was.

To me, Suzie embodied poise and grace. She had the capacity to love and give and forgive more than any human being I knew, with one exception. When it came to Nancy Lynn, she always said, "That's something between me and Jesus."

"The point is, Nina, you and Chuck were asked to do an impossible thing by the only person on earth who could have asked it of you." She took a framed snapshot from the tabletop and handed it to me. She tapped the girl in the center of the photo. "Marie gave Charlie to you. She didn't ask me or give custody to her parents. She asked you, and no matter what goofy rules Nancy Lynn made you promise to abide by when you signed those adoption papers, the fact remains that Marie chose you."

We sat for a long time, taking in the memories that surrounded us. Looking back, it was hard to believe we had known Marie for only two years.

"When did you do all this?"

Suzie followed my gaze around the room. "A while ago," she said.

"How have I never seen it?"

"I don't know," she said, sliding off her Sperry's and tucking her feet into her chair. "I guess this was my come apart," she said, looking embarrassed.

I looked around again, trying to take it all in.

"The day Charlie was born," her voice softened, "you know I'd been struggling to get pregnant, and here was Marie. About as perfect of a person to be a mama and with a perfectly healthy pregnancy. I just couldn't understand why." Suzie pressed her palms together like she was praying and then curled one hand over the other against her mouth and took a deep breath.

"We stayed as long as possible, but John had to work. We made the eleven-hour drive back to Nashville in just over nine hours and we might have spoken a dozen words to each other the whole trip. He took me home. He took a shower and then left for the hospital." She paused, closed her eyes for a moment, and then opened them again. "He left me here, and I kicked a hole in that wall," she said, pointing sideways but not daring to look in that direction. "He always told me the walls were practically sawdust," she said and shrugged her shoulders, still in the memory.

"He got home the next evening and found me sitting at the kitchen counter, staring at a hole in the wall the size of my foot. He hugged me and said he didn't like that wall much either and started crying right along with me. We'd lost so much already that year, and then to lose Marie," she shook her head. "The grief almost destroyed us."

She wrapped her arms around herself. "When we put it all back together in the remodel, he added this space for me and called it my 'runaway room.' I spend less time here now, mainly because of the girls and everything else," she said, gesturing behind her. "But it's always here. When I need to remember her and remind myself that she was real, I can always find her here."

"Charlie looks more like her every day," I said. "I'm not sure what I expected. Maybe that she'd look more like Walt, but I swear. Sometimes, when I catch her at a glance, I have to do a double-take. She looks so much like Marie." I touched Suzie's copy of the picture that Charles had pulled from his wallet. Hers rested in a glass block frame that had "Forever" etched across the bottom. I let my fingers trace the simple script as we sat in an easy silence. "I wish it had really been forever."

Suzie grinned. "I think Nancy Lynn gave me that frame as a wedding gift. As ugly as she was through every bit of that, I thought about throwing it away. It actually made it into the pile," she said, raising her index finger for emphasis.

"You could have just thrown it away," I said.

"That was a small part of it," she said, holding her thumb and index finger up about a centimeter apart. "Charlie's mother's picture is in a frame she gave me. Really, it's sort of my passive-aggressive middle finger to her." She smiled.

A laugh I hadn't expected and didn't recognize escaped from my mouth, and my whole body began to shake with laughter.

She closed her eyes and dropped her hand. "To them both." A grin appeared on her lips. "Truly! It was just her in the beginning, but now they're both culpable." She shook her head, "I just can't believe how long this went on."

"I know it feels that way looking in from the outside," I said, feeling the last sixteen years wash over me, "but being on the inside and living with it every day," I squeezed my eyes shut as tears wet my cheeks again, "it doesn't feel like a bundle of lies."

The silence between us was heavy since this was one of the only things Suzie and I had ever disagreed on.

Memories of Suzie flooded my mind. I heard the heat in her voice. I was with her in the present, able to smell the Burberry scent that touched everything in her runaway room, but I was also with her in a memory from sixteen years before.

I felt Suzie's heart pound beneath my hands and the fabric of her cotton T-shirt and denim jacket as I pressed against her to keep her from flying at Nancy Lynn.

"You're completely unbalanced Nancy!" she hissed. "I swear, I regret the day I introduced the two of you!" she said, snatching her head back and forth between Nancy Lynn and Walter. "And you," she said and locked her eyes on Walt, a man who was a shadow of the man he'd been just days before.

Walt sat in a chair beside his wife, a wife no one knew he still had until she reappeared two days before.

Nancy Lynn stood ramrod straight next to him. Her hands rested on the bump of a belly that had yet to be explained. Her lips were pressed so hard together that the edges were losing their color. She had an ever-present up-tilt to her chin that made her look like she was constantly rolling her eyes at you.

"Suzanna," she said, accentuating each syllable with practiced affluence. Calling people by their full names, regardless of their preferences, was one of a handful of oddities we'd all grown used to when it came to Nancy Lynn.

I met her for the first time the day I moved into our shared dorm room. She introduced herself with such formality, reaching out to shake my hand. Then, in a swish of light, flowing fabric, and Chanel N°5, Nancy Lynn's mother swept into the room and called for her beloved only daughter 'Lynnie' in a fake British accent. Nancy Lynn flinched with every 'Lynnie dear' and 'Lynnie darling.' I'd only known her for fifteen minutes but already recognized a tension between her and her mother that ran deeper than the Grand Canyon.

I felt the same deep, exhausting tension again as I stood between Suzie and Nancy Lynn that day.

"Suzanna, you've always been so prone to the dramatic." Nancy Lynn said with a perfected calm that was proven to send her former boarding school roommate into a rage. "Honestly. What else could you have expected? If the child is to remain in this family, according to her mother's wishes," she said, wrapping the word 'wishes' in air quotes with her manicured fingernails, "I mean, you can't expect for us to have all of Walter Lee's indiscretions out all over the place for all to see. I mean, what is our baby supposed to think?" she said, patting her belly and wearing a nasty sneer on her face. "That child..."

"Charlotte!" Suzie screamed.

Nancy Lynn's mouth dropped open in surprise as though she'd been slapped. "That child's name is Charlotte?"

Suzie continued in a forced whisper through clenched teeth. "Charlotte Baker Mavin. And she has two parents," she said.

Without taking her eyes off Nancy Lynn, she threw her arm behind her at a point beyond the closed door. "One is dead, and the other is—" She drew her body around in a half circle. Everyone in the room watched as she pointed her finger at Walter, a man who sat practically invisible, slumped in a chair, eyes glued to the table like he was studying the patterns in the grains of wood. "And the other..." she repeated. All of us, even Nancy Lynn, waited for Walt to say something, but his eyes never lifted. "And the other is the coward sitting next to you," Suzie said. Her words softened as they filled with pity. Her body began to relax, and slowly, I released my hold on her.

Nancy Lynn blinked, shook her head, and said, "We are not keeping the child," she said, resting her other hand on Walter's shoulder. "It might be better that she is adopted outside of this family." She closed her eyes and rubbed her belly again. "A clean slate," she whispered and opened her eyes. "A new beginning for everyone," she said, looking at Suzie with defiance. "Charles and Nina know the conditions of the adoption. They're free to decline," she said, looking around the room.

For a long time, no one said anything. Then Nancy Lynn nodded her head and said, "Good." She turned to the large conference table, straightened several stacks of paper, and centered an already straight pen on top of each stack. She clasped her hands together gently in front of her. "If everyone's good, we can sign."

Without waiting for anyone to respond, she walked to the conference room door, pulled it open, and said, "We're ready."

A moment later, a sweet looking woman entered the room, appearing oblivious to the drama she'd walked into. "Okay," she said. "If everyone can take a seat, we'll get started."

When everyone had taken their places around the table, the woman went on. "Hello everyone." She said with a one-handed wave. "My name is Robin Loope. I have served as the Ricks family's attorney for twenty years. Ten months ago, shortly after they married, I helped Marie and Walter get their wills in place. Then, six months ago, when they learned they were pregnant, they amended their wills. On a personal note, I was extremely fond of Marie. I've known her since she was a child. I got to watch her grow up into an amazing young woman. Walter, it was my absolute pleasure to help the two of you begin your life together."

Walter looked up and met her eyes. A few moments passed before he dropped his head into his hands, retreating into himself.

"I am so sorry for your loss," Ms. Loope said. She took a breath, turned back to the room, and went on, "The wishes set forth in Marie's last will and testament are what we will be honoring today."

Ms. Loope paused, letting everyone digest her words before going on. "As I understand it and as the paperwork in front of you indicates, this is a closed adoption. Under normal circumstances, upon the death of a child's biological mother, custody would pass without contest to the biological father. However, this case is not typical. With the death of Marie Collie-Ricks, custody of Baby Girl Ricks should pass without contest to the biological father, Walter Mavin." She shifted her paperwork. "As I understand it, Walter Mavin is declining custody because of," she paused briefly, double checking her papers, "mental instability."

She said each syllable as though she didn't quite believe what she was reading. "Going back to the conditions of Mrs. Ricks's will—"

"Miss Ricks!" Nancy blurted in a high, shrill voice. Her cheeks turned pink. For the first time since she'd set foot in the lawyer's office, she was visibly rattled. "It was Miss Ricks," she repeated in a less abrasive tone, placing a hand on her belly and touching the table with the other. "She was not married," Nancy Lynn said, pressing her fingers hard against the table. "She was pregnant and not married."

"Nancy Lynn," Walter said, touching her arm. He'd spoken so little since Marie's death and his voice sounded rough and unused.

Robin Loope continued. "As I was saying, according to the conditions of Mrs. Ricks's will, in the event that either of the biological parents are unable to care for Baby Girl Ricks, it was the mother's wish that her child be raised close to or with her biological family. That would mean, custody would transfer without contest to the paternal uncle and aunt, Charles and Nina Mavin."

She lifted her eyes from the papers resting on the table in front of her and turned to face Charles and me. "Is this a responsibility you are equipped to take on?"

Charles took my hand under the table, and without hesitation, together, we said, "Yes."

"The conditions!" Nancy Lynn said in the same shrill voice and patted the table again to emphasize her point.

"Nancy Lynn," Walter said again, the force in his voice growing more intense.

She shook her head to reject his words and continued, "But she didn't say anything about the conditions." Her tone grew more emphatic with every word.

Ms. Loope pressed her lips together and waited for Nancy Lynn to finish. Then, with deliberate calm, she said, "Ms. Mavin." She waited for Nancy Lynn to give her full attention before she continued.

"Ms. Mavin, you may think that you are in charge here, but let me assure you, you are not."

Nancy Lynn's mouth dropped open in shock.

"In fact," Ms. Loope said. "Ms. Mavin, let me make it clear to you that you are a guest at this proceeding."

At this, Nancy Lynn straightened, "Excuse me?"

"Yes, Ms. Mavin, I understand that not being in charge may be a unique position for you, but please know this isn't my first rodeo in the arena of domestic adoptions." She paused briefly to tap her stack of papers and lay them back on the table, then turned back to the room.

"As you can imagine, this is an extremely unique situation. I understand every family dynamic is different, but something just didn't feel right about this one." She tapped her finger to her lips and then focused directly on Nancy Lynn. "You see, I did my research and found that your husband signed divorce papers twenty months ago. Divorce papers that, for whatever reason, you neglected to file."

It was our turn to be shocked.

I didn't understand.

"But we all went to your wedding," I said, looking at Walter for answers. "I was there!" I said, unable to hide my confusion and frustration.

"Yes," Ms. Loope said, nodding her head as she looked around the room. "I guessed that would be the case, but as you can see, not everyone in the room is surprised," she said, letting her gaze settle on Nancy Lynn, who stared back at her and Walter, whose head was bowed.

Ms. Loope went on. "Ten months ago, Mr. Mavin and Ms. Ricks applied for and were granted a state of Maryland marriage license." Ms. Loope shook her head. "Some of you may be wondering how they were able to do this if Mr. Mavin was still married to—" she gestured at Nancy Lynn. "It may surprise you to know that states don't talk to each other when it comes to marriage. If both had taken place in Tennessee, it would have been discovered eventually. However, since Walter's first marriage took place in Tennessee and his second marriage to Marie happened in Maryland, it's possible that Ms. Mavin neglecting to file the signed divorce papers may never have been discovered."

She looked back at Nancy Lynn. "Your actions, although not illegal, are inexcusable. You have absolutely no place in this room. If—" She stopped herself and reached out for the table for support and to regain her composure. "Ms. Mavin, you are here as a guest. Moving forward, I will ask you to remain as such. Meaning, from this point forward you will remain a silent observer. Are we clear?"

Nancy Lynn stared, mouth open, stunned. When it was clear that her silence would not be allowed to serve as her answer, she responded with a subdued, "Yes, ma'am."

With their understanding in place, Ms. Loope turned to Walter. "As ridiculous as the conditions of this adoption are, they were submitted by you, Mr. Mavin." She paused, waiting for his confirmation. "Mr. Mavin, they were submitted by you, correct?"

Walter nodded, but this wasn't good enough.

"Mr. Mavin, because of the circumstances of this convoluted situation, you're going to have to verbally confirm that these conditions are from you and only you," Ms. Loope said.

The room went silent as though all of us were holding our breath, waiting for his response. Nancy Lynn sat perched on the edge of her chair, clutching her belly in both hands, not daring to speak.

"Yes," he said, and his words were clear. "I'm sure this doesn't make sense to any of you." His voice broke, and he shook his head. "I just lost everything. I can't even take care of myself. A baby…" He paused as though drawing strength from the bottom of a well. "Charlotte has no business being entrusted to me. Marie knew what she was doin'."

His own words appeared to throw him off balance, as if he'd never dreamed he'd ever say her name out loud again. He'd released a ghost into the room. Losing control, he shook with silent sobs.

Ms. Loope cleared her throat softly, "I understand how hard this must be for you all. Although this is a difficult situation, the fact that Charlotte will remain within her biological family is what we should consider a win." She patted the stack of papers. "It is my hope that with time and distance from today and the events of this week, these conditions will be reevaluated." Her voice was warm, and her words were not unkind, but the look she gave Nancy Lynn could have frozen the warmest sea.

"It's crazy," Suzie said, pulling me from my memories. "I can still remember that sweet old lady who ran the adoption meeting."

"I was just thinking about her," I said, smiling.

"Ms. Loope," she said, drawing out the single syllable of her name.

I closed my eyes, picturing her round face, "But I don't remember her being old, like my mom's age, right?"

"I guess so," she said, shaking her head with a smile. "I just remembered how she handled Nancy Lynn," she said with a laugh.

I had to laugh with her, and before we could stop it, she and I were full-on laughing that rare, deep from within, soul-cleansing, therapeutic laughter, a laughter that could have lasted so long that one, or both of us would have forgotten why we'd been laughing in the first place. But that didn't happen.

The sharp sound of the pocket door hitting its stop plate jerked the room into silence as quickly as a burning candle wick goes out when it's pinched with wet fingers. We both turned to see Leia and Charlie standing in the open doorway in shocked silence.

22

Marie

April 2002

My hands shook as I set the cup on the counter and walked into the bedroom. "Okay," I said in an unsteady exhale.

"Okay." Walt's voice was bright, and I heard him get up from the bed and walk toward me.

I stepped out of the doorway and let him pass. I crossed the room to our bed and lay down on my back. I pressed my hands into the mattress and willed myself to think of anything else.

As a child, in the months before I completely lost my sight, I liked to sneak up to the second-floor hall to listen to Evelyn play piano while Mr. Pluto sat beside her and turned pages. She played Beethoven's *Moonlight Sonata*, Debussy's *Clair de Lune*, and Gershwin's *Rhapsody in Blue* when she was feeling particularly sassy.

I loved the way the chords felt against my back and the palms of my hands as I pressed them into the plush antique rug as I lay quietly under the piano while Mr. Pluto and Evelyn pretended they didn't know I was there.

Back then, change was coming, and I was scared because all of that change was happening to me.

Now, as I lay in wait, I was part of that change. This wasn't happening to me; it was happening because of me. I didn't have to be afraid because I chose to love and be loved. I could let myself be happy and even excited for the change that was coming. Another memory pushed its way to the surface.

I was ten years old, and all I could visually discern were faint shadows. I'd tagged along with Mama while she watered the plants in the big house. An unfamiliar song caught my ear, and I couldn't resist. I made my way upstairs and let the music draw me to it like a ribbon across the open space to where I knew the piano bench would be.

A familiar but unexpected hand took my arm, and without a break in the melody, somehow, Mr. Pluto led me to sit beside him on the piano bench. He settled his right hand back onto the keys as I reached out and touched my fingers to the underside of the piano's keyboard to feel every note as his fingers moved faster and faster, and then more slowly, until finally, the space around us was quiet.

He lifted his hand from the keys and his foot from the pedal, and we just sat there. Even though I was young and had known him for only a year, I knew enough to know that Mr. Pluto was a patient man. He could and would wait for me to find the courage to say what was on my mind.

My heart thundered in my chest. "I didn't know." I pressed my hands against the piano bench and tried again. "Your fingers move so fast, like one of those pianos that play by itself," I said. "I didn't know you could play like that. What was it?" I asked. Having found my voice, I asked another question before I lost my nerve. "And who turned your pages?"

He laughed a hardy, friendly laugh. "That was *Prelude in C Sharp Minor* by Rachmaninoff, and there are no pages."

"No pages?" I asked in disbelief.

"No pages," he repeated.

"Oh," was all I could manage.

I was sure I didn't know anything about anything when it came to the piano,
but I was certain his performance was amazing. "How are there no pages?"

"The pages are all inside my head," he said.

"But there's music somewhere, right?" I asked, trying to understand.

"I'm sure there is, but I've never seen it."

"No music? But how do you know what to play? No music?" I asked.

"Nope, no music," he said. "And I don't really know how it works. I've always been able to hear a song and then just sit down and play that same thing."

"Wow!" I said.

"Yeah, it is pretty 'wow,'" he agreed, but not in a show-off kind of way like the girls who used to jump rope double Dutch and act like they were queens of recess.

"It was so good," I said, still searching my vocabulary for the right words and coming up short.

"Well, thank you," he said, giving my shoulder a hardy pat. I heard him slide the cover over the keys.

"So…" I started but was afraid to ask.

"So, what?" he asked.

"Well, how come I haven't ever heard you play before?"

"That's a tough one," he said, and I heard him rubbing the whiskers on his chin that I remembered were always there in the afternoons just before dinner time.

We sat for a while. I'd learned to wait. Pluto wasn't a man who spoke often, but when he did, you didn't want to miss it. The sounds of the old house chattered around us, with floors creaking, the grandfather clock in the downstairs hall ticking, and the water running somewhere on the floor above us. The house was stretching and breathing around us. I sometimes imagined that Edgevale was more than just a house. I imagined her as The Lady on the Hill, a living being that had called each of us to her, a lady who would remember us and keep us safe.

Pluto took a deep breath and finally spoke. "Marie, this may not make sense to you, but you're a smart young lady, so I think you might understand." He slid the key cover back and twinkled the piano keys, making up a melody as he spoke. "Sometimes you do a thing because it makes you happy, and you just love to do it. It brings you a kind of joy that you just can't measure. Even when the thing gets hard, you don't get mad doing it. The challenge makes you love it even more. Does that make sense?" he asked, waiting for me to answer.

I thought for a second and then said, "Like Daddy making his puzzle boxes." I didn't say it like a question, but he answered just the same.

"Yes, exactly. Just like that." I heard him rub his whiskers again. "That's why Ms. Evelyn plays the piano. She loves it, and it makes her so happy. When she gets a new piece with a particularly tricky part like that section in Granados's *Cancion de Mayo*, she works on it for a month."

I laughed, remembering how she'd played that one bit so much that The Ladies were humming it at knit club without even realizing they were doing it.

He laughed with me. "She damn near drove us all crazy, but to her it was magic. And when I get to sit beside Ms. Evelyn and turn pages, I get to be right beside her. I get a front-row seat to watch her do the one thing in the world that makes her most happy, and right beside her is a pretty special place to be." He paused for a moment before going on. "For me, it isn't like that. For me, the piano is a sanctuary." He moved his fingers down the keys. "Do you know that word?"

"Like with Quasimodo," I said, remembering the word from the children's book, *The Hunchback of Notre Dame*. "Like a safe place?" This question was because I didn't understand how an object could also be a place.

"Yes," he said. "A safe place." He repeated my words. "Playing piano is how I sort out my feelings. It doesn't bring me joy, but it brings me peace."

I let his words settle in the air around us.

"I don't play often because I don't often have to work through my feelings. These days, things are good."

I stirred his words in my mind, letting them dissolve and then hoping to form them into an idea that I couldn't quite reach. I let my fingers rest against the cool of the ivory keys.

Three octaves below, Pluto played five notes up and down.

I let my fingers echo what he'd played, and as I brought the stair-stepped notes to life, my mind was able to relax enough to let an idea start to come together.

Without saying anything, Pluto played the same keys, except this time, it was different. Even though I couldn't see his fingers, I could tell he left out two in the middle. What I'd later learn was a triad. Again, I repeated what he'd played, and that same half-formed idea broke apart like a cloud and then reformed in a way that finally made sense.

There was something I could physically do to process the frustration, envy, loss, fear, and anger. If I sat still and listened carefully, if someone could teach me, if I could learn to let the world around me take shape, break apart, and then reform into something I could understand, even at ten years old, I could survive this really hard thing and maybe even come out stronger on the other side.

I spun my bracelet a few times and took a slow, deep breath, wanting to be sure I asked my question in just the right way. "Have you ever taught anybody how to play?"

"No," he said, and his tone was hard to read.

"Oh, that's okay," I said, unable to hide my disappointment. "That's okay." Even now, so many years later, I remember how hot my face was and how embarrassed I was. I remember willing myself not to cry.

Pluto touched my shoulder, and that was the permission my tears needed. As quickly as I could swipe them away, new tears took their places.

"Marie," he said in a tender tone, "it's not that I don't want to. I just haven't ever taught anyone before." His voice was earnest and sincere. "But, Marie," he said, "if you want to learn piano, we can find someone to teach you."

"No," I said and shook my head. I wanted to disappear. The heat of my entire body was melting me into the floor underneath the piano bench. "It doesn't matter. It's fine. I'm fine. I don't care. It's fine."

"Marie!" Pluto said. His voice was stern but kind. "If it's important to you," he paused, taking a steadying breath. "If it's important to you, I'll try."

"Really?" I said. I couldn't hide the soul-warming smile I felt coming from deep inside me. For months, there hadn't been much to look forward to, but now, for the first time in a long time, there was something to be excited about.

"But I have to tell you, I'm afraid," he said.

"Why?" I asked, hoping the reason wasn't because he didn't think I could learn.

"Well, what if I'm no good at teaching?" he said with a laugh.

Before I could respond, the sound of my mother's voice made me jump.

"Marie, hun, where are you?"

"We're up here, Greta," Pluto said at a volume just above his normal speaking voice.

I heard her feet hurrying up the carpeted steps to the second floor. "Oh, Mr. Colgate, I hope Marie isn't interrupting." Her tone was light but directed more at me than Mr. Pluto.

"She wasn't disturbing me at all, Greta." He played a run up and down the keys in front of him, and even though the notes were low, they felt light and happy and full of promise. He played the keys again, only this time he moved a note in the middle, and for a moment, the chord sounded wrong, but in the right kind of way.

"Actually," he said, and took his hands away from the piano, "Marie and I were just talking, and I think, if it's okay with you and Billy, I'd like to teach Marie."

"Really?" Her words sounded like hiccups.

I heard the surprise in her voice, but Mr. Pluto thankfully continued.

"Yes!" he said, and this time he sounded sure. "Learning music is good for so many reasons, but most of all, it's good for a child to have a place to sort out her feelings." I heard him slide the key cover back into place. "I'm no expert, but I expect our Marie will have lots of feelings to sort out in the years to come."

"Mr. Colgate," Mom was quiet while she thought it through, "I expect you're right. Yes, I agree. I think the piano would be good for our Marie."

Even at just ten years old, I knew that Edgevale was a special place that made people brave. I knew that day on the piano bench with Pluto, and I knew it as I lay waiting for Walt.

The bathroom door clicked closed, and Walt lay down on the bed beside me. He ran his hand through my hair, tangling his fingers in the ends, and kissed me as I lay on my back with my hands clasped together on my stomach.

"How long do we have to wait?" I asked.

He rolled onto his back and took one of my hands in his. "The box says up to ten minutes."

"Are you scared?"

"No," he said, and his voice was full of confidence. "Are you?" he asked, turning to me. He reached over and wiped away a tear. "Talk to me, Marie."

"Do you think it's because you've done this part before?" I asked, hoping it didn't come out wrong.

"No," he said and squeezed my hand. "I'm not scared because I'm so freakin' excited."

He slid his arm under me, and I rolled toward him and let him hold me. I rested my head on his shoulder and tangled our legs.

"Walt, what if she has RP?"

"Marie," he said and then paused. I knew that pause meant he was considering his next words carefully. "Two things. One is that I don't want you to get your hopes up."

"I know," I said more quickly than I probably should have. "I mean, it's totally possible that I'm not even pregnant."

"Oh, I'm sure you're pregnant," he said, and the way he said it made me laugh. "What I meant was that you said, *'she.'* You'd better not get your hopes up because this baby could be a boy."

I laughed, and he kissed me again.

"So, what was the other thing?" I asked.

"The other thing is," he said, and his tone was more serious. "If you are pregnant and this baby, our baby has RP, then that's fine. It's more than fine because that means our kid has a chance at being as amazing as you are."

"Walt," I said, interrupting. "I'm being serious!"

"I am too, Marie," he said, not backing down. "I know it's hard for you to believe this about yourself, but I think you're the most incredible human being I've ever known. If our baby has the chance to be like you, I'll take it. I'll take it every single time."

I closed my eyes, hoping I could manage not to cry anymore. That was exactly what I needed him to say.

He rolled me gently onto my back, and I felt him over me.

"What if it's negative?" I asked.

"Then we get to keep trying."

I bit my bottom lip and smiled. "That sounds like it could be fun."

I pulled off the tank top I'd slept in, and he sat up to let me pull his shirt up and over his head. I put my hands on his cheeks and pulled him to me, kissing him, trying to say all the things that I couldn't find words for.

He pulled away, and I felt him smile. "I thought so, too."

The rest was a blur that I would never forget. The feeling of him over me. The feeling of him inside me, first slow and then, at my insistence, more urgent. I held him as my body shook around him, and I felt myself pulse against him.

He rolled me back on top of him and took my hips in his hands, the smallest movements sending waves of electricity through me. My hair fell in a curtain around his face. He brought his hand to the back of my head and brought my lips down to his. Just before they touched, he said, "Again?" like a question.

I moaned, still tingling from the first. "Again," I whispered. He pushed his hips up, and I let my body rock against his.

Afterward, we lay together, my head on his chest as I listened to his heartbeat.

"That was way longer than ten minutes," I said.

"That's right! I forgot!" He kissed the top of my head, and slid out of bed naked, and walked to the bathroom.

I felt my pulse quicken. My ears were ringing so loud I didn't hear him cross back to the bed. He took my hand and turned it palm-side up. Now, my heart was slamming against my chest so hard that I felt dizzy with anticipation.

With his index finger, Walt drew a line from the outside of my palm to the base of my thumb. Then I felt him touch the base of my middle finger and draw another line down to make a 'plus.'

I made a fist, bringing it to my lips, trying to hold onto the moment.

He leaned down, kissed my neck, and whispered in my ear, "You're gonna be a mama."

23

Charlie

December 2018

When we found Mom and Suzie in hysterical fits of laughter, I hadn't waited around for an explanation. I turned on the spot and walked away. The echo of her laughter ringing in my ears and the image of her head thrown back in delight was burned into my heart. Blind or not, I will never forget the joy I saw reverberating within the four walls of that small space.

I floated on autopilot out of Leia's parents' closet, back through her parents' empty bedroom, through the kitchen, and up the stairs. I jumped at the sound of the girls' bedroom door slamming. I thought for sure that I'd turn to find Leia had followed me up the steps and slipped into the room behind me. Surely, she'd been the one to slam the door, but other than my reflection in the mirror that hung on the back of the bedroom door, I was alone.

I'd never, until this moment, understood the expression 'so mad you're seeing red,' but as the space around me came back into focus, the edges of everything were singed. The edges of my world wouldn't focus. My heart made my chest hurt deeply.

A light tapping on the door registered somewhere behind me, and I felt Leia's hand on my back.

"Charlie, what happened?" Her words were slow and measured—a stark contrast to her normal rapid-fire chatter.

I backed up until my body was against the door, and I sank to the floor. I balled my hands into tight fists in the thick carpet and rested my head on the door. "Everything!" I cried.

She sat in front of me and placed her hands neatly in her lap. "Well, let's start at the beginning." She looked more like her mother than I'd ever remembered.

"The beginning?" Through my tears, I heard an odd laugh escape. "Well, I guess that would be the day I was born, right? To some woman named Marie!"

Leia's eyes grew wide.

There was a small round pillow in my hands that I had absolutely no memory of picking up. I threw my head back, pressed the pillow to my face, and screamed her name as loud as I could. "Marie! Marie! Marie!" Over and over and over, I screamed. And when there was nothing more to scream, the words came tumbling out.

"The beginning, right?" A scary, frantic edge was sliding into my tone, but as with an avalanche, there was no stopping the slide. I put a finger up so quickly that Leia flinched, but she never took her eyes from mine, pleading with me to go on.

"My beginning," I said, shaking my head and feeling myself growing even more hysterical. "My beginning started the day I was adopted."

Leia's face went pale. Her mouth dropped open.

For as long as I'd known her, which was basically forever, she'd been a devoted lover of plot twists and surprise storyline shifts in the Nancy Drew novels she loved. But in the thick of this real life "who done it," her loyalty to me never wavered.

"Oh yeah, and that's not it," I said, still shaking my head. "That's not the end of this stupid, effed-up story."

She waited in silence, her eyes urging me to go on.

I lowered my head, not really knowing how to say what came next. "My real father," I shook my head again, anger beginning to give way to sadness. I let myself cry. "God, this is so effed up it's embarrassing!"

"What, Charlie? What's embarrassing?" she asked. She raised her eyebrows so they lifted halfway up her forehead. "And this is FUCKED up, not effed up," she said. "Just tell it like it is."

I nodded in agreement and gave her a weak but sincere smile, so thankful for her, so thankful she was here. I pressed my hands deep into the carpet, knowing I needed to tell Leia everything, but before I could, I felt rhythm against my palm and knew someone was climbing the stairs leading to the girls' shared bedroom.

I closed my eyes and saw Andrew's face. I remembered how it felt to have his hand pressed gently on mine. I saw him in my mind, finger pressed to his lips and his eyes telling me to breathe. Telling me to wait. Telling me to listen to both inside things and outside things.

My heart rate began to slow, and before Leia had a chance to ask me again, we heard a gentle knock.

"Charlie," my dad said from the other side of the door.

As much as I wanted to respond to him, nothing came out when I opened my mouth to speak. I couldn't begin to say out loud what was whirling around in my head and heart.

"Uncle Chuck, she's..." Leia said, searching for something that wasn't an outright lie. She searched my face for something to give him, but when I dropped my head to my knees, she improvised. "She needs some privacy!?" The end of her statement rose like a question.

I felt a small thump, which I was sure was his forehead against the door. "Charlie, I'm so sorry!"

My heart ached for him. Our ride home from the hospital had been quiet. After he stopped the truck outside Suzie's house, he turned to me in the passenger seat and tried to explain. "I don't think your mom ever really dealt with what happened. I don't know. We had you, and, well, I think she put all her energy into being your mama."

He was looking out the windshield at something neither of us could actually see. I was sure it was a faraway memory, but for him, it was close enough to touch.

I watched him without blinking, afraid I'd miss something. His hands gripped the steering wheel like he was forcing himself not to reach out, not to go back to that time, and to stay present with me.

"This is not your fault," he said, shaking his head and turning to me. "You need to understand that. None of this is your fault. It all happened *to* you, not *because* of you."

I nodded, even though I didn't believe him. How could I believe anything either of them said? I looked back down at my hands in my lap and remembered that when he unlocked the doors, I jumped out of the truck like it was on fire. I needed to see her face, to hear her voice, then I'd know if he was covering for her. I'd know if her truth matched his.

The image of her laughing flashed in my mind, and I started to cry again. Buzzing from my coat pocket shook me back to the present.

I pulled my phone from my pocket, and Margot's picture appeared on the screen. I wondered, not for the first time, how she knew I needed her.

Before sliding my finger across the screen to answer her call, I said, "I just need some time," and without waiting for a response, I pushed myself off the floor and crossed the room to Leia's bathroom. I sat down on their bathroom rug and answered the call.

"Hap—"

"Margot," I said, interrupting her. "I need you." I pressed the phone to my face as if that would bring her closer to me.

"Charlie?" she said, confused. "What's wrong?"

The sound of my sister's voice released something inside me. It gave me permission to feel the magnitude of the last hour. "You and Nora need to come," I sobbed quietly into the phone.

"Okay," she said confused. "We can leave first thing in the morning and be there for lunch," she said without hesitation. "What's up?"

"No!" I insisted, shaking my head even though she couldn't see me. "Like, don't ask permission. Don't tell anyone. You and Nora pack your stuff. Bring some extra clothes for me… Leave now! I need you."

Because of what I'd put them through over a week ago, I expected a protest and for her to ask for more information, but neither happened. I imagined her, shoulder to shoulder with Nora, calculating time and logistics.

"Okay, we'll be there after dinnertime. Like, around nine. I'll call you when we get there so you can let us in so we don't wake up Suzie's girls."

"No," I said, shaking my head again. "Text me when you pull up and I'll come out." In my mind, a plan was beginning to come together. "Don't even turn off the car."

I felt her concern through the silence and thought I heard Nora whisper something in the background. I couldn't say more. "I need to go, but Margot…"

"Yeah?" she said.

"I need you to go to my room and get my Vera Bradley zipper pouch. It's the one I got like a couple of years ago for Christmas, with the red and white swirls."

"Okay," she said, and I heard her cover the phone and say something. "Pop says hello," she said in a sing-song voice about two octaves higher than it had been a moment before.

I cringed over what I was asking them to do, but I knew there wasn't another choice. "It has about three hundred dollars in it. I need you to bring that with you." More certain than ever about my next move and equally certain that Nora was beside Margot, I asked, "And Nora?"

"Charlie?" Nora said.

I smiled at her response, knowing that, just like our mother, she hated when people said 'yeah.' I told her, "Pack for cold weather."

I disconnected the call before she had the chance to ask any questions. Then I turned my attention to my open palm where Andrew had neatly written his phone number an hour before.

I memorized the digits written on my skin. I'd never been brave enough to pick up the phone and call a boy before. I'd never even talked to a boy on the phone unless he was family. But, feeling more confident than I ever had before, I dialed the ten digits, tapped the green telephone button at the bottom of my iPhone screen, and said a quick prayer that he'd pick up.

The next few hours passed slowly but without incident. I managed to stay tucked away in the girls' room, and with Leia's help, I pretended to be asleep on her top bunk.

I listened to Aunt Suzie put Adah and Sylvie to bed, and I ignored her when she said my name before leaving the room.

When the girls had stopped their whispered chatter, and I could hear Sylvie's gentle snoring, I slipped from the covers, lowered myself to the floor, and left the room without a sound. When I reached the bottom step, I waited for Leia's dad to look up from where he was helping her with her homework. "Hey kiddo," he said. He smiled and pointed over his shoulder into the kitchen. "Aunt Suzie left you a plate in the warmer."

I thanked him and looked briefly at Leia to convey an entire conversation in a glance, then walked through the kitchen and mudroom and, as quietly as I could, I walked out the back door.

My night vision had never been great, but in the last month, it had gotten worse. Still, I was able to find my orange backpack tucked out of sight at the bottom of the back steps, exactly where Leia had hidden it a couple of hours before. I pulled the straps over my shoulders and pulled the hood of my navy sweatshirt over my head, tucking my hair out of sight.

I started to make my way around the side of the house, thinking to myself that it had all been too easy, but, without warning, as though I was stirring up obstacles with my thoughts, all the exterior lights went out and left me in the dark. I froze where I stood as my eyes made the slow adjustment. A small flicker from the window over the kitchen sink caught my eye. I squinted and could make out the outline of a person looking out. I stood completely still, knowing the smallest movement would give me away.

With a quick puff of air, someone blew out the candle that always rested in that window, and she disappeared into the darkness.

Able to move again, I rounded the corner of the house, avoiding yard toys and a holly bush I'd lost a fair bit of blood and skin to over the years. My heart sped up when I made my way down the driveway toward the street and saw the familiar outline of Margot's 4Runner quietly idling in front of the neighbor's house. Margot's truck was the same color as Dad's, but hers was a newer model with a third row. She'd found it on Craigslist over the summer, and in an act of defiance, she'd covered her tailgate in bumper stickers, which drove Dad completely bonkers.

I crossed the manicured lawn, and the moment I touched the cold metal door handle, I felt a huge wash of relief, like a kid playing chase when she reached home base. I opened the back passenger door, expecting to jump in and make a quick getaway like in the movies, but I was surprised to find Nora in my seat.

"Your rodeo, kitten," she said, holding her hand out to take my bag. "Front seat."

I handed Nora my bag and hesitated for a second. I'd never be able to take back what I was about to do.

"Oh," she said, grabbing something from the seat beside her and holding it out to me. "Happy Birthday!"

I gave her a warm smile and took the small, balloon-shaped sticker from her. "Thanks!"

She took the sticker back, peeled it off the paper, and pressed it onto my shirt with a smile. "You're welcome!"

Her voice was bright. "We found it at the gas station by the McDonalds when we stopped in Cookeville."

I'm not sure how it happened, but with everything, my sixteenth birthday had completely slipped my mind.

I touched the sticker, smiled at her again, and said, "Thank you!" I shut the door and prayed I could fake the confidence I needed until it was real. I climbed into the front seat knowing that there was only one way forward.

"Forty east," I said, pulling my phone from my hoodie pocket, "but one stop first." I typed out a quick text, pressed send, and then held my phone out to Margot.

"Really?" she said, looking straight into me with her ice-blue eyes. "Charlie, we just drove three hours and that's all you're gonna give us? 'Forty east but one stop first?' Seriously, that's bull shit. We're not going anywhere until you start talking!"

I felt her irritation and closed my eyes for just a moment, drawing strength from a reserve that was running on empty. "Margot, there just isn't time to start sharing all the vaulted information that has been unearthed in the last six hours. I'm not trying to be shady or anything." I said, balling my empty fist. "I'm going to explain everything, I promise, but right now, I just need you to trust me. We just need to do the next thing, and then the next thing after that, and the next thing after that," I said, thumping my fist on my leg with each "next thing." I locked eyes with her and begged her to trust me and not see the parts of me that were mad and scared. I didn't want her to see the Charlie who had no idea what she was doing.

Finally, Margot rolled her eyes, reached out, took my phone, plugged it in, and stuck it to the magnetic mount on her dash. "I've lost my fuckin' mind," she said, shaking her head and shifting into drive. She looked over and was about to say something else to me when Nora screamed, "BRAKES!"

We were all thrust forward, Margot's hands locked at two and ten on the steering wheel, mine pressed tightly against the dash to keep me from smashing into the windshield, and Nora braced between the two front seats.

We all stared bug-eyed at Leia with her hands lightly resting on the front part of the hood, like she'd stopped the SUV with a hidden superpower rather than Margot stomping on the brakes.

She walked with confidence around to the driver-side back door, and without a word she hoisted herself inside and shut the door behind her. She tossed her backpack over the seat into the back and buckled her seatbelt. Looking up at the three of us staring back at her, she said, "What?"

"Um, let's start with the fact that you're in my car?" Margot said. She shifted back into park.

Leia made no signs of moving.

Margot groaned and rolled her eyes. "Seriously, Leia! Get out! We have to go!" She looked at Nora, who shrugged, and then at me for support. "Charlie," she pleaded, "tell her to get out," she said, speaking each word with quick clarity.

I recognized Leia's look of determination and knew that short of dragging her kicking and screaming from the truck, she wasn't going anywhere. "Just go."

"Thank you," Margot said, mistakenly thinking my words were meant for Leia.

"No!" I said, on the edge of exploding with frustration. "Margot, just go!"

From the back seat, without an ounce of emotion, Leia said, "My dad is on call and just got paged. He's gonna walk out our door any second now to go back to the hospital. It's gonna get way more complicated if you're still sitting here with that stick up your ass when he does."

As if on cue, a small slit of light appeared in their front door. With no further debate, Margot put the truck back in drive and rolled unnoticed past the Vandenberg house.

Following the GPS on my phone, Margot made a right toward the Vanderbilt Marriott. We rode in silence as Margot followed each step of the directions until making a final right and pulling under the arched glass awning in front of the hotel.

She turned to me and tilted her head to the side as if to ask, "Now what?"

Worried they wouldn't be there, I looked out the window, but I breathed a sigh of relief when I saw them sitting on the steps talking as they waited.

My heart did an unexpected flip-flop, and I knew I'd made the right choice. They were the only other people I wanted, no, *needed*, to see.

Andrew stood when he spotted me, and in a natural motion, he reached back with his elbow. Without hesitation and with complete faith he would be there, Nathan reached out and took his brother's arm.

I looked back at Margot and Nora's stunned expressions as they watched the boys walk toward the truck. I rolled my eyes with a smile. "Andrew and Nathan Walton. They're coming with us. And you're catching flies. Close your mouths." I opened the door and covered the fifteen feet between us.

"Andrew," I said, knowing and not really understanding why I heard relief in my voice. He was taller than I remembered, and if it was possible, he was cuter than I remembered, too. I felt my bravery begin to falter as we said nothing and stared at each other.

He reached out and pushed my hood back, letting my hair fall into his hand and back over my shoulder. Even with the noise from the street and the buzz of men taking bags and moving cars all around us, the space felt intimate. My skin tingled as he pulled his hand through my hair and held onto the end, looping it around his finger. "There you are," he said. He touched the sticker on my shirt. "Happy birthday."

"Hey, Charlotte," Nathan said, reaching out for my hand, breaking the bubble between Andrew and me in a way that wasn't rude or awkward. The sound of my full name sounded strange in the air and normally I'd have corrected the person and asked him to just call me Charlie, but with all the craziness, the new name was okay. Marie named me Charlotte and everything about the word felt right.

"Hey, Nathan." I took his hand and squeezed it to give him what the occupational therapist had called a connection or reference point. I hoped my gesture also said, "Thank you." I hoped he understood everything I felt but didn't know how to say it.

"Happy birthday," he said, and squeezed my hand back with a smile.

A man appeared beside Andrew with a neatly loaded luggage trolley. Andrew looked at me like he was asking if it was okay for him to leave Nathan with me. I nodded, and he turned and took two backpacks from the cart. "We'll take these with us, and you can load the rest into my truck. Y'all have the keys."

"Yes sir," the man said, accepting the folded bill Andrew discreetly tucked into his hand. "Thank you, sir, and we'll see you both in a few weeks?" he asked.

"Like clockwork," Andrew said. He threw the bags over his shoulder and turned toward Margot's truck.

It struck me how much Andrew sounded like an adult and, even more than that, how the valet had treated him like an adult. I didn't know much about him or Nathan, but still, there was no doubt about the importance of having them with us.

"You ready?" Andrew asked.

I nodded, but before I could take a step forward, he stopped me with a single raised eyebrow and mouthed, "Use words." He gestured with his elbow and then nodded toward Nathan.

It was a friendly but imperative reminder to not just 'walk' or 'lead' his brother but to include him.

I nodded to him and found my voice. "Yes, I'm ready." It came out sounding so formal and robotic that I couldn't help but laugh. Like a magic potion, laughter evaporated my timidness. I took Nathan's hand and put it just above my elbow.

"You okay?" Nathan whispered as we followed Andrew back to Margot's truck.

"Oh, you know," I said.

"Blind leading the blind, right?" he said with a laugh that was so bright that I laughed, too.

With their bags tucked into the small space behind the third row, Andrew met us at the passenger side door.

"So, there's a change in the plan," I said, resting my free hand on the door handle but not opening it. I paused, not sure if I could find the right words. "I just want you to know what you're getting into."

Andrew gave me that same single eyebrow raise and said, "I'm not sure this day could get any weirder."

I must have looked embarrassed by what he'd said because he smiled and added, "Weird in a good way. You have to admit, nothing about this day has been normal."

"This is true."

He smiled as though waiting for me to go on.

"So, my mom's best friend's daughter, my best friend Leia, unexpectedly joined us," I said, still not opening the door.

"Okay," he said, nodding. "More the merrier?" he questioned.

"Although insanely cool in just about every way," I said, taking a deep breath and opening the door, "she's only fifteen."

Leia grinned back at them, sitting up as tall as she could and succeeding at looking one hundred percent her age.

"Oh, shit," Andrew said, frozen where he stood.

"Oh, shit is right!" Nathan laughed, tossing his head back and rising onto his toes, giddy as he likely sensed the story unfolding around us. "I think this might be the beginning of a felony," he said, letting go of my arm.

He folded his white cane and tucked it under his arm.

I reflexively touched Nathan's arm and looked intently at Andrew. "You can totally walk away," I said.

He took a deep breath, held it for a moment, and then shook his head. "Go big or go home, right?" He pulled the lever to move the seat forward to let Nathan climb into the back seat and laughed out loud.

I tried to lean past him to see the source of his laughter.

He reached in, and pulled Wade's black Graco booster out, and held it up to Leia. "Yours?"

Leia rolled her eyes, held up both middle fingers, and smiled.

Everyone erupted with laughter, which was a much-needed break in the tension.

Nora and Leia got into the back seat, leaving room for Andrew and Nathan to take the captain's chairs in the middle row. Andrew and Nathan got in, and I climbed back into the passenger seat next to Margot. I took my phone to reprogram the GPS while everyone buckled their seatbelts and waited for me to tell them what to do next. It was such a strange position for me since I'd never led so much as a line.

I pressed the final button, and the Irish lady navigator's voice directed us to "Exit the car park and proceed to the route."

From behind me, Nathan cleared his throat. "So," he said, drawing out the *O*, "I packed my smart wool 'cause I figured we'd need all the help we could get, but just wanted to know, where are we goin'?"

Looking straight ahead, with confidence growing stronger with every decision I made, I said, "Baltimore."

24

Nina

December 2018

Sleep was impossible as I relived the events of the day. It had taken every ounce of strength in my body to listen to Charles and not wake Charlie up and at least try to explain. Even though this was her birthday, and we'd planned a small family party with the Vandenburgs, and Suzie had gotten all the food and a cake, Charles insisted we leave Charlie alone. He said she asked for space, and we needed to respect that simple request.

I dreamed of this day for sixteen years. I dreamed we would sit Charlie down and in a sweet but scripted way, tell her everything. I imagined every detail—what I would say, where we would be, where we would sit. I even planned to have Charles make Charlie's favorite oatmeal raisin cookies.

I was foolish. I imagined she'd cry some and ask a bunch of questions. I never thought the truth would unravel like this. I never anticipated anger and slamming doors. I could have seen that coming from Margot or Nora but not Charlie. Charlie always took life in stride, never complaining, just adapting. This was big life stuff, and I was stupid to expect a normal reaction.

But as I lay in the dark counting the mistakes I'd made in the last twenty-four hours, I couldn't escape the unease about leaving things so unsettled. I was restless. No, a better word is angry. I was so angry with how we'd left things!

I got out of bed and paced what I knew to be a well-worn worry path in the skinny hall between Suzie and John's front door and the guest bedroom, where I knew Charles was pretending to sleep so he could avoid talking to me.

He was furious with me for leaving the hospital. He showed a level of anger I hadn't seen in a while. Long ago, his anger was directed at Walter and Nancy Lynn, and if we were being honest and because it's a natural part of grief, he was even angry at Marie. But not at me. Never at me. I stood in the door to the guest room and stared at my husband. Surrounded by the sleeping house, I thought of the board book I used to read to the children, *The Napping House*, "where everyone was sleeping." I would press my index finger to my lips and whisper the word *sleeping*.

In the story, one thing after another gets piled onto the cozy bed: a granny, a child, a dog, a cat, and a mouse. Then, finally, something as tiny, selfish, and disruptive as a flea spoils the whole process. It scares and claws and thumps and bumps, eventually breaking the cozy bed where they had all been sleeping.

"Hey," Charles said in a scratchy but unrested voice.

"Hey," I said, leaning my head to rest against the door frame. I felt like the flea—tiny, selfish, and disruptive.

"You know only creepers watch people while they're asleep," he said, tucking one arm under his head and squinting up at me.

"Yeah," I said, giving him the smile I knew he craved.

"What's goin' on in your head?" This was his guy's way of asking what I was thinking.

I shrugged my shoulders. "Sort of like that bed," I said, knowing he'd know what I meant. It was something Wade had started saying when he was two or three.

He'd cry, "Mama, I'm like that bed!" when his emotions got too big for his words.

The first time he said it, I had no idea what he was talking about. After two and a half years, Wade was an entirely foreign creature to me. Even though we had absolutely no weapons in the house, he somehow made guns and swords out of everything. He stomped up and down the stairs for absolutely no reason at all. He blew raspberries on the glass doors and growled when he put together Legos. And when he played outside for any length of time, he somehow developed a smell that could only be described as distinctly "boy."

"What do you mean you feel like that bed?" I first asked our raging toddler.

"The broken one that gets too many stuffs on it!" Wade cried. His arms were ramrod straight, and his foot stomped with every word. "I just need to be cozy." Those were boy words for "I need peace."

Charles patted the space on the bed beside him (his way of asking me without words to forgive him for being angry). "The cozy one or the broken one?" he asked.

"Broken," I whispered, crossing the space between us. I was eager to forgive him and to be forgiven. I crawled in beside him, and he pulled the covers over me.

Our faces were so close I could count his eyelashes. "Can we fix this?" I asked, knowing his answer already but needing to hear him say it. He pushed up on his elbow to lean over me. He kissed the soft skin of my neck. "No," he said, brushing his lips against my ear. "We just have to walk through it."

I felt my skin tingle, my body reacting to his touch without thought.

"But we can fix this," he said, drawing me close to him and slipping his hand under the waistband of my pajama pants. He kissed me gently at first, but the heat between us quickly grew, making my head heavy and dizzy as I slipped into a place where the mess of our world fell away and we were just us.

I don't know how much time passed, but as we lay together with covers tangled around us and clothes in a haphazard pile on the floor, I drifted into a desperately needed sleep.

Just before the darkness of what I was sure would be a dreamless sleep, I heard my best friend yell my name.

The cold hardwood hit my feet as I grabbed at the first thing that felt like clothes. I quickly realized they were Charles's pants. "Here," I said, throwing them across the bed. He caught them and had them on in a remarkably short amount of time. Frustration consumed me as I scrambled around in the dark for anything to put on.

In the dark, Charles handed me my cotton robe that had been hanging on the back of the guest bathroom door. "Calm down," he said.

I pulled it on, thinking to myself, not for the first time, that those words always have the opposite effect.

Suzie began a panicked knock on the door. "Nina? Are y'all up?"

Charles flipped on the lights and opened the door. "What's goin' on?"

"Leia's gone! Charlie's gone! They're both gone!"

25

Marie

April 2002

"**A**w, Miss Marie!"

"Hey, Mr. Lionel," I said, smiling in his direction.

The old man's familiar voice greeted us as we passed through the glass doors and made our way along the long, downward-sloping hall of Pimlico. He had been at the racetrack for as long as I could remember, but even more impressive than that was that Mr. Lionel had been there as long as Fifi could remember.

"You brought 'em back," he said, his voice moving closer.

"I did," I said. We stopped, and I let go of Walt's arm. I reached out my left hand to Mr. Lionel. "But this time, I'm a missus," I said with a smile.

"Oh, shoot!" His words came out like a squeal, and he turned my hand up so my rings were on top. "Whew!" And it was like air rushing from a balloon. "My goodness, girl! You are a missus.! I'm gonna get your mama. She didn't say anything about it when she and The Ladies got here earlier."

I laughed at his excitement and said, "I told her not to. I wanted to tell you myself." I reached back to touch Walt's arm with my free hand. "Mr. Lionel, this is my husband, Walt."

"I remember you from last Sunrise." Mr. Lionel said. He let go of my hand. I heard him grasp Walt's hand.

"That's a special girl," Mr. Lionel said. "I been knowin' her since she wasn't but twelve hands high."

"Oh, I know she's special," Walt said.

Despite the chill in the morning air, I felt my cheeks getting warm. "This year, I brought them all," I said, eager to not be the center of attention.

I waved my arm, "These are my friends Suzie and Nina and their husbands, John and Chuck."

"It's nice to meet y'all," Mr. Lionel said so quickly that his words ran together.

"This is all amazing," Suzie said with genuine awe. "I'm so excited to see the horses."

"You're gonna love 'em," Lionel said. "Let me go ahead and take y'all down to get a tour number."

His sneakers squeaked as he turned, and we started down the ramp to the right and then through the glass doors leading to the grandstands. With practiced agility, he led us through the crowds that I knew had been there since six that morning.

We found my parents and The Ladies in their usual spot against the rail. Over the next hour, we took turns taking the tour, and even though the tour was the same every year, I loved being there and sharing it with everyone.

After we finished and got back to our seats, we sent the guys to find something warm to drink. I sat between Nina and Suzie and close to the railing. The air smelled of new earth mixed with coffee. "I've never really understood the draw for these horse races before this, but now I sort of get it," Suzie said.

I felt my hair lift as the sound of thundering hooves passed only yards away.

We sat for a while, just listening, until Nina said, "Everything here is huge."

"I love this place so much," I said. "I know that sounds weird because it's a horse track."

"I get it," Suzie said.

I took a breath, trying to put into words something I'd always known but never said out loud. "This track is the last place I can remember being able to see. I mean really see."

I felt every bit of their attention on me. "I love this place so much because it doesn't matter how many years go by, I can still visualize this place in my mind and know I'm right. I know nothing has changed."

Nina scooted closer.

I pointed over my shoulder. "I know the top and bottom of the main building back there is painted bright red and covered in glass," I said. "And during Preakness Week, they clean it so often that every morning it looks like a second sunrise reflected back." That image reminded me of the final trip I'd taken with my parents before I'd gone completely blind. "It's no final morning at Glacier National Park watching the sun rise over Josephine Lake, but from what I remember, it's still really pretty." I sighed and went on. "I also know that every year they repaint the railings green and white, and you can still smell fresh paint in the air because they touch them up every night leading up to the big race."

"Oh, Me," Suzie said.

I smiled at the nickname she'd given me as I felt her lean her head against my shoulder and hook her arm into mine.

"I know the flowers they lay over the winning horses are the most incredible shade of yellow and have the most intense black centers. Sorry," I said, wiping my tears before they got away from me. "I feel like everything these days is making me cry."

"That's because you're growing a human," Suzie whispered.

"Yep," Nina nodded. "Those A.S.P.C.A. commercials with Sarah McLachlan with the abandoned cats and dogs sent me into a spiral only ice cream could pull me out of."

"YES!" Suzie agreed as we all laughed.

"So, does anyone else know yet?" Nina asked, her voice low.

"No," I said, shaking my head. "We talked about it, and Walt wanted to tell you guys as soon as we found out, but because of…"

"Everything before," Suzie said, finishing my sentence.

"Yes, everything before," I said, thankful she'd found a simple way to say something that was anything but simple. "He wanted to wait just a couple more weeks."

I felt Suzie nod. "That makes sense."

"Girls."

The voice of my mother's best friend made me jump, and before either of us had a chance to respond, she was calling us again.

"Girls! We wanna take pictures." The word *pictures* came out like a song, and I couldn't help but smile.

"*Pictures*," Suzie sang beside me and giggled. "I wanna be like Fifi when I grow up. I love her so much!"

"I wanna be like Evelyn and Pluto," Nina said.

"Fifi and Mable have way more fun," Suzie said. "Did you know they've been best friends since they were our age?"

"Yeah, but I don't think I could do this without Charles," Nina said, and something in her tone caught me by surprise.

"Well, when you put it like that," Suzie said, and I knew she must have heard it too.

"Y'all are gonna make me cry again if you keep it up," I said and pushed myself up. "Let's go take *pictures*," I sang.

Twenty minutes later we'd taken photos of every combination of people and even got John, Chuck, and Walt to join us for a couple.

Shortly after ten, we made our way back up the concourse. As with most years before, Mr. Lionel handed us each a glossy flyer and told us all to come back and see him, but when he got to Walt and me at the back of the group, he pulled me into a hug. He shook Walt's hand again and leaned in, speaking only to us and just above a whisper. He said, "You bring that little one back next year, ya hear?"

Both Walt and I stood still. I was stunned by his words and couldn't help but smile and rest my hand against my belly. "How?"

"Old Lionel knows." He patted my shoulder and laughed as he walked with us to the doors. "You just bring her back to see me."

And then we were outside and standing by ourselves, both stunned by his words for the second time in less than a minute.

26

Charlie

December 2018

Margot and Nora didn't waste any time as we merged onto the interstate and headed east.

"So, what's your story?" Margot asked.

"Margot, you're so rude," Nora said from the back seat. "What she meant to say is…" She paused for effect. "Tell us about yourselves." Nora's voice rose and fell like a song as she spoke. No matter what she was saying, you wanted to pay attention. "Where are you from? What grade are you in? How'd you meet Charlie?"

"What's your *name*?" Margot interrupted, her tone deep and abrupt.

I sighed and rolled my eyes. "Excuse Margot, she's super extra about most things."

"What?" she said, irritated. "I'm serious."

"We know," Leia said, and without looking at her, I knew she was rolling her eyes too.

"It'd be nice to know at least the names of the total strangers in my car," Margot defended her response.

"No, it's cool," Nathan said from the back. "We're from Knoxville like y'all. I'm at TSB here in Nashville, but I'm home every weekend."

"What's TSB?" Margot asked.

"Tennessee School for the Blind," Leia said, answering before Nathan had a chance.

I looked at Margot.

"Oh," Nora said. Her single word response echoed the look on Margot's face.

"It's a long story, but I've been there for about four years," Nathan said.

"Oh," Nora said again, and I could tell she didn't know what else to say.

"Anyway," Nathan said. "Andrew's a junior at Farragut High School in Knoxville, but he's doing a flex learning thing."

"Yeah," Andrew said, picking up his side of the conversation. "Flex makes it so I can do my classes from anywhere. I like to be the one who takes Nathan to his stuff."

"That's cool," Margot said. The edge in her voice softened. "How often does he have to be there?"

"It was a lot in the beginning," Nathan said. "But last year, I got into a stem cell trial, so lately, it's been more like once a month."

"So, you're a junior?" Nora asked.

"Yeah," Andrew said. "I don't play any sports or anything. I mean, I like sports. I just don't play them anymore."

"My friend Polly's sister is a junior there," Nora said.

"What's her name?" Andrew asked.

"Mable, but I think she goes by Mae."

"Mae Ledoux?" Andrew asked.

"Yes!" Nora said, excited.

"She was in my Spanish class freshman and sophomore year. I don't really see her much anymore, but I saw that she dyed her hair blue after Thanksgiving," Andrew said.

"Just the ends," Nora said, correcting him. "Her parents went ballistic."

Andrew laughed. "I bet. She seems like a real darling."

"What do you mean by *darling*?" Nora asked.

"Not rebellious," Leia said, answering for him again.

"Exactly," Andrew said. "Anyway, blue hair isn't my thing, but hers looked sort of gnarly." He looked up at me and smiled. My cheeks got hot. I was glad the car was dark.

"So, Nathan, are you going to college next year?" Margot asked.

"I'm moving back home after graduation. Then UTK next fall," Nathan said.

"No way," Nora said, surprised and excited. "Us too! Margot and I will be there this fall, too. Are you living on campus?"

"I haven't really decided yet," he said, and I noticed something in his voice like he wasn't sure.

"Oh," Nora said, obviously caught up in the delight of having something in common. "Well, you totally should. You know, to get the full college experience."

"I think it'd be cool. It's just … the logistics."

"Oh," Nora said, and I heard embarrassment in her words.

"No, it's okay. It's just more complicated for me. I want to live on campus, but our parents…"

"Mostly mom," Andrew added.

"Yeah, mostly our mom is super wound up about it."

"Doesn't TSB have dorms?" Leia asked.

"Yes."

"So, not really that different?" Leia asked.

"Sort of," Nathan said. "TSB was a hard sell for her, and it's set up for blind kids."

"She was so nervous. It took Nathan six months of negotiating to get her to agree to let him go," Andrew added.

"A college campus in the real world is a lot harder for her to get on board with," Nathan said. "I feel like I have to come up with a proposal listing pros and cons and a cost-benefit analysis when it comes to stuff like this."

"Same," I said.

"Remember the iPad?" Leia said.

"Oh God," I said, annoyed by the memory.

"What was the iPad?" Nathan asked.

"It was stupid," I said. Normally, I hated talking about this stuff, but I relaxed, knowing—just like I had when I met him—that whatever I said would be okay.

"At school, I use a CCTV to see small print, and it's huge. They put it at the back of the class. I like having it, but it's an eyesore. I have to sit at the front of the class to see what's going on, but then when we do open-book stuff, I have to get up and go back to the back. I asked my parents about getting an iPad so I could load my books and also take pictures of the board."

"They didn't wanna get it?" Andrew asked.

"They were fine eventually, but they had a billion questions, and I had to take them to the Apple Store. The sales guy was nice, but he didn't know anything about the adaptive stuff, so I was basically teaching him how to use it."

"Story of my life," Nathan said.

"Mom said the guy at the Apple store kept saying 'do you want a job' every time Charlie showed him something," Nora said.

"Yeah, Nate's been through stuff like that," Andrew said.

"So, do you go by Nathan or Nate?" Margot asked.

"Either is fine, but I guess I like Nathan better," he said. How about you, Charlotte? Do you like Charlie better?"

"I think I sort of like Charlotte better," I said, trying to ignore the look of surprise on Margot's face. "I mean, no one's ever really called me Charlotte before, but I like it."

"Then Charlotte it is," Nathan said.

We slid into easy conversation over the next couple of hours until we got into Knoxville.

Andrew and Nathan needed to make a quick stop at their house.

I stared straight ahead as we sat in silence in their driveway and waited. None of us were able to put into words how weird it felt to be so close to home.

A tap on the window made me jump. I turned to see Andrew. He made a gesture to open the window.

"Hi," he said and smiled.

"Hi," I said, smiling back.

"So, don't freak out, but there's someone I need you to meet." Before he could go on, a woman appeared beside him. I couldn't help but notice that even though it was midnight, she looked too polished to be real. I hurried to get out of the car. She gave me a quick once over and smiled.

"You must be Charlotte," she said. Her voice was kind, and her smile was warm. "Andrew told me about your project," she said, and reached out to squeeze my arm. "I really hope you find what you're looking for. I can't imagine what this has been like for you, and I'm glad you asked for help." She pulled me in for a quick hug.

"Take care of my boys and have them call if you need anything." She let me go and kissed both Andrew and Nathan on the cheek. "Be safe, and Charlotte," she said, touching my arm one more time.

"Yes, ma'am?" I said.

She gave it a gentle squeeze. "I really hope I get to see you again soon."

"Yes, ma'am. Me too," I said. I really meant it.

She let go of my hand and touched both of her sons on the shoulder. Without looking back, she went inside.

"Was that your mom?" I asked.

"Yep," he said. "She's a hugger. Sorry if that was weird."

"No, it was fine. She was nice," I said, "And she doesn't care about you leaving with strangers?"

He laughed and opened my car door. "You're not strangers."

I got in and said, "Okay, someone you've known for a few hours."

"I told her where we were going and that you were a friend who needed help. After that, she was good," he said. He smiled and shut the door.

By two in the morning, we'd made it just over halfway and stopped at a Hampton Inn north of Roanoke, Virginia.

Because Nathan was eighteen and Andrew took him to almost all his doctor appointments, they stayed in hotels a lot. He used an app on his phone to get a suite with a bedroom and a separate living room. The girls were in two queen beds in the bedroom area, and the guys took the pullout couch in the living room. We were all asleep in thirty minutes.

A few hours later, my phone began to vibrate and lit the room for the seventh or eighth time in the last hour. As I lay there staring at the ceiling and listening to Leia's rhythmic breathing beside me, I replayed the last twelve hours.

We were miles from home. Fewer than fifteen feet away stood an incredibly cute boy, and he and I shared a completely unexplainable connection.

Unable to lie there any longer, I got out of bed and crossed the room. I lightly touched the end of my and Leia's bed and then did the same with Margot and Nora's bed, using them as guides through the dark bedroom. As quietly as I could, I slipped into the bathroom and shut the door behind me. I felt my body cool as I pressed my back against the door and felt the chill of the tile under my feet. Without turning on the light, I reached out and took three steps into the room, trying to remember.

When we'd gotten there, I'd tried to memorize the space, but as I stood in the dark and stretched my fingers as far as I could, I felt nothing. Fear washed over me. I swallowed hard, pushing down the panic, talking myself down, telling myself, 'It's just a bathroom,' and, 'I can still see.'

I took one more shuffle-step forward and felt my pinky brush against the faucet. It felt electric, like touching one of those glass globe static electricity balls in the kinetic energy exhibit at the science museum—not enough to hurt, but enough to make my hair stand on end. I pressed the handle up to let cold water flow from the tap. I listened to how the sound changed as I let the water run over my hands and felt it heat up.

Yesterday, I met a spunky orientation and mobility specialist at Vanderbilt named Katie Tong. She'd told me that her job was to help people, regardless of where they are on their journey with blindness, gain independence and learn to navigate the world safely. She helped kids who were totally blind learn to use white canes, and she taught adults with limited sight to learn to use assistive technology to navigate places like the grocery store and public transportation. She told me that the best part of her job was when her patients realized that blindness didn't mean losing their independence.

Her words bounced around my mind. It was hard to believe that fewer than forty-eight hours ago, I'd gone with her to observe an orientation and mobility session with a group of kids from TSB. I rinsed my face and remembered their sweet voices singing memory songs about using their canes and learning different textures.

Most of those kids were boarding students who weren't much older than Wade. I couldn't imagine. How could someone just send a child that young away from home? That would be the worst. Then I realized it wasn't. I hadn't just been sent away; I'd been given away.

The silence was too quiet, and the space around me was too dark. Everything was too much.

I reached out and turned on the light. I hadn't realized my heart was pounding until relief washed over me. I had to steady myself against the counter. My eyes hurt as they struggled to adjust to the lights. A full minute passed before my reflection finally began to come into focus. I stared at myself in the mirror, still unable to make out the tears I felt sliding down my cheeks.

The reality of my past and what was ahead of me, the fear that every touch might be just like this, knowing I would have to spend each day filled with this anxiety, knowing things might not be where they were supposed to be, not where I'd left them.... All that, on top of the possibility that I might be sent away or given away, again, overwhelmed me. I wondered how many people there were like me, people who had done what I had done—tried to end their own lives—to stop the hurt. I wondered how many of them failed.

I wondered how many of them had been able to find hope and happiness.

I took a hand towel from where it was folded on the rack and covered my mouth, biting down hard to muffle the sound as I cried. After several minutes, I was able to breathe again. I splashed water on my face, patted it dry with a clean towel, straightened my ponytail, flipped the light switch, and left the bathroom as quietly as I'd entered.

"You okay?"

I jumped at the sound of Andrew's whisper and covered my mouth to keep from screaming and waking everyone else up.

"Sorry," he said, his voice still low. I felt his hand gently on my arm. "I didn't mean to scare you."

"Oh no, it's okay," I said, reflexively reaching to touch his arm as we stood in the dark. "I just didn't know you were there waiting."

"I wasn't waiting. I just thought..." He stopped. I heard his feet on the carpet, and then he opened the door to the hall. The light was bright as it cut through the darkness, but I could see his hand gesturing for me to come with him. Without a moment's hesitation, I stepped into my sneakers and followed him into the hall.

He shut the door behind us without a sound, tucked the room key card into his back pocket, and handed me one of his sweatshirts.

"It's cold out," he said.

I took the shirt from him. I pulled it on and felt myself relax as I breathed in his unfamiliar but comforting scent. "Thank you."

He reached over and pulled my ponytail from inside and drew it over my shoulders, covering but not hiding the fading bruises around my neck. He looked at me for a long moment before asking, "You okay?" His voice was kind, and there wasn't a trace of sleep.

I nodded.

"I just thought I heard crying," he said.

I looked down at the floor.

He took my hand and noticed his phone number still printed neatly on my palm. He grinned at his handwriting. He laced his fingers through mine and said, "Let's go for a walk."

We started down the hall, and I started to talk. "I must have counted wrong," I said.

He'd been nothing but kind to me, and I felt like I needed to try to explain. "They said I should start counting everything, so I left the lights off. It was really dark," I said, trying to steady my voice. "I thought I remembered the number of steps." I looked straight ahead. He must have thought this all sounded so stupid. If he did, he didn't say anything.

We walked for a while and made our way through empty halls and stairways. A peaceful quiet settled around us. Each time we passed through a door, he held it open with one hand and let go of my hand just long enough to guide me through with a hand on the small of my back. We passed through a sleepy lobby and pushed our way through a door at the end of a long, narrow hall that opened onto the outdoor pool deck. I gasped at the cold, but before I could say anything, I was stopped in awe by confetti sized snowflakes falling around us. My grip on his hand got tighter as we stood together knowing what I was about to tell him.

"I tried to kill myself," I said, looking straight ahead. I was afraid that if I saw disappointment on his face, I wouldn't be able to tell him everything. "About six years ago, I found out I have this eye disease called retinitis pigmentosa. It's degenerative, so I knew there was a good chance I'd end up being blind, but when you're ten years old, that doesn't really mean that much. It's just this faraway thing that might happen one day, so it doesn't feel real. Plus, because of all the medical appointments, I got to miss a bunch of school, and even back then, school was the worst." I looked down at the ground where the snow practically glowed.

"The thing with RP is that it's stable until it's not. So, you can go for a long time without a lot of help. You can get by with large print books, a nice tablet, a good computer, and helpful parents and teachers." This was normally where I stopped explaining, but the warmth of my hand tucked into his made me feel brave.

"At the beginning of fifth grade, when you have an individualized education program, an IEP, that's when they start asking the student to get involved. You know, so the kid sort of feels like they have a say in what's going on." I said, moving my free hand back and forth. "It's sort of a joke because, really, the kid doesn't matter all that much. They're just checking boxes to make sure they don't get in trouble. There's the beginning part of the meeting where they talk about your rights and stuff, and then they go over accommodations. Then, they dismiss the student, and the parents, teachers and principal finish up. Only I didn't go back to class." Somehow, this next part felt more embarrassing than telling him I'd tried to end my own life. He looked at me, but I still couldn't look up.

"There was a half-size chair outside the office and sort of like yesterday at Dr. Peeper's office, something inside told me to stay, to be still."

"To listen," Andrew said, like an extension of my thoughts.

"Yes," I said, relieved that he understood. "I sat in that too-small chair with my knees to my chest and listened to this teacher who hardly knew me. He asked how he was supposed to accommodate such 'tedious' needs." My voice hiccupped around the word he'd used, but I pressed on. "He asked the principal at the meeting if this was the 'most equitable use of his time.'" I felt hot tears tingle against my cheeks. "I actually wrote the word *equitable* on my hand in pen so I could look it up when I got home. But I had a pretty good idea by the time he was done."

I felt Andrew's grip on my hand tighten, and I pressed into it, sharing my burden.

"Having or exhibiting equity: Dealing fairly and equally with all concerned." I wiped away tears with the ends of my sleeves as I recited the definition that was burned into my

memory. "He told the whole room he wasn't sure this was the best teacher matchup. He said he didn't feel comfortable neglecting the rest of his able-bodied students and wasting classroom time and resources on a child who could and should be attending a school that was better equipped to handle the burden of a blind student. He said with a blind student in the classroom, the rest of the class would suffer. And in his opinion, it 'wasn't worth the cost.' Basically, he didn't think I was worth teaching."

"What did the principal say?" he said but then backtracked. "What did your parents say?"

"I don't know," I said, shaking my head and feeling heat behind my cheeks. "I didn't stick around to find out."

As soon as the words were out of my mouth, I saw the connection to what my mother had done. And just like it's easier to tell secrets in the dark, here in the snow, with this boy, it was easier to confess what came next than it would have been to keep it balled up inside me. "I hate her for running away, but I did the exact same thing for the exact same reason. I didn't want to hear the truth, and I didn't want to feel the hurt." I dropped my head, feeling heavy with the truth. "Neither did she," I whispered. "I guess in the long run, it didn't really matter," I said, even though I knew now that it really did.

"With RP, when things start to progress, it happens really fast." I paused, hoping the words I had to say would come out right. "When things started to go downhill a few weeks ago, I realized immediately that I couldn't do this on my own, but I didn't want to be a burden on anyone."

He waited as we stood, watching our breath form clouds that lifted and danced until they disappeared high above us.

"Things at school had gotten bad. I was trying to hide the fact that my vision was starting to tunnel, and most of my peripheral vision was gone. On top of that, there was a group of kids, well, mainly one girl, who made being there really, really hard. I don't think this way now, but I felt so alone, and I thought that my family would be better off without me…like the world would be better without people like me."

"What changed your mind?" he asked.

"Margot and Nora, but when I found out about Marie, everything changed. Just before I met you in the hospital yesterday, I found out that my parents have been lying to me for basically my whole life. I don't know all of it, but what I do know is my uncle had a relationship with a woman in Baltimore."

"Marie?" he asked.

"Yes," I said, finally able to look at him. "Marie is my biological mother, and I think, based on what I overheard Dr. Peepers say to my parents, she had RP and went blind when she was younger, too." I stopped, finally knowing how to put into words what I was feeling. "Knowing there's someone out there that has been through this...I need to find her...I need to talk to her. That's why we're going to Baltimore."

We stood for a long time and watched the snow fall around us.

"My mom loves snow," Andrew said without taking his eyes off the magic in front of us. "When we were little, on the coldest nights when it would get below freezing, she'd wake us up and ask if we wanted to make snow." He smiled as he remembered. "I mean, what five or six-year-old doesn't wanna do that? So, we'd crawl out of bed, and she'd give us both a big mug full of hot water. Then she'd take a steamy mug for herself, point to the back door, and the three of us would tiptoe outside."

"It must have been so cold," I said.

"Yeah, it was cold, but we were warm from the hot water and excitement," he said with a laugh. "She'd count down from five, and when she got to one, we'd hold on tight to our cups and throw the hot water up into the air as high as we could." He made the motion with his hand, obviously caught up in the memory.

"What happened to the water?" I asked.

"Instant snow," he said. "The air freezes the water almost as soon as it leaves the cup, and it turns to snow as it falls back to the ground. It's all physics, but we thought we were magic," he said. He shook his head. "She was magic."

He was quiet for a while like he was trying to catch a thought just out of reach.

"I don't know how I'd feel if I found out she wasn't my biological mother." He squeezed my hand again. "What do we do when we get to Baltimore?"

"I'm not sure," I said, saying out loud what I'd been rolling around in my mind for the last few hundred miles. "All I have is her name," I said.

I pulled the folded picture my dad had given me from my pocket and handed it to him.

He brushed the snow off a nearby bench, and we sat down. He flipped it over and I pointed to a typed label stuck to the back. It read, "It's a girl! L to R: Nina Mavin, Chuck Mavin, Marie Collie-Ricks, Walt Mavin – Pimlico, Baltimore, MD. Friday, May 19, 2002."

"Tell me something else about your mom," I said and leaned my head against his arm. He pulled me closer.

He paused, and I felt his chest rise, "She's quiet, I guess, like me. She's a good listener."

I heard his smile in the bright lift of his voice.

"She works a lot though. My dad, too," he said.

"What do they do?" I asked.

"My dad coaches football, and my mom sells houses. They're always going. She stayed with us when we were little," he said.

"After Nathan's accident, when he lost his sight, and everything went crazy with all the doctors and surgeries and everything, money was tight." He kept his arm around me as he spoke. "Things got a little better when Nathan got into the trial at Vandy. I was young, but I could still tell they were having trouble. They fought a lot about money. We had to sell our house. I remember Mom went and bought a bunch of stuff at one of those home stores to get it lookin' nice to sell. Then when it sold, and we were actually moving, she took all the stuff she bought and returned it to get her money back. Then, she used that money to pay for the U-Haul. That's how tight things were."

"I think she really liked gettin' our house ready to sell. It was fun for her. She studied and got her real estate license and started sellin' other people's houses. I think it was hard for them, especially in the beginning, because she was only doin' it part-time. She was basically makin' enough to pay for travel to Vandy and for people to watch me while Nathan was going through all that."

"The craziest part is how it turned out she was really good at sellin' houses. Like really good!" I watched him smile as he talked about her.

"None of that would have happened if Nathan hadn't lost his sight." He paused for a minute and shook his head. "I hate when they say it that way."

"Like what?" I asked.

"I mean, it makes it sound like Nathan misplaced sneakers or socks in the dryer, or somethin' like that." His voice had changed. It was filled with frustration. He took his arm from around me and stood up. He reached for my hand, and I felt the snow crunch under my feet as we walked across the pool deck to the railing that overlooked the parking lot and the interstate beyond.

"What happened?" I asked in a whisper.

The silence between us stretched so wide that I thought he wasn't going to answer. Maybe he wanted to leave what couldn't be changed in the past.

"We both had played Pop Warner football since forever. Like since we were five. I was twelve, and Nathan was thirteen. He'd just moved up to junior varsity. I was still in peewee, so my game was earlier in the day. It was the first really cold Saturday of November, and I was still in all my gear, standing at the edge of the field, twenty yards or so down from my dad. He was calling in plays from the sidelines to Nathan on the field."

Andrew let go of the railing, moving his hands as he talked his way through the memory. "The center snapped the ball to him, and he threw the most perfect forty-yard strike."

I watched him and imagined the ball sailing through the air.

"For a long time, I thought my mind had warped the memory. I thought, there's no way it could have been that perfect," he said, and looked down at me and smiled.

"But it was?" I asked.

"It was!" he said, taking my hand and flipping it palm up. "A couple of years ago, I got the nerve to go back and watch the tape, and it was exactly like I remembered!" His eyes lit up. "It left Nathan's hand in the most perfect arc." He floated his hand through the space between us and into my hand.

My fingers closed around his and held tight.

"Clean pass. No flags. But when I rolled the tape back and forced myself to take my eyes off the ball, off that perfect pass, in the lower right corner of the screen, you could see, clear as day. The left tackle missed his block, and a full second after the ball was away, the defensive end nailed my brother, and that was it." He gently touched his finger to his temple. "Lights out."

I could see every detail. I shut my eyes to trap tears.

"I know," he said and went on. "There ended up being a lot of drama around it because the kid that hit him was actually too old to be playing, but the coach and the kid's parents put the wrong birthday when they signed him up."

"Oh my god! Are you serious?" I said.

"Yeah! It was really messed up! Everybody told my parents they needed to sue, but they wouldn't."

"Why?" I asked.

"It's a stupid reason, or at least a lot of people think it's stupid," he said, rocking back on his heels and pushing his hands into his pockets. "And for a long time, I was really mad about it."

I stayed quiet, even though I wanted to ask him. He'd given me time to tell my story, and I wanted to do the same for him.

"So, my parents are pretty big Christians. I mean, I am, too. At least now I am. Anyway, there's this sort of rule in the Bible that says you're not supposed to sue other Christians."

"But they lied and cheated?" I said, not really knowing what else to say.

"I know," he said. "That's why it was so hard for me to understand. I spent a lot of time being mad about it. I felt like they cared more about this other kid and his family than they did about Nathan."

"What'd they do?" I asked.

"It's sort of a long story, but the short version is that they took it to the church."

"What?" I said, confused.

"It's been sort of crazy to look back at the last five years, but in a weird way, it's all worked out.

"How do you mean?" I asked.

"Well, the force of the kid hitting Nathan, and then the force of Nathan hitting the ground, caused something called 'bilateral retinal detachment.' It wasn't the only injury, but it was the worst by far," he said. "For a lot of reasons, but mostly the damage that was done when his retinas actually separated, him having surgery to repair his eyes wasn't really an option."

"Nathan must have been so upset," I said, thinking about how angry I was about going blind, and there wasn't even anyone to blame. For Nathan, there was.

"You'd think, but that's the craziest part about it," Andrew said, shaking his head. "He wasn't. Aside from the church part of it, really, Nathan was the reason my parents didn't sue anyone—not the league, not the coach, not even the kid's family."

I couldn't hide my surprise.

"I know," he said with a laugh. "Get this! A couple of months later, Nathan found the kid online, and without telling our mom and dad, he asked him and his parents to come to our house. I know you don't really know him, but it's totally like Nathan to do something like that. I mean, they just showed up at our house." He shook his head and laughed at the memory.

"What's funny?" I said with my jaw dropped.

This time, Andrew laughed for real.

I smiled, realizing I'd never heard him laugh an actual wholehearted laugh. There was so much I wanted to know about him.

Andrew went on. "They talked for hours. It was nuts! And you'll never believe it, but they still keep in touch to this day."

"No way!"

"Totally for real," he said. "He's a good guy. Last year, he wrote about the whole thing and how it changed his life in his essay to get into West Point."

"Seriously?"

"West Point called my parents and Nathan at some point to ask if it was all true. The kid started there this past fall," he said, hanging back on the railing and stretching his arms. He rubbed his hands together, cupped them over his mouth, and blew into them. "I'm freezing," he said.

"Me too," I said, even though I hadn't even noticed the cold.

He dropped his hand on top of mine and took it from where it rested on the railing. "Let's go in before we freeze to death," he said, and he led us back across the pool deck and toward the doors.

"Wait?" he said, stopping abruptly and turning back to face me.

"What?" I said, looking up at him.

"Charlotte," he said and stepped close to me.

Hearing him say my name made my skin tingle. It was my name, but for the first time, I wanted to own it.

"Charlotte." He took both my hands and squeezed them. "I really like you." And then, without hesitation, he leaned in and kissed me, just like that. He wasn't scared or nervous. He was steady and sure.

I was so surprised I couldn't move but felt the world tilt and something inside me shift and settle into place.

In an instant, I'd gone from just a girl to the girl Andrew liked. I went from a girl who had never been kissed to a girl someone wanted to kiss, and not just anyone. I was the girl Andrew wanted to kiss.

He pulled away and grinned down at me, "Was that okay? That I...?"

"Yes!" I said, unable to stop smiling. I pulled him toward me and let him kiss me again. This time, I kissed him back so there wouldn't be any doubt in his mind that it was definitely okay.

The sound cut through the silence that floated around us. We jumped apart and turned to see Leia and Nora standing by the open door.

27

Nina

December 2018

"Leia's gone!"

"What?" I said, leaning in, squinting with confusion.

"Leia and Charlie are gone," Suzie said. Her words were slow and deliberate.

"They're both gone!" she repeated, lowering her voice. She spoke even more slowly, which should have injected calm, but somehow it didn't.

I felt an instant wave of nausea at her words, and my heart dropped into my stomach. I was left feeling dizzy and on the edge of something. I wasn't sure if that something was throwing up, passing out, or somewhere in between, but I had to reach out and steady myself against the end of the bed to keep from falling.

"Wait. What?" Charles asked, running his hand through his short dark hair and pulling it forward to lay flat again.

"Focus, Chuck!" Suzie snapped, clapping her hands a couple of times. "I mean gone! Like not in the girls' room! Like, not in the bathroom! Like, not in the den. Like gone, Chuck! Gone!" The edges of her voice were frayed.

I moved between them and past Suzie, looking left and right, halfway expecting to see Charlie pop out from behind the sectional like when they were little and playing hide-and-go-seek. But, deep inside me, I sensed she wasn't there.

Charles went through the living room and into the kitchen. "Have you talked to John," he asked, moving methodically through the space, looking like a detective at a crime scene.

"No, he's in surgery," she said, waving her hand through the air, dismissing his words, pushing away the need for her husband. It was something she'd almost, but not quite, perfected. Suzie had always been fearlessly independent. It's what made their life possible throughout John's rigorous years of training. And now with his demanding surgical schedule, she was often on her own with their girls. Even when life was highly charged and everything was coming apart around her, Suzie brought order to what was otherwise chaos. But not today. Today she was put together with makeup and hair done, but the stress showed in her wild eyes. She was coming apart at the seams, her voice shaking and constant hand wringing.

Suzie and I watched Charles move through her tidy kitchen.

"Have you moved anything?" Charles asked, not looking up from his search.

"No," she insisted, shaking her head.

He lifted a stack of papers gently, moved a plant, and slid aside a tablet charging station, unsure what he was looking for but hoping to find something. He opened a drawer and pulled out a yellow legal pad just enough to read what was written. He nodded once and held the pad up to us to reveal an illegible handwritten letter. "I think this is what we're looking for, but you're gonna have to translate," he said, holding it out to Suzie.

"Oh sugar!" Suzie said, snapping her fingers. She hurried over to him, took the pad, and sat down at the island. "I completely forgot I put all that junk into the drawer. He's always leaving junk on the counter, and I just thought it was junk—"

"Suz!" Charles said, cutting her off. "It's fine. Just tell us what it says."

I saw her jaw tighten as she read through her husband's scribbled note. Without saying a word, she took her phone, tapped it a few times, and put it to her ear.

As we waited, I couldn't help but feel sorry for whoever was about to answer her call.

"Dr. Vandenberg, please," she snapped, still not taking her eyes from the paper. "This is his wife, and it's urgent!"

For a moment, we waited in silence, and then John was on the line.

"What the freak do you mean Leia and Charlie left last night for FLIPPIN' Baltimore!?!" Suzie said with the volume of a whisper and the force of a scream, entering the conversation mid-stream. The phone was pressed to her ear as Charles and I huddled around her, trying to absorb a shred of what was going on.

"John, I will not calm down! You were not the one who went in to wake up our fifteen-year-old child and found her not in her crappin' bed!!!"

Silence followed as she listened, and then, "Oh, yes! Let's talk about that!" she said, crossing the kitchen to the small built-in desk and snatching up the yellow pad. "Let's talk about your bleeping note!"

"Suz," she said, reading John's hastily written, practically illegible handwriting. "Leia and Charlie left last night for Baltimore." She swung the pad back and forth as she repeated John's written words. "BAL-TA-MORE! The dang murder capital of the United freaking States, John!"

Charles and I jumped back to avoid getting slapped in the face.

"Geez-oh-Pete, John!" she said, giving her husband a teen-worthy eye roll. There was a pause, and then, "Oh, please tell Parker thanks for clearing that up. I stand corrected. Number three in the country for murder." Her voice was thick with sarcasm. "You tell him thanks so much from me."

John had either been brought out of surgery to take her call, or more likely, based on all Suzie's colorful and creative curse word alternatives, was on speakerphone being piped directly into the operating room while he had a patient open on the table.

"Oh, fan-freaking-tastic. Thanks, Parker! I'll be sure to tell Elliott how helpful you were in a crisis." She said, confirming that she was LIVE in the O.R., as Phillip Parker had been John's long-time surgical nurse, and his wife, Elliot, was Suzie's close friend.

She returned her eyes briefly to the page and then continued with his message. "She's with the twins, so don't freak out." She slapped her hand on the table three times as she said the words "Don't. Freak. Out? John, I'm nothing BUT freaking out! Our fifteen-year-old child is not in her bed! She's on a gosh darn road trip, in a car, at night, with teenagers!"

The word *teenagers* came out with the same vehemence that one might say "drug dealer." Charles and I looked at each other, offended that the teenagers she was referring to were obviously ours.

"Oh, John," she said, her voice dropping an octave. "I am beyond peeved," she said, lowering her voice into what could only be described as a serious Southern bell. She set the note on the counter between us and continued reading. "I was going to tell you in the morning in person, but I got called, and you know the Sleeping Suzie rule." She rolled her eyes again as she spoke.

She paused as John said something and then went on.

"She's checking in every hour. Call me when you get my note, John." She said with sarcasm laced into every word. She stopped to listen to his response. "No, I didn't skip anything," she said. "Fine," pushing the pad away. "It says, 'Love, John.'" Her anger was still there but was beginning to fade. "John, don't give me that sheep sugar! This is so outside the realm of Sleeping Suzie!" She took a breath. "On top of that, how could you give Charlie permission without talking to Nina and Chuck?"

Another pregnant silence occurred as we all waited, "Oh. Okay. I know." And just like reducing the heat of a raging pot of pasta allows it to settle into a gentle boil, as she listened to John explain, her anger began to settle and simmer. She finally softened enough to make eye contact with me, and I motioned for her to share information. Charles and I were quietly breaking apart inside, only having a segmented version of the story.

She pushed the yellow pad aside, put her phone on speaker, and laid it on the counter. She put her elbows on the counter and pressed the heels of her hands against her closed eyes.

"Suzie, I don't know everything that's goin' on over there, but Leia felt strongly about everything. She flat out insisted on going, to be there for Charlie. She's a good kid. They're both good kids. Hell, all four of them are way more responsible than I ever was at their age. They're just outside Roanoke. She's checking in with me every hour. She's safe. None of this is ideal, but I'd rather—" John stopped mid-sentence.

The tenor of his voice comforted everyone in the room but gave away his position. "I mean, Babe, we've known for sixteen years that the shit was gonna hit the fan. Nina and Chuck, I know you guys were between a rock and a hard place and wanted to protect her for as long as possible. I know y'all already know this, but this is just about the worst possible way this could've gone down."

The kitchen went silent as we all absorbed the unadulterated truth John had dropped into the room. He was never one to mince words. He was direct and honest. That's one of the things I liked most about him, but this time his truth hurt.

Suzie issued a silent but genuine apology for John's abrupt words, lifted her phone, took it off the speaker, and returned it to her ear.

As she wrapped up their conversation, Charles and I tried again to reach Charlie and the twins, but when those calls and texts went unanswered, all we could do was wait.

It was six-thirty in the morning, and we hadn't heard a word from our daughters.

28

Marie

December 2002

I woke suddenly. In the silence of our bedroom, I heard the rhythmic tick of my watch where it lay on the nightstand beside me. I reached for it and flipped the glass cover open, touching its surface with a practiced gentleness. The hands rested together, just past the three. It was 3:18 a.m. I felt the muscles in my belly tighten. I moved my index finger to the braille dot representing the twelve and waited as the second hand passed under my finger.

Two weeks ago, with Mom's help, I packed my hospital bag. Walt and I had finished our last of six childbirth classes and taken the tour of the maternity floor of Johns Hopkins. I'd been strangely proud when two other mothers in the class thought I was only six months along. Then, in the same breath, they'd remarked on how "brave" I was to do this, not being able to see anything. The comment had caught me off guard and left me warm-faced and embarrassed. Before I had a chance to react, Walt told them that I was brave, but it had nothing to do with being blind. As I felt the secondhand pass under my finger again and the tension in my belly released, I remembered how safe I felt while standing beside him. At that moment, I knew that the mean girls of the world could no longer touch me.

We'd gone for our last ultrasound, and finally caved and found out our baby was a perfect little girl. We surprised everyone and revealed the news to them at Wednesday Knit Club. We shared her name, Charlotte Baker Mavin— Charlotte after my mother's mother and Baker for Walt's mother's maiden name. The Ladies of Edgevale went on a monogramming spree, and now her closet was full of jumpers and blankets with her initials. I loved running my fingers along the raised embroidered letters, a lowercase C and B on either side of the large M. Our M.

This past weekend, Nina and Suzie, who was eight weeks pregnant with her first baby, drove up with Chuck and John and helped my mom with my baby shower. They'd also helped us hang six sets of buttercup yellow curtains over the windows and put the finishing touches on the sunroom-turned nursery at the end of the hall next to our bedroom. Nina's twins had made the trip with them and were over a year old and on the move.

The second hand passed under my fingers a few more times. I lay in the dark and remembered how they'd crawled into what was left of my lap as we sat cross-legged on the floor discussing baby names.

Suzie told us all that using mother's maiden names was a big trend. I remembered the deep feeling of happiness when I felt the heat of their tiny bodies on mine and the wave of contentment that covered me as they put their hands on my cheeks and leaned close to my ear and whispered, "Hi-vee." Nina said that was their baby talk for "I love you."

My belly tightened again, and I restarted my internal timer.

Suzie and John were across the hall staying with Evelyn and Pluto. Nina, Chuck, and their girls were sleeping in our guest room.

Our due date was still a month away, but as I lay in bed counting the seconds between contractions, it was clear that Charlotte didn't plan on waiting any longer.

I felt Walt's hand touch my stomach. He didn't say anything for a long while, but I was sure he'd joined me in the counting. When the contraction finally released, he said, "Was that really a minute?"

"Mm-huh," I said, breathing deeply, finding it hard to form a clear thought.

"How far apart are they?" he asked.

I held up five fingers, shook my head, and dropped my thumb. "Four and a half," I said, squeezing my eyes closed, surprised that I felt the next one coming so soon.

"Marie! Babe! Are you serious?" he said, turning on the lamp beside him and jumping out of bed.

"I just…" I said, putting my hand on my belly, not able to finish my thought.

I heard him take his phone from the nightstand and move quickly down the hall. I couldn't make out his conversation, but when he came back into the room, he said, "No, she just woke up, four to five and a minute long. Yes, it's our first baby."

As the contraction eased, I sat up. I needed to move or do something.

"Um, I don't think so," he said to the person on the phone. His voice was all over the room. I heard him pulling on his pants and then sliding his belt through the loops. Then he was beside me, taking my hand to rest it on a stack of neatly folded clothes I'd set out the night before.

Still on the phone, he held my arm while I held my belly and stood to go into the bathroom. I knew I needed to wash my face and brush my teeth while I could still think straight, but before I could take a step, I felt something inside me snap, like the string of a violin being plucked or a rubber band on your wrist being pulled back and snapped against your skin.

Even though I knew to expect it, nothing could have possibly prepared me for the feeling of release and fluid running uncontrollably down my legs.

"Walt!" I cried, frozen where I stood.

"Scratch that last one," he said, and I heard his smile and excitement in the tone of his voice.

He grabbed towels from the bathroom and dropped them on the floor at my feet. I could tell by the solid *thunk* they made when they hit the floor that they were still folded.

"No, ma'am. Her water just broke," he said, putting his hands on my shoulders and easing me onto the towels he'd just dropped. "Okay, we'll be there soon," he said. He ended the call, and I heard his phone land beside us on the bed.

"I'm sorry," I cried.

"Babe, for what?" he said, wiping my tears and pushing my hair from my face.

"The towels! They're ruined!"

"Forget the towels!" he said and tenderly held my face in his hand. He kissed my forehead.

I reached up and touched his cheeks. He hadn't shaved yet, and they were rough against my hands.

He leaned in so that our foreheads touched. "It's baby day," he said, and in his sweet whisper I heard and felt his joy, which gave me permission to relax.

I echoed his words. "It's baby day!" and let him kiss me. Not a quick kiss, but a kiss that started slow, grew more intense, and would have led to more had Charlotte not been literally on her way.

He pulled away, and even though we both could feel another contraction racing toward us, he held me close for a moment longer. "Marie," he said.

I nodded, unable to speak as I held my belly, feeling it tighten under my hand, and breathed through what was coming. I wanted to hear and remember every word he said.

"I never thought I could be this happy."

Those words spun in the air, and the rest were a blur.

I don't know if he knocked on the guest room door. I have no idea if he called my mom and dad. I can't even tell you how we got to the hospital. The pain overwhelmed me, and the world ebbed and flowed around me. There were nurses and then a lady doctor whose voice was somewhat familiar. I heard my mother speaking to me or about me and Walt asking someone to "Please do something for her pain."

They pushed and pulled. Someone helped me sit up, and someone else asked to hold me steady. I smelled our laundry soap and felt Walt's T-shirt against my cheek. I was comforted by his voice.

"Babe," he said, his lips so close to my ear that they drew me out of the pain. "They're gonna give you medicine to make it stop hurtin'," he said in his long, deep drawl. He was scared.

I tried to nod, but the movement caused the bed to feel like it was shifting under me, and I knew I was going to be sick.

He didn't budge as I heaved the contents of my stomach and gave into the pressure of another contraction.

"Can someone please help her?" he pleaded from somewhere far away, even though he was right beside me.

A man's voice from behind me was so calm that the whole room settled into silence around us. The only sound was the pulse of the heart rate monitor connected to my chest and the familiar and comforting, washing machine-like sound that was Charlotte's heartbeat. "We'll place the epidural at the end of this one. Dad…"

His instructions to Walt were gibberish to me as I rode the wave of another contraction, but then Walt's voice was in my ear again.

"Marie, babe, can you make your back like a *C*," he said.

"A *C*," I tried to say, but I'm not actually sure what came out.

"Marie," said the man's voice from behind me. "Hold still. Lots of pressure."

I closed my eyes and felt the pressure he'd promised, then a *thunk* from deep inside my back, and then sweet relief as the pain went from everywhere to nowhere at once.

I felt my body melt into Walt and heard him whisper, "Thank you, Jesus, thank you, thank you."

The room seemed to settle into a comfortable rhythm, and the sounds around me lost their frantic edge. Someone wiped my mouth with a towel, and someone else helped me lie back against the bed. Then, there was a gentle hand on my arm. "Marie, it's Dr. Jones."

I turned in the direction of her voice.

"How's your pain?"

"Better," I whispered, making a thumbs up with my hand where it lay beside me.

"Good," she said, rubbing my arm. "I don't have any doubt that we're gonna be pushing soon, but I'm going to check you, hun…"

I nodded.

"Mom, you wanna help on this side, and Dad, you got that side?" Dr. Jones said as I felt them bend my legs and guide my knees out and up toward my chest.

"Marie, you're doing so well," I heard my mother say with one hand on my shoulder, and I guessed the other on my disappearing leg. She smoothed back my hair and kissed my temple as I heard the whoosh-whoosh of Charlotte's monitor begin to speed up. I felt something deep within me, pushing, heavy.

"All right Marie," Dr. Jones said. "Let's do this."

"Yes, ma'am," I said, delirious with I don't know what. My manners caused the entire room to laugh as I felt several bumps and clicks and sliding metal against the bed.

And then, even though Walt and Mama were there beside me, there was only Dr. Jones and me.

"Okay, sweet girl," she said. "You're not going to feel all of it, but your body's already showing me it knows what to do. I'm gonna give you a three, two, one, and then you're going to push for ten."

"Yes, ma'am," I repeated, unable to think of any other words.

The room went silent, and then came her voice, "Three… Two… One… Push!"

I tucked my chin to my chest, relaxed the muscles in my face, and pulled from somewhere deep within me and pushed with everything I had as she counted to ten.

"Marie, that was perfect," she said, and then she told me to do it again.

Over and over, someone counted, and I pushed. Every time I thought there was nothing left, but every time they told me to do it again, and somehow there was strength. I have no idea how long this went on or how many times someone counted to ten. It could have been five or ninety-five. Finally, Dr. Jones, mid-count, told me to stop as the pressure reached a tipping point and released.

"She's here!" Walt said, his voice breaking through his tears.

Like sweet music, we heard her cry, and I repeated, "She's here," and Charlotte's father, my amazing husband, kissed me.

"Can I hold her?' I asked, noticing my words didn't come out quite whole. I attempted to lift my arms to reach for our baby but didn't have the strength.

I felt unfamiliar hands on my arms, rough but tender at once, and Dr. Jones gave directions in an unfamiliar, severe voice. I felt the mood in the room shift from joy to concern.

From a different direction, I heard Walt say, "What's happening?"

"Everyone nonessential needs to step into the hall. Get N.I.C.U. in here. I need an O.R., stat!"

The oddest sensation of emptiness washed over me. My heartbeat thumped through my body, thundered inside my ears, and pulsed through my fingers.

"What's happening?" Walt repeated, only this time his tone was more frantic.

"Walt," Dr. Jones said, silencing the room. "Marie is losing a lot of blood. Much more than I'm comfortable with post-delivery. I need you and Marie's mother to step into the hall and let us take care of her."

Panic surged through the room, causing my mother to take my hand and squeeze it tight, not letting go.

That same panic pushed Walter, and he shouted, "No! I'm not leavin' her." He took my other hand.

I fought against the panic rising in my chest, and with all that was left in me, I grabbed a handful of his shirt, pulled him close, and whispered, "Go with Charlotte."

I felt his forehead against mine, just as he had done earlier that morning, only this time, I felt the gravity of his tears on my own cheeks and the weight of his shaking hand in mine. My breathing slowed as my eyelids grew too heavy to keep open.

"Walter, we have to go," Dr. Jones said as I felt the bed click and begin to move.

I felt my hand slip from Mama's grip, and I heard her choke back a sob. In the haze, I couldn't put together how everything had gone from so right to so wrong.

And then, there were only Charlotte's cries, Walt's whispering of my name from too far away to reach, and light, everywhere there was light.

29

Nina

December 2002

"I can't stand the smell of hospitals," I said, trying to fill the silence as we waited in the lobby of the labor and delivery floor at Johns Hopkins Hospital.

Walt had knocked on our door just before four to let us know Marie was in labor and her water had broken. She'd barely been able to stand up on her own, let alone walk. Walt was worried she wouldn't make it to the hospital, so I ran across the hall to ask John if we should call an ambulance. John was concerned it would take too long, so he drove them. That way, just in case they didn't make it, he'd be able to help.

After they were gone, Evelyn offered to sit with the twins so Suzie, Charles, and I could all go to the hospital to wait.

Now, just under two hours later, Charlotte Baker Mavin was here, weighing in at a tiny five pounds four ounces and twenty inches long. The last we'd heard, Charlotte was doing great, but after delivery Marie lost more blood than normal. They'd taken her to surgery and sent Walt and Charlotte to get settled in a room. We hadn't heard anything in over an hour, so we anxiously waited for an update and filled the time with mindless chatter.

"I can't stand the smell of hospitals, either," Suzie said. "John's scrubs make me gag." As she spoke, she pulled a zip-top bag of mixed nuts from her purse.

"How can you eat?" I asked.

"I can't not eat," she said. "If I don't, the morning sickness turns into all day sickness."

"Oh, I remember," I said, "but multiply that times two."

Suzie groaned and popped a few almonds into her mouth. "I'm gonna be five hundred pounds by the end of this," she turned to John. "Can you go up there and find out what's taking so long?"

"Suzie, I'm not an OB/GYN, and I don't work for this hospital," John said, not looking up from his newspaper.

"So?" Suzie asked. She picked up her purse and started rummaging around for something.

"So," he said with exaggerated patience. "They aren't going to tell me anything about what's going on. Nina's probably the only one they'll talk to," he said, still not looking at his wife.

Suzie pulled a giant bottle of water from her bag, set it beside her on the chair, and went back to digging. "You'd think after eleven years of training, there'd be some kind of secret handshake," she mumbled at a volume everyone could hear. "Nina, would you please go see what they'll tell you," she said. I'm dying to meet Charlotte, and I wanna see Marie!"

"Will you come with me?" I asked.

"Sure," Suzie said. "Hang on a sec." She lifted her bag off the chair and into her lap. The bag must have been heavy because she blew out, making hair fly up and in front of her face. "If I can just find…" She started pulling random things from her bag and setting them on John's lap. "I know I threw them in here before we left," she said to herself.

She pulled out a magazine, an iPod she'd gotten from her parents as an early Christmas present, a make-up bag, a deck of cards, a small pack of Kleenex, a sweater, a bag of assorted nail polishes, and what I was sure were my copies of *The Last Girls* by Lee Smith and *The Lovely Bones,* Alice Sebold's debut novel that had been on top of all the book lists for months.

"Are those mine?" I asked, pointing to the purse-battered books.

"They are," she said, resting them gently on the growing pile on John's lap.

"Suzie," John said. He set down his paper and put his hand on top of the stack to keep it from falling.

"What?" she said, looking up. She took the books from the top and handed them to me. "These days, the only things I have time to read are baby name books and that one you gave me about baby sleep."

"*Baby Wise?*" I asked.

"Yes," she said, and with a funny grin, she pulled two dog-eared books from her bag. She held up one. "It's good. A lot of it feels like common sense, but it makes me feel more prepared."

"What's the other one?" I asked.

"Oh, John's Mom got it for me. It's called *Bringing up Bee Bee*." She flipped the book to read the back cover text out loud in a French accent.

When she was finished, she held it out to me. I examined its cover, which was cream with a blue, red, and white border. The woman on the cover stared back at me through her fancy oversized sunglasses, and I already hated her.

The baby in her stroller smiled, and there was no evidence that he'd recently thrown up all over her, blown out his diaper, or some lethal combination of the two. "What's it about?" I asked and opened the book. The discovery of a new baby book brought with it the hope of a full night's sleep and the possibility of going to the grocery store with the twins without an entourage.

"It's basically all about how French people raise kids with nearly perfect behavior and manners," she said.

"Really?" I asked. My attention piqued, I did split-second math in my head to calculate a transcontinental relocation.

"Yeah, apparently France has this amazing preschool tradition called the *crèche* that's basically a toddler boot camp.

"Oh?"

"Yep," she said, going back to searching through her bag. "Supposedly, French kids don't pitch fits in restaurants and say, 'S'il vous plait et merci sans *être invité*.'" Her French was boarding school perfect.

"*Ooh la la! Bon bébé*," I raised one eyebrow as I spoke. I perfected the gesture in the ninth grade and knew it drove Suzie crazy because she couldn't do it. The eyebrow always made her smile, because she loved that I could and would do it on her behalf. My French was gritty and native. I'd learned from our French housekeeper and nanny during the four years my dad was stationed in Germany during my middle school years. On our early distance runs, I taught her all the curse words I knew, and she made French the language we used when we didn't want anyone else to know what we were saying, especially Nancy Lynn, who'd elected to take Latin, or what Suzie called "the language of the dead."

"*Oui, ooh la la!*" she said and added the book to the top of the stack.

"You have a problem," John said, smiling and shaking his head at his wife and what he affectionately called her bag of "spare parts." He moved the collection to the space on the table between them that connected their chairs.

"And I'm all yours," she said, smiling up at him. "And I get a pass from being a mess."

"Because?" John said, playfully pushing her buttons and pulling an untied bow tie from the pile.

Suzie sat up straight and took the tie from him. "That is from Berry and Stella's wedding, and you gave it to me on the way home." She flopped back in her chair and said, "And I get a pass because I'm growing a human!" She gestured to the place where a baby belly would be in a few months.

John laughed and was about to say something when a nurse came through the wide double doors and made her way across the waiting area toward us.

"Are you the family of Marie Mavin?" she asked.

"Yes," Charles and I said at the same time as we both sat up straight. The expression on her face was completely unreadable.

"I'm Sarah, one of the labor and delivery nurses who have been working with Marie. There've been some complications, and Dr. Jones asked me to bring you back."

I turned to Charles first and then John and Suzie, but when none of them said anything, I asked, "Is she okay? Are they okay? Marie and Charlotte, are they okay?" My voice sounded small. I felt my face get hot and my stomach turn.

"Dr. Jones will explain everything and can answer your questions. She can also talk to you about next steps." Sarah's words were calm and measured. Her face gave nothing away, but her tone of practiced control terrified me.

I turned back to John. He helped Suzie gather her things. "John?" My fear turned his name into a pleading question.

He looked up, and I saw that his face matched Nurse Sarah's practiced and completely unreadable expression.

"John?" I repeated, and my voice betrayed the panic I was feeling.

Suzie startled me when she touched my arm. "Nina, we need to go."

I nodded, unable to speak, as Charles took my hand. We followed Nurse Sarah through the doors and down the hall. The lights were so bright. The hospital smell that was annoying in the lobby was now completely overwhelming. We passed the nurses' station and I noticed that no one was looking at us. We made a couple of turns and except for the sound of our footsteps, the
halls had fallen silent around us. A woman in scrubs stepped out of a door at the end of the hall. Her head was bowed. She looked up. Her eyes met mine, and that was the moment I knew.

"Hello, I'm Dr. Jones." She extended her hand, and I pushed my hands into my pockets. If I didn't shake her hand, she couldn't tell me what was coming.

Charles reached in front of me and shook her hand. "I'm Walt's brother, Charles, and this is my wife, Nina."

She held his hand for a beat longer than normal and then let go and led us to chairs at the end of the hall. As we all sat down, I noticed that Suzie was holding John's hand so hard that her knuckles had turned white, but he didn't appear to notice, or if he did, he didn't mind.

Charles and I sat next to them. If you call perching on the edge of our seats sitting. The four of us made an *L*, and Dr. Jones took a plastic chair from across the hall, being careful to lift it, perhaps so it didn't make a screeching noise against the floor.

"As you know, Marie had a fast delivery. Baby Charlotte was born just before four this morning. She's healthy. We take Apgar scores, which are measures of a baby's condition after birth. We measure color, heart rate, reflexes, muscle tone, and respiration, each of which is given a score of zero, one, or two. The five individual scores are added together for a composite or total score. Anything above a seven is considered a healthy score. Charlotte scored an eight at both one and five minutes. We cleaned her up, did her heel stick, and brought her to Dad. Because of the nature of her delivery, she was retested at ten minutes and scored a nine. Before we go on, I need you to understand that even though she's a few weeks early, Charlotte is healthy and thriving." Dr. Jones took a moment to make eye contact with each of us before going on.

"Shortly after delivery, it was clear that Marie was in distress. Post-delivery, we expect a minimal amount of bleeding. Marie's bleeding was extensive. We rushed her to surgery and made every effort to find and fix the cause. We did everything we could, but we were not able to stop her bleeding. Marie did not survive."

Her words yanked at a place inside me just behind my navel. I felt like I'd been physically punched, and the blow had stolen all the oxygen from my chest. I heard Suzie let out a pitiful cry, and I saw John reach to catch her as she leaned into him.

Dr. Jones reached out and put her hand on mine. "Can I answer any questions for you?" Her tone was deep and sincere.

I shook my head slowly, not sure how to put any of my questions into words.

"I am so incredibly sorry for your loss." She turned to Suzie and John.

"When will we be able to see her?" John asked as he held his wife as she sobbed quietly into his chest.

"She's just there and whenever you're ready." Dr. Jones nodded toward the door she'd come from. "Walt and Charlotte are there with her, as well as Marie's mother and father."

Before John could finish thanking her, Suzie had collected herself, wiped her tears, lifted herself off her chair, and taken my hand. She pulled me to my feet, and without a moment's hesitation, she knocked gently on the door and let herself into the room. She started to take the half-dozen steps that physically separated us from our best friend, but I couldn't.

She stopped and looked down at our clasped hands, surprised something was holding her back. She looked up at me, and I would swear a million times over that she didn't recognize me. She tilted her head sideways with confusion. Her eyes told me to follow her, and her tears begged me not to make her do this alone, but I couldn't. She loosened her grip, and in a moment I could never take back, I let her hand slip from mine.

For a few seconds, her expression was true, revealing her hurt, but then it was gone, and she walked to the edge of Marie's bed without me. I heard her take a sharp breath. "Oh, Me."

Marie's mother moved from the corner of the room to stand beside Suzie. She didn't say anything trite like, "She's at peace" or "God needed her more," because none of that was true. Marie was the most peaceful creature I'd ever known, and there's no way God needed her more than we did.

I stayed just inside the door until I felt heat and pressure on the small of my back, and I turned to see Charles beside me. With him there, the rest of the room came into focus. I heard the rhythmic vent preserving Marie's organs for donation. Walt sat on a couch on the opposite side of the room. His eyes were closed as he patted the bottom of a tiny bundle that rested against his shoulder.

As though she knew I was thinking of her, Charlotte grunted, and her fist broke free of her swaddle. Her blanket was stamped with tiny blue and pink footprints, just like the ones we'd gotten from the hospital when the twins were born. Walt rewrapped the blanket around her shoulders, being careful to tuck in her arms. He looped the tail of the blanket around and tucked it in. For a moment, he sat without moving. His hands cradled under her head as he looked down at her. I remembered seeing Charles hold our girls in this way, and just like his brother, the look on Walt's face could only be described as amazement.

Charlotte opened her eyes to find him. She yawned and stretched within her swaddle and looked right back at him.

Walt saw me watching him. His expression was hollow. He shut his eyes and dropped his chin to his chest. He opened them again and looked back down at Charlotte.

Without thinking, I crossed the room and knelt next to him. Charlotte wiggled herself free again, and her arm was out of the blanket. I reached out and touched her open palm. Her fingers closed tightly around my finger.

"Hello, baby girl," I said.

"Charlotte," Walt said, his voice a whisper and unfamiliar tone. "Charlotte Baker." His words dissolved into the air. He swallowed hard.

I wiggled my finger back and forth. "So nice to meet you, Charlie Bee," I said, my voice just a whisper. I kissed her fingers and said, "I'm your Aunt Nina, and I already love you so much!"

"Nina…" Walt said.

"Walt, she's beautiful," I said, not able to take my eyes off her.

"Nina," he repeated. "She's gone."

I looked up at him. "No Walt, she's right here." His blue eyes locked onto mine, and I watched him teeter on the edge of something only he could see.

He shook his head once back and forth. "I can't do this," he said, his voice quiet like he was sharing a secret.

I felt my eyes grow wide at his words. "Walt, don't say that." We became the only three people in the room. "Yes, you can."

"I can't do this without her," he said, shaking his head again.

I nodded like you do when you're trying to change a child's mind. "Yes, you can, Walt. You'll have Marie's parents, and you'll have us. You can do this!"

He hesitated for a moment, and then I watched him nod along with me.

"Okay?"

"Okay," he said, and even though he nodded with me, I knew he was lying.

The next seven days came in pieces like a movie film that was badly edited and then thrown back together.

On Tuesday afternoon, Charlotte was released from the hospital, and Walt brought her home to Edgevale House. He stumbled through the motions of learning to be a father while also planning his wife's funeral. Despite her own torment, Marie's mother became a constant source of strength to him during the day, but at night he walked the halls as Charlotte cried.

Wednesday was Christmas, but no one at Edgevale celebrated. After nearly seventy-two hours without sleep, Walt was beyond exhausted. I watched Evelyn scoop baby Charlotte from Walt's arms, and with love, she sent him away to rest, kissing his cheek and telling him that he was no good to anyone without sleep. She settled Charlotte against her shoulder and rocked her as Pluto took his place at the piano and played. Within minutes, the baby settled down, eyes still wide open but contentedly listening. Walt had walked past Charles and me without speaking, then down the hall to his and Marie's bedroom. He didn't bother closing the door before he collapsed onto their bed and fell instantly asleep.

Thursday was quiet. Fifi snapped a few pictures while Walt sat with Charlotte on the steps in the hall.

Marie's funeral was Friday afternoon. Suzie gave the eulogy and then spent the rest of the day holding Charlotte. Then sometime on Saturday morning, Walt disappeared. Charles and I had planned to leave with the girls and Suzie that afternoon, but when Walt hadn't reappeared by dinner, we canceled our plans and began to worry.

On Sunday morning, Greta called us and asked if we could come to see them as soon as we were up. Charles and I threw on clothes and walked with the twins, still in pajamas, up the short path to the carriage house. Greta and Billy gently walked us through their daughter's wishes if anything were to happen to her or Walt.

Then, less than twenty-four hours later, we were sitting in a law office conference room, stunned at the reappearance of Nancy Lynn.

30

Charlotte

December 2018

"Well, hey," Leia said, with that same one-handed wave and southern lilt as her mom. She looked embarrassed that she'd interrupted.

I looked down at my feet and took hold of Andrew's hand. I felt his grip on my hands tighten as though we were both trying to hold onto the last sixty seconds. I said a quick prayer that I would never forget, and somehow, I just knew he was doing the same thing.

"So," Leia said, not moving from the door. I could tell it was an attempt not to intrude any more than she had to, but knowing she didn't really have much of a choice, "I think your mom's called like forty times, so someone should probably call her before she calls the cops. And the continental breakfast opens at six, which is in like ten minutes." Leia said all of this without stopping to breathe. She drew her lips tight which I knew meant she had something else to say.

"What is it?" I asked, starting to worry because Leia hardly ever held anything back.

She took a step toward us and held out a folded piece of paper. "I think I found the address of your birth mother's parents."

"What?" I dropped Andrew's hand in shock. "How? I mean, where?"

She closed the space between us and handed me the paper. "At least, I think it's her parents. I noticed from the back of the photo that her last name was hyphenated, which is pretty unusual for somebody that young, so I searched Google. If it's them then it looks like they've lived at the same address for like, ever."

"Really?" I unfolded the paper.

Eager to share more, she continued. "Yeah, it's in an area called Roland Park, and it's some sort of plantation house they've divided up into apartments. They have a website, and they look nice."

"My grandparents look nice?" I said, confused, trying to take it all in.

She shook her head. "Oh, no. I mean, the apartments look nice."

"What?" I said, trying to catch up.

"Their *apartments* look *nice*," she repeated with emphasis on each word as though I was way slower than she needed me to be right now. "Never mind," she said, giving up. "That part doesn't matter. What matters is that now we know where we're going."

I nodded, afraid of what she was suggesting should come next.

"We're going to meet them, right? To meet your mom, I mean your birth mother, right?" She stepped closer to me. "That *is* the reason we're going to Baltimore, right?" She dropped her voice to a whisper. "Nora and Margot were up there arguing. Margot said you had no idea what you were doing." She looked back at Nora for a second and then turned back to me, lowering her voice more so that only I could hear her. "Margot thinks we need to go back to Nashville."

I looked over her shoulder at Nora. "Do you want to go back, too?" The words came out louder and more aggressive than I'd meant them.

Nora flinched at my harsh tone. "No!" she cried. "We just," her voice shook with emotion, "Charlie, you haven't really told us anything. I mean, a week ago, you," she gestured behind her. "And we were," she said, struggling to find words, "and then you tell us to come in the night and not tell anyone. And now, we're going God only knows where, with people we barely know." She looked at Andrew. "I mean, no offense, but we don't, like, know you, like, at all." Her voice lifted, turning everything she said into a question. "And it doesn't feel like there's a plan." Another lift and another question. "And Mom and Dad are freaking out and worried. And Mom? Mom is so PISSED!"

At the mention of our mother, I felt my stomach clench, and I got that horrible taste in my mouth that you get right before you throw up. "Fuck her!" I said, stone-faced. "And fuck Margot, too!" If she doesn't trust me, she shouldn't be here." The anger had risen in me so fast it was hard to believe that I'd so quickly gone from one of the best moments of my life to one of the worst.

"Fuck me?" Margot asked, appearing next to her twin with Nathan on her arm. Her words were full of annoyance. "Fuck you, Charlie! You're totally unstable! I can't believe I agreed to this shit!"

"Margot!" Nora cried, trying to keep things from completely unraveling.

"What?" she said, turning on Nora. "What does she expect?" she said, raising her voice. "She called us to come get her, not to tell anyone where we're going." She threw her hands into the air. "She won't even tell *us* what we're doing! And on top of that, she expects us to just go along with it, like puppets." She turned back to me. "This is total bullshit, not even to mention this!" She said, thrusting a finger at Leia. She lowered her voice to a hissing whisper. "If we get pulled over or questioned by, like, anyone, we're all in trouble! And Nathan…"

All of us turned to look at him, standing beside Margot.

"Yeah! I figured you hadn't thought about anybody but yourself. He's an adult, and Leia is clearly not an adult," she said, gesturing her hands in a circle at the three of them. "This could affect us all!"

Nathan had been standing quietly beside Margot with his cane in his right hand and his left hand tucked under Margot's arm. He turned to me, and I saw that his expression was kind. "Charlotte, I think it's probably time you start talking. They need to know what's going on, and we all need to know where we're going."

"Okay," I said, nodding, defeated and exhausted by the drama.

Without a word, the six of us returned to our hotel room. Andrew swiped the key card to unlock the door. After everyone had gone in ahead of us, he took my hand and held it for a moment before I went in. He leaned in and whispered, "She's afraid because she doesn't know what we know. As soon as they know, as soon as you tell them, they'll be okay. I promise." He brought the back of my hand to his lips. "You can do this!"

I nodded. He was right. As mad as I was, no one in that room had anything to do with that anger. They'd all come with me, no questions asked. They all deserved to know what was going on. We divided ourselves in a sort of makeshift circle and sat on the edges of the two queen beds. Nathan sat between Nora and Margot. Andrew, Leia, and I sat across from them.

I looked around at everyone's expectant faces and realized there just wasn't a good way to tell this story. I had no idea where to start. I was about to say this when Andrew took the old photo from his pocket and held it out to me. At that moment, it was clear that the only way I could even begin to tell this story was to start with Marie.

I took the photo from him and unfolded it to see the four of them smiling up at me. "Yesterday," I said, voice shaking, "when we were at Vanderbilt, I'd been meeting with the occupational therapist while Mom and Dad were meeting with the doctor. On my way back from OT, before I went back to the exam room, I stopped to get some water." I closed my eyes, letting myself return to the memory. "When I got back, I was going to just walk in, but I heard them talking. They didn't know I was there, and they were talking about me. Honestly, I just wanted to know what they were saying about me, so I waited and listened at the door." I pressed my hand against the comforter to brace myself for what was next.

"I heard the doctor say something about my medical history and ask about my biological grandparents. I thought she was talking about Nana and Pops, but she wasn't." I shook my head and looked down at the picture again. I was on the edge of crying and was afraid that if I looked up, I wouldn't be able to finish.

They were all there because of me. And now they were all about to know everything.

A tear dropped onto the bottom half of the photo, and I hurried to wipe it away. "This was taken sixteen years ago," I said, turning the picture to face them. "That's Mom and Dad," I said, pointing. "This is Uncle Walter Lee. I'm pretty sure he went by 'Walt' back then," I said, pointing to the young guy in a backward baseball cap. He resembled our uncle but at the same time, looked nothing like him. "And this," I said, tapping gently on the young woman who stood between Walter Lee and our mom. "This is Marie."

I looked up to see everyone's eyes on me. I held it out to my sisters and said, "This is my biological mother."

Margot took the photo and held it in front of Nathan so that she and Nora could both see it. "I don't understand," Nora said. "Sixteen years ago, Uncle Walter Lee was married to Aunt Nancy Lynn. Did he have an affair?" she said, looking up at me.

I shook my head. "No, and I actually thought Dad was the one who had the affair when I first found out about Marie being my mother, but he didn't. None of them did. This is all confusing."

Nora took the picture and looked at the people. "I know pictures don't always tell the truth. I mean, look at Facebook and Instagram, but it looks like they were all friends. I mean, as annoying as Aunt Nancy Lynn is, I can't imagine Mom and Dad being okay with Uncle Walter Lee and another woman." Nora looked up from the picture and to me for more.

I continued, "Apparently, Nancy Lynn was super messed up. Y'all probably know more about her than I do, but the short of it is that she left Uncle Walter Lee before y'all were born."

"So, they were divorced?" Nora asked.

"I don't think so," I said, shaking my head. "I don't know. I just know they were broken up enough for her to leave him, and then he moved."

Nora nodded, encouraging me to go on.

"Dad said Walt took a job in Baltimore and moved up there a few months before y'all were born," I said, watching, neither of them able to take their eyes away from the picture. "That's where he met Marie."

"Charlie, she's so pretty," Nora said, finally looking up at me.

"She looks just like you, or I guess, technically, you look just like her," Margot said, reaching across the space between us to hand the picture back. Her voice had softened but was still filled with confusion. "I just don't understand," she said, rubbing her temples. "I mean, this is so…" Unable to find words, she looked up at me. "I mean, Charlie, is there any way you could have misunderstood?"

I shook my head and whispered, "No."

She looked at Nora and then back at me. "Why did they, like, lie about it? They didn't just lie to you. They lied to all of us." Margot's voice broke. She dropped her head, and tears came.

Nathan put his arm around her, and she rested against him and cried.

"What did Mom and Dad say?" Nora asked.

"Mom didn't say much of anything," I said, feeling that frustration return. "At first, it felt like she was glad it all came out. But, honestly, since I told her about the RP last week, she's been acting, I don't know. Different," I said.

Without realizing it, I'd begun folding and refolding the photo until I felt Leia take it from me. "Thanks," I said, grateful she'd kept me from accidentally destroying it. I let my hands drop to my lap, not sure what to do with them. Andrew took the one closest to him and squeezed it gently.

Even with everything going on, Andrew taking my hand didn't go unnoticed by Nora and Margot. The affection normally would have embarrassed me, but today it felt okay.

"I really don't know how to explain any of this except to say that it felt like they were starting to tell me everything, but then, for whatever reason, she just got up and left. Like she was tired of dealing with it or like she didn't think I could handle it."

Nora's jaw dropped.

"Wait. What?" Margot tipped her head sideways in confusion. "Mom *left*?"

I nodded, remembering the look on her face and the sound of her sneakers on the tile as she walked away. We all sat for a long time, frozen by the truth.

Nora broke the silence. "Charlie, I'm really sorry," she said, shaking her head. "I just don't understand. Why would they lie to you?"

Margot interrupted her. "Nora, they lied to all of us," she repeated, waving her arm around the room. "Well, not you," she said, looking at Andrew, "or you," she said, putting her hand on Nathan's knee.

Leia was the next to speak. "Now you guys see why we have to go to Baltimore, right?"

"You think she's still there?" Nora asked.

"Charlie, did Mom and Dad tell you if she had the same condition as you?" Margot asked.

I shook my head. "No, they didn't say she was blind, but I think she was based on what I overheard the doctor say."

I looked at Leia, letting her know that it was okay to share what she'd found online.

"So, Marie's last name is Collie-Ricks. It's pretty unique, so I looked her up. I didn't find her, which isn't completely out of the ordinary. Some people don't like to be on social media. But I think I did find her parents." Leia paused, choosing her words with care. "It's possible—if she's lost her sight like Charlie..."

I felt Andrew squeeze my hand at her choice of words, and I returned the squeeze, letting him know I'd noticed, too.

"...she may still live with her parents," Leia said, "And if she does, it's possible she could still live there."

"I just thought that if she lived with her parents when she met your uncle," she said, gesturing to the twins, "I mean, biological father..." she said, looking at me. "Or I guess," she said, flipping the photo, "I'm just gonna call him Walt. Anyway, since she was probably completely blind by then, or close to it, it's probably safe to assume she still lives with her parents." She tapped the photo and continued. "Like I said, her name is unique, so I just Googled it. I clicked on the first match on the search results and found her parents." She reached behind her and produced an iPad. "I think her dad, who would be your bio grandfather, was William Ricks, and your bio grandmother was..." She turned the screen to face us and said, "Greta Collie," as she pointed to an older, petite woman standing beside a big burly man.

I took the iPad from her. I touched my thumb and middle finger to the screen and spread them apart to zoom in on their faces. Even with her hair drawn back into a bun, it was easy to see that its color matched Marie's. That also meant it matched mine. Her eyes were kind, and her smile was inviting. I moved the focus to the man and had to pinch the screen to zoom out so I could see his whole face. The first thing I noticed was his smile. It was electric, and I easily saw that his smile matched Marie's. Whoever took the picture caught him mid-laugh. William and Greta were both dressed in what looked like Sunday church clothes. His hair was cut short, and he wore dark sunglasses and an orange pair of suspenders. I zoomed in to get a closer look and couldn't help but smile when I realized they were covered with familiar white lettering.

"What is it?" Margot asked.

I turned the iPad to face her. "He's wearing Tennessee suspenders," I said and pointed, "See the Power Ts?"

She and Nora leaned in to see. "Oh, that's cool!" Nora said.

The month before, they'd both applied for early acceptance to the University of Tennessee in architecture and interior design. They'd both acted like it wasn't a big deal because it was just UT right at home in Knoxville, so they weren't going away for school, but I knew they were excited, and the connection wasn't lost on them.

"I know pictures don't tell the whole story, and they could totally be like that old lady in *Hansel and Gretel* and want to eat little kids, but they both look really nice," Leia said, taking the iPad back from Nora.

I nodded in agreement. "Did you find anything out about her," I said. "About Marie, I mean?"

She shook her head. "She doesn't have a presence on Twitter, or Insta, or any of the socials, not even Facebook, and most older people are on Facebook."

"What about her parents?" I asked. "Did you see if they were on any of them?"

She shook her head again. "No, the only thing I found was a Facebook page for Edgevale House."

I looked at her, confused.

"Their apartment house. The one I told you about earlier."

She tapped a few times and spun the iPad back around to show me a beautiful, white, colonial mansion with a gigantic screened front porch and an enormous lawn.

"Wow!" I said, leaning in and flipping through a listing for a ground-floor, two-bedroom, one-bathroom apartment with a study. It looked like something from a magazine. There were honey colored wood floors, and sunshine poured through floor-to-ceiling windows.

Andrew leaned over to see. "It looks like a storybook," he said, reaching over to point at a photo of a large gazebo on the lawn. His arm brushed the side of my chest, and he pulled back, likely embarrassed at the mishap.

My mouth went dry, and every inch of my skin tingled at his accidental touch. He was so close, and I felt stupid to be thinking about it right now, but all I wanted to do was turn and kiss him again. "I thought the same thing," I said, smiling. We shared a look, and I could tell he wanted to kiss me again, too.

"So, this is where we're going?" he asked.

I nodded and said with confidence, "I think so." I looked up at Nora and Margot. "Y'all okay with that, or do you still think we should go home?" My voice was serious but not mean.

They looked at each other and then turned back to me. "Charlie, I'm sorry. I can't even imagine what you've been through in the last week." Nora said and looked at Margot.

"This whole thing is so messed up," Margot said. "I never thought I'd ever say this, but I don't think we can trust Mom and Dad to be real with us," Margot said, looking back at Nora.

Leia shifted where she sat, and everyone turned to her. "I don't know how exactly, but I'm pretty sure my parents were involved or at least knew something about it, so I'm not sure we can trust them either."

Another silence fell over the room as Leia pulled her backpack across the bed. She unzipped an inner pocket and produced a small wooden cube. It looked to be about five inches on every side, slightly larger than the size of a Rubik's cube.

"What is it?" I asked.

"I'm not exactly sure, but I think it's important," she said, turning it in her hands. "It was on the table between them, Mom and Nina. We walked in on them yesterday in the closet. And sometimes, when we're just sitting in there talking, just the two of us, she'll just pick it up and fiddle with it. I've never seen it out of her closet room. But last night, when I was leaving, I was picking up my backpack off the floor and saw it sitting there on the counter, so I took it."

Leia was usually the perfect kid, but in one afternoon, as far as she was concerned, she'd become a thieving runaway.

"I really thought it was a box, and I thought it was important. But I can't figure out how to open it if it opens. I don't know. Maybe it doesn't open. Maybe it isn't important." She pressed her lips together in another classic Mini Suzie Vandenberg expression. "My mom's going to be so mad," she said, tightening her resolve. "I've never taken anything from her before. But I don't care." Her voice shook. "I've never seen this thing just out in the open before, and something in me just told me it was important. Maybe I'm wrong."

She passed it to me, and after a few tries, I passed it to Andrew. It made its way around the circle. Nora was about to pass it over Nathan's lap to Margot. Somehow, he knew and reached for it.

"Let me give it a try," he said, holding his hands out.

We all looked at him and then at Andrew.

"They're all looking at me, aren't they?" he asked, looking directly at his brother.

"They are," Andrew said, grinning.

"Oh, ye of little faith. Hand it over," he said.

Nora was about to set the box in his outstretched hand, but Margot reached across him before she had the chance.

"Okay, I'm just going to…" Margot said and put her hand under his open palm and gently lifted his hand to the cube she was holding.

"Thanks." His voice was soft, and the intimacy of the exchange made Leia look at me and grin. She touched her finger to her lips and raised her eyebrows.

Margot's cheeks went pink, and she took her hands away.

Nathan rolled the box in his hands to examine every inch of its surface with his fingers, not leaving out a single corner or edge. He brought it to his ear and gently shook it. He listened while he alternated shaking it in one direction, then turning it and shaking it again, but the box didn't make a sound.

One by one, he brushed his fingers across the six flat surfaces. Then he did it again, but instead of his fingertips, he moved his fingers backward using the edge of his fingernail. The first five sides were quiet, but when he turned the box to the final side and pushed his fingernails across the surface, there was an audible *tick* as they moved across two invisible grooves in the wood.

He grinned and repeated the movement. *Tick, tick.* It happened again, and his smile grew wider. "Yep, there you are,'' he said completely to himself.

I looked at Andrew, and in astonishment, I mouthed the word, "What!?" He nodded, his expression knowing, and he mouthed the words, "Just wait."

Nathan tilted the box onto its side, resting it in his palm, and with the other hand, he used his index and middle fingers to slide a narrow section upward an inch. He grinned again and turned the box so that what we now knew to be the bottom rested in his cupped hand.

He rotated the top a quarter-turn clockwise and gently lifted the lid. "And that's how it's done," he said in triumph, holding the lid away from the box and holding the bottom out to Margot.

She took it from him and lifted out what looked like a thin silver bracelet. "Is this your mom's?" she asked, holding it up for Leia to see.

Leia shook her head. "I've never seen that before."

Margot held the bracelet out to me. I took it, and without thinking, I slipped it on my wrist.

She lifted a Jacob's ladder of small, connected photo frames from the box.

As Margot lifted, it was clear that every photo contained a different combination of the same three women: Nina, Marie, and Suzie. Everyone turned to Leia.

My best friend took a slow, deep breath, and in a soft, disbelieving voice, she said, "Well, I guess the only people we can trust are the six of us sitting in this room."

"Who is it?" Andrew asked.

With gentle boldness, Leia took the puzzle box and photo ladder from Margot. She examined the first photo carefully.

She nodded to herself and then looked up at Andrew and said, "My mom."

31

Nina

December 2018

The digital clock on the microwave clicked from 7:59 to 8:00, two minutes after the clock on the oven below. Suzie, Charles, and I sat with half-filled glass coffee mugs in front of us and our cell phones grouped together, silent in the center of the table.

In the living room, I could see Sylvie and Adah snuggled together under a blanket on the couch, watching *The Polar Express.* Tom Hanks sang "Hot Chocolate" as the girls bounced to the chugging beat of the locomotive.

"It's eight," I said, reaching for my phone. Even though we'd texted them repeatedly, we hadn't heard anything at all from the twins and Charlie. The only reason we knew they were together and safe was because of Leia's check-in texts to John. We hadn't heard from her since her last text at six.

We'd agreed to wait until eight and then start calling people. I tapped each phone screen, one right after the other. They lit up, showing their clocks reading an identical seven fifty-eight. "Suzie! Good grief!" I said in exasperation.

"What?" she said, sounding equally frustrated.

"Why is every clock in your house a different time?" I said, gesturing at the four clocks in my line of sight. "How do you know which one is right?"

Charles took my phone from me. "We said we'd wait until eight," he said, setting it back on the table. "We told them they had until eight to call us back before we called the police. We need to wait until eight," he said, his tone irritating but calm. He took my hand where it rested on the table. "They'll call."

As though on cue and like he'd planned it, all three phones lit up with incoming text messages. Each of us lunged for them. It took three tries for me to unlock the screen, and by the time I opened the text, both Suzie and Charles had set their phones back on the table to reveal an identical text message.

"We're together and safe. We know everything! We're going to Baltimore to find Marie."

I watched Charles and Suzie dialing their phones to try to connect with them, but each of them went directly to voicemail.

Suzie set her phone back on the table and pressed her lips together before looking back at me. Her voice broke the silence. "Nina."

"What?" I said.

"I thought you said you told her everything?"

"I did. We did," I said, pointing back and forth at Charles and me as I turned to find him shaking his head. "What?" I said, confused, my head spinning, trying to figure out what she meant, trying to remember.

"Nina," Suzie said, shaking her head. Her voice was low. "I don't think any of them know that Marie is dead."

All the blood drained from my face. "Oh, my…" I said, clapping my hand to my mouth, muffling words I didn't want the little girls to hear. I looked at Charles and asked, "Didn't you tell her after I…"

"Left!" he said with such force that I jumped. "No, I didn't tell her. After telling her we weren't her birth parents, and right after she watched the only mother she's ever known run away from her, no, I didn't tell her that her birth mother is dead." With the tips of his fingers, Charles rubbed his forehead and temples. "This is a fucking disaster, Nina."

"Charles," I cried. "I'm sorry." My voice trembled on the edge of tears. "Should we text them?"

"I don't think that's the kind of information we should put in a text," Suzie said and looked at Charles for confirmation.

"I agree," he said, nodding. "Also, I'm worried that if we tell them, they'll change their plan."

"At least if they make it to Greta and Billy's, we know they're safe," Suzie said.

I put my hands around my coffee mug, hoping its warmth would help settle me inside.

Suzie's phone vibrated with an incoming text. She picked it up, read it, and turned it to face us.

It was from John, "Did you get her text? They're going to find Marie. WTF?"

We sat in silence for several long minutes until I couldn't stay quiet any longer. "I never thought of how this would affect Leia," I said, hanging my head.

"I didn't either," Suzie said.

"Suzie, I'm really sorry."

She nodded and patted my hand. "They're all safe. I love that the four of them are taking care of each other."

I took her hand and held onto it like a lifeline. We shared a look that repeated my apology and her forgiveness.

"Do you think they're going to Greta and Billy's?" she asked.

I nodded and looked up at her. "I don't know how they'd know to go there, but yeah. That has to be where they're going." I looked at Charles, who nodded in agreement.

"I hate to bother them, but we probably need to call them," he said.

"Yeah. From what I remember, they're amazing people, but four teenagers showing up unexpectedly on their doorstep probably isn't the best way for them to meet Charlie," Suzie said.

I sat for a moment, flipping my phone end over end as an idea formed in my head. I took a breath. Knowing there wasn't another way, I said, "I think we, or at least I, need to go."

Suzie and Charles waited, not saying a word. They'd both known me long enough to know to wait while my thoughts solidified into an idea.

"But I think," I said, closing my hands around my phone and bringing it gently to my chin. "I think there's one call we need to make before that." I looked at Charles and knew he was reading my mind.

He shook his head, "Nina, I don't think that's a good idea."

I nodded, hoping that going through the motions would convince him.

He continued to shake his head. "She's not going to let him go," he said.

"I think he needs to know at least what's going on," I said. "I mean, he's her…"

"Her dad?" he asked, staring into me with a defensive edge.

I shook my head, temporarily unable to speak, knowing my words hurt him.

Suzie smacked the table with her hand. "Chuck! Seriously?" We all jumped. It had been much louder than any of us expected, especially her.

From the living room came the echo of Suzie's words, "Chuck! Seriously?" Adah and Sylvie said, and then they both exploded into girl giggles, going back and forth.

"Chuck! Seriously?"

"Chuck! Seriously?"

Their laughter broke the tension of the moment.

"Silly girls," Suzie sang with a forced happy eye roll and a smile.

"Mommy, can I have a snack?" Adah asked.

"Sure," Suzie said. "You too, Sylvie?"

"Yes, please," came sweet Sylvie's voice. She spaced out her thoughts one word at a time and said, "One…what…goes…good…together…with…movies."

Her unique, four-year-old speech, replacing *that* with *what*, tickled me every time I heard her talk and reminded me of our youngest child. Wade hadn't crossed my mind in over twenty-four hours. I was about to let myself go down that guilt trip rabbit hole, but Suzie's voice pulled me back to the moment.

"Look, Chuck," she said, lowering her volume but not her intensity. "This isn't about who her parents are, you and Nina," she said, pointing to each of us. "It's about paternity."

She pushed herself up from the table and kept talking as she walked around the island and into the kitchen. She pulled out her thick bottom pan, canola oil, and sea salt from the cabinets and drawers around the stove. Then, she took a giant plastic parmesan shaker from the refrigerator.

I knew her well enough to recognize these as the ingredients, minus one, for her favorite comfort food, parmesan popcorn. So, it was no surprise when she pulled out a metal measuring cup and a giant canister of kernels.

"Chuck, you know this better than anyone." Her voice dropped away while she filled the cup and dumped it in the pan. She measured and poured in the oil and sprinkled in a generous amount of salt. She turned a dial on the gas range until it began to click rapidly. The burner ignited, and she rolled it back to medium, allowing the blue flame to settle gently around the bottom of the pan. She snapped the glass lid into place and then looked up. "Like it or not, Walt is her closest link to Marie," Suzie said, picking up her sentence where she'd left off. "I mean, there are her parents, us, and we all love her, but he loved her first, and for a time, he loved her best."

She moved the pan back and forth on the burner, gently mixing. "For all we know, he may still love her best," she said.

Charles pressed his fingers to his temples. I thought he would protest and give more reasons not to upset the apple cart that was Nancy Lynn, but he surprised us both when he whispered, "You're right." Then he picked up his phone, scrolled through his recent contacts, and tapped his brother's name. He laid the phone on the table between us, and we waited.

32

Charlotte

December 2018

Now that we were all on the same page and had the same goal, it was time to get back on the road!

We decided to split up and let Andrew and Nathan shower and get ready first, while Margot, Nora, Leia, and I went down to the lobby to eat breakfast. Then we switched.

I'd already taken a shower and had just finished blow-drying my hair when Margot stepped out of the shower. She wrapped a towel around herself and stood in front of the mirror beside me. She looked at her reflection for a long time, and then she looked at mine.

"It's sort of weird," she said. "I wondered if things would feel different. I thought I'd look at us and feel different like something was missing like you might not feel like my sister anymore."

For a few long moments, neither of us spoke. We just looked at each other in the mirror. I wanted so badly to ask, "Well, does it?" I held back, though. I waited for her.

She looked away from our reflections and turned to me. "I feel the same, actually better. I used to worry about you so much…but not anymore." She reached up and took my ponytail in her hand and drew it over my shoulder. Just like our mother often did, she twirled it around her finger all the way down and gave it a playful tug. "You're gonna be just fine." She smiled at me with one of her rare and wonderful, full-of-teeth, room-brightening smiles. "But I do have one question for you," she said, turning back to the mirror.

"What's that?" I asked.

She raised one eyebrow. "Where in the world did these boys come from, and with all of our crazy, why are they still here?"

I smiled. "I honestly don't know the answer to either of those questions, but I'm really glad these boys are here."

She laughed and bumped me with her hip. "I bet you are."

"And one more thing," Margot said. "Why does it feel like we've known them forever?"

"I've thought the same thing a hundred times," I said.

She took a washcloth from the counter and used it to pat her face dry.

"He's just really nice," I said.

"They both are," she said.

I took Andrew's hoodie from the hook on the closet door and held it to me for a moment to breathe in the smell of soap, dryer sheets, and something uniquely Andrew that I couldn't place. I allowed myself to get lost for just a moment in the memory of our kiss.

I turned back to Margot. She'd pulled on jeans and a high school cheer T-shirt and twisted her hair into a towel on top of her head. She leaned close to the mirror to pencil in her eyebrows but turned to me and waited for me to respond.

"Sorry, what'd you say?" I realized I must have totally missed something.

She smiled at me and turned back to the mirror. "I just wanted to know what you thought of Nathan?"

I smiled back at her. "Well," I said, turning to put the hoodie on and making her wait for the rest. I turned back to her and the mirror and pulled my hair out of the back. "If you mean, what do I think of him as a person? I think he's really nice and obviously smart, and good with his hands." I took the brush and pulled it through my hair without much resistance. "But if you're asking, what do I think of *Nathan and you*? Well, that's another question entirely," I said, turning back to Margot, giving her a sideways smile, calling her bluff.

Her mouth dropped open.

I set the brush down and rested my back against the counter. "So, which is it?"

"If it was the second, would you think that was weird?" she asked.

Leia and Nora appeared in the doorway. "It depends on why you think it would be weird," Leia said, unafraid to say what she was thinking.

Margot rolled her eyes and turned back to the mirror.

"What?" Leia said.

"Oh my Gah! You're ALWAYS here!" Margot said, drawing out the word *always*, unwilling to hide her irritation with Leia.

Ignoring her, Leia went on. "Do you think it's weird because Charlie and Andrew are a thing?" She made air quotes around the word *thing*. When she saw the embarrassment on my face, she dropped her hands and corrected herself, "I mean, maybe a thing, sort of a thing."

They all turned to me. I spotted my red cheeks in the mirror.

"Charlie, what!?" Nora said, faking surprise.

"Sorry," Leia said with a sheepish smile. In the next breath, she turned back to Margot and went on. "Or do you think it's weird because he's blind, and of the thousands of guys you've gone out with, you've never dated a blind guy?"

"I haven't gone out with thousands of guys." Margot said, not taking her eyes from the mirror.

"Her question's kind of legit though, Margot," I said. "He's not a regular guy. And it's totally transparent that he likes you." That wasn't completely true, but I really wanted to try to get her to be honest.

She capped her eyeliner and looked at Nora, her barometer for right and wrong.

"I kinda think I agree," Nora said. "Margot, he's had a gnarly few years, and even with a crappy situation, he's come through it really well. I know Andrew's his brother and all, but he's made it clear that he thinks Nathan is an incredible guy."

"I just think he's really…" Margot's voice dropped away like she was carefully considering her next words, "Interesting? And anyone can see he's smokin' hot. And you have to admit, there's, like, crazy chemistry."

"Truth," Leia said, interrupting.

"But he's blind. Like he'll never be able to see if I look nice for something like prom."

"He also isn't gonna care if you're in your sweats, so it might not be that bad," Nora countered.

"Good point. I didn't think about that," Margot said, absently tapping a makeup brush against her powder case.

"But for real," I said. "To answer your question, I don't think it's weird. I especially don't think it's weird that he's blind. It's going to be something we all have to figure out and get used to," I said, picking at my nail polish. "I think he's interested in you, but if it's a game for you, then just don't."

She nodded and turned back to the mirror. I could tell she was thinking seriously about what we'd said.

Less than an hour later, everyone was packed, and Nora had pulled the truck around to the front. I saw Margot and Nora sharing a few telepathic looks that only twins share. As I left the hotel lobby and walked outside, I noticed that the early morning snow hadn't stuck to the roads but had left a blanket of white on the grass, trees, and tops of cars. I looked at the hills off in the distance. Everything sparkled like a Christmas card.

When everyone's bags were loaded, I climbed into the front passenger seat and plugged my phone in. When the navigation screen loaded, I tapped the saved point that marked Greta and William Ricks's Roland Park apartment house. The screen was filled with directions and a bold blue line. It was overwhelming to know that the blue line with all its curves and bends, left and right turns, connected Roanoke, Virginia, Baltimore, Maryland, and the rest of my life.

My feelings must have shown on my face because when Nora got back in, she blew on her hands, rubbed them together, looked over at me, and said, "You okay?"

"Yeah," I said, staring straight ahead. "It's just weird. In about four and a half hours, I'm gonna meet my mother. Maybe."

She looked at me, patted my arm, and said, "It's gonna be okay. We'll be there with you." She smiled at me. "And, as many times as these people have to stop and pee, it's probably going to be more like six and a half hours, so there's still time to feel better about it all."

"You're probably right about that," I said, laughing. Inside, I knew it didn't matter if we took four hours or fourteen. I was only going to get more scared, but that didn't change the fact that I had to go. It wasn't lost on me that Nora and Margot had swapped driving, so I turned in my seat to see where everyone else had ended up sitting. Leia was in the seat just behind me, and Andrew was behind Nora. Margot and Nathan were in the way back, shoulder to shoulder, and sharing a pair of earbuds.

Leia gave me a look and leaned in close to whisper, "I guess it's not too weird."

I smiled and said, "Guess not."

I felt Nora shift into drive, and we rolled out of the parking lot. We left the hotel behind, but I knew it was a place I'd never forget.

33

Nina

December 2018

Walt picked up on the fourth ring. "Hey, brother," he said. His voice was deep and familiar, similar to Charles's, but still distinct and unique.

"Hey," Charles said.

"What's up, man?" he said. "You never call this early."

For a moment, no one spoke. In the silence that hung between us, we could hear the buzz around him through the phone—proof that the world outside these four walls was still spinning.

"Charles?" he said, probably thinking the call had been dropped. "You there? Sorry, we stopped to get a coffee on the way in this morning. The drive-thru was killer, so we just parked and walked in. It's noisy in here. I can't hear shit!"

"Yeah," Charles said, "yeah, I'm here." He took a breath and ran his hands through his hair. "Look man, I... I don't even know how to start this, but it's Charlie."

I imagined his reaction so clearly, as though I were in that coffee shop right next to him. I saw him sway where he stood and reach out to steady himself.

"What?" he said in a confused tone. "I mean, is she okay?"

Charles took a deep breath. "No," he said. "No, not really. Not at all," he said, unable to cushion his words. "She told us a few days ago that she's struggling more than normal to see. We drove over to Suzie and John's a couple of days ago. She's been at Vandy for tests. They confirmed her RP is advancing, which is what we expected."

"Oh man," Walt said. The sound around him muffled like he'd cupped his hand around the phone. "Is there anything I can do?" he asked.

He used *I*, not *we*. Some might call it an oversight, but we knew better. Even with Nancy Lynn standing right there next to him. With Charlie, Walt always used the word *I*.

"So, look man, there's more," Charles said, pinching the bridge of his nose before going on. "Man, we had to tell her."

My guess is that Walt stopped where he stood, with the phone pressed to his ear, his coffee in hand, to try to comprehend what his big brother had just said. "I...I don't..."

"She knows everything, everything except that Marie..." Charles said, not able to finish his sentence.

"She knows what? Everything except what?" Walt asked. "Chuck?" he pleaded. A panicked edge had crept into his voice. "Chuck," he repeated. I couldn't remember the last time I'd heard Walt call Charles Chuck. "She knows what?" I was wrong; the panic wasn't creeping. It was racing into his voice.

Charles opened his mouth to speak, but nothing came out. I looked away from the phone and at him to see tears streaming down his cheeks. He buried his face in his hands.

"Nina?" Walt said, voice raised. The tension in his voice was tangible.

"I'm here, Walt," I said, taking over.

"Nina, what does he mean?" He sounded so much like a child it annoyed me. What did he think Charles meant? How could he not know what he meant?

"We had to tell her everything," I swallowed hard, knowing I had to finish, "but she doesn't know that Marie is dead."

Over the phone, there was silence followed by an explosion of commotion. "Oh, shit," he said. I flinched. I thought his words were meant for me, but as his voice elevated with intensity, I realized they weren't. "Shit. Shit. Shit. I'm sorry. I know…it was an accident. I'm so sorry… No, let me…… Nancy Lynn, can you get them a towel or a mop or something? I'm so sorry."

We listened to the chaos and waited.

"Nina. Shit, I'm sorry. I dropped my coffee, and it's everywhere. Hang on." I heard a door open, and then his end was quiet again. "Holy shit, Nina. Is she okay? Is Charlotte okay?" He rarely said her name. Even though it had been the name he and Marie had given her, to hear him say it now was like hearing him try to speak a foreign language.

Sitting next to me, Suzie interrupted. "You can't be serious, Walter Lee!" Somehow, she'd made his double name sound like a curse word.

"Suzie," he said. Her name came out with a defeated sigh.

On principle, Suzie didn't hate anyone, but Nancy Lynn was at the top of that waiting list, and Walter Lee, by association, was right up there with her. Suzie made the point clear whenever possible. I held my hand up to her because she had no self-control when it came to Walter Lee. She snapped her mouth shut and crossed her arms like a child.

"Walt, no, she isn't okay. She left," I said,

"Wait, what do you mean, 'She left?'" he asked.

"From what we know, she and Suzie's daughter Leia called the twins. They came from Knoxville and got them sometime during the night. The four of them are in Virginia. They're going to—"

"Baltimore," he said, finishing my sentence.

"Yes," I said.

"To the Ricks?" he asked.

"We don't actually know," I said, nervously twirling my ponytail into and out of a bun. "Things didn't end well with us yesterday. We didn't know they were gone until early this morning."

He didn't respond, but we heard what sounded like him getting into a car and starting the engine.

"We got a text from them at eight this morning," I said.

"What did it say?" he asked.

"That they're together. That they know everything and they're going to Baltimore to find Marie."

I heard what sounded like another door opening and closing and then a woman's voice. "Walter Lee! What the hell?"

The pitch of Nancy Lynn's angry voice made my skin crawl.

"I had to clean that up—"

"I seriously doubt you cleaned anything, Nancy Lynn!" he said. The irritation in his voice had to be about more than a spilled cup of coffee.

"Well, I had to get the guy to come to clean it up," she said.

"Could you just stop?" he said. I knew she'd ignore him.

"Walter Lee! Seriously!" She was loud and either didn't realize he was on the phone or didn't care. "That was so embarrassing!" she scolded. "I gave that lady my card and told her we'd cover the cost of having her coat and shoes cleaned. You just left me in there—"

He cut her off, something I'd never heard him do before, and shouted. "Nancy!" The three of us jumped at both the sound of his voice and the fact that he used only her first name. Even though we couldn't see her, we knew that she'd also been stunned into silence.

"Nina?" he asked.

"I'm still here," I said with intentional calm.

"I'm gonna go," he said.

"You're going wh…." Nancy Lynn burst across the line, but her voice dissolved just as quickly with what I guessed was an uncharacteristically harsh look from Walter.

"Are you sure?" I said, continuing as though Nancy Lynn didn't exist.

"Yes. It's about time for me to step up," he said. "I'm gonna take Nancy Lynn back to the house, put a few things in a bag, and get on the road. It's a seven-hour drive straight up I-81, but I'll make it in six. Are you and Chuck driving or flying?"

It wasn't lost on me that he knew the exact drive time without hesitation, and I wondered if there was more to him than I'd let myself believe.

Charles shifted in his chair and cleared his throat. "It's almost nine for us. We're coming from Suzie and John's, so we'll probably have to catch a flight."

"Delta has a flight that leaves at eleven," Suzie said, tapping on her phone. "It's a tight connection in Atlanta, but it puts you there just after three."

"That's perfect timing," Walter said. "I'll get y'all from the airport on my way up," he said.

"I'll call the Ricks?" I said, more of a question than a statement.

"Nah, I'll call Billy and Greta," he said, surprising us all in more ways than one.

"Do you need their number?" I asked.

He laughed a laugh I hadn't heard in so long. "Nah," he said. "It's tattooed."

His choice of words were a dusted off antique. That's how Marie described memorizing phone numbers. I don't know how, but she could hear a phone number just once, and she'd have it memorized. I knew he was smiling at the silent echo of her memory.

After we'd gone up the first weekend to check on Walt and to meet her, I'd written her information down in my day planner and told her that Walt had all our information. She asked me to please give her my number in case she wanted to call. I was happy to, but I wasn't sure of the best way, since she wouldn't be able to see it if I wrote it down.

"Oh, no, just say it. I'll remember," Marie said.

I did. Then she drew an X on her chest, repeated the number back to me, and said, "Got it!"

"Seriously?"

"Yep," she said, with the brightest smile. "It's sort of a blind people thing, but your number is now tattooed on my heart."

And it was. She called me every day for the next eighteen months. I'd grown to love her more quickly than anyone before, even Suzie.

As I sat in Suzie's kitchen, I remembered Suzie's initial jealousy at Marie's and my instant connection and friendship. Then Suzie met Marie. Everyone loved Marie, and she'd fit so perfectly into our world, mostly because she wanted to.

I let myself grow dependent on her like you're supposed to with a best friend. I let all my walls down. And then, on December 23, 2002, the phone stopped ringing, and my world went dark without her.

"Okay, we're pulling up at the house," Walt said, pulling me back to the present. "I'm gonna jump off here, take care of a couple of things, and I'll see y'all after three."

"Okay," I said, resting my head in my hands and allowing myself to cry as I let the unexpected and overwhelming relief wash over me.

Charles put his hand on my back and spoke for us both. "We'll see you soon."

He reached for my phone to hang up, but Walt's voice came through the line, causing him to pause.

"Chuck," he said.

Charles's hand hovered over the phone. "Yeah?"

"Thank you," Walt said. His voice was strong and clear, sounding more like himself than he had in sixteen years. "For this. For everything," he said, and then, true to form, he hung up without saying goodbye.

34

Charlotte

December 2018

This leg of the trip was easy, with lots of music and snacks. About an hour into our drive, we stopped at an Exxon station. From the back seat, Margot had demanded that we stop to fill up.

The year before, Margot had taken Wade to a fancy cupcake bakery out in Farragut, a place we Sequoyah kids called "379-too-far." Back then, she had an old rabbit hatchback whose gas gauge was less than reliable. On the way home, she ran out of gas on the interstate. Even though she coasted to safety, the experience was life changing. She was now hyper-vigilant and the self-appointed gas gauge monitor for the world.

Margot went in to pay, and Andrew and I stayed at the pump to fill up the truck. Nora, Nathan, and Leia went inside for the bathroom and more snacks.

When we were back on the road, Andrew produced two small jars of peanut butter. He handed one to Nathan along with a gas station spork. We sat in disbelief as they ate peanut butter directly from the jar like it was totally normal.

"You just wish you'd thought of it first," Andrew said, grinning, with his spork deep in his jar for the fourth or fifth time.

"Exactly!" I said, laughing.

He held his spork out to me.

"No thanks," I said with a smile.

"Your loss," he said and popped another spoonful of peanut butter into his mouth. He looked at Leia and lifted his eyebrows a couple of times.

Leia laughed and unfolded a map she'd picked up at the gas station.

An hour later, we turned east on Highway 7 and then about twenty minutes later, in Berryville, we turned north onto Highway 340. Although the drive through Virginia had been pretty, that's when things started to change. The scenery became breathtaking.

Just past the turnoff, there was a sign for a town called, "The Historic Harpers Ferry." Out of nowhere, Leia, still looking at the map, said, "There's a place up here where three states touch."

"Oh yeah?" I said, half listening.

"Yeah," she said. "West Virginia, Virginia, and Maryland. It looks like it's on the south side of the river, just after it turns into the Potomac." She unfolded the map and refolded it to study a new location. "The river we're about to cross is actually the same river that goes by the Pentagon and the Lincoln Memorial in Washington, D.C."

"That's cool," I said, still not really paying attention. Then, the road made a gentle curve to the right, and the world opened up. I sat up straight and saw the most beautiful river rushing underneath us. "Wow!"

We followed the road as it crossed the Shenandoah River and then curved back around to the left. There was a rock wall on our right, and the river raced alongside us on the left.

From behind, I heard Andrew talking to me, but he sounded so far away I couldn't make out what he was saying. I felt his hand on my shoulder. "You okay?"

He was underwater, and I couldn't breathe in enough air. "You need to pull over," he said to Nora.

"What?" she said. She was watching the road, not looking at me.

"Can you breathe?" he asked me.

I turned to him, and our eyes locked. I nodded. "I just need to get out!" I whispered, doing everything I could to keep from crying, not exactly sure what had overwhelmed me.

"Pull over!" he said with more urgency.

She turned to me for just a moment. "I can't." She turned back to the road. "There's not—"

Leia sat up straight and leaned forward between us. "There's a sign that says *tow shoulder*," she said, pointing across the road.

"What's a *tow shoulder*?" Nora said, shaking her head.

"Like for tow trucks?" Leia said.

"Like if you break down?" Nora said, and it was clear Leia's words didn't have the confidence Nora needed.

"Yeah."

"But I'm not broken down, and I'm not a tow truck!" Nora squealed. "This is not a tow truck," she said, waving her hand around the steering wheel.

"I don't think that's a requirement," Leia said, rolling her eyes. "Just do a U-turn and pull off there!"

"Leia, I can't! There are signs everywhere that say no parking. I can't!" Nora yelled.

"You can!" Andrew said, not yelling but insistent.

"Yeah, you can!" Leia pointed past her again at the other side of the road. "Look, there's a sign!"

Andrew leaned in between the seats with Leia. "Turn around right there at the 'Welcome to Virginia' sign and then pull off onto the shoulder."

"I can't! It's illegal!" she said in a high-pitched voice.

Andrew interrupted her. "Don't think. Just do! There aren't any cars. It's clear. There's space. Just slow down, pull wide to the right, and just make the U-turn. Then, pull off on the shoulder. It's right there." His voice was firm and confident, the kind of clear instructions anyone would follow.

She eased off the gas and pulled her right tire off the side of the road. I felt gravel crunch under us, and I heard her pray, "Oh, please God, don't let us die. Please don't let me kill us." She pulled the wheel, turned the truck one hundred eighty degrees, and eased herself onto the shoulder. The entire time, she was repeating. "Oh, my God! Oh, my God! Oh, my God!"

As soon as the car was off the road and stopped, she threw the shifter into park and brought her hands together and to her mouth. Her entire body shook, and she whispered, "Oh, my God! Oh, my God! Oh, my God!" into her hands as she tried to control herself.

I put my hand on her arm and felt the tightness in my chest release. "You're crazy!" I said and started laughing.

"Charlie!!" Nora screamed. "What the eff!"

I looked back at Leia. "Is this it?" I said, feeling a thousand times better than I had thirty seconds before.

She smiled and nodded. At that moment, I loved that she was my best friend and that she could read my mind. I grabbed her face and kissed her cheek. "I love you, Leia!" She smiled a smile that I would remember forever, long after my vision was gone.

I heard seatbelts unbuckle behind me. I threw the passenger door open and turned back to Nora with a smile. "Come on! Let's go!" I said and took her hand.

"Go where?" Nora asked in passive-aggressive protest, as she was already unbuckling and following me, crawling over the center console and out the passenger side door.

Once we were out of the truck, feet on the ground, Leia took her hand and said, "Let's go stand in three states." Together, they climbed over the guard rail. I watched their heads bob down the embankment.

Andrew connected with Nathan to see if he wanted him as a guide.

"We've got it," he said. Andrew looked at Margot.

"We've got it," she repeated. She raised her eyebrows at Andrew and walked Nathan to the rail. They stepped over and made their way down.

"Are you okay?" he said, searching my face.

"Yeah," I said, nodding my head. "It's just that for a minute, everything felt—big. Like, too big. I just needed some air and to put my feet on the ground." I shook my head. "I know it probably sounds stupid."

"It doesn't sound stupid at all," he said, taking my hand. "Don't let go."

"I won't," I said, nodding.

"I don't care if you feel steady. Don't let go," he said.

"Okay," I said.

He nodded back at me, and just before we hopped over the guard rail, Andrew stopped and pulled me back to him, just like he'd done this morning. He leaned in, put his free hand behind my head, and brought my lips to his. We kissed for a long time, and when he pulled away, we both tried to catch our breath. "You okay?" he asked, brushing my hair out of my face and tucking it behind my ear.

"Yeah," I said, still breathing hard. "I was just…"

"What's wrong," he asked.

"It's just that before this morning, I've never kissed anyone, and… I don't want to do it wrong," I said, hoping he wouldn't see me blush.

He smiled down at me and ran his thumb across my lips. I closed my eyes and kissed his thumb, where it rested on my bottom lip, and touched it with the tip of my tongue. Electricity fired through my body. I knew he felt the current, too. And then his lips were so close to my ear that they touched as he spoke. "You are definitely not doing anything wrong."

He brought his lips to mine again, and my heartbeat pulsed deeper inside me than I thought was possible. This time, it was more intense, and I kissed him back. An echo of Nora's U-turn prayer flooded my mind, but it was different. Nora's prayer of "Oh, my God!" was for the intensity to stop. The prayer my mind shouted over and over was, "Oh, my God! Please let this *never* stop!"

I hooked my fingers into the belt loops of his jeans and pulled him to me. It felt like my body had a mind of its own, taking what it wanted. I pulled him closer and felt him against me. I heard a small moan, and it took a second to realize the sound was coming from me.

"Charlotte," he whispered and kissed my neck along the line of bruised skin that I knew was fading but still there. I tipped my head back, letting it rest against the truck window. I was dizzy. The sound of my name on his lips, the sensation of his hands in my hair, the experience of his holding onto me like I might slip away. "Holy…" his voice dropped away, unable to finish what he was saying.

I pulled away so our faces were just an inch or two apart. "Are you okay?" I whispered.

"Yes!" he said with a playful laugh. "God, yes!" He took my hand and absently circled his thumb in my palm. "I've never felt like this with anyone," he said, his voice still low. "My head keeps saying, 'Slow down. You just met her yesterday,' but everything else…" he shook his head.

"What?" I asked, hoping he'd say what I was thinking.

"Everything else wants more of you. Every other part of me can't get enough." He shook his head. "For the last two years, all I've been doing is going to school and being there for my parents, being there for Nathan. It's like I've been there for everyone except for me. You know how when you go a long time without drinking water, it isn't a big deal until you realize you are thirsty?"

I nodded once, not trusting myself to speak.

"I've been thirsty for a long time."

I hung on to his words, needing to hear that someone wanted me or maybe even needed me. I hadn't thought that he might be the same. For someone to want nothing from him, for someone to want just him and need him just as he is.

"I know," I said, running my hand through his hair, down his arm, and back to his waist, pulling him back to me.

As we kissed, a feather of insecurity slipped into my thoughts, and I pulled away.

"So, you haven't? I mean, you've never?" I said, embarrassed to ask him but needing to know.

"No," he said and shook his head. "The first girl I ever kissed was in the snow by a hotel pool in Nowhere, Virginia."

I was completely speechless.

We heard the others calling for us.

He ran his hand through my hair and stopped at the bottom to hold only the ends. "I don't want to move from this spot, but we probably should," he said and kissed me again.

I nodded. "I don't want to either, but you're probably right," I said. I couldn't resist pulling him back to me. I felt him against me. At his touch, I couldn't catch my breath, but it didn't matter. A piece of me was on the edge of the opening. I wanted to pull him closer and press more deeply into him. I was so thirsty and just like he'd said, I just wanted more.

"Are y'all coming?" someone shouted from the distance, interrupting the moment.

I pulled away, my fists full of his shirt, leaning my head against his with my eyes shut tight, trying to hold onto this moment.

He buried his face in my neck, wrapped his arms around me, and breathed me in. We stood like that for a while to let our heart rates slow down and our breathing settle, and then, finally, he pulled away and took my hand in his. "Let's go stand in three states."

Together, we climbed over the guardrail and made our way down the steep embankment to the edge of the river below.

"Charlie, this is incredible," Margot said, holding onto Nathan. They'd sat down on the bank, and he had his arm around her. "If you close your eyes, you can feel how big it is from inside you," she said.

Holding Andrew's hand, I closed my eyes. I felt the gentle vibration of the earth under my feet, heard the roar of the water as it rushed by, felt the freezing spray of mist that settled across my skin, and smelled the muddy earth around us. The river was so loud you'd never know there was a road fewer than twenty yards above and behind us.

"According to my GPS, this is the point where Maryland, Virginia, and West Virginia all come together," Leia shouted over the river. She took a stick from the ground, drew a circle to mark the spot, then stepped inside and smiled.

We took turns to stand on the circle. Afterward, we stood and admired the river and its power as it pushed ahead.

Without looking at me, Margot stood up, still close enough to Nathan that her leg was touching his arm, and said, "This really is incredible, Charlie. Thanks for letting us come along."

"Of course," I said, deciding not to point out that they were the ones who came to get me. Without them, I'd probably still be at the Vandenberg house being shuttled back and forth to Vanderbilt.

"No, I'm serious," she continued. "It's totally clear they would have taken you anywhere you needed to go, and you would have been fine, better than fine." She said, nodding at Nathan and Andrew. "But I really am glad you let us know what was going on. That you let us help you, or at least come with you. I mean, I don't know what Marie will be like, or why she's stayed away. It's possible that Nancy Lynn and Walter Lee had a lot to do with it."

Her loyalty wasn't lost on me. Margot had only called them by their first names, dropping the titles of aunt and uncle. It was nice to know I wasn't alone. I turned to look at Nora and Leia. They were pointing at a log and watching the current shuttle it downstream. They were only a few feet away, and I could see their lips moving, but I couldn't hear them over the roar of the river.

Nora looked back at me, and our eyes met. I mouthed that we should probably get going and pointed back to the road. She nodded, took Leia's hand, and they steadied each other on their way up. Andrew and I turned to make our way to the car.

"Wait here," Andrew said.

While he was climbing back over the rail, I felt a calm wash over me, and the feeling of urgency began to recede for the first time in weeks. I was certain now that I would always be able to feel how big and incredible the world was, but I never wanted to forget what the world looked like. I turned back to the river for one last look and was surprised to see Margot and Nathan so close together that their silhouettes had merged into one. They were too far for me to make out the details, but I easily filled in the gaps with my imagination.

Andrew took my hand from behind and leaned close to whisper, "Come on, let's get back to the truck."

I turned to him, but before I let him help me back over, I asked, "Are they?" My voice was filled with excited surprise.

He put his finger to his lips just like he'd done on the floor in the hallway at Vanderbilt. He lifted me over the rail like I weighed nothing, and we hurried back to the truck. He opened the door, and I hopped inside, and before he had a chance to shut the door, I asked, "Well?"

He leaned in close and nodded. "They are," he said with a smile.

35

Nina

December 2018

It hadn't dawned on us that it was the day before Christmas Eve, a day people often refer to as Christmas Adam until we'd booked our same-day flights for a thousand dollars each.

When I entered our travel information, I jokingly said to Charles, "You should have been a pilot."

He rolled his eyes and shook his head. "You should have been a pilot." He gave me a playful nudge, and I felt the cold between us begin to thaw. He hadn't apologized for what he'd said in Suzie's kitchen, but that's because I deserved it.

Our flight to Atlanta was uneventful, but as promised, the connection was tight. We had to do a full-out, *Home Alone*-style sprint from Gate B8 in the South Terminal all the way to Gate B27 in the North Terminal, and we were still the last people to board the flight.

We had to sit apart because of the late booking and the completely full flight. Given the stress of the last forty-eight hours, Charles sitting on the opposite side of the aisle five rows back wasn't necessarily a bad thing. The space gave me time to think without pressure. I spent the first half of the hour and forty-five-minute flight destroying my fingernails until the man sitting beside me interrupted.

"You must not fly much," he said.

"No, I actually fly a lot."

"You seem nervous," he said. His words were precise and gentle, with a faint British accent.

I clasped my hands together to force them to be still.

"You're bleeding a bit there," he said, nodding down to my hands.

"Oh," I said, embarrassed and startled at the sight of a darkening red edge on my pinky nail. I reached for my bag and found a small package of superhero tissue in the front pocket. I pulled one out, wrapped it around my finger, and held it there.

"I'm not nervous to fly," I said, shaking my head. "I'm nervous about what will happen once I get where I'm going." I offered him a weak smile.

I'm not sure if it was the tweed sport coat with the leather patches at the elbows or the gray, flat driving cap, but he looked wise. His wide, light brown eyes reminded me of Marie's, which ultimately brought me right back to Charlie. My eyes stung with tears.

"Well, we'll land. Then, we'll all get to walk off the plane. And if Baltimore isn't where you're headed, you'll get to board another plane that will take you where you're going." He looked past me and out the window. I thought he was finished, but then he looked back at me. "And, if Baltimore is where you want to be, then you'll go to work or go wherever it is that you're going to go or do whatever it is you've come to do," he said and raised his finger. "But, if you're really lucky, like me, you get to go home."

He looked at me like he expected me to tell him why I was traveling, but when I didn't say anything, he went on, "I'm headed home to Commodore, Pennsylvania. For the last four months, I've been teaching college freshmen about dead poets and philosophers at Emory University. I'm ready to get back to Jerry and Teeser," he said and lifted a finger for each as he said their names. "And my wife, too," he said, dropping both fingers to replace it with one.

"Jerry and Teeser are your children?" I asked as I peeked under the tissue at my finger.

"Oh, no!" he said, laughing. "My cats!" He looked at me, if not through me, and for just a moment, I experienced *déjà vu*, but the feeling slipped away just as quickly as it had come.

"I don't think I'm in any of those situations,'" I said in a timid voice.

"I see," he said. I expected him to say more, but he surprised me again by saying nothing as though he were waiting for me to go on.

Against every introverted impulse in my body, in a moment of weakness that I would later blame on Charles for not insisting we sit together, I found myself telling this kind, old man everything, or at least what I could cover in forty-five minutes. By the time the flight attendants made the announcement about returning our tray tables and seat backs to their upright and locked positions, he probably wished he'd never spoken to me in the first place.

I talked all the way through touchdown in Baltimore, and I didn't stop until we'd finished our taxi and had come to a complete stop at the gate. The seatbelt indicator gave its familiar alert, and the lights blinked off, releasing the cabin into a flurry of activity. Passengers all around us unbuckled, stood to gather their bags, and filled the airplane aisle to wait for the doors to be opened.

I pulled my backpack from under the seat in front of me and hugged it as I waited, staring out the window and into my blurry thoughts. I hadn't noticed the plane emptying around me until I felt a hand on my shoulder and looked up to find Charles had stepped into the row behind me and reached over to get my attention.

"You ready?" he asked.

I nodded but waited while I watched the professor unfold himself into the aisle. He was tall.

"You must be Charles," he said, holding out his hand to shake.

I saw confusion wash over Charles's face.

Unable to delay the future any longer, I pushed myself to stand, bending my head sideways as I stepped out from under the overhead bins. "Yes, this is my husband, Charles, and this is…" my voice trailed off, and I felt my face grow hot with embarrassment. "I'm so sorry," I said. "I don't think I ever asked your name."

"Not at all. I should've introduced myself. I'm Tom Figgans, but my students call me Professor Fig." He patted my arm and gave us both a smile.

"Charles Mavin," he said and took his outstretched hand. "But I guess you already know that."

He nodded and let go of Charles's hand. He gathered his worn leather bag from the overhead bin and rested its strap over his shoulder. The bag completed his look. If he were a painting, he would be called "The Academic." He turned to us and rested his hands on each of our shoulders. "George Bernard Shaw used to say, 'If you cannot get rid of the family skeleton, you may as well make it dance.'" With that, he turned and made his way down the aisle.

Charles and I stood and watched him go. Professor Fig was doing that awkward sideways shuffle that all full-sized people do when exiting an airplane so they don't bang their legs and hips on the armrests. When he reached first class, where the space between the rows got bigger, he squared up and continued. He patted each seat back with his free hand as he passed—something Marie used to do and something Charlie would be taught to do. He stopped at the front row just before the bulkhead and did a half-turn to face us. "Shaw also said, 'Take care to get what you like, or you will be forced to like what you get.'" He tipped his cap and gave a salute. "Good luck to you both." With that, he turned the corner, disappeared through the galley, and was gone.

Once we were off the plane, Charles texted Walter. Walter was about twenty minutes from the airport, so on the way out, we stopped and got a chai tea for me and a coffee each for Charles and Walter.

With the drinks in a carrier, we waited at a bench by the giant glass windows just inside and to the left of a set of sliding glass exit doors. Every time the doors slid open, a blast of December air rushed in to warn us of the Baltimore cold.

We'd been standing at the windows for fewer than five minutes when Charles's phone buzzed with an incoming text.

Charles pulled out his phone and read the message. He tucked the phone back into his pocket, shouldered his bag, and reached for my hand. "He's here."

36

Charlotte

December 2018

After a couple of turns, we were back on the road. Departure was a lot less traumatic and dramatic than arrival had been. We were headed back north and had just passed the 'Welcome to Maryland' sign.

We had been on the road no more than two minutes when Margot squealed from the back seat, "Kettle Corn!!!"

"Boiled Peanuts!" Leia shouted, matching Margot's enthusiasm.

They both had lunged into the space between the front and middle rows and pointed across me and out the window at a row of brightly colored signs that lined the right side of the road like a pilot's landing strip. A moment later, they'd convinced Nora to pull off the road again and into a gravel lot. The entire space resembled a tiny corner of a Renaissance fair.

Nora maneuvered the truck and shifted into reverse to back in next to a row of neatly parked cars.

Margot had already pulled on her coat. She leaned over the seats and gave Nora a playful kiss on the cheek. "Dad would be so proud of your parking job!"

Nora waved her away with false annoyance and held up her hand, palm out. "Five minutes!"

"Yay!" Margot said with a cheer.

"Margot, I'm serious! We have to get there before dark!" Nora said again and held up her hand again, wiggling her fingers. "Five minutes!"

Margot nodded and clapped her hands together with excitement.

This was such a role reversal for the two of them. Margot was normally stern and kept the two of them on track, but I was equally startled and happy to see her joy fill the space around us.

She pulled Nathan out with her. "Anyone else wanna come?"

Surprised but excited by the open invitation, Leia grinned at me and grabbed her jacket. "Want anything?" she said.

"I'm good," I said, smiling back at her.

"Five minutes!" Nora shouted as Leia closed the door and ran to catch up with Nathan and Margot.

Nathan had taken Margot's arm and crossed the gravel space to where the vendors were set up. They stopped for a moment at the craft tables. From where I sat, I couldn't really tell in detail what was happening, just that they'd stopped.

Instinctively, without me even having to ask, Nora started narrating. "I can't tell what it is, but Margot picked something up from that table and put it in Nathan's hands. She must be telling him about it." We watched them for a moment. "She's actually really good with him," Nora said, putting words to exactly what I was thinking.

"She really is," Andrew agreed. "She's sort of a boss at it."

Nora laughed, "Margot pretty much makes herself the boss of everything, so we probably shouldn't be surprised."

"It's weird letting him go," Andrew said. "I've been his eyes since the accident, especially after I got my driver's license and took over getting him to most of his appointments. I'm kinda nervous watching him be led by somebody else."

He stared out the window at them. "I keep thinking that she's going to forget and run him into something or not know to tell him about something."

"That's kind of how we feel when we see you with Charlie." Nora said, looking out the window as she spoke, but when she was finished, she turned and looked back at Andrew.

He nodded, letting her know without words that he'd heard her and understood what she meant.

She looked back out the window. "Whatever it was, they put it back," she said.

We watched them make their way over to a tent where two men stood watch over giant metal pots while they talked to a few people gathered around them.

"They look like brothers," Andrew said.

Nora turned her head sideways like she was getting a better angle. "Yeah, maybe so," she said, leaning over the wheel and squinting. "Look at that facial hair!" she said, gesturing with her hands below her chin, giving me an idea of what she was talking about. "It's impressive. If they aren't brothers, they're definitely related," she said. "The bigger dude, the one with the longer beard, is talking with his hands so much that it looks like he's about to take off."

I turned and snatched Leia's iPad from her seat. I swiped to the right to open her camera and pointed it in their direction to watch for myself.

It took a few minutes for them to reach the front of the line, but when they did, the man and Margot got into a conversation. They were talking so intently that she didn't even notice when Nathan leaned down to Leia and whispered something in her ear.

"Where's he going?" Andrew said, sitting up straight.

"No idea," Nora said.

Andrew started to reach for the door to intercept them. I grabbed his hand and held it. "Wait, let him go. You're here just in case, but let him do this," I said, keeping his hand tight in mine.

I could tell it took physical will for him to trust my words and stay where he sat. We watched Nathan and Leia recross the lot and return to the booth where they'd stopped first.

Nathan leaned in and spoke to the woman behind the table. She nodded several times and then reached out and took his hands. She placed something in them. He inspected it. He shook his head and handed it back to her. He said something and moved his hands as he spoke like he was describing what he was looking for. With intense concentration, the woman watched him and listened. When he finished, she looked down at her inventory, nodding as she searched. Finally, she plucked something off the table and set it in his hand with care. He went over the item carefully and then gave the woman a nod.

He spoke to Leia. She nodded and turned to check on Margot, who was still in an animated conversation with the man at the kettle corn table. Leia turned back to Nathan and said something. The three of them—Leia, Nathan, and the woman at the craft table—exchanged a few words. Leia nodded, squeezed Nathan's arm, and hurried back to the table with Margot. Leia appeared to order herself a bag of peanuts.

Andrew moved to get out of the truck again. I squeezed his hand again. "Wait," I said. My voice was sterner than I'd meant it to be.

He looked at me. Our faces were so close that I could read the concern in his eyes. With one glance, he was begging me to make him stay and, at the same time, asking for permission to go to his brother's rescue.

"I know you want to go get him," I said, holding his eyes in mine, "but you have to let him do this!" I said, pointing out the front window. "You need to know he'll be okay. You're an amazing brother, but he needs to know he can do this kind of stuff without you."

He stared at me, still unsure what to do.

"You have to let him do this," I repeated and held his hand even tighter, willing him to stay but also knowing that there was nothing I could do to keep him there if he was determined to go.

He waited, perched on his seat like a rocket ready to launch.

We watched Nathan pull out money, unfold it, and hand it to the woman. She made change for him in her cash box. We saw him speak to her again, and her face lit up with animation. She took the money back and then carefully handed him each bill of his change separately. He took each bill, folded it, and tucked it into his wallet. He said something else to her. She laughed, reaching for a jar beside the cash, and guided his free hand to it. He felt the opening and dropped the last bill she'd given him inside.

The woman came around the table and handed him a small white bag. He tucked the bag into his coat pocket, and the woman let him take her arm. She walked him back to the tent and delivered him without interrupting the kettle corn man's story. He reached out, and to the surprise of everyone inside the truck, he took Margot's arm on the first try. Margot looked up at him and smiled. She took his hand and held it while they stood waiting for her food.

Nathan leaned down and spoke to Margot. She nodded and said something to Mr. Kettle Corn. They all looked toward the truck, and as though on cue, we all lifted our hands and waved. They burst into laughter.

The kettle corn man scooped her popcorn into a long, clear plastic bag and wrapped a twist tie around the top. He handed it over to her. She thanked him, and the three of them turned and hurried back. As they walked, we could see their breath in clouds trailing behind them. And when they opened the car door, the cold air rushed in, and we all made space for them to get in as fast as they could.

Once all were safely tucked into their seats, Nora turned to us and asked, "If you're ready to get on the road and not stop anymore, raise your hand."

Without a sound, we all raised our hands to placate her.

"Good!" Nora said, pulling out of the gravel lot and back onto the highway. "It's just after eleven now and about two

hours away, so if we do a drive-thru for lunch, I think we can
be there by two."

"Sounds good," I said, feeling more confident than I had
felt in the last week.

"Are you ready for this?" Nora asked me.

I nodded. "I think so," I said, shrugging my shoulders. "I
mean, I feel pretty crappy about just showing up to meet her
without calling or anything, but I don't want her to have the
chance to say that she doesn't want to meet me."

"I seriously doubt that will happen," Nora said.

I shook my head. "I just don't know. I mean, why do you
think she hasn't tried to reach out to me?" I asked, taking the
strings of Andrew's hoodie, winding them, and then
unwinding them around my finger. I had already decided,
regardless of what happened after we had to go back to real
life, he would never get it back. "I mean, if they were all so
close, what could have happened to mess it all up? What
could have broken it to the point that she and Walter just,
like, gave up?"

"I don't know," Nora said. She didn't take her eyes off
the road, but I could tell by her tone that she was considering
my question like she'd asked herself the same question, and
just like me, she'd not been able to come up with a good
answer. She drummed her thumbs on the bottom of the
steering wheel. "I don't know why I feel this way, but I think
when everything comes out, Nancy Lynn is going to have
had something to do with all of this."

"I don't know," I said, still wrapping and unwrapping
each of my fingers just to have something to do with my
hands. "I don't get how one person could have that much
power over anyone." I took a breath, hoping my next
sentence would come out the way I meant it. "I mean, Nora,
you didn't see her."

"Who, Nancy Lynn?" she said, confused.

"No! Not Nancy Lynn," I said, shaking my head.
"Mom," I said. "I mean Mom. She didn't want to talk to me
about it so badly that she literally ran away from me. She ran

all the way from Monroe Carell back to Suzie's house to avoid talking to me. That's like fifty blocks."

She was quiet for a while, and the air between us felt charged. Without her having said a word, I knew she was going to try to play devil's advocate.

"I just…" she started, but she stopped when she saw me shaking my head.

I held my hand up to stop her.

"What?" she said. "There are so many different sides to every story. Like Mom and Dad say all the time, whatever they do for us falls into categories. Either to teach us or—"

"Keep us safe," I said, completing her sentence. I loved that she was helping me see the situation from a different angle, but I hated that she was probably right.

"All I'm saying is there's probably more to the story than we could even dream up. So, rather than letting your imagination go wild with worry, let's meet her and let her try to explain. The same goes for Mom and Dad and even Walter. If I were caught in a mess, at the least, I'd want the chance to explain my side of the story."

I nodded and sat quietly. I tried to understand our mother's side of things while I listened to Leia, Nathan, Nora, and Andrew debate about each other's iPod music selections.

The strangest feeling of peace washed over me. An unexplainable calm filled me up. No matter the reasoning behind any of their decisions, these were my people. Everything that had happened before these last couple of days had all been necessary. Without it we might not have made it here or might not have made it here together.

I felt stronger for having decided to go, and I no longer felt alone. The reality was that I had never been alone. I was at peace with myself and felt joy hearing everyone cracking up as they played the Allie Quick edition of 'Name the Next Lyrics.'

Nathan was smoking everyone because he was a secret mega fan. He had every single one of her albums and even had his favorite deluxe version on vinyl.

These were my people, and if it took all of this to find them, it was worth it.

37

Nina

December 2018

Charles and I left the airport waiting area and walked through the doors. Six lanes of hustling people and shuttle buses stretched in front of us. The cold made my cheeks tingle as the wind rushed through the tunnel of concrete pillars. A yellow-vested traffic officer stopped traffic, and we crossed with a group of other travelers to the median separating the two lanes of airport shuttles from the two lanes of hotel and rental car shuttles. Beyond that, rumbling toward us where we stood at the edge of the arrivals loading area, was Walter's diesel king cab Ford pickup truck, white with an orange Power T plate on the front.

He pulled to a stop, hopped out of the truck, and came around to take our bags. He set them in the back seat and turned back to hug me. He slapped Charles on the back and pulled him in for a hug, too. We all climbed in, the two of them in the front and me happily in the back. "Good flight?" he asked, rubbing his hands together and holding them in front of the heater vent.

"Yeah," Charles said, handing him a coffee.

Walter took it, removed the green stopper, and took a sip. "Thanks."

"Sure, thanks for the ride," Charles said.

"Of course. It's crazy how the timing worked out so well." Walter said.

His southern drawl was even more pronounced than usual. A tell that his nerves were bubbling just below the surface. He checked the mirror and eased back into traffic through a series of large, sweeping left turns to make his way out of the airport.

Anxious energy filled the space between the three of us until Walter seemed to not be able to stand it anymore. "The GPS tried to take me through the city to get up there," he said, drumming on the steering wheel with his fingers. "It says it's four minutes faster to take the beltway around the west side of the city and then down 83."

Charles and I sat and listened to him rattle. We knew Walter had always been a talker, and that meant that we knew he just needed time and space to talk it out and work through everything.

"So," he said with more rhythmic drumming on the steering wheel, "that's what we're gonna do."

Unable to watch his brother suffer any longer, Charles finally spoke. "We haven't heard anything from them since this morning at eight. Did you hear anything from—"

"Billy and Greta?" Walter asked, interrupting. "No," he said, then corrected himself. "I mean, I talked to them as I was heading out of Shelby this morning. I told them what I knew from you and that the four children might try to connect. They said they'd let me know, but I haven't heard anything back."

"Were they surprised to hear from you," I said, finding my voice.

"No," he said and looked at me through the rearview mirror. "No, they weren't surprised," he said, "I talk to them at least once a week."

"Really?" Charles and I said at the same time, both completely unable to hide our surprise.

"It's not me," he said, like a confession. "Greta's been after me for sixteen years. She stayed with me but was patient, and she's about the kindest person I've ever known. Plus, she loves that little girl somethin' fierce." I caught his reflection in the mirror. He was blinking back tears. "But I guess she's not so little anymore and looking more like Marie every day."

His blunt words and sincerity surprised me. As far back as I could remember, he hadn't ever asked for a photo of Charlie. In fact, when Charlie was a baby, he lived near us in East Tennessee because he worked for the Tennessee Valley Authority. We would visit them, or they'd occasionally visit us, not often, and he was always gone for work. Then, when Charlie was three, Nancy Lynn moved them two hundred miles east to Shelby to start an upscale wedding event facility.

They bought about fifty acres of relatively flat pastureland. The land had an old farmhouse that took two years to renovate from top to bottom. They turned it into a bed and breakfast. The land also had two barns. One was small and used to store tractors and other equipment, and the other was for horses, and it was huge. They gutted them, transformed both into event spaces, and built a steel and glass chapel that connected both barns. The place was incredible, and as much as I hated that they left town, neither Charles nor I could believe the transformation. What they'd created was stunning.

Once the renovations were complete, it still took several years to get things going. Still, everything took off when an old boarding school friend of Nancy Lynn's booked her wedding there after she announced her engagement to reality star turned actor, Thomas Gough.

The bride's dress cost over one million dollars, and the groom's mother insisted on having doves deliver the rings. So, Nancy Lynn and Walter hired two doves from an animal talent agency in southern California. The story was that they flew in on a private plane and had their own handler.

Every bit of the event was a production, and they complained about it for months, but it was the event that put their space on the map. It wasn't the Biltmore, but ten years later, their weekends were booked throughout the year, and they had a cancellation standby list in the spring and fall.

The business started out with just the two of them and a handful of part-time help. We honestly thought their marriage wouldn't survive the stress. But now they had over twenty on staff and another ten or so subcontractors for larger events. Their success made it easy for Walter to cancel and send his regrets for not showing up for family gatherings.

I sat and tried to mentally process what he'd said and remember the last time that I'd seen him and, more importantly, the last time he'd seen Charlie. I spoke in a carefully metered calm and tried to put my thoughts into words. "I didn't realize you stayed in touch with them that well."

He didn't hesitate a single moment before answering. It was like he'd been anticipating the question and was jumping at the chance to talk about it. "About six years ago, I think. It was the year Charlotte turned ten. I got a yellow envelope in the mail from Greta. A bundle of pictures that you'd sent her."

He pronounced the word *pitch-er*, the same way you'd pronounce the baseball position, pitcher.

Traffic was heavy as we made our way north. Walter flipped his blinker and slid one lane to the right, moved around a dump truck, and then slid back to the left and back in front of the truck he'd just passed. He did this with such ease, like a dancer on a stage. He never appeared to be looking around, yet you know he did because he'd gotten it right every time. His muscle memory reminded me that, for a time, he'd called this city home. It was something that I often forgot. There was a piece of him here that was free of Nancy Lynn.

"Greta had tucked a note in there with the pictures and said something about how it had only been a couple of months since she'd gotten pictures from you, but she was shocked by how much more grown-up Charlotte was." He gripped the steering wheel and looked straight ahead. "She said that she understood why I didn't ask you for photos, but since I'd never responded to her with so much as a hello, she hoped I didn't mind that she'd sent 'em to me."

As he spoke, I heard and saw his frustration. My heart sped up as I anticipated, but I tried to deny what was coming next.

"You see," he said, "I didn't get any pictures." He gripped the steering wheel with one hand and banged his fist against it with the other. "Greta has been sendin' me pictures since we left Knoxville when Charlotte was three." He took off his baseball cap and ran his hand back and forth through his hair, then put the cap back on. "That's seven years of pictures I'd never gotten, much less ever seen."

Charles and I waited for him to go on.

"When I got home that day, I asked Nancy Lynn about it. If we'd gotten 'em, and she said we did, and she got rid of 'em.'" He looked away from the road and at Charles for longer than was probably safe and said, "Can you believe that?" His voice broke, but he pushed through. "Can you believe that she fuckin' burned 'em?" He looked back at the road and shook his head at the memory, "I never thought…" he said, still shaking his head, "not in a million years. I never thought she'd ever do somethin' like that. It took every ounce of strength I had not to explode that day. In fact, I actually got in my truck and left. I had to sort out what was goin' on in my head. Goin' back was one of the hardest things I've ever done. But what other choice did I have?" The defeat he felt at the memory broke my heart.

"I couldn't abandon our kids," he said, referring to his and Nancy Lynn's daughters, Anna Claire and Mary Katherine. "I had to go back. I had to get past what she'd done," he said, shaking his head. "I mean, she left me! She served me with divorce papers. She pushed me to sign them! She said she was done. And then she never signed the damn things herself. It felt like it was a game to her. Like, let's see how far I can push him. Like, *what else can I make him do*? The week before everyone came up to Baltimore for the wedding, Marie and I went down to the courthouse. We did the whole marriage license thing, and it all went fine," he said. "I mean, y'all know. Y'all were there."

I closed my eyes and remembered the day.

They'd gotten married on the day before Valentine's Day, five months after they'd gotten engaged. It was a Wednesday, which we all thought was crazy, but because they'd met on a Wednesday and the knit club was on Wednesday, the date made perfect sense to them.

Suzie and I helped Marie into the dress again. At the ceremony, Suzie and I watched Marie, with her mother and father on either side, walk between the rows of white folding chairs to the gazebo that was tucked into the lowest corner of the lawn of Edgevale House. There were fifty or so people there, including all Edgevale House residents. The night before at the rehearsal dinner, Marie and Walt had called them The Ladies of Edgevale, and everyone had laughed.

Walt's voice pulled me from the memory. "I thought the divorce paper situation, which meant I couldn't move on, was the worst thing she could have done. Then the pregnancy...forging my signature to use the frozen embryos...her showin' up actually pregnant when she struggled gettin' pregnant and stayin' pregnant for so long." He shook his head.

Charles and I sat stunned. I heard both anger and relief in his voice—anger at the act and relief to finally be able to tell someone.

"I thought that would be the end." His voice broke again, but he went on. "She apologized. She said all she'd ever wanted was to be a mother. She said it had made her go crazy. She said she'd been seeing a therapist, and she was much better. She still loved me and said she would raise the baby on her own, but then she called it 'our baby.' That sent me over the edge," he said.

Charles and I hung on to his every word. This was a part of the story we'd never heard. When Nancy Lynn had shown up five months pregnant, we'd always assumed the worst about Walter, that he'd cheated and that what people were now calling '9/11' had brought him back to his senses and back to Marie. He'd never denied it. In fact, he'd never even spoken about it at all. But now he was telling us the truth.

"I'd just lost everything," he said. "There was nothing left in me to give her, but still, she wanted to be with me. She wanted to take care of me."

He took the exit and merged onto I-695. I watched him gather his thoughts before going on. It was not until that moment that I truly appreciated what he'd been through.

"I always knew she struggled and could never come to terms with how she left me," he said with a practiced calm. "Even now, she hasn't really worked through everything that happened—really anything that happened in those first couple of years. We never talk about it. When she came back, she said she'd been seeing a counselor or something, but since then, as far as I know, she hasn't talked to anyone. She doesn't want anything to do with anyone who had anything to do with Marie."

"I think," he said, considering his next words, "no, *I know* that she's tried from the beginning to separate our families. She's tried to keep me from getting to know Charlotte and being a part of her life. I let Nancy Lynn pretend that those two years never happened, like Marie never existed…" his voice broke away as a sob caught in his throat, but he pressed on, "…like Charlotte never existed. I don't remember a lot of what happened in the days after Marie's death," he said. "But I know I was wrong. I was wrong to forgive Nancy. I was also wrong to agree to any of those shit rules when y'all agreed to take Charlotte. I was wrong on just about everything that had to do with Charlotte. And I was wrong for letting Nancy push me into it."

I sat back, absorbing everything he'd just said. After Marie's death, I thought Walter was a coward, that he was nothing like his brother. I had no respect for him.

I thought he took the easy way out. I thought he ran away. But now with every passing moment drawing us closer to the inevitable, it was clearer to me than it had ever been before. He lost everything. He wasn't a coward. He was a hurt human. He'd given us Charlie, knowing she was safe and loved, and he'd done what was necessary to survive. Our lives would have been so different if we'd told the truth from the beginning. The realization humbled me.

We said nothing for several minutes. I watched him wipe away tears as they rolled down his cheeks. "She's not happy I left," he said, talking about Nancy Lynn. "I told her it was time to put all this to bed. I asked her to come with me," he said, shaking his head again.

"What'd she say?" Charles asked.

"Oh, she went ballistic," he said, with a laugh that had a crazy edge to it. "I'm worried about her, but I'm done with this bullshit. It's time for us all to grow up. I should have stepped up sixteen years ago, but I'm thankful to God y'all did." His words had started to break apart again, but he kept talking.

"I was worried about Nancy Lynn taking this out on the girls, so I called Mom and Dad. They drove over from Knoxville," he said. "The girls were at a friend's house having a sleepover last night, so I just called them and told them it was a surprise, but that grandma and grandpa were gonna pick them up and bring them back to Knoxville. It'll be the first time they've had Christmas there since we moved away. They were so excited they didn't ask any questions. Small mercies, right?"

He continued, "There's an event at the farm this evening, and even though I don't think she'd do anything crazy to mess that up, I went ahead and called her best friend to come get her and told our event manager, Bart, that we were gone for the weekend. They'll be fine without us. They'll probably do better without us being there like this."

I shut my eyes and let the gravity of everything he'd told us press into me like a weighted blanket.

38

Charlotte

December 2018

An hour and a half after we'd left the kettle corn and boiled peanut sellers, Nora asked for quiet as she navigated off the highway and onto a road called Northern Parkway.

Leia had been engrossed in her iPad, but about ten minutes after we turned off the highway, she leaned forward between the front seats and pointed at an iron fence on the right side of the road.

"I think…" she said, looking back and forth, "Yeah! Look up there. Where the brick posts start up there with the iron fence in between." She pointed again to a space through the trees.

It was hard to see, but there was a dirt road or something not far from the road. Maybe the distance between the big lines on a football field: ten yards, maybe fifteen.

"What is it?" I asked.

Nora eased to a stop at a red light. "I thought so!" Leia said, excited. "It's Pimlico!" She pointed to one of the least ostentatious marquee signs I'd ever seen.

A simple red and black sign announced the dates of Preakness Day, Black-eyed Susan Day, and Spring Meets.

"The photo of your parents was taken just over there," Leia said. "This is the back side of the track."

The light turned green, and Margot accelerated with the traffic, keeping her eyes on the road while everyone else turned and watched the track slide out of sight. She got another red light at the intersection and slowed to a stop at the corner. She tapped her index fingers on the steering wheel and bit her lower lip. When the light turned green, she didn't move. Nora looked at me and then turned back to Andrew and Leia.

"What?" I asked and turned around to look at them.

Leia's eyes went wide with understanding, and she started to nod. "Yes, definitely yes!"

The determination in her voice surprised me.

Nora shifted her gaze to Andrew, who tilted his chin down and raised his eyebrows as high as they'd go. "Why not?" he asked, shrugging his shoulders.

I looked back and forth between the three of them. "I'm so confused?"

A raggedy, rattling truck behind us broke the moment, honking his horn, annoyed we weren't moving. Nora jumped like it was gunfire, and Leia shouted, "Go!"

Instead of following the GPS and going straight through the intersection, Nora checked her mirror and squealed, "Hold onto your diapers!" She hit the gas and turned right across traffic from the left lane.

The entire back seat erupted into a confetti of playful protests as the raggedy truck driver laid on his horn again with disapproval.

I wasn't sure if it was fear, excitement, or both, but either way, I stayed quiet. I felt my face tingle and my ears get hot. I knew, without anyone saying it, that even though this was my adventure, whatever was about to happen was going to be out of my control.

We made our way around what looked like the backs of the pitched roof, stable buildings and empty overflow parking lots on our right.

It didn't escape my notice that we weren't in the best part of town. A small voice inside said to be afraid for our safety, but the voice was overridden by the growing list of things I never wanted to forget. I never wanted to forget this beautiful melting pot.

Inside the truck, we were quiet except for Leia's calm and direct navigation instructions, which were in complete contrast to her normal disposition. I knew this trip was changing me, but now I could see that it was changing and growing everyone with me.

We made a series of right turns until finally turning onto Hayward Avenue. The white buildings of Pimlico rose in front of us. Nora followed the signs to the parking lot in front of the blocky, glass main building. She pulled around, backed into a space in the front row, then turned off the engine.

"Ready for a getaway?" Andrew asked.

Nora pulled her coat from between the seats and pointed her finger at him. "You'll thank me when we get kicked out of here for being too young, and we have to run."

"Good point, Dale Earnhardt," he said with a smile and handed me my coat.

From the back seat, Nathan shouted, "Nora, don't listen to him. You can drive our getaway car anytime! You've earned it, girl! You've got mad skills behind the wheel."

"Says the blind guy," Andrew said, making his brother laugh.

"I think I have an idea about seeing where the picture was taken," Leia said, settling the laughter around us. She held up a picture from the puzzle box and turned it to face me.

I took it from her and held it close to look. I hadn't seen it earlier.

"It was loose in the bottom of the box. I think it was added later because the picture quality is better, like it was taken on a nicer camera, and it's a different size." Leia said,

I looked at her with surprise, "They were all there. I mean here. They were all here?"

She nodded. "I think," she said. "I've thought about it a lot. Just hear me out."

I braced myself, knowing there was no telling what was coming next.

"If we can talk to someone, I don't know, like a manager or somebody like that ..." she paused and looked at me, forcing me to return her stare.

"And do what?" I asked.

She sighed and then took a deep breath. "I think if you tell them about what's going on with you, that you're going blind and you're adopted and you found this picture of your bio mom and dad..." She cracked her knuckles, probably nervous she'd said too much or gone too far.

I just looked at the picture. It scared the crap out of me to admit all of what she'd just said out loud, especially to a perfect stranger. I could barely admit most of it to myself, and telling someone else made it real. But the truth was I wanted to see the spot where that picture was taken just as badly as everyone did, and at the moment I couldn't think of a better plan.

I looked up at her. "Let's do it."

"Really?" Leia said.

"Yeah, I think it's a good plan, and it might work." I pulled on my coat and hat and smoothed my hair. "Let's go before I chicken out."

It was so much easier than any of us could have imagined. An older man met us just inside the doors. His name was Lionel, and he told us he'd been working at Pimlico since the early seventies.

His bushy gray eyebrows rose and fell as I told him our story, leaving out the parts about my parents lying about everything and feeling an annoying sense of loyalty to them.

Without any explanation, he passed through our group and waved for us to follow him. While we walked, he told us several times, "This ain't somethin' I'm s'pose to do, but for you girl, I walk you out myself! It ain't like anything you've seen before! You jus' gotta see it to believe it!"

And he did. He took us down the ramp to the track entrance, where the winter wind whipped and whistled through empty bleachers. We were able to walk all the way to the fence.

"Lemme see that pitcher of yours again. We'll find your spot," he said.

I handed him the photo, and he studied it. He turned it sideways and looked at it for another long second. "Come on," he said, hustling us down the bleachers and following the fence line. He stepped off the end, and I noticed the ground change from concrete to brick under our feet.

"What's this?" I asked.

"Winner's circle," he said over his shoulders, not slowing down. This man was easily eighty years old but was moving like he was much younger. Finally, he stopped and held the picture up in front of him, matching the picture with the edge of the brick wall that he'd noticed in the corner of the photo. "Right here!" He said, gesturing with his hand for us to come and stand where he was pointing. "You got yo camera?" he asked, holding out his hand.

There was nothing rude about him, but I felt unsettled that he was able to know the next moment before we'd even gotten through the one we were in.

I fumbled in my pockets to find my phone, but before I found mine, Andrew handed over his, and Leia pulled her Polaroid from her bag. We came together in a row. Nathan, Nora, Margot, Leia, me, and then Andrew at the end.

"Say, 'Ol' Hilltop,'" he instructed as he snapped pictures with each of the cameras we'd handed him. Then the kind old man escorted us back to the main lobby and told us to come back in May for the Preakness, when we could take the tour. And just as quickly as we'd walked in, we walked out.

39

Nina

December 2018

The even hum of Walt's tires against the interstate allowed me to slide into that space between asleep and awake. I felt the truck slow down as we took an exit and followed the signs to Northern Parkway. We took the left side of the fork toward Rolling Road. My stomach did a quick flip-flop as the exit dropped down a sharp hill and then scooped up to the traffic lights.

I was so familiar with this space and place. We'd been in that exact spot more times than I could count, and even though I hadn't been there in many years, every bit of it felt intensely personal and wildly recent and familiar. I rested my head against the seat and let the memories of Marie fill the spaces in my heart.

I heard her sweet laugh. I smelled the scent of her citrus shampoo. "This isn't real," I said to myself. I didn't dare open my eyes, knowing if I did, she wouldn't be there.

Even though I knew with every bit of me that she wasn't there, I felt her warm hand take my arm inches above my elbow, just like she'd done a million times before. I told myself again and again. "This isn't real! This isn't real!"

"You know I can hear you."

My eyes snapped open, and, in the flesh, right beside me, sat Marie. She looked so much like Charlie, but it could only be Marie. Pretty, spunky, strawberry blonde, teeny tiny Marie.

"Hi," she said, like it was totally normal for her to be sitting next to me.

When Charlie was a baby, I saw Marie all the time. I saw her so often that I thought I was losing my mind. I went to a counselor a few times hoping it would help, but I never told Charles. I never told anyone, not even Suzie. Eventually, I stopped seeing Marie everywhere, and then I stopped seeing her at all.

I closed my eyes tight and turned sideways in my seat, pulling my knees to my chest and resting my back against the door. I repeated, just like I had before, "This is not real. This is not real. This is not—"

"Nina," she interrupted, her face inches from mine. "I'm dead. I've got all the time in the world, but you have about seven minutes to figure out what to say to her." As she spoke, she sat back and raised seven fingers, then turned them to face me. Her brown eyes were bright and clear. I waved my hand in front of her face.

She reached out and took my hand, and it was warm around mine.

I looked at the front seat. Neither Walter nor Charles made any indication they'd heard anything. "If this were really happening, they would have heard us, right?" I said out loud. "If I'm dreaming..." I pointed at Marie. "And if you are a ghost, your hand would've gone right through mine, right?"

She shook her head.

I covered my eyes, just like a small child would do to shut out the scary parts of a movie. I hugged my knees and rested my forehead against them and took slow, deep breaths and whispered as I cried, "This can't be real."

I felt her move close to me, place her hands on my forearms, and gently separate them. My knees dropped to the sides, and I crossed my legs in front of me. But still I kept my eyes shut tight. My whole body buzzed with anticipation until I felt her lean in close.

In the gentlest voice, she said, "Just because I'm not really here doesn't mean this isn't real." She touched her fingers to my chin and lifted my face to hers.

I opened my eyes to see her smiling back at me.

"Hi," she said, brushing my tears away with her thumbs and kissing my cheek. "Oh, how I love you, dear friend." Her voice was steady and sure.

"I miss you so much," I said, barely able to string words together.

She nodded, "I know."

It wasn't lost on me that she hadn't said she missed me, too, and in that moment, it hurt not to hear her say it to me. I would later look back and know that it wasn't possible for her to feel the loss. None of that hurt existed for her.

"You can see?" I said half a question and half a statement.

She leaned in and whispered in my ear, "Nina, 'For now we see in a mirror dimly, but then face to face. Now I know in part; then I shall know fully, even as I have been fully known.'" Her voice was soft but confident.

I shook my head. "I don't understand." It felt like she was speaking in a riddle.

She put her finger to her lips and then touched one hand to my heart, and with the other, she touched her ear. "Listen," she said, still in a whisper. "For now, we see through in a mirror dimly, but then face to face. Now I know in part; then I shall know fully, even as I have been fully known.'"

I recognized the Bible verse, 1 Corinthians 13:12, from the eulogy Suzie had written sixteen years ago. "So, you're okay?" I asked through my tears.

"I am more than okay," her smile confirmed her words.

"How is this happening?" I said and shook my head, trying to make some sort of sense of this. "Am I dying?" I asked. I heard my voice grow frantic. "Am I going crazy?" I said, realizing that must be it. "The stress. Is it making me lose my mind?"

Marie stayed calm through my hysteria, and when I was finally finished and once again focusing on my breathing, she shook her head, "You're not dying." Her voice was so cheerful that I felt confident and relieved when I heard her words. "I'm here because you need me."

"Marie," I said, finally able to settle my voice. "I've needed you so many times. Why now?"

"Because *she* needs *you*," she said, "and you're sort of in a bit of a mess."

I shook my head. "She needs you."

"Well, since that's not a real possibility, you must help her."

"I just feel like we've messed this whole thing up so badly," I said, finally leaning into our conversation. "I mean, Marie, she ran away! She hated me so much that she called her sisters, grabbed her best friend, and took off. She'd rather try to find complete strangers to get answers than come back and work things through with Charles and me."

"Aw, Chuck," she said, tilting her head sideways. She turned and leaned between the seats and stared straight at him, inches from his face. She turned back to me. "He's seriously going gray!" she said and then turned to Walter. "And you," she said, touching his cheek. She took a piece of his hair that wasn't tucked into his backward ball cap and twisted it once around her finger.

At her touch, he turned to face me. I could tell he thought I'd touched him, but when he saw me pressed into the corner of the back seat, he turned back around without a word.

"He really is so handsome," she grinned back at me. She sat back down and faced me again. "Look, you know me. I'm not going to tell you that you did the right thing. You all let Nancy Lynn run the table," she said, pointing her finger in a circle to include everyone in the truck.

"I know," I said, agreeing with her.

"I can't tell you how to make it right, but the best way to find your way out of a jam is to take inventory and use what you've got."

When I didn't respond, she tapped me gently on the forehead and said, "Think."

I smiled. "I guess the biggest thing is that, by the grace of God, Charlie is amazing."

Marie laughed out loud and brought her hands together. "She is!" she said, placing her hand on her chest. "The delight of my heart." She dropped her voice to a whisper. "She's the best thing I ever did."

At her words, I felt a wave of sadness for my friend. For the baby girl she never got to nurse. For the mother who never walked her child into a classroom. For the girl who never held her mother's hand. For the young lady who would never know her biological mother. I envied the fact that Marie couldn't feel grief overwhelm her.

She saw me slipping and took my chin in her hand. "No," she said, her voice firmer. "You have to stay here."

I could only nod.

She let go and shook her own head. "Don't be jealous of me," she said in a whisper, reading my mind. "I mean, don't get me wrong, where I am, well, you'll see someday," she said. "But Nina, you're here, and while you're here, you have to *be* here!" She pressed her hands into and against my knees. Deep inside, I felt the warmth she brought.

I nodded and heard myself saying, "There was a man on the airplane."

She nodded, and I sensed her intensity as she focused on my words, which made me think our time was short.

"He told Charles and me that If we couldn't get rid of the family skeleton, we may as well make it dance."

She nodded, and I went on. "I think that's a super weird way of saying to make the best of the cards you've been dealt."

She surprised me by clapping her hands in delight. "I was hoping you got that!"

"Wait. What?" I said. I was so confused.

She ignored my confusion. "He also said," she paused, and when she spoke again, her voice sounded like the old man from the plane, "Take care to get what you like, or you will be forced to like what you get."

I stared at her, my eyes wide and mouth wide open. I struggled to piece events together, like someone trying to find the right key on a janitor's ring. And then, the right keys slid into place, the barrel turned, and the door opened wide. "That was you?" I asked.

I experienced *déjà vu* on the plane because I had heard the phrase before. The story was Marie's, from when she and her mother took their last trip before she went completely blind.

Marie was ten years old when her doctors said she had six to eight months of functional sight remaining. She and her parents made a list of ten places she wanted to see. They went to Disney World, the Grand Canyon, the Oregon Coast, and Niagara Falls. They visited Yosemite, Zion, and the Great Smoky Mountains National Park. They watched the ball drop in Times Square on New Year's Eve and visited Mackinac Island for the Fourth of July.

Their final destination was Glacier National Park. They stayed at the famous Mini Glacier Hotel and took a Red Bus tour of the park and a boat tour of Josephine Lake. Greta drove the entire length of Going-to-the-Sun-Road, and they walked the boardwalk and gravel Trail of the Cedars. On the final morning, Marie told us that she remembered standing on the balcony of their hotel room and staring without blinking at the water when a perfect reflection of the mountains rose on the other side. She said that even at ten years old, she knew that even if she'd been able to see for a hundred more years, she'd never see another place on earth so beautiful.

On their way home to Baltimore, Marie sat between her mother and a kind old professor who'd been on his way home to Pennsylvania to see his cats and wife, in that order. That's why the story was familiar.

"You remember?" she asked, eyebrows raised, hopeful. "Professor Fig? From Commodore, Pennsylvania?" she said, holding her hands out palm up, like she'd already given me everything I needed.

I shook my head, not believing what I was hearing. "That was you."

"Please tell me you haven't forgotten all the fun we had?"

I shook my head, unable to hide my smile. "I remember everything," I said.

She looked toward the radio, and the music came to an abrupt stop. She turned to me and grinned, "Look," she said in a whisper, pointing out the window behind me.

I turned to look, and without thinking, I asked, "Can you stay?"

The truck slowed, and Walter made the sharp turn onto West Griswold Lane, a narrow access road that was basically an alley put in when the land around the manor house was subdivided and sold.

"I don't know," she said. I watched her smile grow even more electric as we followed the road as it curved wide and around to the right. "But if I can't, this was enough."

With no leaves on the trees and a light dusting of snow sticking only to the grass, the red bricks stood out as The Lady came into view to welcome Marie home.

40

Charlotte

December 2018

In a few short, silent minutes, we'd crossed the bridge over I-83, and my phone's GPS directed us to turn right onto Falls Road. With that turn, the area changed from sketchy to stately. Less than a mile later, we made a left turn onto Harvest and entered a different kind of place.

There was snow on the ground, but the streets and sidewalks were clear, and the sunshine through the trees made everything sparkle.

There was a man running, and he waved as he passed a bundled-up woman pushing a modern stroller that was covered in fuzzy blankets. Two children trailed behind the woman and pulled plastic sleds. They talked and gestured wildly with what appeared to me to be stories of the hills they'd just conquered.

Leia leaned forward. "So, this is the part of the map I studied," she announced mostly to Nora. There's going to be a Y in the road up here, and you'll go to the right." She pointed at a spot on the screen. "That's Edgevale House, so just past the Y, make a quick left. It'll look like an alleyway, but it's a street that was probably added where the original drive—"

"Too much!" Nora interrupted. "I literally just need, like, the next step only."

"Sorry," Leia said. "I got carried away."

Nora glared at her. "Extra!"

"Go right here," Leia said and then clamped her mouth shut.

"Perfect," Margot said and took the right side of the *Y*.

"And now a left, ri-ght…" Leia said, drawing out the *i* in right before she pointed past Nora and said, "Here. Turn here."

A small stone and wood monument sign that read "Edgevale House" was positioned just inside a horseshoe of low, manicured hedges.

"Where?" Nora asked. "Right here?"

"Yes," Leia said, pointing again.

"Here? "

"See the sign?" Leia's calm instantly relaxed Nora, and she nodded and made the turn just in time.

"Holy crap! This is skinny!" she said. The word *skinny* raised her voice two and a half octaves to rival the mice in *Cinderella*. She drew her elbows in close to her sides like that would help her truck 'think skinny' and stay away from the old stone wall that began to gradually rise on the right.

Andrew leaned up beside me. "Is that it?" he asked, pointing up at a gigantic colonial brick home at the top of a hill that was surrounded by a blanket of snow.

Nora slowed to a crawl, another attempt to avoid nudging the stone wall with her truck. Her slowing down also gave us all the chance to get our first good look at Edgevale House as it appeared between the trees. We made our way along the driveway that crawled up the hill in a wide, sweeping circle around the house. The road took us around the back to a paved parking lot. Farther down, we saw a carriage house that had clearly been updated. The parking lot was full, but Leia noticed and pointed to a cobblestone drive that had been cleared of snow and circled around to the front of the house.

Nora nodded again and eased off the pavement and onto the stones. She pulled around to the front of the house and parked at the end of a white gravel path that had also been cleared of snow. The path led up to the enormous, screened porch.

I braced myself, holding tight to the door handle and the armrest. Before I could lose my nerve, I opened the door, climbed out, and walked around to the front of the car. I reached the point where the driveway met the path. I had barely put one foot on the gravel when a woman appeared at the open screen door at the top of the steps.

Her smile was familiar. She looked so put together, but it felt wrong to even think that because she wore a jogging suit. The jacket and pants were color coordinated and fit her perfectly, not too tight and not too loose. She had on a full face of neatly applied but not overdone makeup.

I stood still, sure it was possible to see my heart pounding through my coat.

She was petite, only a couple of inches taller than I was. The ends of her hair lifted with the winter wind, and I watched the sun turn strands into a beautiful mixture of strawberry blonde and light gray that looked hand-painted by subtle brushstrokes. She laughed and pulled a clip from her pocket, then twirled her hair around into a stylish, messy twist and snapped the clip into place.

Still laughing and smoothing down her jacket, she said, "Well, hello, hun." The greeting sounded like a question.

In the same way that a deer stops before it decides to run, I paused and took a small step backward.

She appeared unable to take her eyes away from me like she was looking for something inside me. But with a blink, the moment was gone and replaced with curiosity as she saw the rest of the group forming behind me. "Well, come on in," she said, motioning for us to follow her. "We're on the sun porch this week, and I'll need your gentleman friends to take a couple of chairs in from the parlor," she said.

I looked at my sisters, who had been my guideposts, and the people I followed since I had the ability to follow.

They nodded.

I turned to Leia, her face alight with nervous excitement and pride that she'd navigated us here. Nathan stood at Nora's side, and Andrew tucked my hand into his. Without intending to, we'd formed a circle, and without words, they'd each confirmed they were with me. I nodded and turned to follow the woman I'd never met.

She held the screen door for me until Andrew took it from her with a smile and held it for the group while I walked on. We crossed the porch, went through giant, heavy double front doors, and walked into a spacious center hall. This wide space held an enormous center staircase that rose and wound around us three stories above. I turned in place, trying to take it all in. I was sure I had never been in here before, but every fiber of who I was felt tied to every inch of this place.

"Charlie," Margot had left Nathan's side for the first time since 'Three States,' and she'd dropped her voice to a whisper. "This is…" She lifted a framed snapshot from a table tucked into the nook of the stairs.

Leia and Nora crossed the hall in different directions, finding shelves filled with more photos and a table with an album that was lying open in a place of honor between two large vases of winter roses.

"…you," Nora said, finishing Margot's sentence without looking up from the album.

Leia stepped back to look at something on a top shelf.

When Andrew realized she wanted a better look but couldn't reach it, without words, he left Nathan at my side and went to help her.

As the certainty of the importance of this place overwhelmed me, the warmth and weight of Nathan's hand on my arm felt like the only thing keeping me from floating away.

He somehow must have felt me sway where we stood because he whispered down to me, "Don't you go anywhere, girl. This is just gettin' good."

Andrew and Leia crossed the hall together and returned to where we stood. Leia held out a twin to the photo box that she had taken from her mother. I took it and tried to open it like Nathan had earlier, but nothing happened. I tried again, trying to replicate his movements exactly—still nothing. The lid wouldn't budge.

"I built them to be identical twins, not sisters," I looked up to see the shadow of an older man making his way through the hall.

"What does that mean?" I asked.

He didn't answer but just tapped the side of his head.

We all turned to Margot and Nora, expecting them to understand what he was saying. They were twins, after all.

I handed it to them, and while they both looked at it, I watched them. There were subtle differences in their appearance, hair up versus hair down, eyeliner choices, and even an eyebrow piercing, but none of these things could cover up the fact that they were mirror images of each other, from their dimples on opposite cheeks to their opposite dominant hands.

"Sisters look alike," I said. "Identical mirror twins are mirror images of the same strand of DNA," I said.

Nathan squeezed my arm, and I felt him lift onto his toes, excited at the discovery. "It's a reversal!" he said.

I took the box back and handed it to Nathan. He reversed the moves he'd made earlier. He found the groove quickly and tipped the box on its side. This time, rather than sliding the insert piece up by one inch, he slid it down by one inch. He tipped it back and turned the lid a half turn counterclockwise, lifted the lid again, and held it out to me to lift out the accordion of pictures we all knew would be inside.

The top photo took my breath away. It was Walter sitting and holding a baby on his knees. The photo had been taken from the side. The baby lay on her back on his lap, looking up at him as he cupped her head in his hands.

The pretty, daisy-chained flowers on the wallpaper in the background of the photo were an exact match to the paper on the steps beside us. It had been taken here, in this hall. This meant I had been here before.

The second picture was the same baby but now with Walter and the beautiful woman from the porch.

I pulled the folded photograph from my pocket and compared it to this new one. There were remarkable similarities, but although they were subtle, the differences were there. Her eyes were blue, and the woman from the photograph that we knew to be Marie had brown eyes, just like mine.

One after another, I lifted the photos from the box, one of the baby by herself and one with a couple that was not much older than my parents. Although each photo was different, all of them, at first glance, had two things in common. First, the baby, who I now believed was me, was in every photo. Second, Marie wasn't in a single one.

Without a sound, the man had made his way through the hall to meet us. "Those were taken the day we brought you home." He held out his left hand and pointed to the steps. "Here."

"You're William...Billy," I said, in a voice I didn't recognize.

"I am," he said. He looked in our direction but not quite at us. It was a posture that I'd gotten used to the more I spent time with Nathan. I realized William was blind, or at the very least visually impaired, like me.

"And Greta," I said and turned to where she stood in an open set of French doors that led to a sunny hall.

"Yes." She nodded as she watched me without blinking as the final piece slid into place like one of Billy's puzzle boxes.

"And Marie?" I said.

They waited, watching, not daring to speak for fear they would rush what was coming.

It felt like there was a loosely knit scarf unraveling in my hands. I looked around, feeling more certain than I had about anything else in my life. If she had been able to be there, she would have been. "She's gone?"

"She is," Greta said. She held my gaze.

I nodded with sadness and loss, but I also felt whole for the first time in my life.

"Now, come with me," she reached out and cupped my cheek in her hand. It was an intimate thing to do to someone you've only just met, but somehow it felt like the only right thing. I touched her hand with mine and nodded, not trusting myself to speak, feeling the tears in my eyes.

She smiled and took my hand in hers. "The Ladies of Edgevale House have been waiting a long time," she said as she led me down the hall.

I knew without looking that everyone was behind me, so I wasn't scared when we stepped into the warmth of the sunroom. There were no fewer than ten women sitting around the room, all with yarn projects on their laps in various stages of completion.

"Ladies," Greta said, getting everyone's attention, "although it is a big deal, let's pretend it isn't. This is Charlotte." She looked at me with the sweetest and most proud smile, asking permission.

I smiled at the group. "I'm her granddaughter," I said, beating her to it.

Her smile grew, and she embraced me and rubbed my arm. "Yes." She swallowed back a few tears. "My granddaughter."

"Okay," she said, wiping away tears and clapping her hands together. "Take a seat anywhere." She pointed to an open space, "Extra chairs over here," she said, directing Andrew. "Billy, can you please get the starter kits from the closet on the left?"

"Be glad to," he said, disappearing back through the French doors.

Then she turned and introduced us to The Ladies around the circle. "This is Delphine Prost, one of my oldest and dearest friends."

"Greta!" she said with a sigh. "It is lovely to know how dear I am to you, but I'd appreciate you not telling everyone I am the oldest." She turned back to me. "You can call me

Fifi. Clearly, Betty is older," she said, pointing at the woman sitting to her left.

The circle burst into laughter, and Betty, who was perched on a floral print couch next to Delphine, threw a rude gesture in her direction, causing the room to laugh even harder.

In a much quieter voice, she said, "My dear..." Fifi paused, overcome with emotion. She took my hand in hers and squeezed it before she went on. "You are going to hear this all the way around, but let me be the first to say you look so much like your mother, like Marie," she said, correcting herself.

"It's okay," I said and squeezed her hand back. Somehow, I knew that she and every woman in this room needed to know.

"You..." Her words caught in her throat, and she shook her head, unable to speak.

She held my hand a bit longer, squeezed it tight, and then let go.

"Now, I don't want this to feel like a receiving line at a wedding reception," Greta said. "If it's okay with you, you'll just get to be an honorary member of the knit club, and we'll talk to you like you've been here forever." She led me to an empty seat on one end of a light blue, crushed velvet couch.

"That sounds good," I said.

"Sit, sit," Greta said, waving everyone else into the empty spaces. She patted the shoulders of each twin. "Nora and Margot, right?" She looked between them, "No, wait, reverse that. Margot and Nora."

They looked stunned that she had gotten names right without a guess.

"It's the dimples," she said, pointing to her cheeks. She sent them to the empty ends of a long, French country sofa near a matching loveseat.

"And you, sweet girl, must be Suzie's oldest daughter," she said, holding Leia by the shoulders at arm's length. "My goodness, you favor her, but I think, much like your daddy here," she said, tapping the side of her head just as Billy had done before. "A thinker, I bet."

"Yes, ma'am. Thank you for having us," she said with manners that would have made her mother proud.

"Oh, my dear…" Greta paused, waiting for Leia to answer a question she hadn't asked.

"Leia," she answered.

"Leia," Greta said. "I have always told your mother she needed to bring her girls and that handsome John."

"You knew them?" Leia said, still working hard to wrap her brain around everything.

Greta held up a finger. "I did…I do," she corrected herself. "A friendship like the one Marie had with your mothers," she shook her head, searching for the words, "a friendship like that has the ability to stretch, like a ribbon, across miles, years, and generations." She kept shaking her head. "It astounded me then, and it astounds me today."

She turned Leia and gently sent her in the direction of the couch to the left of mine.

Her focus settled on the boys. Nathan had placed his parlor chair at the end of the couch where Margot sat.

Andrew had settled on a space across the circle from me next to a neat, put-together woman with excellent posture, light brown hair, freshly applied lipstick, and beautiful statement jewelry.

"I'm Andrew Walton," he said to the woman he'd set his parlor chair down beside, even though it was actually an answer to Greta's questioning eyes.

"And I'm Linda Morris," she said in a way that was so genuine that it made you feel like she'd been waiting her whole life to meet you. "It is nice to meet you." She turned to me. "I was your mother's teacher from about the middle of fourth grade until she graduated high school."

"Wow," I said, realizing what Greta had meant when she said they'd been waiting a long time.

Greta picked up the story, "Yes, the Lindas were quite the pair!" she said, smiling.

"The Lindas?" I asked. "There was more than one Linda?"

"Oh yes. There were two of us," Linda Morris said. "I was the softie, and Linda Brooks, well, let's just say your mother couldn't get anything by her." She laughed. "But she's no longer with us."

I wasn't quite sure how to respond.

"Linda!" came a voice from two seats to my left.

I leaned forward to see a woman with long, sandy blonde hair half up in a clip and the other half down and spilling over her shoulders. Even though she was sitting, I could tell she was tall.

"I'm Evelyn Colgate," she said, with her palm to her chest. Then she patted the knee of the person next to her. "And this is my husband, Pluto. We lived across the hall from your mother."

I leaned farther out and was surprised to see a man of about the same age sitting next to her. In place of a knitting project, he held a magazine and had a newspaper tucked in beside him.

He looked completely out of place among The Ladies of Edgevale House, but he also looked comfortable and even happy to be there.

Evelyn went on. "Linda has made it sound as though Linda Brooks is 'no longer with us.'" She made air quotes around her words. "Well, Linda is most definitely not," she pointed up, and I took that to mean she was talking about heaven. Her eyes sparkled with the story that was coming.

"Oh," I said, feeling relief.

"It was quite the scandal," she said.

"Really?" Leia said and leaned in, not wanting to miss a detail.

"After Marie graduated from college and moved into the big house, there was an incident." Evelyn paused, and it appeared she was considering her audience. "Let's just say the man that sweet Marie thought was an intruder most certainly was not.

The room burst into laughter again.

"Anyway," Evelyn said, maintaining her poise. "Mr. Not An Intruder turned out to be an important person at McDonogh School."

She paused to knit a stitch or two. "And if you're wondering," she said, holding up her pointer finger, "there wasn't anything nefarious about their relationship." She did another quick stitch and then held her finger up again. "And he proposed to her less than a week later."

Pluto rubbed her knee as the room filled with laughter again.

"He retired not long after, and we don't see much of her these days. They spend the summer in Ocean Pines out on the bay and winter down in Florida." Evelyn said.

Billy came back in with a box of neatly lined up, clear, zip-top plastic bags.

Greta stood, took the box, and thanked him with a kiss. He sat in a chair next to Greta's end of the loveseat as she handed out six knitting starter kits.

"Did you know that Walt and Charles were both knitters before I even met them?" Greta asked.

"I didn't know that," I said, unable to imagine my dad or Walter with knitting needles.

The woman sharing the loveseat with Leia jumped into the conversation with excitement. "Oh yes!" She had a child's voice, even though she was an older woman. "I'm Claudine Santangelo, but everyone has always called me Lucky. Can you believe someone would do that to a child?"

I shook my head, not sure what she meant.

"Like that girl in the Jackie Collins novels?" Nora said.

Lucky squealed and clapped her hands together, "Yes!"

"Who's Jackie Collins?" I asked.

"A British romance writer," Nora said. "And you tell me I need to read more."

Mable laughed as we all turned to her. "In the seventeen years I've known Lucky, you are probably only the third or fourth person to know who Lucky Santangelo is."

Nora smiled at Lucky. "Glad I could bring up your numbers," Nora said with a wink.

"Me too!" Lucky laughed.

She turned to Delphine. "Fifi, do you remember the day Walt moved in?"

Fifi laughed. "How could I forget? That was the day Mable ruined everything!"

Through her laughter, Mable said, "Fifi, I told you then, and I'll tell you now, it was my turn!"

"Your mother sat on that couch, only it was on the front porch because it was summer," Fifi said, pointing at where I was sitting.

Mable leaned over and patted me on the knee. "Knit club is on the porch in the summer," she said as an aside.

Fifi continued like Mable hadn't interrupted. "I know because that's where Marie always sat. It was her favorite spot." I watched her face soften as she relaxed into the memory. "We watched him fix her dropped stitch, and we watched her fall in love."

The room fell into a reverent silence as they remembered Marie.

"She was remarkable," Pluto said, taking Evelyn's hand. "Your mother had a way with people." He swallowed hard as he looked around at all the tears. "We know you don't know us, but you should know that through the pictures your mom has shared with Greta and Billy over the years we've known you, loved you, and prayed for you since before you were even born."

Evelyn nodded, still unable to speak.

"Or at least I think that's what The Ladies of Edgevale would say if they'd stop crying!" he said with a smile.

Again, the room was full of laughter, the kind of laughter that fills you up, heals your heart, and gives you courage for whatever comes next.

As they settled down, the room returned to playful conversation. We talked for a long time about all sorts of things. As we talked and the afternoon stretched, I watched the shadows move and lean their way across the room. Even though I knew it was cold outside, the room felt warm, like a place meant for sleepy Sunday afternoon naps.

I shut my eyes, feeling the hint of pain at my temples, a promise that a headache was coming if I didn't do something. I listened to the sweet lilt of Linda's voice as she walked Andrew through his first line of stitches for the third time.

The day had started so early, and it felt like I'd lived a lifetime between then and now. This was the first time I'd let myself take just a second to relax.

I thought it was just a moment, but it must have been longer because the conversations around me skipped and didn't quite make sense.

I felt a gentle hand on my shoulder, and Greta whispered, "Are you okay?"

"Yes, ma'am, I'm just..." I started, feeling embarrassed and looking for the right words. "I'm sorry, I just suddenly got so tired. I guess the day is catching up with me. Is there somewhere I could lie down just for a bit?"

"Of course," she said, patting my hand. We stood, and I took my bag from the floor.

"Do you want me to come with you?" Margot offered. "I don't mind at all."

"I'm fine. I'm just really tired. It sort of just snuck up on me. I can hardly keep my eyes open. I think I just need to lie down for a few minutes. Thank you, though."

"Okay." Margot said. "I can come check on you in a few."

"It's okay, really." I thought it might bother her not to come with me, but I wanted to be by myself. I couldn't stop my mind from spinning. All I wanted was to close my eyes and make the spinning stop.

I followed Greta down the hall and through a set of French doors into what felt like a sunny sitting room. We walked past a small kitchen and down another narrow hall. We passed a closed door, and farther down at the end of the hall was a bedroom.

Greta reached for my bag. "I'll just set this right here at the end of the bed," Greta set my bag down on a cushioned bench. "And I'll just shut these," she said as she walked to the windows and pulled the curtains closed.

I watched as she crossed the room.

"And there's a bathroom right in here." She rested her hand on the door frame. Her shoulders rose and fell as she took a deep breath.

Even though all I wanted was to close my eyes and just stop feeling everything, I could tell it was the opposite for her. She needed to feel it all. She'd been waiting for a long time to feel everything.

I took a few steps to close the distance between us, took hold of her hand, and whispered, "Thank you."

She turned and rested her hand on my arm. "I'm just so glad you're finally here." Her eyes shined with tears.

I was going to tell her, "Me, too," and hug her and wait for her to leave. I was going to get my migraine medicine that was always in my bag, and I was going to take a tablet, and if that didn't help, I was going to take another, and if that didn't stop the hurt, I was going to take another. I was going to take another and another and another until I couldn't feel... until the roaring all around me stopped. But instead, I found myself holding onto her sleeve and saying what I hadn't been able to since we'd arrived.

"I thought I'd find her here. I thought she'd be able to tell me what happened. I thought I'd hear her voice and everything would make sense. I thought—" I stopped talking, afraid if I went any further, I wouldn't be able to stop.

Greta reached up and rested her hand on my cheek. "That's too much for one girl to think all on her own."

I nodded, not trusting myself to say anything else.

She nodded, too. "I'm gonna let you rest. We're close by if you need anything." She smiled and turned to go but stopped at the door. "We moved to Edgevale when Marie was little. Maybe a couple of years older than your baby brother. She grew up here, and even though she's been gone for some time now, I still see her all around." She rested her hand on the doorknob and looked back at me, really taking me in. "Not in a weird ghost sort of way, but like an echo of her in all her favorite places. It's a special place," she said, closing her eyes and breathing in the moment. She opened them and smiled at me again. "I really am glad you found your way here."

Once she was gone, I stood in the bathroom with my eyes closed and head resting against the door frame for what felt like a long time, trying to steady myself. I opened my eyes and caught a glimpse of my reflection in the mirror above the sink. Everything about me was the same. Walking closer, I reached up and touched the edges of the bruises around my neck.

They were now barely visible, especially if you didn't know they were there. But I knew.

I opened the mirror to the medicine cabinet behind me. There were only a few things inside: a toothbrush still in the package, a small tube of toothpaste, dental floss, a bottle of acetaminophen with the plastic still around the top, a bar of Dove soap still in its box, a mini deodorant, and little bottles of shampoo and conditioner. It was all the stuff you'd have for someone visiting in case they forgot something. I took the acetaminophen from the top shelf and heard the pills rattle like teeth inside.

The last forty-eight hours pressed so heavily against me. She was supposed to be here to tell me who I was supposed to be. I was supposed to find her, and she was supposed to tell me it would all be okay. I'd come all this way thinking it would fix everything inside me that was broken and wrong.

The plastic seal pulled away easily, and when the raised arrows on the rim of the bottle were pointing at each other, I took the top off easily.

Everything I felt so sure about had unraveled so quickly. I'd taken everyone I loved on what I thought would be an adventure to answer all the questions I had, but I'd only created more questions and destroyed the trust they had in their parents.

I tipped the bottle and felt the pills tumble into my hand in slow motion. Each pill felt connected to the people I'd dragged with me. Their faces flashed against my closed eyelids.

Margot and Nora dropped everything and came to get me. Leia, who would have followed me to the ends of the earth. And Nathan and Andrew, who deserved someone so much stronger than me, a friend as strong as they were. I'd dragged them seven hundred miles on a wild goose chase. All for nothing.

I opened my eyes and was startled to see a flash in the mirror and feel movement behind me. I turned to see who was there, but no one was there.

"Who's there?" I said to the emptiness around me.

A single note ping made me jump, and the hairs on my arms stood on end. The sound had come from a small music box on the dresser to my left.

I let the pills slide back into the bottle and set the bottle on the counter. I walked to the music box as though being pulled and couldn't help but reach out and touch the glass piano sitting on a mirror. It was cool under my fingers. I lifted it and turned it on its side to find a winding knob on the bottom. I twisted it a couple of times, and it began to play what I instantly recognized as "Moonlight Sonata." I went to place it back on the dresser top and noticed that a brass key had been hidden underneath. I set down the music box and took the key.

I looked around the room and saw a keyhole in the top drawer of the dresser, but when I pulled on the handle, the drawer slid open easily, and there were hand towels and washcloths neatly folded inside.

Key in hand, I turned and looked around the room, still unsettled about the medicine bottle that I'd left resting on the bathroom counter and the feeling that I wasn't alone. I didn't see anything that was locked along the walls—just the long dresser where I'd found the music box and key, an armchair that looked like it might rock, nightstands on both sides of the bed, and a tall dresser between the bathroom and the closed door that was probably a closet.

I walked over to it and tried to fit the key into the lock, but of course, it didn't fit. The lock was much newer than the key in my hand.

I turned, leaned my back against the door, and slid to sit the same way I'd done at the hospital. I hugged my knees and rested my forehead against my arms. I sat for a long time and must have dozed off because I jumped at the sound of the key hitting the floor and bouncing forward to land on the rug.

A creaking noise to my left drew my attention, and I turned to see a slinky orange cat making its way into the room. He wound his way around the legs of the dresser and then crossed the room and disappeared under the bed only to reappear on the other side. He had a blue collar with a bell that jingled as the bed skirt brushed against it. He sat down and stared at me like he was sizing me up. After a long moment, he made his way over to sniff my shoes, turned, sniffed the key as he passed, and hopped on top of an old chest at the foot of the bed. Then he turned to face me, positioning himself like a sphinx.

When I pushed myself to my knees to reach out and pick up the key, I found myself face to face with the keyhole in the trunk.

I held it up and saw that the metal plate on the trunk matched. Without stopping to think, I slid the key into the lock, and it turned. I felt something inside my chest flutter like butterflies in a box.

The cat, still watching me, stood up and hopped from the trunk to the bed.

The lid didn't make a sound as I lifted it and looked inside.

I'm not sure what I expected, but it was definitely not what I found. There were rows and rows of old CDs with rubber bands bundling them into groups.

I pulled a bundle from the middle, and there was a note in neat, mid-sized print that read, "101.9 WLIF 2002 Rebrand Commercials." I set them on the floor beside me and noticed that the group I'd taken out revealed that the discs were stacked at least two levels deep.

I pulled out a few more bundles that also had handwritten notes: "Orioles 1998-2001" and "103.1 WPOC 1999, 2000, 2001 Commercial-Country." Two bundles were labeled "Audible Auditions 1997, 1998, 1999, 2000, & 2001," and a single disc was labeled "9/11 PSAs." Underneath there was a small silver radio/CD player.

I lifted it out. None of the notes made any sense to me, but because I knew what 9/11 was, I started with the one at the top of that stack. The rubber band made a weird stretching noise as I pulled the top one out, and the disc clicked as I popped it out of the case. It took a second to open the player, but when I finally figured it out, I was surprised to find that there was already a CD inside.

"Holy shit," I whispered, reading the words printed neatly on its shiny surface. "Walt & Marie Fun 2001." "Walt & Marie" winked up at me like they'd been waiting sixteen years for me to find them written there.

The cat watched me as I closed the lid and scooted across the floor to the nightstand. I followed the lamp cord down to where it was plugged into the wall and yanked it out. As quickly as I could manage, I fumbled the player's plug into the outlet. My heart raced as the machine started to make crunching sounds, and the digital display started flashing a double red eight as it came alive. I pushed the decorative pillows out of the way and climbed onto the bed while kicking my shoes off and letting them fall to the floor with a thud.

Instead of running away with all the movement, the cat moved closer as I crossed my legs in front of me and leaned over, holding my breath as I pressed the play arrow and listened as the disc inside spun to life.

The first voice that came through the speakers was like my dad's, only different. It was slower and somehow more familiar to me in a place deep inside.

"Test, test," he said and cleared his throat. A sound swiped across the microphone, and then he spoke again. You could tell he'd moved closer. "This is an interview," only the way he said it, there was no *T*. He said, "innerview."

I heard a woman's laugh, and as she moved close to the microphone, the cat moved closer to me. He placed his paws on my leg, and without thinking about it, I let him curl himself into my lap and listen.

"So, you're interviewing me, or I'm interviewing you?"

"I'm interviewing you," he said.

"Okay," she said, and I heard the smile in her voice. "Did you push record?"

"I think so," he said. I heard tapping, "I push this one, right?"

"Yeah, and then this one to cancel background noise," she said.

"Got it," he said. A moment later, the sound got crisper. "Okay, state your name for the record."

His voice was mockingly serious.

She dropped her tone to match. "Marie Collie-Ricks."

I knew who she was, but hearing her say her name gave me goosebumps.

"Okay, Marie, tell me something I don't already know."

"Okay," she said, "but you have to promise never to tell my mom."

"What about Fifi?"

"Nope! You can't tell anyone."

As they spoke, I heard them get closer to the recorder and closer to each other. I curled into a ball and relaxed into the pillows. As I listened, I felt the cat settle into the space between my knees and chest and start to purr. I closed my eyes, sure that if I closed my eyes I'd be able to see them.

"My favorite color isn't pink."

"Lies," he said, laughing.

"No, really, it isn't!"

"No, I don't believe it," he said, still laughing. In my mind, I saw him shaking his head.

I felt her sit at the end of the bed, one foot still on the floor and one leg tucked under her. I opened my eyes to see.

"Was it yellow?" I asked, unable to take my eyes off her. She was so much like me but still just different enough.

"How'd you know?" she asked. And like the scattered fragments inside of a kaleidoscope, something shifted inside me and went from beautiful nothing to beautiful something.

"It's always been my favorite, and I just thought…"

She nodded, and my words slipped away.

"I know this is a dream," I said, unable to look away or even blink, not wanting to risk her not being there when I opened my eyes again. "I thought you'd be here. I wanted you to help me."

She pulled her other foot up onto the bed and crossed her legs in front of her. I sat up to mirror her. For a moment, nothing else in the world mattered.

She reached out and touched the silver bracelet on my wrist.

"It was in the box," I said. "Aunt Suzie's photo box." I felt the tips of her fingers against my skin, and she felt so real. "It was yours, wasn't it?"

"It was," she said, nodding. "But it's yours now." She closed her eyes, and we both sat still for what felt like a long time, her hand resting on my wrist and my heart beating right there under her fingertips.

"Are you okay?" I asked, and it felt like I was tiptoeing on the edge of crazy.

She opened her eyes and looked deep into mine. "I never got to hold you." The words came out small, and she knotted her fingers together as though she was holding onto the moment. "I heard you cry, but I was never able to touch you." It looked like it physically hurt her to be so close.

"I didn't know," I said, with tears on my cheeks. "I didn't know about any of it."

"I'm sorry I wasn't here." Her words were so full and honest.

"I thought you'd be here at Edgevale House. I thought you'd be able to tell me who I am."

She shut her eyes again and reached out and took my hand in hers. I felt her and the warmth of the mother-daughter connection between us. She could have said something stupid and insignificant, something that most adults would say without thinking, just to make me feel better, but she didn't. She spoke the truth.

She opened her big brown eyes—my big brown eyes—and more certain than I'd ever heard anything said before, she stated, "You are mine!"

I nodded and looked down at her hand in my hand. I was wanted. I was loved. I was hers.

I felt the rumble of something that I knew was outside, but that I could somehow feel deep inside, like I'd felt it before.

"But that's not all," I said, looking up at her.

She shook her head just once and tilted it toward the dark corner of the room.

I sat up with what felt like a real electric current running through me. The CD player had cycled through the tracks and was now silent, the display glowing "STBY." Someone must have come to check on me because the blanket was over me. The place at the end of the bed where Marie had been sitting was now empty, but I still heard the echo of her voice.

I wasn't alone.

41

Marie

December 2018

I can't tell you about all the times I've fallen in love, but I can tell you about the last time I fell in love.

Most mothers experience this when their babies are born, but I didn't have that chance. That wasn't in His plan for me. I fell in love for the last time as I stood breathing in the familiar space around me, unseen by everyone but Nina, who somehow held an invisible string connecting us through time and space.

At that moment, I felt everything. Even though I knew with every fiber of my soul that it wasn't possible, I felt a heartbeat in my chest, air in my lungs, and a tingle in my skin. Even though I knew it wasn't real, it felt more real than anything I'd ever experienced before.

I watched Poky languidly stretch himself into an arch and then walk off the side of the bed. He wove himself between my legs and despite his age, he made an effortless jump to the back of the chair.

"She's…." I squeezed Nina's arm, but she didn't need me to complete my sentence.

She nodded, never taking her eyes off our beautiful girl.

The world around us slowed to a stop. I had to remind myself not to wish it never to end, but rather to delight in the power of right now.

Charlotte turned to find Nina, knees curled into the armchair in the corner of the room that Walt and I had planned to bring her home to sixteen years before. I watched them each take in the other, surer with every passing moment that we'd made the right decision in the months before she was born. The decision had been emotional, as those sorts of adult conversations often are. No one could replace us. No home would be the same as ours, but we'd decided that if anything were to happen to us, Nina and Charles would give Charlotte the love and support she needed. They were family. She would grow up with her cousins who would be like sisters.

Nina shifted in her chair and crossed her legs in front of her. She leaned forward and drew in a deep breath, getting ready to speak, but Charlotte beat her to it.

"I heard them," Charlotte said, her voice small but determined. "They sounded happy—like really happy."

Nina smiled and nodded, "They were."

"They made a recording," Charlotte said, glancing back at a small CD player on the nightstand behind her.

Nina nodded.

"You can't do that to me anymore," Charlotte snapped.

The edge to her voice caused Nina to sit up straight and her gentle smile to disappear.

"Okay," Nina said, with such sincerity that Charlotte couldn't argue. She set her feet down on the floor and leaned in, remembering, "They made a lot of recordings. It was sort of their thing."

Charlotte got off the bed and went around to the large chest at the foot. She swung the latches and lifted the top. "Was it her job or something because there are a thousand of these," she said as she pulled out a bundle of discs and held them up.

"It was," Nina said, unable to hide her smile. "She worked for a radio station and made commercials for all kinds of things, like the animal shelter and local restaurants. When she was pregnant with you, she started to narrate audiobooks. She even did a few spots for the Orioles, I think."

I could tell by the look on her face and the brightness in her tone that she'd let herself slip into a memory, but when Charlotte didn't respond, Nina settled and clarified, "The baseball team here in Baltimore."

"Oh," Charlotte said and turned away, looking back into the chest. "So, these are all her." Her words came out softly like she was talking to herself.

They sat for a while—Charlotte examining the large print labels of the CDs and Nina watching her in a way that could only be described as relief. I could see her waiting for the right moment and courage.

"Charlie," she said, sliding off the chair and onto the floor beside her. "These are all yours. They were sorted and put away for you."

Charlotte nodded, pressing her lips together. It was something Nina used to do, like holding onto her next words to make sure they were just right before she let them loose into the world.

"Charlie," Nina said.

Charlotte looked up at her mother, waiting, needing her next words to be right.

"I'm sorry."

Charlotte opened her mouth like she wanted to say something, but nothing came out.

"Your mother..." Nina closed her eyes for just a moment and then opened them and looked at me.

I nodded, doing what I could to urge her to go on.

"Marie, your mother, was..." She ran her hand through her hair, tangled her fingers in the ends, and held on tight. "I don't even know how to start, except that she was the best person I've ever known. And losing her was the hardest thing I've ever had to walk through."

"I know," Charlotte said. "I know why you did it, why you lied. I mean, I think I do." She set down the discs and turned to face Nina. "I don't think it was right, but I think now I get it."

Nina started to defend herself but then changed course. "She was my best friend, and when they got married, she was my sister. I talked to her every day. Back then, probably even more than I talked to Aunt Suzie."

Charlotte listened, brown eyes looking deep, searching for cracks, finding none.

"When she died, we were told that she and Walt had made a plan. If anything happened to them, they wanted you to be with us." Her voice slipped into a whisper. She took a breath, swallowed hard, and pushed forward. "To this day, I don't know how Nancy Lynn managed to take so much control, but Walt showed up with her and this list of rules." She held out her hands as though she were holding an invisible basket. She knotted her fists and went on. "If we wanted to honor Marie's wishes, we had to follow these rules."

"What were the rules?" Charlotte asked.

She dropped her hands into her lap, and I imagined Nancy Lynn's basket of rules falling, shattering into a million pieces on the floor between them.

"I don't remember all of them now, but the most important one was that we had to agree to keep the adoption a secret, or at least your biological parents a secret. I think," she said, pulling at a string on the end of her shirt, "we'd just buried your mom. We were so afraid that we'd lose you." Her voice broke, but she spoke through her tears. "That's not an excuse. We had so many chances to tell you the truth. There was a clause that gave us the ability to tell you if it became medically necessary. We could have." She swallowed and sat up straighter, forcing herself to stop and start again. "We should have told you as soon as all this started. We kept meaning to..." She stopped, her words leaving a trail like a stone being skipped across a river.

"But you got sick," Charlotte said with certainty.

"What do you mean?" Nina said, lost in the fog of memory.

"When you went away. Nora and Margot said they heard you and Dad arguing. He told you to go and get better. That your heart was sick." Charlotte kept talking, never taking her eyes off her mother. "Because you missed your friend." She dropped her eyes to her lap. "I know that sometimes everything can look fine on the outside, but you can be sick on the inside, like in your head and your heart. Like from sadness or not knowing how to fix something that feels really broken."

Charlotte nodded to herself, and Marie sat still, holding her breath. I saw that she understood that her daughter's words were, in part, forgiveness and, at the same time, a confession.

"But you're okay now?" Charlotte asked.

"Yes," Nina nodded and then, realizing her answer was too quick and added, "I will be."

"Okay," she said and nodded. "That's good."

"And you?" Nina asked, treading so carefully.

"I'm okay," Charlotte said without blinking or looking away. "You know the next year is gonna be hard, right?"

"I do," Nina said.

"And the leaving when it gets hard part?" Charlotte asked,

"I won't," Nina said without hesitation.

They sat for a few more seconds, and neither looked away. Then, finding what she was looking for, Charlotte closed the distance between them and fell into her mother's arms.

Charlotte's relief was tangible, and with it came an onset of questions. "How did you get here? How did you get here so fast? Is Daddy here?"

Nina pulled away and held her at arm's length. "Yes, Daddy's here. We flew. It was sort of an adventure, which I'll tell you all about later, but there's something you need to know."

Charlotte nodded, holding her stare.

"Walt is here."

The look on Charlotte's face reminded Nina of riding a roller coaster for the first time, a thing you'd dreamed about being tall enough to do for as long as you can remember. She'd started this journey to unwind the knots of her truth and confront the people who had spun the lies. Now, it was right on top of her. The feelings were almost too much to hold onto.

"Here," she said, more to herself and the space around her. "He's here," she nodded and pressed her hands against the floor beside her. Without warning, she said, "Okay," again, more to herself than anything or anyone else, flexed her hands, balled them into fists, and walked out of the room.

Back in the center hall, she retraced her path back to the sunroom with Nina right behind her. She stopped at the door and took a quick look around.

"How long was I asleep?" she asked with her lopsided smile.

Andrew looked up from his lap. "Apparently, I'm a better knitter than your dad," he said. It was a smile meant only for Charlotte, and it lit up his whole face. "You wanna sit?"

She smiled back at him and said, "I want to, but I can't."

She looked at Charles. Charles looked at Nina. Nina looked at Charlotte and then looked out the window. I couldn't take my eyes off her as she looked with Nina across the snowy lawn and down the hill to where I knew he would be.

I saw the muscles in Charlotte's jaw tighten, and her expression darken. Before giving herself a chance to change her mind, she turned and disappeared through the door, leaving the room in stunned silence.

Nina gave them all a pleading look and turned to follow, knowing the entire room would be right behind her.

As she walked, Charlotte slipped a hairband from her wrist and snatched her hair into a quick ponytail that shifted back and forth as she made her way down the hall and out the front door.

She stepped onto the front porch of my parents' home and took my breath away. The winter air hit her in the same way because I saw her cheeks turn pink, but she didn't slow down. In fact, it appeared that she picked up speed as she crossed the porch and pushed open the screen door. She was already down the steps and crossing the gravel path when the door snapped closed behind her. She slowed for a moment, and only when she passed the huge white truck in the drive. It was empty, but she didn't have to see the owner in the driver's seat to know whose it was.

Again, anticipating what was about to happen, I felt everything beat in my chest. I felt winter air in my lungs. I felt the tingle of snowflakes on my skin. Even though I knew it wasn't real, I was there. I saw my child.

So many people had told me what it would feel like to see and hold my baby for the first time. They told me to expect an instant, internal answer to the question, "Will I know how to love this child like she needs to be loved and deserves to be loved?" They also told me that those first questions of insecurity would immediately be replaced with a new one that was just as important. "How could I possibly love anything more?"

I left Nina's side and closed the distance between Charlotte and me. She'd already made it halfway down the hill when I caught up, but only because she'd stopped when she saw Walt standing at the *hem*, just outside the gazebo and only steps away from where we got married. I stepped in front of her, which allowed us to stand eye to eye, but Charlotte looked past me, through me, and down at Walt, willing him to turn.

I looked at Nina over her shoulder, and she nodded, urging me to let her go. I turned back to Charlotte and reached and touched her face for just a moment. She brought her hand to her cheek where my fingers had been. With every piece of me that connected me to this earth, I willed her to see me. I wanted to fill the doubt that I knew she hid in her heart.

From behind her, my mother stepped onto the porch. Daddy waited in comfortable familiarity, one shoulder leaning against the door frame.

Finally, with sweet relief, for the briefest moment, I saw Charlotte shift. She stopped looking through me and looked right at me. She wasn't looking at Walt, who'd turned to face her. She was looking at me. She saw me. I saw her lips move and felt her whisper my name from somewhere inside me.

"Marie," she said, and it was no louder than a breath, but it was everything, and it was enough. She shut her eyes tight and then opened them again. Like a blink, the moment was gone.

I was back at the porch and climbed the four wide, painted, wooden steps and crossed to the doorway where Daddy was leaning. I came close and thought he was watching me. He gave a funny smile, and that's when I knew it wasn't just a thought or a feeling. "You can see me?" I asked in a whisper.

"I felt you first," he said, his voice low, matching mine. "I couldn't see you until you came close."

I reached out and wiped a tear that was sliding down his cheek.

"You did good girl—really, really good," he said.

I leaned into his flannel shirt, soft against my cheek, and breathed in the smell of him. He stroked my hair once from the top of my head to the base of my ponytail. He twirled it around his finger and ran his hand all the way to the ends in the most endearing and familiar way like he did when I was little. The gesture meant more than anything he could have said.

I stepped away from him and felt something inside me slide sideways and fade. I felt that whatever had brought me here was telling me my time was short.

I turned and was beside Charlotte again, where she stood watching Walt.

She stepped forward. I watched her eyes flare with anger. She walked toward him. Her first couple of steps were timid and slow, but as she advanced on him, Walt must have seen the fire in her eyes because he took a single step backward, losing his footing on the low step up to the gazebo platform. He turned to catch himself, but when she was only a couple of feet from him, he turned back to face her, ready, knowing he deserved anything she had to give.

Faster than a reflex, she lifted her hands, slammed both fists into his chest, and screamed, "Why?"

At the sound of her pain, my heart broke apart, and I could see his did, too.

At the same time, Nina and a boy on the porch moved toward her to help. Charles reached out to hold Nina back, and Margot and Nora each held the boy's arms to keep him from going to her.

"Why are you even here?" Charlotte cried.

He opened his mouth to speak, but she didn't let him.

"I've been here for sixteen years! Sixteen birthdays! Sixteen Christmases! Five thousand, eight hundred forty-one days! I thought about it the whole way here," she cried, pounding her fists into his chest over and over, and he never moved. He never blocked her. The force of her blows pushed him backward until he was trapped against the gazebo railing.

"I was there the whole time!" she said, pointing her finger into his chest at every moment of their shared past all at once. She stepped back from him, wiping tears from her face. Still crying, she pointed to the floor below her feet where he and I had taken our wedding vows and whispered, "I was here!" The sleeves of her hoodie had slipped over her hands. She balled the loose fabric in her fists, brought them to her face, and screamed into them with everything she had left.

The commotion had brought everyone to the porch, and they watched in stunned silence as the wind swirled around two hurt people.

Charlotte pulled something from her hoodie pocket and thrust it out to him. The accordion of photos she'd taken from inside unfolded in front of him as she held it inches from his face.

Tears ran down her cheeks, openly with the innocence of a small child, wanting desperately to understand. But then, without warning, her face darkened. "What happened to him?" she asked, teeth clenched, voice low, like a growl, so angry she was shaking. "He looks like he loved that baby."

Walt looked back at her and nodded. He set his jaw, but tears streamed from his eyes.

She snatched the photos back from him and pointed to one. "That's you, right?" she demanded.

He nodded and mouthed the word "Yes."

"And that's me, right?" She said, pointing at the baby cradled in his arms.

"Yes."

She pushed the picture back into his face, "Where did you go, and how could you leave me?" She dropped the pictures, which shattered into a million pieces on the floor between them. She hit him again, but this time, when her fists hit him, she collapsed into him, sobbing. She had nothing left.

I watched him put his arms around her and apologize over and over.

He looked up, and our eyes met. I saw recognition on his face. I saw him trying to gauge if I was something only he could see.

I nodded, encouraging him.

With a gentle hand, he moved her so he was looking right at her, right into her eyes. He took her face in his hands for a moment, and she let him wipe her tears with his thumbs.

"Charlotte, it wasn't just one thing." His words came out in a rush. "It was a million things." I heard the shake in his breath, "Alone, all of 'em..." He let go of trying to put together his thoughts. He lifted his cap, messed his hair forward and back, and then flattened it before putting it back on. "On their own, they were manageable, but all put together," he said, bringing his palms together flat, "they were just too much to carry." He looked down at the pictures as he spoke. "I didn't know how to be strong without her." He looked back up at her. "I still don't, and for that, I'm sorry. When I lost Marie, I lost my faith, I lost myself, and the worst of it is, I lost you. After Marie died, I saw her everywhere. The store, walkin' around the neighborhood, and here," he said, opening his hands wide to Edgevale House and the land around them. "Always here. She's always here." His words came out as a sobbing whisper.

"Charlotte," he said, and her name in his voice felt like a salve on her brokenness. "I let other people tell me how to live without Marie. I let them tell me what was best for me and what was best for you, and that was wrong," he said, shaking his head. "I can't take it back, but I can spend every day from today until forever tryin' to make things right again."

Charlotte gave him a slow nod, not in agreement but an acknowledgment of an agreement.

"And that's only if you even wanna know me. And you don't have to answer now. Take time. As much time as you—"

"I don't need more time," she said, interrupting him.

Her voice was strong, and her face was serious and unreadable. I could see Walt holding his breath.

"I want to know you, but it doesn't have anything to do with you," she said, her voice rising with emotion as she turned to look over her shoulder and back up at Edgevale House. "I want to know you because I want to know her."

Charlotte turned back to Nina and Charles, her hands in fists at her sides. She closed her eyes, choosing her words. "I am so mad about what you did. You forced them to lie to everyone!" she said, throwing her arm out to the side and behind her. "They lied to everyone, the twins, Wade, and your girls. You made Leia's parents lie, too," she said, pointing back at her best friend. "You hurt so many people!" Her chest heaved, trying to take in air as her anger reached its peak, and her face began to soften.

"But you'd lost your best friend. You were broken, and I know what being broken feels like." Her hand went reflexively to her neck, where I noticed a red mark on her skin just under the edge of the turtleneck she wore under her hoodie.

She turned to see her sisters, her best friend, the two boys who had believed in them enough to come all this way to help, and she said, "I can't imagine what I'd do if I lost any of them," she said. She turned back to Walt. "There has to be grace for that. There has to be a chance to make things right again. I don't know what that looks like, but I think we can figure it out."

Walt reached out, and she let him take her hand. "Charlotte, Marie was the love of my life. She changed my life in ways I didn't think were possible and didn't believe I deserved. Everyone loved her, and she lit up every space she touched." He looked back and up at the house and then turned back to Charlotte. "From the moment I met her on that porch up there until the moment she left this world, she made me a better man. I loved her more than I've ever loved anything or anyone." He shook his head before going on. "I failed her, Charlotte, but most of all, I failed you."

She watched him without speaking, eyes wide, letting his confession soak in.

"I loved her." He shook his head again as though he was fighting his loss to make way for his present and future. "I love her. I will always love her. And you…" He paused to take a steadying breath and took her shoulders in his hands. "I love you." He was steady and sure. He locked eyes with her and repeated his words. "I love you. I have always loved you. I will never stop loving you."

She nodded once, taking his words as a promise.

Walt nodded, and without warning, she stepped into him, glass from the photo frames crunching under her sneakers, and wrapped her arms around him. He held her for a long time and whispered words only she could hear into her hair.

A short time later, they started up the hill, not touching each other but close. They made their way up the steps, across the porch, and back inside, greeting The Ladies as they walked.

I stayed on the gravel path and watched the younger of the brothers take Charlotte's hand and say, "You are amazing." I watched her pull him close and kiss him. As I felt myself slip away, I heard her call my name.

"Marie!"

I smiled and lifted my hand to wave.

She left the boy on the porch and hurried down to the bottom step, where I met her. "I saw you," she said, trying to catch her breath. "Earlier. I saw you. I thought it was a dream. I wasn't sure if it was real, and I was afraid."

I reached out to her and felt myself fading.

"Do you have to go?" her question was soft like a child.

I nodded and took her hand. She closed her eyes and rested her palm against my chest, where we both felt what I'd thought was my heart beating, but when she pulled my hand back across the space between us and placed it on her chest, I felt the rhythmic pulse and realized it had always only ever been hers.

The boy appeared beside her. Without taking my eyes off her, I let go of her and stepped away, my fingers sliding out from under hers.

She smiled and reached out to take his waiting hand.

With the last bits of me remaining there, I heard myself repeating my father's words back to her, "You did good, girl. Really, really good!"

42

Nina

May 2019

I gripped my steering wheel as I felt a wave of excitement pass through me. I smiled in anticipation. I'd been preparing myself for the next three days since the day Nora and Margot were born.

I looked at Wade in the rearview mirror. He was playing on his iPad while we waited for Charlotte in the high school parking lot. "Are you excited for this weekend, buddy?" I asked, hoping he'd want to talk to me.

"I guess," he said, not looking up from the screen. "But do I really have to wear a tie?"

"Yeah, that's what Margot picked for you," I said.

He rolled his eyes, still not looking up. "Why does she get to tell everyone what to wear?"

"Well, because, buddy, this is—"

"Nathan said he didn't care what I had on. He said, 'Wade, you can wear swim trunks for all I care. I'll never know the difference'," Wade said, lowering his voice to imitate Nathan. "But Margot's like, 'Wade Mavin, if you show up to my wedding in swim trunks, so help me, blah blah blah." His mimic of Margot was so accurate that it made me laugh out loud.

The phone rang, breaking into our conversation. I pressed a button on my steering wheel.

"Wade's wearing swim trunks tomorrow," I said, answering Suzie's call, as always, in mid-conversation.

"What color? Adah will want to match," she said.

I laughed. "Are you almost here?"

"Yeah, we actually just pulled into your driveway," she said.

"Oh good. I'm getting Charlotte from school, and we'll be back in a few. Just go on in."

"Is she excited to be done?" she asked.

"I think so," I said, letting my voice and thoughts drift.

"You okay, mama?" she asked, hearing the shift.

"Yeah," I said, shaking away my thoughts. "Just lots going on. Lots of change."

"Hey, Courtney just pulled in," she said, referring to the wedding planner. "How does a twenty-two-year-old wedding planner drive a Tesla?"

"Charles asked the same thing," I said, laughing. "I think someone in her family maybe owns the dealership."

"Lucky girl," she said. "Speaking of lucky girls, is Margot here?"

"If she isn't right now, she should be soon," I said.

"Oh wait. She and Nora just pulled in behind me. All is well. I'll see you in a bit," she said and hung up.

I leaned my head back against the headrest and closed my eyes. I cracked the windows to let in the early May air and let myself take a moment to walk through the memories of the last eighteen months.

After that first trip to Baltimore, Walt filed for divorce. Nancy Lynn had threatened to make the process miserable. When he let her know that he'd spoken to a lawyer and there was no statute of limitations on the theft of embryos, she became extremely compliant. She agreed to the uncontested divorce with joint custody of their daughters. When it was final, she bought him out of their business, and within a month, he'd moved back to Knoxville.

Charlotte had gone completely blind only two short months after that first trip to Baltimore, much faster than any of us could have ever expected.

We'd made a couple of trips back in those first couple of months. Even though we'd expected it and even though it destroyed Charles and me, she fell in love with Marie's parents and with Edgevale House.

Charles and I both had big reservations, but she was adamant about seeing them more. Just like with her name, we realized it was non-negotiable and began making the trip at least once a month. I think we'd hoped the new would wear off, but it didn't.

She became just short of obsessed with graduating early and going to college closer to Greta and Billy.

Without mentioning it to us, she connected with Nathan's vision therapist and found a private tutor. The first we heard anything about it was when the tutor, Stella Allbright, called us wanting to set up monthly payments.

Charles was livid, and had Suzie and Leia not been visiting. The resulting conversation would have gone much differently. As it was, Charles, red-faced, steam practically shooting from his ears, with clenched teeth and fists, had said, "In the future, would you please let us know if you're committing us to spending hundreds of dollars a month?"

Without even looking in his direction, she'd said, "So don't keep important details a secret from the guy who didn't tell me I was adopted for like sixteen years? Got it!"

He was stunned by her words and had no response. Really, what could he say? What could either of us say? Looking back, I think that we'd been completely delusional about what returning to normal life would be like. I think that conversation was what sent us back to Mitchell Kent for therapy. We still saw him together on a weekly basis.

In that first year, Charlotte learned to read and write braille. With the help of an aide, she returned to school on track to graduate early. There was a fire in her that both amazed and terrified us.

I jumped at the sound of tapping against the glass and turned to find Charlotte at the passenger door. I unlocked the doors, and she opened them to let Scout, her three-year-old German Shepherd, hop in before she climbed in and shut the door behind them. Scout settled herself into place and rested her head on Charlotte's foot.

The most recent milestone was that Charlotte had been accepted to Johns Hopkins University. She would start in the fall, and Nathan's younger brother Andrew, who had also been accepted, was planning to go as well.

We'd spent so long in a bubble of no boyfriends; now, having two of them in our home as almost permanent installations was odd. They were perfectly nice boys, with manners and gentleness with our daughters that everyone noticed, but it was nonetheless unsettling to know that we were no longer the center of their world.

When Nathan and his parents invited us to come for dinner back in early February, an engagement wasn't even on our radar, but as with most things in the last two years, it was happening with or without us. We chose to be supportive and excited, and here we were, four short months later, a wedding planner in our driveway, my firstborn's wedding gown hanging in my closet, and Charlotte with a devoted boyfriend by her side, both of them preparing to move out of state and start college in August.

My head was terrified for either of them to go, but my heart knew they were both ready.

"What?" Charlotte asked.

"What?" I said, startled.

"We've been sitting here for like five minutes, and I can feel you staring at me."

"I'm not staring at you," I lied.

"Yes, you were," Wade said from the back seat.

"See!"

"Traitor," I said, turning to look at him.

He shrugged, still engrossed in the iPad. "Charlie would let me wear swim trunks."

He was the only one who still called her Charlie. The truth is, he was the only person she allowed to call her Charlie.

"What's wrong?" she asked, sounding exhausted.

"Just lots of big life stuff," I said, reaching over to squeeze her hand.

"You're so dramatic," she said, rolling her eyes. "It's just a wedding. They're literally living in married student housing like three miles from home!"

"I know! I'm fine! I'll be fine."

"You sure?" she asked, her voice losing its teen edge and gaining a mature softness. "Good," she said, squeezing my hand back before letting go. It was just one word, but it felt like she meant it, and that was enough.

43

Charlotte

August 2019

I took the green and orange knit quilt from my bed, folded it, and laid it neatly on top of the last tote with all my other bedding and towels.

I'd brought it with me on our first trip back to Edgevale House, and I'd learned that Evelyn Colgate was the friend of my parents who made it. She'd recognized it and told me about how she'd given it to Marie and Walt as a baby gift before I was born, and she was thrilled that somehow, in the shuffle, it had been with me through everything.

A knock on my open bedroom door caused me to turn.

"Hey Charlotte," Margot said, and I heard Scout's collar jingle as she stood up to greet them.

"Hey! What're you doing here?" I asked, surprised. We'd had dinner as a family last night, and since Margot had a doctor's appointment this morning, I hadn't expected to get to see her again before Andrew and I left for Baltimore. She put her hand on my arm, pulled me into one of those oh so rare hugs, and said, "Just wanted to see you one more time," she said.

"Aw, you're gonna miss me?" I said and hugged her back.

"Yea, that, and I wanted to be sure you weren't taking any of my stuff,"

"You got married and moved out. Anything left behind is common property." I hugged her back hard. "Thank you."

"Thanks for what?" Wade said, and I could tell, by the shift in the location of his voice, first, from the hall outside my room and then across and on the other side of my room, that he was moving fast.

"That I got to see Margot and Nathan one more time before I leave," I said.

He slid in beside me and wrapped his arms around my waist. "Just three weeks, right?"

I knelt beside him, and he sank to the floor to meet me. He rested his palms on my cheeks, and I covered his hands with mine.

"Three weeks," I said, holding up three fingers, hoping to settle him. "Remember the paper chain we made."

"Yes," he said, and I felt his shoulders shake as he nodded.

"But just one a day," I said.

"Just one," he said, and it sounded like a question.

"Just one," I repeated.

"Okay," he said, and I heard the shake in his voice.

"Hey, Little Man. Just three weeks," Andrew said. The sound of his voice and his hand on my shoulder gave me physical relief.

I'd let myself grow so dependent on him. That dependence had been the source of our only argument, and when I say argument, I mean I yelled, and he listened and let me yell. I'd been terrified that he'd get tired of always being the caretaker, first with his brother and now with me.

Then, with his characteristic calm, he sat in front of me close enough to kiss but not and said, "Charlotte, every minute of me learning from Nathan was all for this. You don't get to take that from me. I'd choose you every single time." He took my left hand, turned it palm up, and touched the place where he'd first written his phone number. "I chose you that day, and I wouldn't change a single thing."

Then he spun Marie's silver bracelet to where we'd had it engraved the day he'd gotten his letter of acceptance to Hopkins.

"Three weeks," Wade said, pulling us back to the present. He lifted himself from the floor and left the room. He banged on the door a few times on his way out, and then shouted, "Y'all better not change your minds or be late, either."

Andrew laughed, and helped me to my feet, and asked, "Is that the last tote?"

"Yeah. The lid's by the closet on the floor."

"Got it," he said, and I heard him snap the lid shut on both ends.

I mentally did a final sweep of the space. My electric piano, three totes, and two suitcases were already loaded into Andrew's truck. Walt had moved back to Baltimore a few months ago and was planning to meet us at the dorms to get everything unloaded.

Leia left The Book with me when she and her mom left that morning. I slipped it into my backpack, pulled the zipper closed, and lifted the heavy bag from my corduroy chair. I let my fingertips brush against its ridges before picking up a sweatshirt from where it rested on top. We left my room, but just outside the door, I stopped short and said, "I think…"

"Did you forget something?" Nathan asked.

"No," I said, not sure how to put my feelings into words. "Can you guys give me a minute?" I said. "I won't be long. I just need a minute."

"Yeah, no worries," Margot said, seeing more than I was able to say.

Andrew said, "Take your time."

They left, Andrew first, his heavy footsteps with the tote, and then Margot and Nathan behind him.

"I won't be long," I repeated, more to myself than anyone.

I let my practiced fingertips run gently over the engraved surface of the silver band. It had been on my wrist since that first day at Edgevale House. I spun it again, this time taking a moment to read. Jeremiah 29:11 had been Marie's favorite Bible verse. She was with me and would always remind me that I have "hope and a future."

Discussion Questions

1. Most of the main characters experienced major growth or change over the course of the novel, which allowed them to be their authentic selves. Of the three narrators—Marie, Charlotte, and Nina—who do you believe had the most significant change and why?

2. Walter Lee Mavin also had a character change in the novel, although in a different direction. How do you believe his true character aligns or contradicts how he is portrayed in the beginning of the novel and the end?

3. Suzie's character traits remain the same throughout the novel. How does her consistent character aid the growth and development of the other characters?

4. Do you feel the relationship is healed between Charlotte and Nina by the end of the novel? Why or why not?

5. There is an underlying theme of loyalty throughout this novel. Which relationship do you feel best embodies loyalty?

6. Most of the conflict that Charlotte encounters in this novel is due to a "failure to act" by the adults

7. in her life. Although many characters are culpable for her predicament (including, of course, Walter Lee, Nina, and Charles), who do you think bears the most responsibility for Charlotte's hurdles?

8. There are two occasions when Charlotte seriously
    questions the value of her life and contemplates
    ending it, although she ultimately acts on these
    thoughts in varying degrees. One incident is at the
    opening of the novel. The other is toward the end.
    How are these two incidents different? Describe how
    you, as a reader, are sympathetic and/or relate to
    either or both of these incidents.

9. When Marie has an unexpected appearance at the end
    of the novel, do you feel that she is really present, or
    do you feel that Nina is so heartbroken by Marie's
    absence that she projects what she feels Marie would
    have said in that situation?

10. Likewise, when Charlotte is interacting with Marie,
    do you believe she is projecting what she needs to
    hear from Marie in order to heal?

11. As a reader, what actions by the characters make you
    feel as though their "good intentions" fall short in
    adequately justifying their behavior?

12. Charlotte experiences the crushing realization that
    the adults she loves the most have created a web of
    layered deception that has spanned her entire
    life. Why do you believe Charlotte is still willing to
    put so much trust in Andrew, a stranger, while she is
    dealing with so much dishonesty and secrecy from
    others?

13. How does this story change your understanding of
    people who are vision-impaired or blind?

Acknowledgments

Without these people, this book would not be what it is.

My Editors: Jody Dyer, Janice Laurino, and Sara Bice

My Beta and Galley Readers: Greta Stetson, Katie S. Van Arendonk, Tim Endsley, Nikki Cummings, Andy Moore, Anne Monroe, Anna Kovach, Joanna Presley, Katherine Moore, Sandy Campbell, and Debbie Stetson

My Subject Matter Experts: Sarah Higgins, Esq., Dr. Allyson D. Schmitt, Dr. Paul Brezina, MAJ Suzanna Hagler, US Army, and Dr. Tong Chang

About the Author

Lili Vincent was born the second of four kids raised by their single dad in Memphis, Tennessee. She graduated from Overton High School for the Creative and Performing Arts..

Lili started at the University of Tennessee in Knoxville as a Communications major before graduating in 2002 as an English major with a focus in Rhetoric and Writing. In those first communications classes, she fell in love with writing.

Lili was a member of Alpha Phi Omega National Service Fraternity, served as a coxswain for the University of Tennessee Rowing Team, and studied abroad in Normandy, France. In her senior year, one of her short stories was published in the university's literary journal, *The Phoenix*.

In 2005, Lili married her college sweetheart. After stops in Memphis, Tennessee, Baltimore, Maryland, and Ann Arbor, Michigan, Lili, her husband, and their three daughters returned to Knoxville in 2014. They adopted a puppy, two cats, and a flock of chickens.

Today, Lili and her family live on a hobby farm. On most days before six in the morning and after eight in the evening, she can be found writing, but during the day, her sunny office is used for homeschooling her daughters, overseeing piano practice, and occasionally enjoying an early afternoon nap.

Follow Lili Vincent here:
Facebook: WanderingLili
GoodReads: Lili Vincent
Instagram: wanderinglili
TikTok: @wanderinglili

From the Author

Dear Reader,

I finished the first draft of this novel in November of 2020 during the National Novel Writers Month (NaNoWriMo). That fall, my girls were in the lockdown version of school, there was a sourdough starter taking up valuable space in my countertop-depth refrigerator, and I was teaching the real Ladies of Edgevale how to use Zoom. My mother had been dead for just over four years. I'd surfaced from grief thirsty and eager to learn as much as I possibly could about her. She was diagnosed with juvenile open-angle glaucoma at four years old and was completely blind by age seven. There isn't space here to do her justice, but in short, she was fascinating and furiously frustrating.

Our relationship was overwhelmingly complicated. I loved my mother deeply and still do. However, at the same time, I was terrified of her capacity to dazzle in one moment and destroy in the next. She was remarkably flawed and heartbreakingly broken.

She was the product of choices made on her behalf by people who did their best to protect her in a world that was not built for the blind. The more I learned about her, the more I asked myself, *What if?*
I stacked every decision I wish had been made for my mother, and those *what-ifs* became Marie. The rest is history.

I sit in awe at the end of this journey and look back and wonder, *How did I get here?* But the answer always comes quickly. I have a great team and the best family and found family. Their support has been incredible, and this novel would not be what it is without them.

To Jody and her team at Crippled Beagle Publishing and Lauren at Lauren Balmer Marketing Services, thank you for taking my dream and making it real! Thank you to the real-life knit club ladies and every woman who stood in the gap when my mother couldn't. Linda and Anne, and your dear husbands Max and Larry, you ARE my family! Thank you, Greta, for being my Baltimore phone-a-friend, and Katie for your hospitality and being my feet on the ground in Nashville. And Sara, your friendship truly takes my breath away. I lost a dear friend in my early forties, and I thought I was finished making friends because the loss was too hard…and then came you. I love you dearly, and this novel wouldn't be what it is without you.

Thank you to my family—my sisters for taking my calls when I thought the whole thing was falling apart and I was losing my book, and my brother for teaching me the best curse words and reading every single draft. Thank you to my girls—Eleanor, MJ, and Abigail, you are my heart divided into three, walking around outside my body, living, breathing, and becoming the most dazzling people. I didn't know what I didn't know. Thank God that now I know!

And to my husband, Jeremy, thank you for putting up with the late nights and understanding when I just couldn't step away from writing, even to sleep. Thank you for supporting my obsession with tea. Thank you for listening to me rant about the "teenagers in Virginia" who had taken up residence in my brain. Thank you for making my computer work when nothing I did would.

Thank you for making this world accessible for me. Thank you for loving me and always giving me the best. You are my very best yes! I can't wait to do it all over again!

Finally, a little about the writing. As an author, I operate under the understanding that for me, a story is a found thing. I understand now that this isn't unique to me. Many authors feel that for a time, an author is simply the caretaker of a precious thing. When I find an idea, it's my job to dig it out without destroying it in the process. If I choose to walk past an idea, it isn't lost; it will simply find someone else to do its excavation. I am so thankful that I got to tell the story of Marie, Charlotte, and Nina.

Reader, I want you to walk away from this novel with hope. I want you to know that forgiveness has the capacity to heal the broken and that love has the ability to give rest to a weary heart. Our ability as humans to give the gifts of love and forgiveness cost us nothing, but love and forgiveness have the potential to make all the difference.

With so much love,

Lili